# ONE for the Money, TWO for the Sluice

*A Fr. Jake Mystery*

EQUUS

**Albert Noyer**

**Books by Albert Noyer**

*The Saint's Day Deaths (2000)*
*The Secundus Papyrus (2003)*
*The Cybelene Conspiracy (2005)*
*The Ghosts of Glorieta / A Fr. Jake Mystery (2011)*
*One for the Money, Two for the Sluice / A Fr. Jake Mystery (2013)*

# ONE for the MONEY, TWO for the SLUICE

*A Fr. Jake Mystery*

# Albert Noyer

**Plain View Press**
3800 N. Lamar, Suite 730-260

http://plainviewpress.net
Austin, TX 78756

ISBN: 978-1-935514-72-5
Library of Congress Control Number: 2013935302

Cover art: Painting by Albert Noyer
Visual elements of the plot, clockwise: Sluice gate mechanism, hoof pick, picket signs, Isabel Trujillo, Colt.45 pistol, Civil War excavation finds
Cover layout by Pam Knight

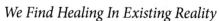 *We Find Healing In Existing Reality*
Plain View Press is a 36-year-old issue-based literary publishing house. Our books result from artistic collaboration between writers, artists, and editors. Over the years we have become a far-flung community of activists whose energies bring humanitarian enlightenment and hope to individuals and communities grappling with the major issues of our time—peace, justice, the environment, education and gender. This is a humane and highly creative group of people committed to art and social change. The poems, stories, essays, non-fiction explorations of major issues are significant evidence that despite the relentless violence of our time, there is hope and there is art to show the human face of it.

*With sincere thanks to the writing group:*
*Jennifer, Carolyn, Roy,*

*and*

*Dedicated to the loving memory of*
*Roy Zarucchi*

## Map of Providencia

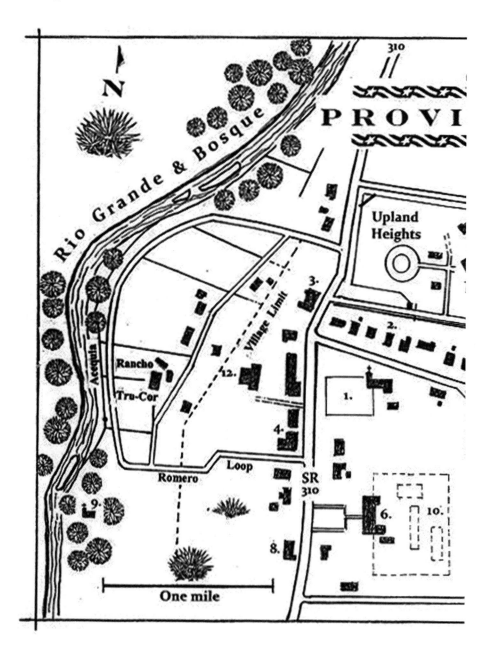

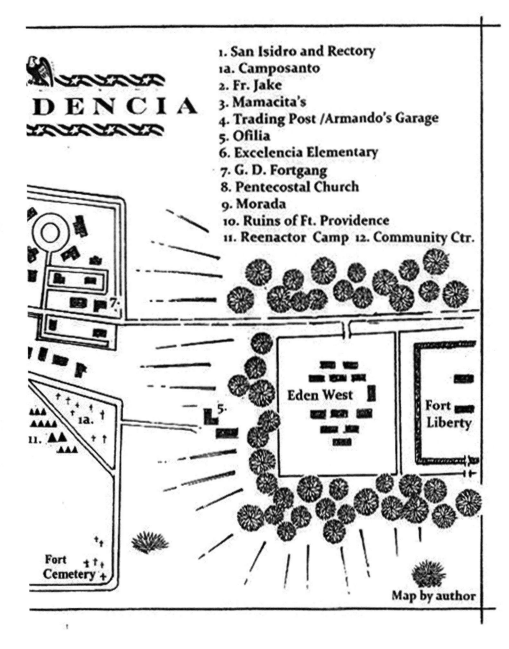

**DENCIA**

1. San Isidro and Rectory
1a. Camposanto
2. Fr. Jake
3. Mamacita's
4. Trading Post /Armando's Garage
5. Ofilia
6. Excelencia Elementary
7. G. D. Fortgang
8. Pentecostal Church
9. Morada
10. Ruins of Ft. Providence
11. Reenactor Camp 12. Community Ctr.

7.

5.

1a.

11.

Eden West

Fort
Liberty

Fort
Cemetery

Map by author

# Prologue rancho tru-cor / 1997

A September sky blue as the background in a New Mexico painting by Taos artist Ernest Blumenschein spread over Don Fernando Trujillo de Sevilla's Arabian horse ranch and the nearby Rio Grande *bosque*. An early morning breeze brought in a faintly stagnant odor from the summer-shallow river that mingled with the more pleasant grassy scent of a last seasonal cutting from the ranch's alfalfa fields. Doña Isabel-Maria Cordova y Trujillo prepared with her husband to exhibit stallions at an Arabian Horse Association competition in Albuquerque. The petite woman looked elegant in her down vest, twill riding breeches, and knee-length boots—a riding outfit designated in horse owners' magazines as "The equestrian lifestyle look."

"Fernando!" Isabel called to her husband from the bottom of a ramp that led to the entrance of a slant-load horse trailer. "We're ready to guide *Vencedor* inside now."

The Don glanced up from checking the front hitch mechanism. "*Bueno, mi amanta*," he called back to her. "Is Vando in front, holding the stallion's halter?"

"*Si*, Fernando."

"Where are Dulcinea and Mrs. Nevarez?"

"Our daughter and her nanny are standing back, well out of any danger," Isabel reassured him.

The stylish equestrian couple had readied two Arabian breeds to enter in the AHA Nationals Association competition, held this year at the New

Mexico State Fair grounds in Albuquerque. Married in 1990, the vivacious, dark-haired Isabel-Maria and Leo Carrillo-handsome Don Fernando had moved from Socorro onto her father's ranch, where her husband was manager. Unexpected tragedy struck six years later: Doña Isabel's parents were killed in a wrong-way accident on Interstate 25 that was caused by a drunk driver. After his wife inherited the ranch, Fernando renamed the property Rancho Tru-Cor, a contraction of **Tru**jillo and **Cor**dova family names, yet also suggested "True *Corazon*," the true closeness in their hearts of his and his wife's love for one another—and mutually for Arabian horse breeds.

When Fernando came around to the ramp, Cervando "Vando" Benevides, the burly ranch boss, tipped his cap in deference to his titled *patrón*. The Don nodded acknowledgement, looked at the waiting stallion, then smiled and embraced his wife. "*Amanta*, do you think *Vencedor* may win a ribbon, or perhaps even more, a trophy?"

"*Con certeza*...most certainly." Isabel gave her husband's shoulder a playful push in rebuttal of a question she considered silly. "After all, his name means 'Conqueror'."

"*Te amo*...I love you." Fernando slipped an arm around his wife's waist and turned to look toward their five-year-old daughter, standing with an older, gray-haired woman. "Mrs. Nevarez," he warned, "hold tightly to Dulcinea's hand as *Vencedor* is walked up the ramp."

"*Si*, Don Fernando." Eusebia Nevarez clutched their daughter's hand and held it up to satisfy her long-time employer.

The Don signaled to Vando, then released Isabel. "*Amanta*, I must get something from the barn. Stand on the right side of the ramp, a bit back of the trailer's door."

Puzzled, she asked, "You won't watch *Vencedor* enter inside his travel stall?"

"Vando is perfectly capable of doing that," he replied amiably, then walked away.

She blew her husband a kiss. "*Marido, te amo*."

"*Igualmente*," he called back, without turning toward her.

As Vando led *Vencedor* clumping up the ramp, Isabel stood on grass alongside and slightly to the rear of the horse. At the trailer's entrance, the chestnut stallion paused without warning, then whinnied and reared upright. Its poll, a vulnerable spot at the top of the head, struck hard against the upper metal frame of the doorway. As the now-blinded stallion kicked out its hind legs in shock and pain, Vando stumbled backward into the trailer. *Vencedor*'s right hoof flailed back and struck Isabel in the forehead. Mortally wounded by the blow, the woman crumpled to the grass, bloody and unconscious. The Arabian steed's huge bulk toppled off the left side of the ramp, opposite to Doña Isabel's body. The "Conqueror" lay quivering in its terminal death throes.

Watching, Eusebia gasped in stupefied horror, then picked up Dulcinea and hurried with the child back to the ranch house.

At the barn, Don Fernando heard the commotion and came outside to determine its cause. "No! No!" he wailed on seeing the results of the accident. "¡Mi amanta...mi amanta!" He ran and knelt alongside his dying wife. Sobbing and cradling her head in an arm, he ignored bright blood that seeped onto khaki jodhpurs and the embroidered front of his horse exhibitor's shirt. They were of no importance; his beloved Isabel was dead.

# 1 providencia / june 28, 2010

Wearing a short-sleeve, light-blue clerical shirt with Roman collar insert, Fr. Casimir "Jake" Jakubowski stepped out onto the front porch of his New Mexican adobe *casita*. Using an envelope to shield his eyes against a morning sun, the priest glanced at a sky bluer than his shirt.

Driven by a western breeze, light-gray clouds, remnants of an early morning rain, scudded toward the east and opened up a vast, deep-azure Southwestern firmament. In his front yard, patches of ochre grass, which had received scant moisture since a final April snowmelt, now sparkled with beads of water. Scattered raindrops glistened on his old house's worn porch stairs, and spotted the hood of "Nissy," the priest's 2004 Nissan Altima, parked on the gravel of a side drive.

Fr. Jake stretched his arms and inhaled a pungent odor of mixed juniper and sage that overlaid the air, then jested aloud to no one in particular, "That rain last night brought out a scent that could be bottled and sold as men's after-shave lotion. Is this rain an early beginning to the monsoon season that Armando mentioned?" *Monsoon? Michigan's abundant, heavy rains were never described that way, so when I heard him call rainy weather here by that name, I wondered who he was kidding. This is New Mexico, not New Delhi.*

That past April, the seventy-year-old, Polish-born priest had decided not to retire and requested that his Detroit archbishop allow him to continue serving the modest lakeside parish in Michigan, where he was assigned. Somewhat irked by Fr. Jake's well-known liberal slant on Vatican II church reforms, yet aware of his valuable ministry to Mexican migrant farm workers, the Prelate suggested that, "Since probably half the people in New Mexico speak Spanish," Fr. Jake should take a sabbatical leave and spend a year helping a sickly New Mexican pastor: Fr. Jesús Mora served a church at the small Rio Grande community of Providencia. However, fearful that an outsider would make changes in the conservative parish, the Michigan *norteño padre* had not been warmly received. Yet Fr. Jake gradually became instrumental in helping solve the pastor's unexpected murder, and working to revitalize a dysfunctional parish.

Fr. Jake ran a hand through steel-gray hair and looked across the street, beyond his church of San Isidro, toward the former pastor's rectory, a small, metal-roofed adobe house, then silently re-read a letter he had received the previous week. It was written on stationery of the New York University Department of Anthropology.

Dear Father Jakubowski;

My name is Jayson Baumann. I'm Catholic and an M.A. graduate research assistant at NYU. I was excited to hear about the Civil War era forensic anthropology discoveries at Fort Providence and received a departmental stipend, plus permission from the Bureau of Land Management to work the site for three months. I was at Ft. Craig when the bodies of Negro 7th Cavalry soldiers were discovered there. Since, beginning on 1 July, I will be in need of an inexpensive (ha, ha) residence for this period, the Archdiocese of Santa Fe suggested I contact you as the person perhaps best able to suggest appropriate lodgings—"

At an irruptive beep-beep of an automobile horn, the priest looked up. Detective Sonia Mora slowed her mud-stained red Plymouth Neon to a stop at his curb. The Socorro Sheriff's Department officer was the niece of Fr. Jésus Mora, the murdered pastor whose body had been found in his chapel on the fifteen day of the past May.

Fr. Jake refolded the letter and walked down to open the car's driver-side door.

"Morning, Detective." He grinned approval as he pointed to his watch. "You're right on time."

"Always try to be, Father Jake." Sonia smiled and extended a hand. "How are you? I see you got a haircut. Did you go to Belén?"

"Didn't have to. After yesterday's Mass, a parishioner offered to trim my locks. Mister Melendez is a retired barber now working part time out of his home."

"You look good."

"For being seventy-something?"

"No, I didn't mean—"

"I'm kidding, detective, and they joke that fifty is the new seventy...." The priest pulled open the door and stepped aside. "How are *you*, Sonia?"

"Okay, I guess," she told him with a non-committal head shrug. "It's my day off and I might have had other plans."

Fr. Jake nodded in the direction of the church. "We have a lot of work to do over at the rectory."

"Right, I got your call..." Sonia stepped out of her Plymouth wearing a plaid, long-sleeved summer shirt, belt-less denims, and leather sandals. The petite detective with green eyes and a clear olive complexion had tucked her lustrous black hair under a tan Baker Boy summer cap. She adjusted the visor to ask, "What's this all about, Father? I knew I'd have to clean stuff out of my uncle's rectory sooner or later, but why right now?"

He held up the letter. "Seems a budding anthropologist needs a place to stay for three months and figured a poor parish priest would know the whereabouts of cheap lodgings."

"What?" Sonia's eyes narrowed as she shook her head. "The guy can't live in my...my late uncle's rectory."

"No, no. Sonia, this *casita* I'm living in belongs to San Isidro Church, so I thought I'd move into the rectory and rent out the place to...to"—he checked the name on the letter—"to Jayson. That's J-a-y-s-o-n. Jayson Baumann."

"Well, okay..." She voiced hesitant agreement. "I guess that makes some sense."

"Good. I have a key to the rectory and I'm here to help you sort through your uncle's belongings in any way I can."

"Thanks, Father, but I don't know what I'll do with all his broken-down furniture, or any non-priest clothes he owned."

"A charity resale shop would take whatever you don't want."

"You're right, of course. I...I'm still not thinking logically when it comes to my murdered uncle."

"Understandable, Sonia. By the way, how is Agent Herrero? Juan?"

"The DEA re-assigned him to their Washington D.C. office." Sonia masked her disappointment by turning away to pull a cordless hand vacuum from the Plymouth's back seat. "Shall we go over and start?" she asked, her inflection curt. "And would you carry in those boxes on the passenger side?"

"Gladly." *I hoped that Sonia might have found someone to ease the loneliness in her life. Now a fellow law officer I thought might help her is stationed over two thousand miles away.*

"Father, shall we go?" At the priest's hesitation, the detective's question emphasized her irritation at a lost day and the beginning of an unpleasant task ahead.

"Sonia, I'll be right there." Fr. Jake went back to lock his front door, then stacked the cardboard boxes inside each other and followed Sonia's wet footprints in the grass to the adobe rectory's front entrance.

Set in motion by a light breeze fragrant with sage, a band of tattered yellow crime scene tape fluttered across the weathered doorway. "Jeez," Sonia complained, "I *told* Deputy Griego to take that tape down. It's been over six weeks since my...since Father Mora's death."

"Here, let me..." Fr. Jake opened the main blade of his Wenger pocketknife, cut through the tape, and bunched it into the smallest box. As he turned his key in the lock, he heard the expected scurrying of mice and looked back. "Sonia, it's liable to be quite nasty in there."

"I figured the place to be that," she sighed, "but I'll have seen much worse at crime scenes."

"I'm sure you have." The priest put down the boxes and eased the warped, blue-painted door open—to a suffocating wave of warm, foul-smelling air, buzzing with flies that were agitated at being disturbed.

Sonia dropped the vacuum, brought a hand to her mouth, and hissed though her fingers. "Father, open the damn windows!"

Holding his breath, Fr. Jake went over to snap up a tattered window shade and brush cobwebs aside. Despite his efforts, the rusted cam lock held tight. He turned back at her. "Sorry, it won't open, but I'll leave the door ajar for ventilation and to give us more light inside."

"Okay, but I...I apologize for the outburst, Father."

He chuckled at the impromptu incident. "*Te absolvo* Let's look around at what has to be done."

The air in the living room smelled musty, yet the worse odor came from the rectory's cooking area. Sonia led the way past sheet-covered living room furniture that had belonged to her grandparents. Rodent droppings speckled the soiled creases. As the priest followed her into what was a kitchenette, predictably, more flies and a hornet swarmed up to harass their uninvited intruders.

Except for a small dull-green barrel cactus, several withered geranium plants on the sink-board were dead. A stained refrigerator door was partly open: its feeble yellow bulb illuminated a plastic milk jug chewed through by mice. The congealed sour puddle beneath was riddled with black droppings.

Bitten-open food storage dishes were scattered on the wire shelves or lay on the wooden flooring among yet other black pellets. The lower left vegetable storage bin held the oozing remains of what might have been leaf lettuce, half a green pepper, and celery stalks. The right side meat holder mercifully was empty.

Fr. Jake went to a door that led to the back yard outside, unlatched the bolt, and wrenched it open. "Morning air that's still cool ought to help dispel the stench."

"Hope you're right…" Sonia stepped outside to clear her nose of the noxious odor. "Father Mora certainly didn't believe that cleanliness was next to godliness. Isn't that supposed to be biblical, Father?"

"Sort of," he answered from the doorway. "Psalm 51 speaks of God preferring a clean heart, but that other 'proverb' seems more from the eighteenth century Enlightenment." *Sonia isn't calling the priest 'uncle' any longer. She had said they weren't close, yet perhaps it's also a way for her to continue dealing with his loss.* Fr. Jake looked back inside at the clutter and groaned. "It will take a bevy of Merry Maids to make this place livable!"

Sonia laughed despite her dark mood. "That's 'Molly Maids,' Father, but I'll find a couple of local *viejas* instead to do the major cleaning." She went back into the kitchenette to suggest, "Let's start in Father Mora's closet and see if he left any clothing I could donate."

"The Saint Vincent de Paul Society would gladly accept them. Is there one here in Providencia?"

"I live in Socorro," she snapped. "Ask one of your parishioners about that."

"Fine, I will." *Sonia is touchy, but these old memories about her uncle are bound to be painful.*

The rectory's cramped bedroom closet held a minimum of clothing: two sets of black clerical shirts and trousers, gray dress slacks, short-sleeved sport shirts, and a tattered dressing gown hung on wire hangers. No more than three sets of shoes lay on the floor—two pairs of black oxfords and one of well-worn canvas slip-ons. On a shelf above the rack, next to a straw hat and three baseball caps, two department store clothing boxes, which might have held the slacks or sport shirts, were stacked one above the other.

Sonia pointed to them. "Can you reach those cartons, Father? Hand them down to me and I'll open them on the bed."

"Sure…" The priest coughed as he tilted the topmost box and dust filtered onto his face.

Sonia stepped back. "Easy there, Father! Is it heavy?"

"Not particularly...feels like it might hold papers, magazines, perhaps some pamphlets. I can put it on the bed."

Sonia ran a finger across the dusty top. "There still must be a towel in the bathroom. I'll wipe off the cover before I open it."

The second box was heavier. Both had DALTON'S, a department store name, embossed on the lid. After cleaning off the first box, Sonia eased up the cover and laid it aside. Inside, a rusted paperclip held yellowed newspaper clippings of Reverend Jesús Mora's ordination in St. Francis Cathedral at Santa Fe. They were dated June, 1979. In photographs of the new priest, taken after his Ordination Mass, Father Mora stood unsmiling with his mother and family members. His complexion was sallow and he already looked ill and emaciated.

"I was a teen-ager at the time," Sonia recalled. "The drive to Santa Fe with my cousins was fun, but the service was so long and boring. You should know, Father...all incense, and candles, and prayers."

"Yes, well, even the freshly minted Reverend Mora doesn't look too happy."

"No, and I remember a *primo* joking that my uncle became a priest just to please his mother."

"That does happen," Fr. Jake affirmed. *And not always with happy results.*

The detective sifted through a sheaf of envelopes. "Congratulatory cards from family members. Oh, here are some articles clipped from Catholic publications about the pope and Vatican II reforms."

"Those look like TIME magazine covers underneath the clippings."

"Let's see.... You're right, Father, and the latest on top is January 20, 2002. *How Your Mind Can Heal Your Body.* Then, *Can the Catholic Church Heal Itself?* April 1, 2002.

Fr. Jake recalled, "That last cover story was about the priest pedophile scandals. I read it. We...we all read it."

"Those cases settled now?"

"Settle-*ments*. Some archdiocesan bishops spent millions in compensation to many, many abuse victims."

"1997, *Does Heaven Exist?*" Sonia read the title aloud, then paused to look up. "Father, do you priests doubt that?"

"No. Genesis describes it as the firmament and dwelling place of God, yet doesn't give any details. A mystery isn't easily explained. You, detective, of all people should know that. Look at this next article, *The Generation that*

*Forgot God.* April 5, 1995. It's about Baby Boomers going back to church. There were plenty of discussions among my fellow priests and, I don't mind telling you, a lot of whiskey consumed, trying to figure out how to lure fallen-away Catholics back to the fold."

"*Buena suerte* on that one." Sonia wished him luck and continued looking through her uncle's clippings. "Here's '*What Does Science Tell Us About God?*' and '*Who Was Jesus*'?"

"Detective, just as I do, Father Mora read and saved what he thought was important to him."

"I suppose… Jeez, look at this last one!" Sonia shook off a dead insect and held up a TIME cover portraying a satanic theme. "Clipped to this is an article from a local paper, dated 1992, about the disappearance of Aimée Parker. Remember, when we searched the rectory, we found a photo of her and that note to Father Mora in his desk over there."

"I do. What's the TIME story about?"

"'*The Occult Revival*', June 19, 1972. It's subtitled, 'Satan Returns'."

"Unexpected reading for him, but let's see…" Fr. Jake closed his eyes and calculated a moment. "If your uncle was ordained in 1979, he would have been in college at that time."

Sonia's brown eyes further darkened at the implication. "And learning about a Black Mass?"

"Detective, Aimée's death and her possible connection to Father Mora, or a Black Mass, was solved, so that's 'an emptied collection basket,' as we priests quip whenever discussing irrecoverable past events."

"Perhaps, yet the perp's trial is still pending," she reminded him.

"True. Sonia, hand me your towel, please." Fr. Jake brushed dust off an edge of the second lid. "Wonder what's in this other box?"

Sonia jiggled the top off. Inside, a narrow, inch-thick rectangle of purple satin had been wrapped around a flat object of the same dimensions. A cross on top, embroidered in oxidized silver thread, glinted softly in morning light from the window. Next to it, another package wrapped in a stained white sheet looked more bulky.

Fr. Jake recognized the satin material. "That one bundle is covered by a priest's purple stole, like those used in Lenten services."

"Really? What other surprise could be inside?"

"Unwrap it, detective." *Sonia's uncle saved an article about the disappearance of a married commune girl he was counseling. What else is she expecting to find?*

Sonia undid the cloth, which protected a leather-covered volume bearing the hand written title, *Hermanos Pentitentes*. Underneath, the title *Hermano Mayor* was smaller.

"*Penitentes?*" Fr. Jake whistled his surprise. "Same as those men who built the *morada* we saw in the *bosque*."

"Except that the word '*Penitentes*' is something of an insult," Sonia explained. "They prefer being called *Hermanos*...Brothers." She flipped through the stiff pages of the journal, pausing briefly to scan some of the writing, and then handed the book to the priest. This is called a *cuaderno*, a notebook or memorandum about rituals. I noticed a collection of *albados*... hymns sung in Spanish that commemorate the passion of Christ during Holy Week. There are prayers to the Virgin Mary, too."

"And '*Hermano Mayor*'?"

"That means, 'Elder Brother', the leader of a local Brotherhood."

"So one might conclude that Father Jesús Mora once was a high-echelon *Hermano?*"

Sonia brushed back her hair, a look of confusion on her face. "The *Hermandados* were mostly found in far northern areas of Old Mexico, where few priests were available."

"Yet, the *morada* we have here indicates that the *Hermanos* are still active in Providencia."

"More or less," Sonia conceded, "so I can guess what's in that white-shrouded bundle, Father."

"Items the Brotherhood uses in their rituals?"

"Let's find out..." She unfolded the cloth to reveal thorny branches from a rosebush that were twisted into a crown. Next to a small flute, a plastic bag held sharp obsidian blades. A short flagellum had seven strands with roofing nails attached to the ends. Sonia took out the whip and stone blades to hold up. "All these were used to draw blood and imitate Christ's passion on Good Friday."

"More than a bit excessive," Fr. Jake commented dryly. "During Lent, most Catholics fast a little and some might attend Friday evening Stations of the Cross services."

Sonia held up the whip a moment, shook her head, and then replaced it in the box. "The media tends to sensationalize the supposed aberrations of the Brotherhood, yet the chapters are really there to help a community during the year. While bloodletting still may be true, when this was part of Mexico, the Chihuahua Diocese bishops wrote to condemn some *Hermanidad* secret devotions. Their letters describe in detail what transpired—"

"Father Hakub?" A questioning voice at the front door calling the priest's name interrupted the detective. "Father Hakub, you in there?"

The priest recognized the voice. "Armando, here in the bedroom. Sonia, he calls me by the first part of my last name Jakub-owski and pronounces it in Spanish."

"Don't think I haven't noticed that." Sonia rolled her eyes as she replaced the covers on both boxes.

Armando Herrera sported a light moustache and goatee, and parted his dark hair in the middle. He appeared in the doorway with a swarthy, heavy-set companion wearing muddied work clothes and rubber boots. "Oh... hi... detective." The young auto mechanic greeted Sonia, breathing in gasps, as if he had run a fair distance. "I...saw your car...in front of Father's *casita* and then the rectory door open. I...figured you both came over here."

Father Jake stood up. "I'm moving into the rectory, Armando. We're sorting out things I won't need and whatever Detective Mora wants to keep or give away of her uncle's."

He glanced around and shook his head at the clutter. "Father Hakub, you're gonna need a lotta Clorox to make this place smell good. Look, I'm sorry, but this ain't...isn't...a visit." He turned to the man behind him. "This here is Cervando Benavides. He's *jefe*...ranch boss...over at Don Fernando's place."

Cervando clawed off his straw cowboy hat. The Hispanic man's broad face had perfectly arched, heavy eyebrows set over squinting eyes. His curved moustache drooped over a full-lipped mouth. A rosary dangled around his neck and one brawny arm bore a tattoo of the Virgin of Guadalupe. Embarrassed, the man shifted from foot to foot when Fr. Jake extended a hand and greeted him in Spanish, "*Mucho gusto, Señor Benavides.*"

"Father, it's okay to talk English," Armando told the priest. "And everybody calls him Vando. Detective...it's good you're here, too."

"Oh?" Sonia stood to adjust her cap back on. "Armando, you sound upset. Did something happen I should know about?"

"Yeah, that's why we came. Vando was up early checkin' the *acequia madre* on the ranch. You know, seein' where the mother irrigation ditch might need cleanin' out. He ran over to my shop and told me to call a priest."

Surprised, Fr. Jake wondered, "Why would Vando need a priest? Is someone dying?"

"Not exactly…" Armando sucked air through his teeth, ran a nervous hand through his hair, then stammered, "He…Vando…thinks he found a…a unborn dead baby in the water."

## 2 don fernando' s ranch

After several moments of stunned disbelief, Sonia asked Vando, "An unborn dead baby? Sir, how old did this...this fetal infant appear to be?"

Armando replied for the ranch boss, "Like I said, detective, Vando told me it looked like it wasn't hardly born yet."

"Please let Mister Benavides answer," Sonia cautioned. "Sir, about this baby or fetus?"

Reluctant to answer the woman, Vando fingered a rosary around his neck and stared at Sonia. "*¿Esta Usted una detectiva?* Don't look like one to me." His mocking tone reflected the idea that a beautiful female also could be a law enforcement officer was beyond imagining.

Sonia pulled her ID from her jeans back pocket and held it out to him. "*Detectiva* Mora, with the Socorro Sheriff's Department. Sir, tell me about this fetus you say you found."

"*Dios*," Vando replied, "it was *muy pequeño*, an' I thought it was maybe dropped by a *javelina*. I found 'em before. You know, the sow splits from the herd when birthin'. There's lotsa prickly pear by the ditch. Them is their favorite *comida* an'—"

"Sir," Sonia interrupted, "how did you determine it might be a human fetus?"

Vando's eyes widened and his arched brows rose at what was obvious. "How you think? I looked at it closer, saw it was a...a *niño*."

"A boy. Then what did you do, Mister Benavides?"

"What else? Fished it outta the ditch." The foreman tugged at his shirt collar to make a point. "I wrapped it in my bandana before I went over to Armando's, an' put a rock on it to keep everythin' from blowin' away."

Sonia slowly shook her head at this well-intentioned interference. "Sir, that was not a good thing to do. You tampered with a possible crime scene."

"*Dios, detectiva,* you got coyotes…snakes…even turtles over there," he said, critical of the lack of smarts in people not familiar with open land. "Don't you city types know nothin'?"

Sonia ignored his insolent remark. "Why did you want a priest to come first and not the sheriff?"

"I thought a *padre* might wanna baptize the *niño.*"

"And I will," Fr. Jake said, "as soon as I can get over there."

"Father, we'll all go." Sonia turned back to Vando. "Sir, Armando mentioned that you work for Don Fernando Trujillo de Sevilla."

"*Sí,*" Vando nodded vigorously. "*Soy jefe del rancho y mayordomo de l' acequia. ¿Comprendo Español, detectiva.*"

"I do understand Spanish," Sonia told him," but please answer my questions in English."

Fr. Jake was not familiar with Trujillo's name. "Sonia, do you know about the man Vando mentioned?"

"Don Fernando owns about a thousand acres and raises Arabian show horses. We've had a few calls from his place, mostly about fence vandalism."

"Is that part of the land that Father Mora lost to Tex Houston's quitclaim deeds?"

"No, the Don's property line is at the western boundary of Providencia, and then cuts a short way across the Rio Grande. Fernando is strictly Socorro County…" Sonia picked the two Dalton boxes off the bed. "We've got to get over that ranch. Father, I'll put these in my car's trunk, while you lock up the rectory."

"Fine, Sonia, and I'll get my stole and a bottle of holy water from the house."

"All right, but hurry, and then we'll all go to the *acequia.* I'll drive."

Armando hesitated. "Detective, I was doin' an oil change when Vando came to tell me about that dead *niño.* The guy's still waitin'."

"We should get over there," she said, "but you needn't come along, since you were not at the scene."

The mechanic nodded his thanks. "Vando said the baby was found at the south end of the Don's *rancho.* Take South Romero Loop to get you there."

"Thank you, sir."

With Vando in the back seat and Fr. Jake sitting up front, Sonia Mora turned her Plymouth left onto Highway 310, then right at Providencia Grocery & Gas, on the corner of the unpaved Romero Loop. Armando's auto repair shop was at the rear of the store.

The early morning rain mercifully tempered the choking dust clouds that automobiles raised on gravel roads. After a half-mile's jarring ride along the rutted surface, a white rail fence on the right marked the beginning of the Don's Arabian horse ranch. Several hundred yards in, an ornate, wrought iron gate blocked his private access road to the main ranch house. As Sonia continued on toward the waterway, Romero Loop turned sharply north at a point where the Rio Grande *bosque* appeared beyond the muddied waters of the irrigation ditch. The lush band of cottonwoods, willows, and thick underbrush, stretching along both banks of the river, displayed a color palette that varied from yellow-green to darker foliage hues. Fr. Jake had noted that these were softer hues than those of Michigan's dark pine and oak forests. Closer in, reddish salt cedar stands encroached towards the *acequia's* far edge. From the direction of the *bosque*, a mourning dove called above the buzz of summer insects. An acrid smell of leafage heated by the June sun mingled with a fishy odor drifting in from the river. Sonia half-turned her head toward Vando in the back seat. "Sir, how much farther?"

The ranch boss leaned forward. "Up ahead, *pronto*, at where white fence crosses *acequia*. *Hacer alto para una* sluice. Stop there. Don Fernando, he got a mile of water rights along the Rio."

Sonia braked to a stop at the waterway, just beyond the turn in the road and near the red hand-wheel lifting mechanism of a sluice gate at one end of the irrigation ditch. In late June the water level was low, a result of depleted Colorado snowmelt and some two hundred miles of diverted upstream Rio Grande water. Unlined with concrete, the *acequia* encouraged green vegetation to flourish along its edges, yet ranch hands had kept the waterway fairly clear of water plants that might clog the circular sluice entrance. Dragonflies skimmed the surface of the slow-moving waterway as the three left the car. Grasses on this side of the channel, dried by a warming sun, flattened underfoot as Vando led the way toward a blue bandana lying on the grass.

The man knelt to brush circling flies and hornets away from the covering with his hat, then used it to shade the kerchief. Fr. Jake adjusted a green stole around his neck and unscrewed the cap from his holy water bottle.

Sonia slipped on a pair of latex gloves, bent down on one knee, moved the rock aside, and slowly eased back the corners of the bandana. The pale fetus underneath was about three inches long, with head, arms, legs, hands—and unmistakable male genitalia visible. "Between three to four months along, I'd say." She looked up at the priest. "Father Jake, use only one drop of water and don't touch the victim…the fetus."

"I have sacred chrism….anointing oil."

"No oil, Father, nothing that might contaminate the scene."

"Thank you." The priest stooped to shake a single drop of water on a tiny forehead, then made a sign of the cross over the partially formed body. "Juan Doe," he began, "I—"

"Father," Sonia interposed, "just 'Baby Doe' will do."

"Baby Doe, I baptize you in the name of the Father, and of the Son, and of the Holy Spirit. Amen."

Vando repeated a mumbled "Amen," then Sonia carefully folded the bandana back over the pitiful human form.

Fr. Jake stood and closed his baptismal kit. "Detective, do you think this is a miscarriage or an induced abortion?"

"Father, the result of a miscarriage isn't usually tossed into an irrigation or drainage ditch, is it?"

"No, of course not. How long has the fetus…has Baby Doe…been in what we would call a sluice in Michigan. In the water, do you think?"

"Considering the victim's intact condition and what Mister Benavides said about predators, I'd estimate only since the very early morning hours."

"I could celebrate a funeral Mass."

"Father, only after the medical examiner is called in and finishes his work." Sonia turned back to Vando. "Sir, exactly where was the victim found?"

*Aqui*…" Vando shoved his hat back on and strode in his heavy boots to a thick stand of bulrushes that pushed through a gentle current near the water's edge. "Here I find the *niño* in *La Isabel*."

Puzzled at the name, Sonia repeated it as a question, "La Isabel?"

"*Si*. Don Fernando, he call the *acequia* for his dead wife, Isabel-Maria. She was kill in horse trailer accident."

"And he named the *acequia* in her memory? Isn't that sort of weird?"

"*Detectiva*, many do that. *La Chica*…*Los Tres Caballos*. Name like that."

"I see. Sir, would last night's rain affect the *acequia's* water level?"

26

"*Dios*, no." He shook his head, while absently scratching a Virgin of Guadalupe tattoo on his forearm. "*Lluvia*…rain…too light. Barely soak in ground."

"Thank you." Sonia inspected grass underfoot as she walked a hundred yards north, in the direction from which the waterway flowed. She stooped to pick up a short length of branch-wood, weighed it in her hand a moment, then called back, "Father Jake. Tell where this piece of wood floats."

He flashed a "thumbs up" to her, then watched the sluice's rippling surface. When the stick bobbed beyond him, toward the center of the *acequia*, he shouted, "It floated past me."

"Okay…" Sonia walked back another several yards until she found a similar small branch. After she threw it near the water's edge, the current caught the wood and swirled it in gentle arcs, until it gradually spun closer to shore, and became snagged up in the bulrushes near Fr. Jake and Vando.

The priest called to her, "It's caught near shore at about where the fetus… about where Baby Doe was discovered."

"Good. Both of you please walk over here."

Vando came up to her first. "*¿Detectiva, que paso?* What are you doing with the *madera?*"

"Sir," she explained, "I found pieces of wood about the size and weight of the fetus. Allowing for a slight difference in buoyancy, I figured the victim would drift ashore at about the same place as the wood…' Sonia pointed to the *acequia's* edge. "This is close to where Baby Doe was thrown into the water."

The detective looked around the acreage. On this side of a white fence near the north end of Don's land, a revolving center-pivot irrigator watered a circle of bright green alfalfa. Crows, fluttering black dots in the watery mist, quarreled over earthworms that squirmed to the surface. Two Arabian horses grazed beyond the sprinkler. On a rise of ground to the east, a windbreak of scotch pines partly concealed Don Fernando's sprawling ranch compound.

Sonia asked the foreman about a smaller water-filled channel that led from the main ditch. "Mister Benavides, this is a transverse irrigation ditch, correct?"

"*Si*, it pump water to pond an' flower garden of Don Fernando."

She pointed to the evergreens and building. "His place is that big house over there behind those pines?"

"*Si.*"

Fr. Jake noted, "There's a gravel path alongside this *acequia* leading from the house to the main waterway."

"*Mi patrón* an' his daughter sometime walk there."

"I see that," Sonia nodded. "Father, I'll go back to my car and alert the O.M.I. in Socorro. Mister Benavides, you wait by the *acequia* until the medical examiner arrives. Don't touch anything. Meanwhile, Father and I will inform Don Fernando about the victim we found on his property."

Vando abruptly grasped the priest's arm in a firm grip. "*Dios*, you no go too, *padre*! Since his wife die, Don Fernando got no use for any priest. No *Católica* anythin'."

Fr. Jake gently shook free. "I'll chance that and go with the detective."

"Sir," Sonia repeated, "please go wait for the medical examiner to arrive."

"*Si*," he scowled, "but *padre*, you no say I not warn you."

After Vando started back toward the waterway, Fr. Jake massaged his arm. "The man is strong as an ox. Sonia, when I finished reading my breviary this morning, I didn't connect myself with the final verse, yet now that I've heard about the Don's possible agnosticism, I'm not so sure it doesn't apply to him."

Sonia recalled, "I remember that you try to see if your reading sort of predicts events. So what did this verse say?"

"The reading was a psalm. 'Mark this, you who never think of God, lest I seize you and you cannot escape.' That certainly relates to what Vando told me about the ranch owner's attitude about priests and Catholicism in general."

Sonia turned to walk up the gravel path. "Well, *Padre Hakub*, let's go see if that 'biblical boot' does fit the foot of Don Fernando Trujillo de Sevilla."

## 3 rancho tru-cor

As they walked nearer to the main house, Sonia calculated, "Father, I'd guess that place at about five thousand square feet."

"It's certainly larger than anything I've seen in my Michigan parish."

Beyond the scotch pines, a fountain and pond in front of the house was centered on a circular asphalt driveway that led from a gated entrance on Romero Loop Road. No water splashed from the fountain; only stagnant water festered inside the basin. The priest and detective circled away while swatting at mosquitoes that swarmed at them from floating green scum. On the left, a wide garage/workshop looked large enough to park three automobiles. To the right of the garage, a porch-covered entrance led to the ranch owner's living quarters. A sign above the stairs identified the property:

**RANCHO**

**TRU-COR**

Colorful coat-of-arms from the Spanish cities of Seville and Cordoba identified the residents' family origins.

"'Tru-Cor' must be the abbreviated surnames of Trujillo and Cordova," Sonia surmised. "The ancestral families of the Don and his late wife."

Fr. Jake scratched a mosquito bite on his neck. "If there's a groundskeeper, the man isn't doing a very good job in maintaining that fountain."

"As you just found out," Sonia noticed, "it's a breeding place for mosquitoes now."

At the front entrance, Fr. Jake gave gentle raps on the door with a brass door-knock in the shape of a horse's head. Moments later a woman in late middle age, with short-cropped, gray hair, opened the door part way. She suspiciously glanced at the woman with the priest, before demanding of him, "*¿Que quiere, Padre? What you want?*"

"*Señora,* we're here to see Don Fernando."

"You want money, *Padre?*"

Fr. Jake smiled and shook his head at her question. "No, no, *señora.* We wish only to speak with the Don."

Her thin lips moved silently before she agreed. "*Si, momento.*" After she turned to go into the house, Fr. Jake pushed the door further with his foot. The open portal allowed a glimpse of a long entry hall, and beyond to an open room where cedar-beam truss-work vaulted the high ceiling.

Sonia said, "I didn't have time to show her my sheriff's ID."

The priest eyed her work clothes and quipped, "*Detectiva,* you're not exactly in uniform. The woman thought we were here begging for charity."

In a few moments, Don Fernando appeared at the door. The rancher wore khaki riding breeches, a sleeveless polo shirt, and high boots. A leather equestrian helmet he had in one hand dangled from its chinstrap; his other hand held a pair of suede gloves. Overall, the man might have passed for a middle-aged Leo Carrillo, and possibly as charming: handsome, manly features, dark wavy hair, graying at the temples, a thin pencil mustache along his upper lip.

Any charm he might possess drained from the Don's blue eyes when he saw the priest. "*Padre,* no one here is dying. If you and that young woman are collecting alms, I'm not contributing to anything that has to do with the Catholic Church."

Sonia held her ID case up to him. "Sir, I'm Detective Sonia Mora, Socorro County Sheriff Department."

Don Fernando looked at her informal clothes, then scoffed, "What, you're undercover? Detective, I haven't called your office to report any fence vandalism."

"Sir, this is much more serious. May we come in?"

The Don frowned and tilted his head toward Fr. Jake. "The *padre,* too? Why are both of you here?"

"Father Jakubowski has become part of an investigation."

"Father Jaku—" Fernando allowed himself a faint smile on recognizing the name. "Of course. You're that Anglo priest from up north, who took Jésus Mora's place at San Isidro."

"Correct, Don, and Detective Mora is Father Mora's niece. She's not in uniform because she came to clean her uncle's belongings from the church rectory."

Sonia slipped her ID case back in a pocket. "Sir, may we come inside?"

"Of course, detective." The Don's charm returned as he stepped aside with a sweeping gesture of his helmet. "I was about to exercise one of my Arabians, but we can talk in my study." He turned to glare at the priest. "I warn you, *Padre*. before I find out why you're here with law enforcement, you'll first sit through my story of why I left the Church."

Fr. Jake glanced for permission from Sonia. When she did not object, he agreed amiably, "Fair enough Don, yet you won't be the first person to tell me that kind of story."

"I'm quite sure I'm not." Fernando laid his helmet on a side table, and used his gloves to signal to the elderly woman who had answered the door. "Mrs. Nevarez," he asked pleasantly, "please bring us coffee with *empañadas* or *biscochitos*."

With a murmured "*Si*," she scurried off to the end of the hallway, stepped down, and entered a doorway to the right of the family room.

Fernando identified the old woman. "Eusebia Nevarez has been in the family for years and years. She was my daughter's childhood nanny, really, in a sense, her 'foster mother' after my wife, Isabel, died. Well…. Let's talk in my study."

The Don led the way through the entry hall, and past the vaulted space ahead that was a family entertainment room: a stone fireplace centered on one side had a leather sofas, chairs, and tables facing the open grate. A TV / Hi-Fi music center filled the opposite wall. French doors at the far end led to a patio.

The glass eyes of two Oryx heads, mounted above the fireplace, stared blankly into space.

The Don's study was to the left and down a short hallway. The dark-paneled room held a computer/work area, with shelves of books on law, animal husbandry, horse breeding, a few classic novels, and several volumes in both English and Spanish, lining three walls. A fourth wall displayed a multitude of colorful award ribbons presented a various local and national Arabian horse shows. The shelf at the top held silver and gold trophy cups won at these competitions. Beneath his prizes, a large mahogany table was crammed with photographs of Isabel-Maria Cordova, Don Fernando, and an infant daughter. Most pictures were of the petite, beautiful woman standing alone, or posing in her equestrienne outfit with a favorite Arabian mount.

Thirteen small, electric votive candles flickered at the center of the bizarre memorial —one for each year since Isabel's death.

Fr. Jake stopped at the closest photograph. "Your late wife? Cervando Benavides told us she died in an accident."

"That's true, in nineteen-ninety seven."

"I'm so sorry."

"Standard response of regret, eh, *Padre?*" Don Fernando chided in a sarcastic voice. He picked up the photo and kissed his wife's image. "I'd like to tell you about *mi amanda*...my beloved. Isabel died in a terrible accident—"

"Sir," Sonia cautioned him, "I'm not officially assigned to the investigation that will come out of this, but probably will be given the case. With your permission, I'd like to ask a few preliminary questions."

Fernando nodded accordance and put back the photo. "Only, detective, after I have my say to the *padre.*"

"Sir, please summarize what you'll tell him."

Fr. Jake looked at her. *Sonia hasn't mentioned Baby Doe yet and the Don didn't ask for any specifics about our visit. Perhaps she hopes to learn something about the fetus from what Don Fernando reveals to us.*

Fernando indicated chairs, then sat down behind his desk and looked at the priest with the eyes of an accuser. "*Padre*, Isabel-Maria Cordova's family was our neighbor in Socorro, yet we also were close friends. Isabel was four years younger than I, but we attended the same Catholic school. Neither of us had brothers or sisters."

"Both of you were raised as an only child?" Fr. Jake asked.

The Don continued without responding. "My father was an attorney who did legal work for Isabel's father, Francisco Cordova. He owned a feed and tack store in Socorro, and also this Arabian horse ranch acreage. In high school, during summers, I worked for him both in the store and over here. After graduation, I majored in animal husbandry at New Mexico State in Las Cruces, then joined the ranch full time." He paused to brush imaginary lint off his polo shirt. "I did well and Mister Cordova promoted me to manager in nineteen-eighty-eight. Isabel and I married two years later."

Sonia ventured, "Sir, Mister Benavides mentioned a daughter."

"Dulcinea." The Don smiled at his thought of the girl. "My Dulci. I call her 'Sweetness.'"

"How old is she, sir?"

"Dulci is eighteen—"

Eusebia Nevarez returned with a tray of apple *empañadas*, a coffee urn, gold-rimmed china cups, and small matching plates. Conversation paused while she poured the coffee. In filling the cups, her gray face sagged and thin lips twitched. Red blotches disfigured an area around the older woman's left eye, as if a skin infection was left untreated. After pouring three coffees, Eusebia wiped her hands on her apron and faced the priest, waiting for him to sample her pastries.

Sonia noticed. "Father, have you tried *empañadas* yet?"

"No, but they look like the *pierogi* my mother baked."

"I believe these are apple-filled. *¿Esta bien, Señora?*"

"*Si, detectiva, manzano*," she replied without smiling.

"Father," Sonia urged under her breath, "try one for the nanny's sake."

He took a bite of pastry and sip of coffee, then nodded appreciatively to Eusebia. "*Delicioso, Señora, y tambien el café.*"

Eusebia muttered a barely audible '*gracias*'and padded back to the kitchen.

Don Fernando continued where he paused, "As I said, Isabel and I married in 1990. Dulci had just turned five when her grandparents were killed on I-25. Wrong way driver. Broad daylight. Drunk. The Cordovas... they ...they were coming here from Socorro for Dulci's fifth birthday party. I...I had gotten her a pony."

"Horrible," Fr. Jake commented. "Again...my...my sympathy."

Don Fernando sipped coffee without a comment, but Sonia added, "It's an ongoing problem in New Mexico. Sir, after her parents' deaths, your wife inherited the ranch?"

"Yes. Isabel was a superb equestrienne..." He stood to bring back a different photograph of a beautiful woman in riding clothes, holding the reins of a white stallion. "*Mi amada....*"

"Mister Trujillo, tell us about the horse trailer accident."

"Isabel went to Mass every morning," he told Fr. Jake as if he had not heard Sonia's request. "She even had a private chapel dedicated to the Virgin built onto our bedroom. Maria was her namesake. We tithed to the Church. Isabel was active in both the Archbishop's Finance and Pastoral councils. There was nothing my darling Isabel wouldn't do for the Catholic Church."

Sonia repeated, "Sir, about the accident?"

"Yes. Excuse me..." He paused to turn his head and wipe his eyes. "We... we were loading a four-horse trailer for an AHA show in Albuquerque."

"AHA?" Fr. Jake questioned the unfamiliar initials

"Arabian Horse Association." The Don indicated his awards collection with his coffee cup. "Many of those are AHA. As I was saying, Vando was inside the trailer. Isabel stayed at the side ramp, behind *Vencedor,* the last horse, guiding him up the incline. For whatever reason, the stallion suddenly reared up at the entrance and hit his poll on the top of the door."

Sonia asked about the term. "Poll, sir?"

"It's a crucial joint, detective, at the top of the head, between the atlas and skull. Any blow there to an animal, even a large one like a horse, is as a deadly karate chop would be to a human. The animal is blinded."

"I see." Sonia tasted her coffee and shifted position in the chair. "Please go on, Mister Trujillo."

"*Vencedor* lashed out with his hind legs. The nearest right hoof caught Isabel in the head. She...she never regained consciousness. *Mi amada* died in my arms in an ambulance on the way to the hospital."

"Sir," Sonia ventured softly, "I'm sorry for your loss."

"Sorry, yes!" Don Fernando reacted with anger. "What human being with any feelings at all would not be sorry? *Padre,*" he challenged, "can you explain to me why God allowed that to happen to Isabel? Or to her deceased parents, since we're speaking of accidents?"

"Centuries ago Job asked the same question," Fr. Jake replied. "The Lord may help us, but humans must find solutions to the problems they create. You can't blame God—"

"Then who?" Fernando demanded, his handsome features now an ugly mask of hate. "We both were heavily involved in the Church... *his* church. Isn't God supposed to watch over those who love and serve him?"

Sonia thought it an appropriate place to tell Fernando her reason for questioning him. "Sir, we aren't here to discuss theology. Earlier this morning, your ranch boss, Cervando Benavides, discovered a human fetus in your irrigation ditch."

After a pause in which Fernando returned his wife's photograph to the table shrine, he repeated as a question, "A human fetus? Detective, what are you babbling about?"

"Mister Benavides discovered a fetus in your *acequia,* and then went to Armando Herrera's shop in order to summon a priest. That's why Father Jakubowski is here with me."

"A fetus? I...I can't believe that." Fernando slumped back in his chair. "How—?"

Sonia asked, "Who, besides Mister Benavides works here as a ranch hand?"

The Don's hand shook as he finished his coffee and set the cup down. "Detective, there are three stable workers. Gilbert Begay, a Navajo. Lorenzo Lujan, and Mathias Crisp. Two Green Card seasonal workers from Mexico tend the fields. The Torrez are a husband and wife couple."

"We'll question all of them in due time," Sonia told him, "but, if I may, I'd like a word now with Dulcinea, your daughter."

"No, I can't let you do that." Fernando's dead stare and firm tone suggested he always had his way, even with law enforcement officers. "Dulci isn't well and besides, what does finding this…this fetus…have to do with her?"

"Sir, the questioning is routine."

"Dulci is under a doctor's care." Agitated now, Fernando shook his head as he stood up. "No! I can't let you upset her."

Sonia finished the last of her coffee, then stood and faced him. "The names you mentioned are the only household members and workers you have on the premises. Is that correct, sir?"

"That is correct, detective." The frigid tone of his reply indicated questioning was over.

"Sir, thank you…" Sonia turned to the priest. "Father, we'll go now—"

"Fernandi." A woman's mellifluous voice from the doorway interrupted a response. "Fernandi, you are not going to tell that *detectiva* and the *padre* about me, Lareina 'Queen Millie' Jaramillo?"

A slim woman with smooth, expressionless Indio-Mexican features, wearing an ankle-length black dress, stood in the doorway. Despite her gentle reprimand to the Don, Queen Millie was not smiling.

# 4 queen millie

As a youthful-looking, fiftyish woman stepped gracefully into the room, window light caught her eyes. Her left iris shone dark brown, almost of the same darkness as the pupil. The iris of her right eye was light blue.

"Ah...yes. Millie, that is, Miss Jaramillo is a...a healer," the Don explained with barely concealed nervousness. "She...she's a practitioner of *curanderismo*."

"Like Ofilia, Armando's aunt," Fr. Jake recalled.

"*Si, Padre*," Queen Millie said. "I hear of *una vieja curandera* in village."

Sonia looked at Fernando with a disapproving frown. "Mister Trujillo, you told me that your daughter was under a doctor's care, not that of a folk healer."

Millie retorted first with simmering scorn, "These fancy doctors, they don't know everything. Me, I study Mexican *curanderismo* with El Perito. He learn from the great El Niño Fidencio in Esperanzo, Estado de Sierra Leon..." She held up an elk-skin bag dangling from a belt at her waist. "Also I know Nahuatl cures—"

Sonia insisted, "Miss Jaramillo, do you have valid medical credentials? Are you treating Don Fernando's daughter?"

"When I get work visa, Immigration ask me that," she smirked. 'I tell them my father was *Americano* mine engineer. See"—she pointed to the right side of her face—"I have blue *gringo* eye." They laugh, say, 'Maybe if you have eye color of Green Card, we believe you'."

The detective turned back to Fernando. "Sir, I still would like to speak with your daughter."

"No! I forbid!" Millie stepped back with her arms spread to block the door. "Dulci suffer *susto*, bad fright that become worse and worse. Now is *desasombro*. Her spirit-soul wander away during sleep. Sometime, too, in daylight."

"'Spirit soul'?" Sonia asked. "That doesn't sound like a medical condition."

Fernando was defensive. "Detective, what Miss Jaramillo refers to is that Dulci was five years old and present when her mother was killed. She watched from a safe distance with Mrs. Nevarez, who immediately took her back to the house after the accident. Of course, my daughter was upset, yet she seemed quite normal until a few years ago. Dulci underwent menstruation at a later age. She was fourteen and changed about that time... became moody and withdrawn."

"At womanhood," Millie explained, "*susto* vision come out from mind. Dulci not eat, lose weight. Bad sleep. That when the *susto* turn to *desasombro* condition."

Fr. Jake said, "It sounds like you're saying that Dulci repressed the memory of her mother's horrible death until puberty. Don, you've no doubt had her examined by a physician?"

"Of course, and by several pediatric specialists. Dulci's abrupt decline baffled all of them. Nothing helped until I...well...until I heard about Miss Jaramillo and invited her to treat...to help... my daughter."

Sonia requested, "Sir, before we leave, I would like to speak briefly with Mrs. Nevarez. Father Jakubowski would be present."

The Don glanced at Millie, who nodded slightly. "I...I wouldn't object to that. Her living quarters are at the rear of the house."

"Adjacent to your daughter's room?"

"No, Dulci is next to Miss Jaramillo's quarters. My daughter is in one room beyond mine." Fernando fussed with his shirt cuffs a moment, then stood up. "Come, I'll take you to Mrs. Nevarez."

Queen Millie stepped aside with a stiff smile. "*Hasta, Padre...detectiva.*"

Eusebia Nevarez stood at the kitchen sink, washing the family's breakfast dishes.

Don Fernando gently told her, "Eusebia, this detective would like to ask you some questions about what was discovered on the ranch this morning."

"*Si*, but I keep working," she replied without looking around.

Sonia turned to Dulci's father. "Thank you, sir, please go on with what you were doing. We'll see ourselves out."

"Yes. Keep me informed." Fernando touched his forehead with two fingers in a kind of salute. "Good day to you both."

After he left the kitchen, Sonia told the housekeeper, "Mrs. Nevarez, a fetus, an unborn male child, was found in the *acequia* this morning."

The old woman gasped and brought a hand up to her mouth. "¡*Ave Maria Purisima, esta La Llorona!*"

"Pardon?" Fr. Jake questioned an unfamiliar name.

"Father," Sonia explained, "La Llorona is a woman in a Latino folk tale, who wanders the countryside weeping and moaning as she searches for her lost children. Some parents try to keep their youngsters from misbehaving by threatening that La Llorona will come to punish them, if they act up."

. "In this day and age?" Fr. Jake was skeptical, but reconsidered. "I must admit that back in Poland there are similar tales for persuading children to behave."

"My parents never tried to frighten me with that story." Sonia turned to the nanny. "*Señora*, do you know of any pregnant girls living close by?" After the old woman shook her head in ignorance of anyone in that condition, the detective said, "I'm sorry, but I must ask you about Don Fernando's daughter."

"Dulcinea? ¿*Por que?*"

"It's for my investigation. *Señora*, does the girl get out much? Is there a boyfriend?"

"*Sancta Maria, no, detectiva.*"

"Does she have many friends at school?"

"Not go to school. Teacher come here three time a week."

"A male?"

"*No, una mujer. Maestra.*"

Fr. Jake asked, "Is Dulci also taught by Miss Jaramillo?"

"¿*Èsa hechicera?* Nevarez's face clouded over as she spat out her scorn for the woman, "*Impostor... Embaucador.*"

Sonia translated, "You call her an imposter? A cheat?"

"*Si.* I call her *La Hechicera. Encantadora.*"

"Enchantress?"

"She say Dulcinea have *almizclera* sickness."

"Muskrat sickness? Why does Miss Jaramillo say that?"

"*Detectiva*, Indio shaman believe animal cause person to be sick. Muskrat can make *menstruo* problem."

"Menstruation?" Fr. Jake understood. "The Don did say that his daughter's declining condition began around that time."

"*Si, Padre,*" Nevarez confirmed. "We have many *almizclera* in Rio and *acequias.* Make person's mind mix up. No energy, like Dulcinea."

Skeptical, Fr. Jake nevertheless asked, "And what is the cure, *Señora,* for this illness that muskrats bring?"

"*Padre,* you see bag *La Hechicera* have? Fill with things from river… funny shape wood, stones, dry plants. She make *altarista* in room. Not for saint, like Francis or San Camilo, *patrón* of sick people. Put many thing of Dulcinea there, with mud animal statue, skull."

"A muskrat skull?" Sonia asked.

"Maybe, *detectiva. Mal.* Bad to do that!" Eusebia shook her finger. "I no like Millie."

"Mrs. Nevarez, why does the Don keep Miss Jaramillo around?"

The old woman glanced past the kitchen before whispering to Sonia, "*Hechizaro.*"

"She's bewitched him?"

"*Si, detectiva.*"

Sonia stood up and motioned to Fr. Jake that further questioning would be useless. "*Gracias, Señora.* If I'm assigned to this case, I may need to speak with you again."

Outside on the driveway, Sonia waved away mosquitoes at the fountain's stagnant pool. "Look at that floating green scum. As you pointed out, Father, if there's a groundskeeper here, he or she isn't doing a good job."

"After what we've seen and heard, Don Fernando may not want the fountain turned on. It would be another reminder of his deceased wife."

"Weird, since he has a table full of mementos about her. Let's see if the M.E. is still down there."

The Mobile Crime Scene Lab and medical examiner had finished their work and left. Beyond the buffer of pine trees, Sonia noted, "I see the C.S. Lab strung crime scene tape along the *acequia* bank, from where I estimated the victim was thrown in, to where it…where Baby Doe was found."

"You mentioned that distance in your phone call?"

"Yes." The two walked in silence over now-dried grass to her Plymouth Neon, parked near the waterway. "Buckle up, Father," she said, after unlocking the door. "Are you still wondering why I don't get this old car washed very often?"

"You told me it was because its decrepit condition throws lawbreakers off the scent."

"Like, it's not really decrepit," she said, mimicking a teen age voice. "But like, would a cop or detective own a car this dirty?"

"I guess not, Sonia."

"Bingo, Father."

*Bingo?* He laughed at her recollection of a largely forgotten parish activity. "Not much of that game is played these days, even in church halls. Too many casinos out there, competing for senior citizens' cash. We have gaming in Detroit and across the river in Canada."

"Then how *do* you raise money for your parish?"

"Guess you've never Googled 'Church Fundraising Ideas.' Let's see… selling restaurant and movie cards. Raffles are legion, and candy bar and popcorn sales are favorites. Candles, scratch cards, and silent auctions are only a partial list of dozens of fundraising items that are available."

"Jeez, Christ must be turning over in his grave."

"What, Sonia?" he demanded sharply and looked over at her. "Is that a joke?"

She flushed at his reprimand and apologized, "Real sorry, Father. The guys say that, but it…it isn't funny."

"No, it is not." A moment after Sonia started the Plymouth and circled back around the road, the priest asked, "Tell me more about this woman, La Yor…Yor—"

"La Llorona…double 'L' with a 'Y' sound."

"La Llorona, then?"

"Good, Father. Well, there are as many stories about her as there are *viejos* to tell them. Basically…one or maybe two of her children drowned and she roams around the countryside at night, wailing and searching for her kids. The *Acequia Madre* in Santa Fe is one of her favorite hangouts."

"No wonder Mrs. Nevarez thought of La Llorona, when we mentioned the ranch's sluice, the 'Mother Ditch'."

"Right. Depends on who tells the story, but the old gal dresses in either a long white or black dress, with a shawl covering her head. Some say it's more of a hood. "

"Detective," he chided, "you sound a bit irreverent."

Sonia slapped her forehead in mock regret. "I guess that's twice now, Father. As I said, my parents never frightened me into behaving with spooky stories."

They had reached the corner of the Romero Loop and the Highway 310. As Sonia made a left turn with the Plymouth, she inquired, "So, Father, what did you think of…Queen Millie…was it?"

"Well, it's certain that Eusebia Nevarez doesn't like her. Probably because Millie has pretty much moved in and replaced her in Dulci's life."

"And maybe as the Don's new '*amada*'?"

"To replace Isabel? Charitably speaking, he could just be desperate to find someone…anyone…who might help his daughter. According to him, physicians couldn't do anything."

Sonia recalled, "Fernando said that Millie's room adjoins his."

"'Let him or her who casts the first stone…'" Fr. Jake lightly touched her arm. "My turn to apologize, Detective Mora. I didn't mean to imply anything about your spin on their relationship."

She reached over to pat his hand. "No offense taken, Father Jake. In solving cases, every possibility is explored. Such as, that Mrs. Nevarez thinks Millie bewitched him."

"Do you believe that?"

"Father Jake, in police work we see individuals who go bonkers for no apparent reason. Call it lust, bewitchment, whatever, but sexual attraction can be a compelling motivation. And when I asked to speak with Mrs. Nevarez, 'Fernandi' glanced toward Millie as if asking for permission."

"That's true. Sonia, when will you know if you'll be assigned to the Baby Doe case?"

"Possibly as early as today. I'll call in, but we haven't cleared out your rectory."

After they passed the church parking lot that faced the highway, and Sonia turned onto Calle San Isidro, Fr. Jake felt a chill run through his body. "Uh, oh. See that olive drab Hummer parked in front of my place?

"Properly, a military Humvee, Father, and an older surplus model. What of it?"

"I saw it up at the survivalist compound. Perhaps the owner hid up there and came back to…to even the score with me for the raid on his drug running operation."

Sonia slowed the Plymouth. "Duck down, Father. I'll drive past and then turn around to come up behind the vehicle. Now do you see what I mean about just another dirty red car not attracting much attention?"

"Thank God for that…."

To be out of sight, Fr. Jake bent down as far as possible, his forehead resting on the car's dashboard. Sonia stopped at the end of the Calle, unlocked the glove compartment, and took out her Glock G19 Compact revolver. She turned the car around and slowly approached the squat rear end of the parked Humvee.

## 5 dave and breanna

Holding a sheriff's ID in her left hand, the Glock revolver low in her right, Sonia used caution in walking along the vehicle's left side, toward the open driver's window. Her gaze followed a man's gray eyes, watching her arrival in his side view mirror.

Standing slightly back from the hatless driver, Sonia held forward her ID. "Sir, Detective Mora from the Socorro County Sheriff Department. Keep one hand on the steering wheel and show me your license and car registration with the other." She glanced past him at a woman passenger. "Ma'am, put both your hands on the dashboard."

"What's this about, detective?" the driver asked with an innocent smile. "We're just waiting to see the Reverend who lives here."

"Sir, hand me your license and car papers."

"Sure thing." The man, who looked to be in his early twenties, with blond hair and squinting eyes, reached inside the breast pocket of a tan camouflage jacket and handed over a New Mexico driver's license, the Humvee's registration, and an insurance card. "Everything's in order, detective."

"David Allison," she read, comparing the license photo with the driver. *Round, almost boyish face, small mouth, scars, but a hard look in the eyes. That uniform was bought in a military surplus store, yet he may have been in the service and seen combat.* "Sir, you have a fairly new driver's license with an address on Center Street in Belén?"

"It's a motel," he admitted, then indicated the woman, who looked some ten years older than him. "My friend, Breanna Springer. We're staying at the Zia Motel while I look for work."

Sonia handed back his documentation, then tucked the Glock in her waistband. "Sir, why did you wish to see Father Jakubowski?"

"Jacob who?" Allison glanced at Breanna and chuckled. When she did not share his mirth, he turned back to Sonia. "We have a favor to ask of the good Reverend. Look, detective, if this is about us being in the survivalist camp, we were held for almost two weeks and questioned. We got released yesterday, because those DEA cops realized that we had no connection with Billy Ray Scurry's narcotics operation. I told them it was just the old guy and his stupid sons running it, and we knew nothing about what was going on."

Sonia asked, "Sir, are there any weapons in your vehicle?"

Allison's gray eyes looked directly at her. "No, Ma'am, there sure aren't."

"Please wait here." Sonia walked back toward her car. Fr. Jake lay slumped down on the passenger side. "It's okay," she called to him through the open window. "This couple just wants to speak with you."

The priest opened the passenger door, eased out, and came around to her side. "Sonia, who are they? How do they know me?"

"You were partly right. They were members of the Fort Liberty survivalist camp, but evidently not involved in drug trafficking. While you talk to them, I'll go over to the rectory and sort out more of my uncle's...of Father Mora's...things."

"Fine, Sonia. I'll join you as soon as I can."

As Fr. Jake walked up to the Humvee, Allison opened the door and stepped out. The priest recognized the young man. "You were at the fort with Scurry on the night of the raid. His son brought me up there at gunpoint."

"I'm Dave Allison," he said extending a hand. "Real sorry about that, Reverend. I had no idea what Colonel Scurry was up to. You know, about the drug running and all."

Fr. Jake returned his grasp. "Son, Scurry wasn't an Army officer. Billy Ray was a private in the first Gulf War and, in fact, was given a bad conduct discharge."

"B.C.D.? Imagine. Sure had me fooled. Oh"—he pointed to the woman on the Humvee's passenger side—"That's my friend, Breanna."

Fr. Jake nodded acknowledgement. "Dave, what did you want to see me about?"

"Reverend, can we go inside your place?"

"Of course. I'll put on a pot of coffee."

"That would be real nice." Allison leaned in the car. "Come on, Breanna. We're going inside the Reverend's house."

Inside the *casita*, the couple looked around at what obviously were second hand furnishings. "Nice place you got here, Reverend," Allison remarked.

"You're being kind, Dave," the priest acknowledged back the kitchen. "I was preparing to move into the San Isidro rectory, when Detective Mora and I had to go out on a case."

"Yeah? What about?"

Fr. Jake avoided an answer when he came into the living room. "Coffee'll be ready shortly. Sit on the couch, both of you and I'll take the armchair. Now, how can I help you?"

Allison sucked in a breath. "Well, Reverend, it's real sad. I served in Iraq from '07 to '09. One of my buddies was from around here and we, well, we joined Scurry's bunch a few months ago."

Breanna added, "Not really knowin' what a scum bag the S.O.B. was."

"Go on, Dave."

"Well, Reverend, my buddy died suddenly just before the DEA raid. Those Pentecostals in the adjoining commune make coffins, and they have a big freezer room to store meat. I bought a coffin from them for burying him."

"What? And your friend is still in their freezer?"

"Well, with the raid and all—"

"Excuse me, Dave, I think the coffee's done." Shaken at the bizarre story, Fr. Jake stood up to fill their cups. "You take milk and sugar?"

When both nodded they did, the priest returned with three steaming mugs on a wooden tray.

Allison smiled. "Thank you kindly, Reverend."

"Dave, most people call me Father Jake. Feel free."

"Maybe I'll just keep it 'Reverend' like my mom would want."

"Fine. What is the name of your deceased soldier friend? How old was he?"

"Dominic Salazar. He was an E-7 Platoon sergeant. Age? Probably around thirty."

"Is there a death certificate?" Fr. Jake asked.

The man glanced at Breanna. "Yeah. The Pentecostals have a doctor and he was there when Sal...everybody called him that...when Sal died. The doc put down that it was pneumonia."

"And what would you like me to do, Dave?"

Breanna, who had commented once and then fidgeted by winding and unwinding strands of long, dull-brown hair, answered for him in a melodic drawl. "Rev., seein' as the sargint was from around here, we wondered if he could be buried out yonder in your graveyard."

Fr. Jake asked, "From where 'around here' Breanna?"

"Don't rightly know."

"I'm a new priest here. Was Sergeant Salazar from Providencia or a parishioner at San Isidro?"

Breanna shrugged her ignorance of Salazar's origins and looked at Allison. "Sugah, do y'all know?"

"Sal never talked about a specific place," Dave answered. "All I know for sure is that he said he was from this area and his dog tag was stamped 'C' for 'Catholic.'"

"I could check the parish records, but I'm not positive that Father Mora kept them up to date."

Breanna said quietly, "We just can't keep poor Sal in that freezer forever, Rev."

"No, Breanna, we can't," Fr. Jake agreed.

Allison ran a hand through his blond hair, then spread both hands apart in a plea for help. "Reverend, you're the only one I could think of to ask. And, I mean, Sal *was* Hispanic."

"He could be a Catholic from Mars, Dave, and still be buried here if I authorized it. Let me talk to Armando Herrera, a parishioner. Do you have a phone at the Zia?"

"Yeah…" Allison pulled a motel business card from his wallet and handed it to the priest. "Write the number down and Room 105."

"All right. Meanwhile, drink your coffee."

"Reverend…" Allison stood up and motioned to the woman. "Breanna and I will drive over and take a look at your cemetery."

"It's down there at the end of the Calle San Isidro."

"We know," she said.

Fr. Jake wrote the motel's phone and room number on a note pad and handed back the card. "Dave, Belén must have a Veterans of Foreign Wars post. I could call to get you a flag and probably a graveside honor guard."

"I dunno, Reverend, we got a flag. And us joining up with Scurry was a big mistake, but those VFW guys, they might not understand."

"Of course, as you wish. Ah, Dave," Fr. Jake ventured, "I have a five o'clock Mass on Saturdays. You don't have to be Catholic—"

"Reverend, we just might be there." He looked toward his companion. "What do you say, Brea?"

"Just might, sugah. Rev., we were thinkin' that July Four would be an appropriate date for the funeral. You know, the Fourth o' July bein' Independence Day an' all."

Allison reinforced her request. "Yeah, and with Sal dying after serving his country."

"The holiday date is a Sunday," Fr. Jake reminded them, "so a funeral wouldn't be held then. Besides, I'm scheduled to see Civil War re-enactors in the afternoon. How would Monday the fifth be? That's a week from today."

"Guess that suits us fine, Reverend," Allison said. "Right, Brea?"

"Sure, Sugah, close enough." She stood up with him. "Let's do it on the fifth."

"I could ask Armando to recruit some of his friends as pallbearers."

Breanna smiled for the first time. "Super. We were hopin' for somethin' like that to honor Sal."

Dave Allison opened the door. "Thanks Reverend. Much obliged."

"You're welcome and I'll be in touch." From his porch, Fr. Jake watched the Humvee turn around and head toward the *camposanto*, then went back inside to clear away the mugs. "Hmm, neither one touched their coffee. Well, I'd better go help Sonia pack up what Father Mora left behind."

Fr. Jake met the petite detective halfway to her car, carrying the department store boxes. He reached out. "Here, let me...."

"Thanks, Father, I've got them. I'm only going to take these now and come back later for clothes and whatever else. You still have a few days before that anthropologist arrives. I'm leaving you the cooking utensils, but you'll want a new mattress and blankets. You can keep the roll-top desk and dresser, but the living room furniture ...well...frankly, it stinks. Find something newer."

"Thanks, Sonia. I'll get the car door for you."

As they walked to her Plymouth, the detective said, "The discovery of Baby Doe changed what I was going to do today. I'm heading back to Socorro." At the car Sonia put the two boxes in the trunk, eased herself into the driver's seat, and looked up at Fr. Jake. "Oh, what was it that David Allison wanted?"

"An army buddy of his died and he asked me to conduct a funeral."

Sonia rubbed her chin in surprise. "I didn't think Allison was from around here."

"He isn't, but he says that his friend was. Dominic Salazar."

"Salazar? That's a common surname, with probably over two hundred in the Albuquerque phone book alone."

"Dave's woman companion was older. Breanna didn't say much until they were about to leave, but I think she's one tough cookie. That gal may wear the pants in the family, as the saying goes."

"Both ex-military?"

"Possibly. Dave's way of speaking was Midwestern. Hers had a gentle drawl that might have been West Virginian."

"Hey," Sonia quipped, "you're getting to be quite observant, Father, just like a real detective." She started the engine, eased the Neon into Drive, and held her foot on the brake. "If I'm assigned to the Baby Doe case, I'll call you tomorrow. I may want you to be there when I talk to Dulcinea."

"The Don's attitude probably soured his daughter on priests. Remember?"

"Still...." Sonia slowly eased her foot off the brake pedal. "Well, thanks, Father. I'll be in touch."

"God bless." The priest watched her drive off, then went back to spruce up the rectory as best he could with whatever cleaning supplies Pastor Mora left behind.

O

Later that afternoon, Fr. Jake walked to the Providencia Grocery & Gas to pick up something for his supper and speak with Armando Herrera. The young auto mechanic was in his shop behind the grocery, working in the engine compartment of his Camaro.

When he noticed the priest, he wiped his hands on a blue work rag. "Hi, Father Hakub. I'm still cleanin' grit outta my car's air filter. What happened over at Don Fernando's?"

"The fetus was a male, but beyond that we don't know much. The Don's housekeeper thought that Sonia and I were taking up a collection."

"That would be Eusebia Nevarez."

"Right and the Don wants to hold up a crucifix whenever a priest comes near him."

Armando laughed and slapped the Camaro's fender. "Like clergy people was vampires or somethin'."

Fr. Jake smiled. "That *was* a poor example of mine in trying to describe his dislike for priests. In any case, the Don blames God for the accident that killed his wife."

"Yeah, Isabel was *muy bella*, really beautiful. Since then he don't... doesn't...come around when his BMW needs fixin'. Sends one of his ranch hands instead."

"Somewhat of a recluse, then?"

"For sure, Father. How's his daughter doin'?"

"Fernando wouldn't let us see Dulcinea. Neither would the Mexican *curandera* woman who's treating her."

"That would be Queen Millie," Armando surmised. "My *tia* Ofilia is a *curandera*, too, and she doesn't like her one bit."

"Is it professional rivalry between Ofilia and Millie?"

"Y' know Father Hakub, like there's different kinds of doctors, *curanderismo* has different kinds of people practicin' it. *Tia* works with plant cures, but some *curanderos* still go on tryin' to contact dead people. Maybe Millie does."

"Is that true, Armando?"

"Look, I don't know that much about it, but it's something not to be messin' with..." He glanced around for the priest's car. "You here because somethin's wrong with Nissy?"

"No, the Nissan you sold me is running very well. I need a favor."

"Sure, Father, anythin' I can do."

"A veteran of the Iraq war died recently. Dave Allison, a friend of his, wants him buried in our *camposanto*. The name is Sergeant Dominic Salazar."

"Salazar?" The mechanic shook his head. "Don't ring a bell. Where's he from?"

"Allison isn't sure."

"What can I do, go try and find his family?"

"No, Armando, since that might be impossible. We'll need pallbearers to carry the sergeant's coffin from the church to the grave site."

"Oh, sure, Father Hakub. I'll round up some *Hermanos*."

"You mean *Penitentes*?"

Armando frowned at hearing the term. "Father, the Brotherhood doesn't like to be called that. It would be like me callin' religious guys that are different from us 'Weirdos'. Like...like those Pentecostals up there in their commune."

"Sorry, Detective Mora implied as much. Have you joined the Brotherhood again?"

"Well, you know, the *Hermanos* help out people that need it. Like in that reading at church yesterday about lovin' your neighbor. You said it meant we should all help one another."

"Armando, you'd make a fine theologian by cutting through all the doctrinal murk. Yes, Saint Paul summed it up in his letter to the Galatians by warning that if they went snapping and tearing at each other they could destroy the whole community."

"And it's bad enough here in Providencia with all the young people leavin'."

"I'm sorry to hear that."

Armando wiped a spot of grease on the Camaro's fender. "So when is this Salazar funeral?"

"July fifth. Probably at ten o'clock."

"Don't worry, Father Hakub. I'll get some guys there."

"Thanks, Armando, and I'll mention it at Mass. The sergeant volunteered to help defend this country and should have at least minimal recognition at his funeral."

"You're right there, Father."

"Now I'll go see Carlotta about what I might eat for supper."

"And I got to finish cleanin' the shit…I mean grit…out'a my engine."

"God bless…."

When the priest entered the store, Carlotta Ulibarri, proprietress of the Providencia Grocery & Gas, was stashing a line of new frozen dinners in the freezer. The blond, middle-aged woman heard the door open, turned, and wiped both hands on her apron. "'Morning, Father Jake. You're early today for picking up your supper."

"That's because I had to see Armando about something."

"About what?" she asked, then flushed. "None of my business. Come on over here, Father. I think you're eating too much lasagna and want to show you these." Carlotta held up the bag of a frozen meal. "This here's a braised beef dinner with vegetables. Healthy and this holds a couple pounds of it. Might even last you for two, three meals."

He chuckled at her salesmanship. "Okay, sold, Carlotta. I always trust your judgment."

"Then y' know, Father, you oughta wear a hat. Pardon my saying it, but your face is pretty sunburned. Providencia is 'bout a mile high altitude…

thinner air." The woman pulled him by the sleeve toward a hat display rack. "Look over here. You want something in a western style, like this Tri-Conch with turned up side brims?"

This time the priest laughed at her choice. "Not until I take up wrangling cattle."

"NMT cap, then?" she asked. "New Mexico Tech? No, not much shade in wearing a cap. How about an open weave South Beach model?"

"What would my parishioners think of that gaudy hat band on a priest?"

"Okay, Father..." She tried a flat-crowned style on him and cocked it at a slight angle. "This looks good on you. Called a 'gambler hat,' but you don't need to tell anyone."

"As I said, I trust your judgment." He checked the price. "Tag says 'Fifteen dollars'."

"Clergy discount, Father Jake, so make it twelve."

"Sold."

She brought the frozen food bag to the counter. "Anything else, Father?" Her questioning look wondered what he had wanted with Armando.

"Thanks, if I think of something, I'll come back later this afternoon. Carlotta, I went to ask Armando for a few pallbearers to help out at a soldier's funeral next Monday."

The woman crossed herself. "*Santa Maria,* I'm afraid to ask who it was got killed?"

"Does the name Dominic Salazar mean anything to you?"

She thought a moment before shaking her head. "No Salazars living around here I know, and I know 'bout everyone."

"Interesting, neither did Armando recognize the name."

"Okay, Father, with the hat that'll be fifteen, fifty...with tax, sixteen dollars even. The beef dinner costs a bit more than your lasagna, but, like I said, you'll get two, three meals."

"That's fine." As the priest fished a twenty-dollar bill from his wallet, he probed, "Carlotta, what do you know about Lareina Jaramillo up at Don Fernando Trujillo's ranch, or his daughter, Dulcinea?"

She paused with the register drawer open. "Dulci's a sweet girl, but I'd call her anorexic. I mean look at her...no breasts to speak of, skinny legs. And Eusebia Nevarez told me that Dulci was late having her first period." Carlotta took his money with a scowl, then said, "That *curandera* you mentioned calls herself Queen Millie."

"I know. How long has she been treating Dulcinea?"

The woman brushed her hair back as she handed Fr. Jake his four-dollar change. "Millie showed up at a booth during a harvest festival in Belén, I think 'bout…'bout four…five years ago."

"Dulcinea was thirteen or fourteen back then," Fr. Jake calculated.

"I guess. She was there with her father showing his Arabians. Millie kind of enchanted the Don with her fast talk about death-spaces… *conquistadores*…spiritual levels and what she thought was wrong with Dulci."

"Millie moved in with Don Fernando?"

"Sort of, the poor guy was lonely. I mean his wife, Isabel Maria, had been dead for some nine years."

"Armando thinks Millie tries to channel Isabel's spirit."

"Channel?" Carlotta asked, "What does that mean?"

"You, know, try to communicate with Isabel. Perhaps in a trance state."

"Father, you haven't been in New Mexico that long, but out here we take November the first very seriously."

"That's All Saint's Day?"

She explained, "We call it *Dia de los Muertos*…Day of the Dead. When Millie first came in here, she bragged about studying in Mexico at some sacred place with famous healer guys. You know *curanderismo* has a lot of different methods for practicing it."

"So Armando told me. Don Fernando keeps a…a rather macabre shrine to his deceased wife….candles, pictures of her, all sorts of mementos. Carlotta, that kind of extended grieving isn't good for him or especially Dulcinea."

"Who's to say, Father?" she asked, abruptly defensive. "Folks here generally mind their own business."

*End of conversation with an 'outsider' then.* Fr. Jake held up his purchase. "Carlotta, thanks for the health tip. I'm sure I'll enjoy the dinner, and God Bless."

"Bye." She walked back around to his side of the counter to finish stocking the refrigerator with frozen dinners, then turned back. "Oh, and here's another tip, *Padre*. If I was you, I wouldn't mess too much with something you don't know nothing about."

"I'll remember that." *And it's just as well that finding Baby Doe has been kept from public knowledge.*

## 6 dulcinea's dilemma

Barefoot, wearing shorts and a halter top, Dulcinea Isabel Trujillo de Sevilla absorbed the morning sun, while lying in a patio lounge chair and reading a paperback self-help book.

The tramp of riding boots echoed on the flagstone paving. Don Fernando rounded the corner of the house, gently lifted his daughter's sun hat and kissed her forehead. "Sweetness, I'm back from my ride in the *bosque*. Did you say good morning to your mother?"

"*Papá*, mom's dead," she replied without putting down her book.

"I know that, Sweetness. I meant her pictures in my study." When his daughter did not respond, he glanced at the book's title. "'Self Esteem: Finding the Real You.' Did Millie give you that?"

"No, *Nana* Eusebia did."

"Where would she find such a book?" Fernando noted his daughter's thin arms, almost skeletal legs, and prominent collarbones. Her breasts hardly made a bulge under the halter. "Did...did you eat any breakfast?"

"What you told me mom used to eat. A piece of toast and coffee."

"That's great, Sweetness! What would you like to do today? We could go help groom the horses. Would you like that?"

"*Papá* don't!" Dulci slammed down the book and snatched off her sunglasses. "*Papá*, at times like this I believe you think of me as still being five years old. The age I was when Mom was killed."

Taken aback by the outburst, her father retorted, "Nonsense, that... that's not true. You're my big grown-up girl now."

"Then tell me who were you talking with earlier this morning?"

Fernando hesitated a moment before admitting, "A detective and that new Anglo priest at San Isidro."

"What about?"

"Now, Sweetness, you need not concern yourself about any of what we discussed."

"Why not? And, *Papá*, I really wish you wouldn't call me by that sickening, childish nickname."

"My dear, Dulcinea means 'Sweetness' in Spanish."

"I know that, but I'd like it better if you just called me Dulci."

"Of course, Swee—" He sighed and corrected himself. "Very well…Dulci it is." Fernando held out a hand to her. "Now…Dulci…how about going to groom those horses?"

"I suppose," she agreed with little enthusiasm. The girl slipped a bookmark in the page where she left off reading, adjusted her sunglasses, and stood up.

The Don pointed toward a golf cart parked beyond the patio. "We could ride over in that. Wouldn't it be fun?"

"*Papá*, I'd like to walk."

"Very well."

The two went back through the family room of the ranch house. Eusebia was in the kitchen preparing for lunch, but Millie Jaramillo was not in sight. While Dulci slipped into a pair of sandals set inside the front door, Fernando hung his riding helmet on a clothes tree and slapped on a tan cowboy-style Stetson.

Outdoors, a breeze fragrant with the combined smell of fresh-cut grass and heated *bosque* vegetation came in from the west. The warm wind blew away mosquitoes, but rippled the stagnant water in the driveway's silent pond, and set in motion slimy threads of algae that clogged the surface.

Dulci gagged, as she bent over the pond's stone rim. "*Papá*, this water totally stinks. Why don't you have the thing cleaned out and turn that fountain on again? Put some plants in the water, just like I remember it. Even a few koi fish."

"Dulci, you know snakes came to gobble up the fish. Besides, your mother—"

"I know! I know!" she shouted, stamping a foot. "You've *told* me a hundred times that mom was afraid of snakes, but…she…she's not here any more. This is another stupid shrine to her!" Under her sunglasses, tears flooded the girl's eyes. "Mom's dead, *Papá*, so it doesn't matter now! None of what you do about her matters!"

Fernando reddened and glared at his daughter. "Young lady, don't you *dare* talk to me about your mother in that tone—" The Don stopped his harsh reprimand in mid-sentence, regained control, and pointed toward the stables. "Diablo Negro had a slight limp last evening," he told his daughter softly. "I...I wonder how he's doing today." He hesitated, then, with a trembling smile, linked a tanned arm in the girl's thin one. "Well, Dulci, let's go find out."

The two walked in an awkward silence until they reached a white-painted, wooden building with a corrugated green metal roof and the same trim color. Twin dormers on the sloping roof admitted light into an interior that stabled five horses—two Arabian stallions and three mares. A **TRU-COR** weathervane on top undulated in the breeze that came from the west. In the stable area, an odor of manure overlaid the outside's grassy scent, yet it was not an unpleasant smell. Beyond the stable, two mares munched grain feed from troughs in an open air, three-horse "Mare Motel."

Mathias Crisp, one of the stable hands, shoveled compost from a metal-pipe enclosure into a Bobcat front loader tractor.

'Matt," Fernando called over to him, "How is Diablo today?"

The man paused to look up. "Better, sir. That liniment did the trick..." Matt tipped his battered straw cowboy hat to his employer's daughter. "'Morning, Miss."

Dulci turned to look out the door without acknowledging his greeting.

Thirty-two years old, Mathias Crisp had somewhat close-together eyes in an oval face, a full shock of dark hair, and sported a mustache and goatee that surrounded a small mouth with thin lips. The ranch hand had been born in the shadow of the Arapahoe Park Racetrack at Aurora, Colorado, which early-on made horses his passion. But with the track open only on weekends, from Memorial Day to late August, and the dwindling number of visitors due to the economic recession, those conditions—and a failed marriage—prompted him to move south to the racetrack at Albuquerque. However, city life and its painful memories were too much like Denver, so he continued south along the Rio Grande valley, exploring horse ranches as he went. Three years ago, the Coloradan found employment at Rancho Tru-Cor.

"Matt," Don Fernando asked, "Where are Lorenzo and Gilbert?"

"Probably in the stables, sir. I saw Zo fillin' water troughs. Gil was rubbin' down Chorro, the stallion you took out today."

"Dulci," her father said, "let's go find Gilbert. My daughter wants to groom Bombóna, her pregnant mare," he explained to Matt, then glanced around. "Have you seen Vando?"

The stableman grinned and pointed to a barracks-like building that housed the four men. "He's maybe sleepin' it off?"

"Sleeping what off?" Fernando scowled at his probable reference to alcohol, specifically the vodka bottles that Victoria Torrez had brought from bunkhouse trash. "What do you mean?"

"Well, Van was checkin' the south ditch this mornin' and left there in a hurry. When he came back, he looked kinda all shook up, went right to the bunkhouse fast as he could."

"He's supposed to be sprucing up the horse trailer that we're taking up to Albuquerque next month for the AHYA Convention." Angry now, Don Fernando turned to his daughter. "Dulci, you go see Gilbert, while I rouse up that no good *jefe*."

"All right, *Papá*."

When Gilbert Begay saw the young woman enter the wash stall, he stopped smoothing a white finishing brush over the stallion's glossy umber coat. Full-faced, wearing wire rim glasses, the Navajo ranch hand kept his black hair short and brushed over his forehead. Strands protruded from under a baseball cap he wore that advertised Purina Mills horse feed.

He nodded a greeting to her. "How do, Miss Dulci."

She seemed surprised. "You know my name?"

"All us ranch guys do, even though you don't come down to the stables very often."

Dulci took off her sunglasses. "*Papá* doesn't let me come here alone, so how come they know me?"

"Well, your daddy doesn't want any of us married, and we can see you sometimes, sunning yourself on the patio, so...." Gil reddened, walked around to the mare's other flank, and bent down with the brush. "Sorry. I...I shouldn't be telling you all that."

"No, really," Dulci persisted. "What do they say?"

The Navajo straightened, but avoided an answer. "Miss, how can I help you?"

"*Papá*...my father...wants me to groom Bombóna."

"Sure." Gil handed her the brush. "Here, mind finishing up with this while I get the mare ready in her stall over there?"

"You're Indian, aren't you?"

"Yep. Born at Chinle, on the Arizona Navajo Reservation."

Dulci stroked Charro's nose curve. "Why did you come here to New Mexico?"

"Long story, Miss."

"Tell me anyway."

Gil pushed back his cap. "Well, my mother needed help to support herself and my brothers and sisters. I dropped out of high school to serve up fast food at the local burger joint."

"But you work on an Arabian horse ranch now."

"That's because I also volunteered part time at a Chinle veterinary clinic that specialized in horses. That's where I got to love them." Gil grinned at the girl. "Now Miss, I suppose you'll want to know how I got here?"

After Dulci's nod gave him a go-ahead, he continued, "I was twenty-six. With almost half my town living below the poverty line, I gave my mother most of my savings, left Arizona, and headed east. Reached Albuquerque, but couldn't find work. I had almost run out of money, when I met Mister Trujillo...your daddy...at an AHA show at the fair grounds. That was five years ago and I been working here ever since."

"Do you like it on a ranch?"

Gil glanced out the door, then put a finger to his lips. "Don't tell your daddy, but I'd like to go back to Chinle one of these days, get married, and start a small Arabian business of my own."

"Won't that take a lot of money?"

"Miss Dulci, I've been saving it." He handed her the Arabian stallion's reins. "Go put Charro in his stall and I'll bring out Bombóna for you."

Dulci put on her sunglasses. "I...I changed my mind. I'm tired and want to go back to the house. I'll go find my father."

After the girl left, Lorenzo "Zo" Lujan turned off the water faucet. A slightly built twenty-five-year-old, with black hair neatly worked into a braid at the back, Zo was born in Providencia and was the second longest employee working at the ranch. He threw down the water bucket, came over to his Navajo co-worker, and chuckled.

"Man, Gil, that gal is skinny as a *Dia de los Muertos* candy skeleton. An' maybe tastin' as sweet? Right, *amigo*?"

Unamused at the comment, Gilbert replied, "Stow it, Zo. Personally, I feel sorry for her."

"Man, what for?"

"Just *look* at the poor girl, you ¡idiota! Isn't that enough of an answer?"

"Yeah, well, *a mi modo de pensar*, with those flat *chichis*…tits to you, Gil… and ass, she ain't getting' enough *amoroso*'. Know what I mean?"

"*Cabrón*, don't you ever think above a girl's neckline?" Gilbert teased, then continued, partly in jest. "And I don't appreciate the Spanish lingo. You guys came here and caused half of my people's problems, then Anglos caused the other half."

"What? Man, you just called me an idiot and asshole in Spanish."

"So you'd understand, *baboso.*"

"*¡Pendejo!*" Lorenzo turned and taunted him by waving his braid of hair hanging at the back. "*Caña…caña….*"

"Who you calling a prick?" Gil then insulted him in Navajo, "*T'óó dinigis!*"

"Oh, crazy am, I?" Zo retorted, clenching his fists. "I'll show ya—"

Both men mimicked boxing each other, while laughing at the mutual insults that helped break the monotony and loneliness of daily living on the ranch. Don Fernando did not hire married men, and Belén was too far away to drive and return from a workday evening spent with picked-up, or paid-for female company.

A girl's scream sounding from outside the stable ended the jesting. Both men ran out to find the cause.

Dulci, trembling, a hand covering her mouth, stood horrified at the sight of a horse trailer that Vando had driven close to the water faucet on the stable's north wall. The 2-4 horse aluminum transport normally was parked behind the bunkhouse, so it could not be seen from the main house.

"Damn," Gil blurted, "that's the trailer where the girl's mother was killed. Dulci's freaking out…."

Vando Benavides slid down from the seat of a Ford F350 pickup that had pulled the trailer. Near the bunkhouse, Don Fernando had seen what happened and shouted in blistering Spanish to his ranch foreman, then ran back to put his arms around his daughter.

"Dulci…Dulci," he mumbled, "I told that idiot to never bring the trailer where you could see it. I should have sold the cursed thing long ago. I'm so… so sorry you were nearby." Fernando released her and turned his daughter toward the house. "It's almost lunchtime. Let's go back. Why don't you first go rest awhile in your room?"

"All right, *Papá*, if that's what you want."

He reached over to stroke her cheek. "It is, Sweetness."

O

Eusebia Nevarez had set a circular metal table on the patio with brightly decorated Mexican dinner plates and thick, bluish glassware. A wide umbrella overhead shaded diners.

A green chile enchilada casserole, green endive salad, and tortillas would be served with sun tea—oversized tea bags in a glass jar, brewed by heat from the morning sun.

Don Fernando had seated himself with a morning newspaper, but toyed absently with a knife, while waiting for his daughter to come outside for her lunch

After he watched Eusebia pour tea into his glass, he admitted to her, "*Nana*, Dulci accidentally saw the trailer at the stables. She's quite upset."

"I tell you many times to sell," she retorted. "Why keep *carretero del muerte* here?"

"I don't want to forget Isabel, or Dulcinea her mother—"

Eusebia scoffed, "And place where she die, too?"

"No...no. That trailer is always hidden away behind the bunkhouse. Millie says—"

"'Millie say,' 'Millie say'," Eusebia mocked. "You are fool, Fernando. That *encantadora* wrap you like string around tiny finger."

"Millie helps my daughter.... Oh, here she is with Dulci." Don Fernando stood up to pull chairs back for the two women, one on either side of him.

Queen Millie Jaramillo of the brown and blue eyes, looked with disgust at the meal, then lashed out at Eusebia. "Old woman, *vieja loca*, you poison the girl with this *comida*. The salad, okay, but Indonesia rice, tabouli should be for food. Not corn tortilla."

"No, Dulcinea too thin!" Eusebia countered in reciprocal anger. "She must eat *comida* that put meat on her bone. Make healthy again."

"Now ladies...." Don Fernando flushed and motioned for calm with his newspaper. "Dulci is upset enough as it is. *Nana*, perhaps you *could* consult more with Millie about what food to serve."

"On my dead *cuerpo*," Eusebia muttered as she spooned enchiladas onto two of the plates. She passed them to the Don and Dulci, then glared at Millie. "You two-eye *Bruja*, take what you want, or eat nothing. *Nada*...."

"*¡Diabla!*"

"*¡Corróna! Opportunista*...scrounger—"

"I said, enough of that!" Fernando warned the two women, shaking his fork at them. "Millie, you said you would contact Isabel tonight and tell her that Dulci will be showing Bombóna at the Arabian Horse Youth Convention next month."

Millie reached over to caress his face. "*Si*, If you want, Fernandi."

Eusebia scoffed at the possibility of communicating with ordinary deceased humans. "You cannot talk to the dead, only with saints through their *bultos*."

"*Vieja*, what would you know?" Millie helped herself to salad while taunting, "Are you a *curandera*? Have you studied with El Perito? Do you know of the Nahuatl 'death-space' where the dead live? You, childish old woman, only babble of La Llorona—"

"Stop it!" Dulci abruptly cried out and pushed her chair back. "I'm going to my room. You two are always arguing about what's best for me. I need to find out for myself."

Fernando protested, "But, Sweetness, you haven't touched your food."

"I'm not hungry, and...and I told you not to call me that!"

The Don stood up to go with his daughter, but Millie pulled him back down by an arm. "Fernandi, it is the *desasombro*," she whispered. "Soul escape when the fright return today, after she see death-trailer."

"How did you know about the trailer" he asked. "When we came back from the stables, I took Dulci directly to her room."

"I...Dulci tell me," Millie stammered and put an arm around the Don's shoulders. "Fernandi, I do a *barrida* sweep on her this afternoon. Bring soul back to body."

"Tell me how you do that again?"

"I not tell everything I do," she replied with a coy touch to his lips. "I lay Dulci on floor, arm out like a cross, then sweep body with branch *de saliva*, *romero de castilla*, other herb. Sometime whole egg...then say prayer. Maybe take two, three day." The Mexican *curandera* stroked his face with long cool fingers and smiled. "Fernandi, you must trust Queen Millie."

## 7 monsoon season

Above any one of the four vast summer horizons that delineate New Mexico's mountain-and-high desert landscape, a distant smudge of thunderclouds—dark columns of rain spilling beneath—is sure to be a common sight. If local residents mouth the cliché, "We need the moisture," out-of-state tourists hope that drenching rainstorms will not ruin their plans for visiting exotic locations in The Land of Enchantment.

This yearly Southwestern monsoon phenomenon can begin as early as mid-June and last into September. The meteorological cause is a combination of climbing summer Pacific Ocean temperatures in the area of the Mexican Baja Peninsula, superheated air rising over the southwestern deserts, and a change in wind direction that eventually sweeps a moisture-laden atmosphere from the Gulfs of Mexico and California, northward into Arizona and New Mexico. Both states receive up to half their annual rainfall in these crucial weeks, helped, some believe, by prayers and the many flower-decorated images of San Isidro, patron of farmers, which are kept on ranches, farmsteads, and inside mission churches.

During sweltering afternoons that began in the third week of June, clear skies, usually airbrushed to a smooth, deep-blue tint, had gradually built up imposing white clouds in the southwest. A tentative light rain had fallen on the evening of Sunday, June 27th.

Later on the afternoon of Monday, Fr. Jake watched massive thunderheads move in from the direction of Mexico and overlay Socorro, the city south of Providencia where Sonia Mora lived. With a sun obscured by murk, warm summer air had cooled. After a scattering of hail pellets bounced on the flat roof of the priest's adobe, a steady rain fell to initiate the beginning of a monsoon season that he had mocked that very morning. The downpour turned fairly violent—what Gilbert Begay might call in Navajo, *niłtsá bika*, a "male-rain." Jagged electrical flashes and the rumble of distant thunder marked dangerous lightning strikes in the mountains, yet the wetness would minimize danger from forest fires.

O

On Tuesday morning, Fr. Jake took his usual bowl of raisin bran-and-banana breakfast to eat on his front porch and survey the storm's aftermath. On the arid ground, stunted plants and dry grasses were bent over from the force of the hail and rain. Shimmering water puddles lay in the asphalt-paved Calle San Isidro. Gullies of earth washed from driveways formed parallel rows of sandy deltas on the street in front of homes.

The priest wondered if the rain had leaked into his church across the way, when he heard his cell tone ring inside the house. He gulped down a final spoonful of cereal, while hurrying back inside to pick his phone off the kitchen table and answer the caller.

"Father Jake, San Isidro Church."

"'Morning, Father," Sonia Mora greeted in a pleasant voice. "How did you like our monsoon rain yesterday?"

"I thought the name was an exaggeration, "but," he jested, "the monsoon cometh that 'prophet Armando Herrera' foretold to me."

"I told you this happens every year about this time. In a few days you'll see more types of wildflowers than probably ever grew in your Michigan."

"Wonderful! I remember a psalm, something like, 'You sent abundant rain, O God, to refresh all of your creation'."

"Right, so enjoy it while it lasts." After a pause, the detective continued, "Father Jakubowski, I'm calling to tell you that I've been assigned the Baby Doe case."

*Sonia only calls me 'Jakubowski' when it's about a serious matter.* "Well, that's just as you expected, isn't it?"

"Yes, but almost too quickly. I can't figure out if the sheriff wants me out of his way by assigning me over there or—"

"What, 'over there'?" he protested before she could continue. "Excuse me, Sonia, but this is a perfectly charming part of New Mexico."

"Father, I meant on that side of the river…the east bank of the Rio Grande. The real action is over here."

"I'd say you saw plenty of action 'over there-here' in the past six weeks."

"Yeah, I guess," she agreed without much fervor. "It's just that.... Oh, forget it. Father Jake, I'd like you to be with me when I start by questioning Mister Benavides, Don Fernando's three ranch hands, and the two Mexican workers."

He tried to fathom her motive before asking, "Why, Sonia? You know I can't hear their confessions and repeat anything they might have told me to you. We don't even know if the men are Catholic."

"I suspect that Lorenzo Lujan and that Mexican couple probably are. Perhaps even Benavides. It's not that. A priest might...well...help to relax them."

"You mean let their guard down?" There was a rare curtness in the priest's voice. "Perhaps invoke guilt? Sonia, I don't think I like being used like that."

"Fatherrr…" Her sigh of impatience come through on the line. "Father Jake, despite every sordid true or false sin you've heard dumped on you in confession, you're quite naïve about criminals. I need you to…" Sonia's voice quickened. "Sorry, gotta run. I'll pick you up at nine sharp. *Hasta.*"

"Wait…" He glanced at his watch, 7: 45, then let the dial tone buzz for a moment before pushing the off button and folding his phone shut. *Guess in a way I'm flattered by being asked to help a detective solve a case, but this isn't a CSI-type television episode like 'Castle' or 'The Mentalist.' Someone was callous enough to discard a human being, no matter how incomplete the stage of development. Or even desperate enough to do so, since self-preservation is a basic and powerful human instinct. 'Greater love has no man or woman than to give up his or her life' would not apply here.*

O

Fr. Jake sat on his *casita*'s porch to wait for the detective. He examined the new hat he bought from Carlotta, then opened his sketchbook to draw the church's bell tower.

Sonia arrived about fifteen minutes late. As the priest came down the porch stairs, she apologized through the open car window, "Sorry, Father, I like to be on time. Motorcycle accident on the Rio Grande Bridge. Guy tried to pass a pickup, skidded into the railing. I called in for a deputy and EMT medics to be sent out."

"Was it a serious injury?"

"No. The idiot wasn't wearing a helmet, but he'll just be cited for reckless endangerment." She reached across to push the passenger door open. "Hop in, Father and belt up. Oh, good. I forgot to tell you, but I see you're wearing a priest collar."

"On the phone you sounded like this was official business." He noted the detective's charcoal one-button blazer pants suit, open-throat blouse, and black Greek sailor's hat. "You're certainly dressed for business."

"Right…" Sonia released the hand brake and put the car Drive, then nodded toward his head. "That a new hat you're wearing?"

"Yes, Carlotta more or less talked me into this 'gambler' model."

"Appropriate, maybe when working on a hunch?"

"What do you mean?"

"I'm not sure yet…." Sonia swung the Plymouth around toward Highway 310, braked at the stop sign, then turned left toward South Romero Loop. "You sleep well, Father?"

"Not really, the sight of poor Baby Doe kept running through my mind."

"Same with me," she admitted, "and I'm not too optimistic about the autopsy lab results being useful."

"Can paternity be determined through the DNA of a fetus?"

"I was told it's possible during the thirteenth week of pregnancy, and guessed at Baby Doe being right on that border line."

"So, detective, taking DNA from the ranch hands might not prove anything?"

"That's the gamble." Sonia drove on in silence, turned up Romero Loop until the car reached the paved driveway to Don Fernando's ranch. She swung to the right. "Here we are at the Tru-Cor entrance."

A wooden arch above the gate had the same sign as had been over the porch entry to the main house:

R A N C H O

TRU -COR

Each side of the whitewrought iron gate wings bore the same names and crests of Don Fernando and his late wife's familial origins in Spain, Seville and Cordova.

Sonia parked her Plymouth on the near side of the broken fountain. As she and Fr. Jake got out of the car and walked past the stagnant water, mosquitoes swarmed up at the prospect of a fresh meal.

She swatted at an insect harassing her ear. "Jeez, the Don should clean that pond out…get a few mosquito fish in there to control these pests."

"He seems still too fixated on his dead wife."

"Right, Father. I noticed that and it's definitely not healthy."

After Sonia gave a few raps with the horse-head doorknocker, Eusebia Nevarez opened the portal a crack and peered out. Her watery brown eyes looked red and inflamed, like the blotches on her face.

"*¿Si, detectiva?*"

Sonia held up a notepad with the names of the ranch hands. "Ma'am, please tell Don Fernando that I would like to question his workers."

"He not here," she replied. "Gone with Vando y Mathias to Belén for horse supply."

"So who is present ma'am? Lorenzo Lujan, Gibert Begay, and the Mexican couple?"

"*Si.*" The housekeeper noticed Fr. Jake and opened the door a bit further. "*Buenas dias, Padre.*" An ingrained respect for his priestly office, not exactly friendliness, was in her formal greeting.

Fr. Jake tipped his hat to her. "*Buenas dias, señora.*"

Sonia asked, "Ma'am, where is Lorenzo Lujan now?"

"Zo maybe wash stall of Charro, while Gilbert exercise stallion."

"*Gracias*, thank you. If the Don returns, tell him where we are."

"*Si.*"

In going toward the stable, the two walked on grass still wet with overnight rain. A splashing sound came from the stall that Lorenzo scrubbed down, wearing a white tee, jeans, and rubber boots. A distressed raffia cowboy hat covered his head. But the ranch hand was clean-shaven, with his oiled hair twisted into a neat braid in back. On noticing a man and woman approaching, Lorenzo turned off the hose nozzle.

Sonia held up her police ID. "Mister Lujan? I'm detective Mora from the Socorro Sheriff's department. This is Father Jakubowski. Sir, I'd like to ask you a few informal questions."

"Wh...what? Why?" Zo barely concealed his nervousness. "Lady, I'm not in no trouble am I? If it's about that *pendejo* barkeep in Belén—"

"Sir"—Sonia held up a hand to quiet him—"I'm here investigating a possible homicide, not you personally."

"Then why talk to me and bring along a *padre*? I got nothin' to confess about killin' nobody!"

"Sir, where is your room?" Sonia's question bordered on impatience at the ranch hand's defensive attitude.

"In the bunkhouse, lady, where else?"

"Please take us there."

"I dunno. The Don he don't like visitors to—"

She raised an index finger and frowned. "Mister Lujan, take us to your room."

"*Bueno*," he mumbled at her stern warning tone.

Built of the same white clapboard-and-green trim as the horse stables, the bunkhouse for ranch hands—roughly a 13' by 60' rectangular building divided into a recreation room, five apartments, kitchen, bathroom facilities, and a connecting hallway—was located about forty feet north of the stable that sheltered Don Fernando's Arabians.

Sonia took out her spiral notepad to write down observations of the interview.

Lorenzo stopped some twenty feet from the bunkhouse and pointed to the ground. "That day, after you was here, Dulci freaked out right about on this spot," he recalled. "Van, he drove a horse trailer the poor kid's mother was killed in right out here in front. I never seen the Don so mad."

"Understandable, yet why would Mister Benavides do that?" Sonia asked.

Zo shrugged a shoulder in ignorance. "Forgot, I guess, or didn't know she was here. I was supposed to wash the trailer, but I always do that in back."

Sonia looked toward the bunkhouse. "That screen door on the left is where you enter?"

"*Si*. Goes to our TV room."

"Let's go in, sir."

A residual smell of cigarette smoke came from the twisted butts that littered the floor. Empty soft drink containers lay scattered on dusty Bamboo Tan linoleum that covered the cement floor of the recreation room. Aside from a card table and folding chairs, minimal furnishings—a heavy couch that faced a *trastero*-style cabinet, housing a TV set—were of heavy, faux-distressed Mexican manufacture.

Zo squirmed, just short of an apology at the disorderly room. "Vickie, she comes in to clean on Fridays."

"Vickie?" Sonia flipped a page of her notepad to recall the name. "Victoria Torrez?"

"*Si*, the *Mexica*."

"Where do she and…Estabán…her husband live?"

The ranch hand pointed out a window on the right. "That single-wide over there."

"I see." Sonia glanced along the hallway at five closed apartment doors. "Sir, which room is yours?"

"This here first one is Van's place. Mine is next to him."

"May we go inside?"

Zo shuffled his feet and looked away. "Aw…it's kinda messy in there."

Fr. Jake touched his arm. "Lorenzo, I'm sure Detective Mora has seen worse. It's important for her investigation."

"Well, see, *Padre*, I do some of the weekend cookin' that Vickie don't do for the guys. The kitchen's at the far end an' I ain't always got time to straighten things up in my place."

"Lorenzo, please open your door," the priest insisted.

"Aw' right, but don't say I didn't warn ya."

Light from a single dirty window in the north wall gave muted light to an 8' by 9' space fouled by the strong smell of stale smoke from an ashtray overflowing with cork-tip Marlboro butts. Unwashed underwear lay scattered on an unmade bed, along with dirty socks and a soiled blue work shirt. Lorenzo self-consciously pulled a blanket over the clothing, then stood in front of a wall display of photographs of female models, cut from swimsuit issues of magazines. As he tried to shove a wastebasket of empty Corona bottles under the bed with a booted foot, he mumbled, "The Don, he don't like us drinkin' either, but a guy's gotta—"

"Sir," Sonia interrupted before he could finish, "I'm not here to check either your housekeeping or lifestyle. Does your window open?"

"*Si.*"

"In the other rooms too?"

"I wouldn't know, but they should."

"Sir, do you bring women in here."

"*Mujeres?*" Zo snorted in frustration and shook his head. *No tengo ningún chicas aqui.* The Don, ever since his wife died, he don't let us have girlfriends."

"So I understood." Sonia went to his Mexican-made bedside table. *Latina*, a Spanish-language woman's magazine lay alongside a scarred wooden lamp base. "May I look in the drawer of your table?"

"Be *mi* guest….got nothin' to hide."

Sonia checked the drawer's contents: a bottle of aspirin, spare keys, two ball point pens, loose Q-tips. She wrote in her notepad, than look up at the ranch hand. "Sir, do you, know any women who recently might have suffered a miscarriage or gotten an abortion?"

Obviously surprised at the question, Zo exclaimed, "¡Jesucristo, no, detectiva! No way!"

"All right, sir. May I see the kitchen?"

"Si, at...at the end of th...the hallway." He stammered his answer, seeming upset by the woman detective's questions about pregnancies.

Breakfast dishes lay in the gray water of a stainless steel sink, next to a stove and refrigerator. One side of the room had an open cupboard for storing food cans and boxes. At the southeast corner, five chairs, a table with ketchup, mustard bottles, and napkins stood under a five-lamp chandelier that had been made from a wagon wheel. A closed door was at the north wall of the kitchen.

Sonia asked him, "Where does that door lead?"

"Out back, where I dig garbage into a mulch pile. Plastic an' other stuff go to a landfill south of town."

"Thank you Mister Lujan, that will be all for now. Would you please ask Gilbert Begay to come up here?"

" I dunno," Lorenzo hesitated. "Gil's exercisin' Charro."

"Sir," she told him, again sternly, "this is a murder investigation."

"Oh, sure detectiva. I...I'll send him up." Zo nodded farewell to Fr. Jake and went down the hallway toward the entrance door.

Sonia returned to his room and riffled through clothes in a wardrobe. "Couple pairs of shoes...black Sunday suit....winter jacket." She opened a dresser drawer and tallied, "Underwear and socks. Everything is a total mess, yet nothing out of the ordinary or incriminating. Father, let's go wait for Gilbert in the TV room."

As they passed Vando's door, Fr. Jake asked, "Are you satisfied with your investigation?"

"Of Lorenzo? For the present, but I didn't find any condoms in that drawer of his, so if he screwed any girls around here...." Too late, Sonia regretted her slang. "Pardon, Father. If the guy had sexual relations—"

He stopped her with a laugh. "Detective, I assure you that I know the term, and Lorenzo seemed almost in shock at your question."

"That's a point in his favor, but the man knows more Spanish than he's letting on."

"How did you figure that out?"

She pointed out, "The captions on those pin-up cheesecake photos and all his magazines were in the lingo. Also he didn't hide a Spanish-language *Playboy* printed in Mexico, and copies of *Siempre Mujer* and *Maxim* far under the bed."

"You didn't mention finding Baby Doe to him."

"No, I wanted to see his reaction to my questions about any pregnant women who might have lost a fetus."

"He seemed genuinely shocked."

"True."

While Sonia and Fr. Jake waited for the Navajo ranch hand to arrive, the priest picked up Styrofoam cups off the floor and crammed them into an almost full wastebasket. The morning was heating up, with a higher than normal humidity. As the priest fanned himself with his hat, circles of perspiration darkened the armpits of his clerical shirt. Sonia unbuttoned her jacket and looked around the room, taking notes, then put her pad on the card table and waited by the screen door.

"Getting warm in here, Father, and I didn't notice a swamp cooler on the roof."

"Swamp cooler?"

"Kind of a cheap air conditioner we have in the Southwest…. Ah, here comes Mister Begay."

Gilbert Begay, wearing the green baseball cap that advertised Purina horse feeds, blue work shirt, and jeans, took off leather gloves as he wiped his cowboy boots on a worn fiber mat just inside the door. When he nodded acknowledgment to the woman and priest, a silver and turquoise bracelet on his right wrist reflected the light.

Sonia held up her ID. "Sir, this is Father Jakubowski and I'm Detective Mora of the Socorro Sheriff's Department. I was assigned to investigate the death of a Baby Doe found in the *Acequia Madre* here."

"*Bįįh yáázh*…a fawn?" Gil asked in disbelief. "Don't you have animal control guys to do that, detective?"   .

Sonia realized his confusion. "Sorry, I didn't make myself clear. Yesterday morning, your ranch boss, Mister Benavides, discovered a human fetus lying in the *acequia* water."

"What?" Gil seemed stunned and took off his Purina cap. "That… that's terrible. What kind of woman would do that?"

"Or man? Sir, that's why I'm investigating the victim…Baby Doe's… death."

"Baby Doe? Oh, sure, like on TV they call unidentified corpses 'John Doe'." Gil nodded toward the priest. "Is that reverend here so the guilty person will confess?"

"Mister Begay, I'm Father Jake," he said, extending hand.

The Navajo's return grip was lukewarm. "Reverend, *just* call me Gil."

"Fine, but, Gil, I'm not here to elicit a confession."

"No," Sonia affirmed. "I asked Father Jake along because he was helpful in solving a previous case."

"So, do I need a lawyer, detective?" Gil grinned at his own question. "Saw that line on 'Law & Order C.I.'."

"At least twice per episode," Sonia added without smiling. "No, sir, a lawyer won't be necessary. I'm trying to determine if you men might have seen or heard anything out of the ordinary two nights ago."

"Ma'am, we all sleep pretty good. Ranching is hard work."

"I'm sure. Sir, may I take a look at your quarters?"

"Yeah, I got nothing to hide, except maybe a dust bunny I missed in sweeping up."

Fr. Jake said, "We understood that Victoria Torrez cleans the bunkhouse."

Gil chuckled before clarifying, "Reverend, that's just the TV room, kitchen, and toilet. She's not allowed in our rooms."

*That accounts for the condition of Lorenzo's place.* Fr. Jake glanced at Sonia, surmising that she shared his thought about housekeeping.

The Navajo man had no hesitation in unlocking and opening the door of a room that smelled pleasantly of lingering smoke from a sage bundle freshening the air. The half-burned stump lay in a white pueblo bowl decorated with brown glyph designs.

Gil had made his bed and covered the sheet with a bright cotton Zapotec-style blanket. When Fr. Jake went to examine geometric designs on a wall hanging, the Navajo explained, "That's a *Bis Da Łitso* weaving…Two Grey Hills to you…from the rez. My favorite design….those white, brown, tan, and black colors are all natural sheep wools."

"It's truly outstanding work," Fr. Jake agreed.

Gil waited while the detective looked in a plaited yucca-fiber basket on his night table that held several greeting-card-size envelopes.

Above the bed, a John Nieto giclée print titled, "American Survivor," depicted a horse-riding Indian wearing a war bonnet and draped in an American flag. The web of an intricate dream catcher caught light in the window. A new-looking 18" Sylvania TV that could play DVDs stood on a desk that faced the bed. Two granite rocks held several books upright: *Navajo Code Talker; The Trail of Tears; Guidebook to Native American Tribes.* A Compact Disc of R. Carlos Nakai flute music lay next to the television.

Gil noticed the priest's interest. "Reverend, you're not from around here, are you?"

"No, I came from Michigan."

"You have many 'Indians' up there?" His question bore a trace of innocent sarcasm.

"Hurons...Chippewa...Ottawa, although I don't think they're a large presence. A local story was that Chief Pontiac is buried on an island in Orchard Lake. That wasn't too far from my parish."

"Yeah, he was Ottawa..." The Navajo took the *Guidebook to Native American Tribes* off his desk. "Pontiac is kind of a folk hero to a lot of us, because he managed to unite several eastern tribes in a common effort to throw off British control, and damn near succeeded." He opened the book, thumbed through the pages, read a moment, and then shook his head. "Naw, nobody is certain about where the chief is buried. He was killed by one of us at Cahokia in Illinois country."

While Gil spoke, Fr. Jake picked up a small, sculpted figure dressed in leather clothing, with a grotesque mask as a face, and an antler headdress. "What does this...this doll represent?"

"Put it down, it's not a doll," Gil ordered bluntly, then tempered his annoyance. "It's a Deer Katchina, Reverend, which represents a spiritual entity to Native Americans. You ever hunt deer or elk in Michigan?"

"Afraid not—"

"Gentlemen..." Sonia had allowed the two men to talk while she looked around the room and outside the single window. "Gentlemen, let's get back to the present. Sir, what is that igloo-shaped structure outside?"

"Haven't you seen a *táchééh*, a sweat lodge, before, Ma'am?"

"No, but I've heard about them. May I look at the interior?"

"Sure, come around through the kitchen."

Deerskins and a tarpaulin covered the bent willow poles of the oval, eight-foot long structure. Gil held open the door flap so Sonia could bend down and look inside.

He explained to her, "That round pit in the middle is where I put twelve heated rocks and then ladle water on them to create steam. Well, there's a ceremony involving prayers and tobacco, but I won't go into that."

Fr. Jake recalled. "It's like a sauna that many Finnish people have in Michigan's Upper Peninsula."

"I guess…" Gil dropped the door flap and straightened up. "Anything else, detective?"

"Just what I'm asking all the ranch hands. Do you know of any local pregnant women who might have miscarried or gone through an abortion procedure?"

"No, Ma'am, I don't," he answered firmly, tugging his cap back on. "Can I go back to exercising Charro? Mister Trujillo has me keep a record of my time."

"Yes, sir, you're free to leave."

"'Then, *Ahéhee'*. That's 'thank you' in Navajo. Good luck in finding who's responsible."

The two watched Gilbert walk back to the exercise arena a moment, before Fr. Jake asked, "Sonia, did you learn anything that might help your investigation?"

"Lorenzo Lujan is fastidious in his person, but a sloppy housekeeper. Gilbert Begay has a neat room, yet is less concerned with his appearance."

"But into the 'Indian thing,' if I can put it that way—"

"Don't, Father," Sonia warned, shaking her head. "We have nineteen Native American tribal pueblos here in New Mexico. All attempt to preserve old traditions, while trying to make a living…survive really…in what is still a white man's world."

"What about all those Indian casinos that I've heard about?"

"Mixed blessings, I suppose. A couple of them are in default on their loan payments."

"What will you do now, detective?"

"Look along the *acequia*, while I wait for the Don to return. Maybe try to talk Mrs. Nevarez into letting me see his daughter."

"And Queen Millie?"

"I'll move with caution when questioning her…" Sonia went to retrieve her notepad from the card table in the TV room. "As Mrs. Nevarez believes, our *curandera* lady has 'bewitched' the Don."

"Well, detective, I should get back and a start moving my things into the rectory. That young anthropologist, Jayson Baumann, is arriving the day after tomorrow."

"I'm afraid that Father Mora's old couch and chair are still in the rectory."

"They'll have to do for awhile, since I'm renting out the parish's *casita* furnished with what Armando scrounged for it."

When Sonia offered to drive him back, Fr. Jake declined. "*Gracias*, but I'd like to walk. See how well my new sun hat works out."

"Okay…" She touched his sleeve. "Look, Father, I'm sorry, but being in Socorro and all, I haven't been able to contact anyone to clean the rectory."

"*No problemo*, Sonia. I'll swing by Armando's garage and ask him. Let me know if you learn anything from questioning the other suspects."

"They ain't suspects, Fadder," she corrected in her mock-macho accent. "An' you gotta quit watchin' them police programs where they solve every crime in an hour."

He laughed with her. "You've tried to make that point before, detective. Good luck with your interviews."

"I'll let you know about whatever I find of interest."

O

Fr. Jake found Armando Herrera taking a mid-morning break on a bench in the shade of the north wall of his repair shop. He munched a bear claw sweet while sipping a cup of Carlotta's piñon coffee from the grocery.

"*Buenas dias*, Armando."

The mechanic looked up from reading the *Valencia County Herald*. "Hey, 'mornin' Father Hakub. Want coffee?"

"No thanks, Armando, I'm here to see if you can help me at the rectory."

"Sure, Father. Me and a coupla guys will bring over a new mattress and blanket. What else do you need?"

"Detective Mora didn't have time to find anyone that might clean the place. I'll pay, so do you know any *viejas* who might like to earn some pin money?"

"I probably do, but y' know, *Tia* Ofilia is gonna' want to come over an' do a *velacione*."

"A what?"

"It's called a '*velacione*.' Auntie will stay up all night over there, burnin' green an' purple candles, callin' on a saint to get rid of any bad vibes in the place. I mean, after all, Father Mora *was* murdered."

"So his ghost might come and haunt the place?"

"Treat it as joke, if you want, Father. I'm just sayin'—"

"No, I'm sorry. I do respect your customs, but could you find someone to work on the rectory this afternoon and tomorrow, Wednesday? I'll need to move in on Thursday, as I'm renting the *casita* out to a graduate student in archaeology for the summer."

"Archaeology? That's what Cynthia Plow does when she isn't teachin' kids."

"Yes, and she'll probably be delighted to have his professional help."

"Yeah…" Armando stood up, finished his coffee, and wiped his fingers on a paper napkin. "Yeah, I guess, talkin' to a archaeology pro…. Father, I gotta get back to work, but I'll call *tia* about cleanin' the rectory."

"Thanks, Armando." *Ouch! I've probably hit a nerve.* Fr. Jake watched the young mechanic walk around the corner. *I'm pretty sure Armando and Cynthia are becoming more than just casual friends. He may see the man as a rival.*

# 8 velacione

By mid-morning of June 29, Fr. Jake had cleaned out the worst of the refrigerator gunk in the rectory kitchenette, scoured the sink, and swept the floor of mouse droppings and sandy dirt. *I don't think I want a cat, but I should buy mouse traps next time I go to Carlotta's for groceries.*

After returning to his *casita* for an early luncheon sandwich of turkey ham and Swiss cheese, the priest went back to the rectory to remove the yellowed, rodent-feces spotted sheets that covered Fr. Mora's old living room sofa and chair, and shake them outside. He found the furniture upholstered with brown mohair and in usable condition, presumably because of the old protective covers and the fact that the reclusive priest had few visitors.

Sonia Mora had emptied her uncle's roll-down desk of his files and letters and left it in the bedroom. Fr. Jake had set up his *altarcito* to San Isidro atop Fr. Mora's worn ponderosa pine dresser. The wood showed the scars of age and usage, but three empty drawers would hold most of the priest's clothing. Now, all of his belongings lay piled on the bed, to not interfere with the housecleaning of the women who came to help.

○

At precisely 1:00 o'clock.that afternoon, Armando's aunt, Ofila Herrera, showed up in front of the rectory door. She brought two elderly women with her, whom Fr. Jake had noticed at Mass, yet not met. While her companions—twins with the alliterative names of Carmella and Carmelita Cardonas—carried buckets, rags, a mop, and cleaning supplies, Ofilia brought only her wooden tray of curative herbs and potions. The small woman with gray hair cropped short, wearing a blue floral-print house dress, beamed at the priest.

"*Buenos tardes, Padre* Hakub. How your *comézon?*"

"*Señora,* happily my rash is gone." He grinned and extended his left forearm to show where the redness had been. "See?"

"*Bueno.* Where else you hurt?" Ofilia waved a gnarled hand over the herb packets and jars in her tray. I have *remedio* here for you."

"I'm fine, Ofila, and grateful to you and your lady friends for helping get the rectory in shape."

"*Si.*" She placed her tray on the couch. "Carmella, Carmelita good worker."

Fr. Jake turned to the twins. "Ladies, I thank you."

They returned a shy smile, spoke to each other in Spanish, and padded in bedroom slippers toward the kitchen with their cleaning supplies.

Ofila went into the bedroom, then frowned as she took wilted dandelions off the priest's patron saint's shrine and held them up. "*Padre,* you have *altarcito* for San Isidro, but not nice flower for him. You thank the *santo* for bring rain?"

"*Si, Señora,* I did."

"*Bueno.* Soon you have nice new flower for him."

"So Detective Mora told me." Fr. Jake took the dead blossoms from her to put in a wastebasket next to the desk. "Now that the afternoon monsoon rains have started, I should have Armando take down the saint's picture from that cottonwood tree next to the church. Oh, and *Señora.* I…we, that is, should have another *mayordomo* as caretaker of San Isidro. How do I find someone willing to do the work?"

"*Padre,* you no find. We ask good parish family who will accept honor of be *mayordomo* and *mayordoma.*" Ofilia went back to the living room, her wrinkled face scrunched up as if tasting something rotten, and holding her nose. "Not smell good in here. I light sage bundle like Armando bring to your *casita.* Tonight, I use incense, light three candle…" She chuckled. "Or maybe you need five for this *velacione.*"

"*Señora,* your nephew didn't tell me much about this purification ritual. What is involved?"

"You find out…" Ofilia made a shooing motion with both hands. "Now, *Padre* you go away, we must *hacer trabajar.* Where you keep your new *sombrero?*"

"In the closet. You know about my *hat?*"

"Everybody know what Carlotta know about sell you *sombrero*," she cackled. "Go now, take *sombrero*, come back three, four *horas*."

Fr. Jake laughed at the old woman's stern order in a mixed English-Spanish vocabulary. "Very well. Cynthia may still be in her classroom. So I'll go tell her about her new archaeology partner."

"Vamoose, now. Vamoose, like cowboy say in movie. Go, *Padre*, go!"

O

Fr. Jake found Cynthia Plow at Excelencia Elementary School, arranging students' pottery projects in a hallway showcase near the principal's office. The red-haired fifth grade teacher and amateur archaeologist had tired of her "Plain Jane" looks and clothing; she had recently switched from eyeglasses to contact lenses, styled her hair in a shorter length, and tinted it a bold henna color. Today she wore white slacks, a turquoise blouse, and brown sandals. It was a striking change from the way she looked and dressed only two weeks earlier.

"Good morning, Cynthia," Fr. Jake called out to her, tipping his hat. "What are those plaques you're putting on display?"

"Oh, hi, Father." She straightened to hold up a five-inch ceramic square. "Kids used to make ashtrays in art class, but I discourage that. These are kitchen trivets for placing under hot pans and dishes. For this project, they decorate them in a repeat pattern."

"I see that red and green chile motifs are a favorite."

"Right, but the children even learn a few new words in the process."

"Such as 'trivet'?"

"Yes, and also 'slab method,' 'glaze,' 'kiln' and other pottery-making terms. Here in New Mexico we're fortunate to have Native American pueblos that produce fine pottery items."

"I haven't visited a pueblo yet."

"Then, Father, we should go to Santo Domingo on the fourth of August for the ceremonial corn dances."

"Of course," he recalled, "August fourth is Saint Dominic's feast day, thus 'Santo Domingo'."

"Right, but last year the tribal council changed the name to 'Tewa Pueblo', the name of their language group. The feast day attracts one of the largest gatherings of Native-American people in the state, who perform ritual dances and sell their craftwork. You won't see anything elsewhere quite like what they do." In her enthusiasm, Cynthia touched his arm to make her point. "Father Jake, there are so many exciting new things for you to see here!"

"I'm beginning to realize that, Cynthia. My Detroit archbishop said this was a kind of sabbatical, and that's a year in which to learn new things. I could bring my sketchbook—"

"No, unfortunately, that isn't allowed, nor is taking photographs. The pueblos are sovereign nations with their own set of laws." Cynthia closed the showcase door, locked it, gathered up the scissors and roll of paper to return to her classroom, but turned back to the priest. "Ah...not to pry, Father, but I've seen Detective Mora's red car around your place a lot over the last few days. Has a crime been committed that the village should know about?"

The priest avoided a direct answer. "Well, since I'm moving into the San Isidro rectory, Sonia has been coming to clean out Father Mora's belongings. I've rented the *casita* for three months to an anthropology graduate student from New York University. I came to tell you that Jayson is interested in your dig. He said he was at Fort Craig at the same time the three Buffalo Soldiers' bodies were discovered."

"So was I, Father. What is his name again?"

"Jayson Baumann."

Cynthia thought a moment, then shook her head without looking at the priest. "Sorry, doesn't ring a bell, but I'm excited to be working that closely with a professional."

"He'll be here July first. Have you discovered anything new in your excavations?"

"I haven't worked the site recently, but pretty soon the BLM will put up a tent over everything and rope off the area. I'll try to do a little more digging before they get around to that." Cynthia switched her roll of paper to the other hand and frowned. "Father, maybe this Jayson is a person they're sending to continue my excavations."

"His letter to me implied that he would only be here for three months."

"If he's a grad student, he'll have to get back to NYU by September. Oh, about another thing. Armand had already told me about Detective Mora coming to collect her uncle's belongings, but there are...well...rumors that something happened up at the Arabian horse ranch on Romero Loop."

"Don Fernando's place." Fr. Jake sucked in a breath. "Cynthia, the details are still hush-hush, but if you know of any women or pubescent girls who were pregnant and aren't any longer, you might want to contact Detective Mora."

"Does the sheriff's department suspect there was a self-performed abortion, or a clandestine miscarriage kept from the child's father?"

"I'm sorry, Cynthia, but I can't say more." Fr. Jake glanced at his watch. "I'll leave you to your work and, if you don't mind my saying so, the new 'Cynthia Makeover' is stunning!"

At his compliment, she blushed to a shade close to her hair color. "Thanks for noticing, Father. Armand likes it too."

"So I would think unless he's blind. Well, God Bless, and I'll introduce you to Jayson Baumann when he arrives."

○

That morning, a stretch of high altocumulus clouds had crept into a pale, milky-blue sky from the southwest. Now, by mid-afternoon, growing clusters of cumulonimbus that resembled giant cauliflower heads had massed on the horizon, their dark gray undersides heralding imminent downpours of life-sustaining moisture. To the north, toward the jagged Jemez Mountains, curtains of rain already slanted down from a blue-black sky blanketing the horizon.

○

During that night of June 29-30, flickering yellow candlelight could be seen through the bedroom window of the murdered Fr. Jesús Mora. Now, Ofilia and her two women co-workers were back in the adobe, after they had carried the dead priest's stained mattress and bedding outside and laid it at a distance, perpendicular to the building. Sonia had taken her uncle's crucifix with her, and the women removed other faded and cobweb-hung religious pictures from the walls and placed them with the bedding.

Inside the rectory again at dusk, the old *curandera* began her *velacione* ritual by placing three lighted green candles in a triangle on the floor and within the bed frame, where Fr. Jake's new mattress would rest on the springs. Then the three *viejas* knelt before the shrine of San Isidro to chant the Apostle's Creed in English, recite a *Padre Nuestro*—the Lord's Prayer—and *Las Doce Verdades del Mundo*. "The Twelve Truths" was chanted in Spanish as a kind of comprehensive litany of Salvation History, from Moses and the Ten Commandments, to the martyrdom of the twelve apostles.

For a *sahumerio* purification incensing ritual, Ofilia lighted a pan of glowing charcoal, then spooned incense granules that she had prepared over the coals. While Carmella and Carmelita followed, reciting prayers to St. Joseph, patron of homes, the old *curandera* carried the smoking pan and incensed every room, closet, and corner of the adobe house. Fr. Mora had been an ill, dysfunctional pastor, thus the ritual was designed to destroy any negative influences his spirit might have left in the rectory to harass a new occupant.

The women's vigil lasted until dawn. As a final *velacione* rite, Ofilia allowed a white candle to burn in the bedroom for the rest of Wednesday. She told the priest not to enter the rectory until the next day, the first of July.

O

On the evening of the last day of living in his *casita*, Fr. Jake listened to a night rain, while reading from his breviary. The priest wanted to study the verses of Thursday's Psalm 18 for possible clues about how the initial day in his new home might turn out to be. He read aloud:

"'The Law of the Lord is perfect, it revives the soul.

The rule of the Lord is to be trusted, it gives wisdom to the simple.

The precepts of the Lord are right, they gladden the heart'."

*So far so good. All positive counseling.*

"'The command of the Lord is clear, it gives light to the eyes'—"

The ringing of his cell tone interrupted his reading. "San Isidro Church," he answered. "Father Jake speaking."

Sonia Mora's voice sounded apologetic. "Hope it's not too late to call, Father."

"Not at all, detective. How can I help you?"

"I've arranged to question Don Fernando tomorrow morning. Could you be there?"

"Sonia, you know he doesn't like priests. Won't he clam up if I go with you?"

"I'm hoping for the opposite and I need to speak with his daughter. Look, I'll meet you at the rancho at ten 'o clock."

"All right. Ofilia has finished her purification of the rectory, but she says that I can't go inside yet."

"Why not?"

"She stopped by to tell me I couldn't go in, but not *why* I couldn't enter. Ofilia is letting a white candle burn in there all day, and she's opened every window. I suppose that's to give any left-over ghosts an easy way out."

"Father J a k u b o w s k i…." Sonia's condemning tone was a gentle reprimand for him not to belittle local folk customs.

"You're right, Sonia. The rituals might be a clue to one day solving a crime."

"What makes you say that, Father?"

"I'm not even sure."

"About tomorrow?"

"Okay, Sonia, see you at ten. God Bless."

When the priest returned to his reading, the rain had stopped. The Psalm ended by declaring that the statutes of the Lord were more desirable than gold, and that they were sweeter than honey from the comb.

*I doubt that Don Fernando has read that psalm, but let's see how well his answers are to be trusted.*

# 9 don fernando

Wearing tailored jeans with a silver AHA belt buckle, a short-sleeved red shirt, and cowboy boots, Don Fernando met the detective and priest at the door of the entrance hall to his ranch's living quarters. The usually dapper equestrian's face was haggard, his eyes bloodshot. A two-day growth of beard crept toward the thin moustache above his mouth.

Stone-faced, the Don extended a limp hand to Fr. Jake. "*Padre*, Detective Mora asked if you could be here and that makes little difference to me." He stepped out on the porch stairs to glance at the sky. "Clouding up already, so the air is still relatively cool. Detective, shall we talk outside on the back patio?"

"That will be fine, sir."

The three walked in silence through the vaulted entertainment room, past the fireplace, where a taxidermist's glass eyes on the two mounted onyx heads stared blindly at the opposite wall. Eusebia Nevarez did not appear in the kitchen, and no one else seemed to be occupying the house at this time.

Fernando opened the French doors to the patio. "Let's sit here…" He adjusted an umbrella to provide shade over the wrought iron table and chairs. "Sorry," he apologized, "I can't offer you any refreshments. Vando drove Mrs. Nevarez, Dulci and…and Millie to Belén for supplies. They'll stay there for lunch."

Fr. Jake found it unnecessary to glance toward Sonia to know that she had the same thought: *The Don sent away anyone not yet questioned. What is he or they trying to hide?*

"Mister Trujillo, we're fine as is," Sonia told him as she pulled out her spiral notebook and a ballpoint pen from a pocket. "Sir, how *is* your daughter? Dulcinea?"

"How?" he sneered at her question. "How would you be if you saw your mother die in a horrible accident?"

"Sir, that was thirteen years ago. I pulled the police files on that accident and read them."

"What?" Don Fernando's eyes squinted at her in smoldering anger. "For what reason would you do that, detective?"

Sonia flipped open her pad. "I'll explain in a moment, but I must again ask, officially, if you know of any local pregnant women who might have had a miscarriage or an abortion."

"Local pregnant women?" Fernando glared at her a moment, then said, "Really, detective, I feel quite insulted. Why would you ask me such a question?"

Fr. Jake told him, "Because the fetus…Baby Doe…was found on your property and in your sluice."

Fernando glared at him, but ignored the remark. Sonia indulged the priest's intrusion, but sucked in a breath of impatience before continuing. "Sir, the fetus could have been discarded in any number of places, but the person chose your property to do so. I'm conducting a criminal investigation of a punishable offense. The statute is, 'Human fetal remains shall be disposed by incineration or interment'."

The Don sat down, moved the umbrella a little to the right, and then slipped on sunglasses from a case clipped to his belt. "So then, detective," he said in a slow, deliberate tone, "it's your job is to discover who broke the law."

"Yes sir, that's correct, both now and perhaps at the time of your wife's death."

"My wife's death!" Fernando snatched off his glasses at the unexpected question. "What…what a monstrous accusation to make. No one broke the law. Isabel died in a tragic accident."

"Sir," Sonia asked him in a calm tone, "doesn't Belén Equine Veterinary Clinic treat your Arabians?"

Fernando stared at the detective a moment before answering, "Yes, they have for years now. What has that to do with anything?"

"I'll paraphrase a section in the rules and regulations handbook published by the New Mexico Veterinary Commission. 'Disposal of a dead horse – Autopsy' 'In the event a horse should die on the premises of the owner….

the veterinarian may order an autopsy to be performed on said horse for the purpose of ascertaining the cause of death'." Sonia held up a file. "Belén Equine performed an autopsy on *Vencedor*."

"Yes…yes," he agreed. "I was totally concerned about my wife at the time, but I later learned of the autopsy. The first time you were here, I believe I said that the cause of the *Vencedor*'s death was an injury to his head, when the stallion bolted at the trailer's entrance door."

"Sir, did you read the report yourself, or did someone tell you about the autopsy?"

The Don replaced his sunglasses. "I suppose that Cervando could have informed me, but I don't recall. You see, detective, I was involved in planning my wife's funeral."

"I understand, sir, yet what Mister Benavides might not have revealed to you is that the veterinarian's report noted an unexplained three millimeter puncture wound in *Vencedor*'s right brachioscephalicus neck muscle."

"So?" Fernando shrugged an obvious explanation, "It's an injury probably caused by barbed wire. That happens frequently to horses."

"No sir, it was a puncture, not a laceration wound."

After shifting in his chair, Fernando demanded in an irritated voice, "Detective, I don't know what you're getting at, but I was there. I've just explained to you once again that *Vencedor* suddenly bolted upright and hit his poll on the top of the door. The stallion lashed out with his right hind hoof and stuck Isabel in the head. Is this what you came to talk about, or is it that…that fetus you mentioned?"

"Both, sir, but I was hoping to question Mister Benavides today and also your daughter."

Fernando firmly shook his head. "No to that, detective. I don't want Dulci re-living that terrible accident yet again."

Fr. Jake remarked, "As far as I can determine, you force her to relive it every day with that macabre shrine you maintain to your dead wife in your study."

"That's it," Fernando snarled through his teeth. The rancher backed away from the table and stood so quickly that his overturned metal chair clanged on the patio stones. Trembling as he slipped his sunglasses back into their case, he nevertheless warned Sonia with deadly calm, "This interview is over, detective. You'll need a court order to talk to either Cervando or Dulcinea." He pointed a shaking finger toward Fr. Jake. "And don't ever bring that damned priest here with you again!"

"Thank you, sir." Sonia stood to replace the file in her briefcase. "We'll let ourselves out."

Outside in front, both walked in silence past the polluted fountain and got into Sonia's Plymouth. They had reached the iron gate to Rancho Tru-Cor before Fr. Jake apologized. "Sonia, I'm sorry I spoke up like that. I probably shouldn't have come."

"Wrong, Father," she countered without looking at him

"Wrong? Why is that? I had no idea you were going to bring up Isabel's accident. Isn't that opening up what they call on TV a 'Cold Case'?"

"Also in *real life*," she emphasized, turning left on Romero Loop. "Don Fernando never answered my question relating to any knowledge of Baby Doe, yet before entering his stallion in that AHA competition, he would have inspected *Vencedor* and noted an injury to his neck. That would be reason enough not to enter the event. Our Don either is lying or knew that there was a puncture wound that the judges might miss."

"Perhaps, yet isn't there a third possibility?"

Sonia pushed her cap back and glanced sideways at him. "Go on, Father."

"What would you do if you were suddenly jabbed with a sharp object? You'd jump up, correct?"

"Point taken, go on." Neither one laughed at Sonia's pertinent yet unintended pun.

Fr. Jake continued, "Vando was on that side of the horse and at its head, presumably guiding the animal into the trailer. Isabel was behind *Vencedor*, but with Fernando, Eusebia, and little Dulcinea far away on the opposite side. They couldn't actually have seen what Vando was doing."

Sonia's eyebrows rose at his analysis. "I won't even speculate just yet, but you're thinking like a detective again. This is June thirtieth. The Fourth of July is coming up, but I'll try to get that get that court order to interview the ranch boss as soon as possible. Aside from Cervando, I'll need to question all three other witnesses to the accident."

"Three witnesses? Surely Dulcinea was too young to tell you anything of value."

"Perhaps, yet the most important person could be the child's nanny, Eusebia Nevarez."

## 10 jayson baumann

At 10:20 A.M. on July 1, an Albuquerque yellow 505 QIK-RIDE taxicab pulled up in front of San Isidro Church. The cab driver and a young man wearing a bush jacket, Indiana Jones-styled fedora, and laced-up field boots got out. After the passenger pushed back his hat, looked around, and pointed to Fr. Jake's house, the cabbie wrestled a bright red WT Drop Bottom Cargo Bag from the car's trunk.

Through his living room's front window, Fr. Jake watched the man as he paid the cab driver with three bills slipped from his wallet. *That must be Jayson Baumann spending over a hundred dollars for his ride here. He sounded quite amiable in his letter and I've made this place as presentable as possible. Shouldn't be a problem renting him the casita.*

The priest went to glance in his bathroom mirror and run a hand through steel-gray hair, adjust the white collar on his blue clerical shirt, and then came out to welcome the NYU anthropology graduate assistant.

As Jayson wheeled his heavy cargo bag up the walkway to the porch, Fr. Jake went down the stairs to help him. "Jayson Baumann? Welcome to Providencia. I'm Father Jakubowski..." He bent to help lift the bag up the stairs. "Let me help you."

"*Padre*, I can manage," Jayson countered. "Just hold that screen door open."

"All right."

In the living room, Jayson retracted the handle of his luggage bag and glanced around with a look that did little to conceal his disappointment. "Pretty small, *Padre*. What, again, are you asking for this...dum ...this place?"

"The *casita* belongs to the parish, Jayson. I thought three hundred a month, utilities included, would be fair. After all, you won't be here in the daytime, and I didn't think you needed anything larger."

The grad assistant pursed his lips and half-shrugged a reluctant acceptance. "Then, *Padre*, guess this will have to do."

The priest held in annoyance at the anthropologist's rude manner. "Look, Jayson, drop the '*padre*' bit. Call me Father Jakubowski or just 'Father Jake'."

"Well, okay...Father. Say, you got a pretty good Slavic face that tells you're from Poland."

"Guess an anthropologist would notice. Ah..." The priest pointed to a small space off the living room. "That's the kitchen. Would you like coffee or cold lemonade?"

Jayson gave a cursory shake of his head. "I'm good...anxious to check out that dig."

"So, when did you become interested in archaeology? Was it in high school? Which one did you attend, Jayson?"

"Manhattan's Aquinas Academy," he absently replied, still glancing around the small house. "It's Catholic. You ever hear of it pad...I mean, Father?"

"No. Does a religious order run the school?"

"Christian Brothers used to, pretty much. Now the faculty is about eight-five percent laymen."

"And lay women?"

"Pardon?"

"Women. Do women teach there, Jayson?"

"Oh. Yeah, the Drama Club, I think, but everything's all pretty much macho-male. Me, I was in the photography club and got involved with the school's Peer Ministry."

"Peer Ministry." A bit surprised, Fr. Jake nodded satisfaction. "That's very commendable."

"Yeah, I straightened out some of the nonsense that those phony interpreters of Vatican II were preaching to us in class and at lunchtime."

"Hmm, really?" *Phony nonsense? Better not go there, Father.* "Jayson, can you sit down before I show you around the *casita*? It's warming up outside, so are you sure you don't want that cold drink?"

"No, I'm good, Father," he refused.

"You were born in New York?"

"Yeah, Manhattan. I grew up there. Dad's in Wall Street. My mom has a psychiatry practice."

"Thus your family is quite well off. Where do you live in Manhattan?"

"An apartment on Ninety-eighth Street overlooking Central Park…" Jayson bent down to check along the base of the adobe wall nearest him. "You have roaches here?"

"No, it's too dry for them. Field mice, maybe, although they haven't bothered me. Look, why don't you sit down a minute?"

"Okay." Jayson took off his fedora and sailed it like a Frisbee onto the couch, sat next to it, and took up the conversation. "Father, I know what you're getting at. 'Spoiled rich kid—"

"Didn't cross my mind," Fr. Jake told him with a straight face and settled in his armchair.

The young man continued, "After high school a couple of us guys took off for California, like '01 to '02 was a sort of sabbatical coming-out year for us."

"So you could experience real life after attending an all-boys' Catholic school?"

"Well, yeah, kinda…" Jayson chuckled and winked at the priest. "Coming back we stopped off in Albuquerque for a weekend to sight-see. That's when Indian exhibits at the university museum got me interested in archaeology."

"A kind of career-awakening epiphany, was it?"

"You could say. Anyhow, in the fall of Two-thousand-two, I enrolled in NYU's Department of Anthropology. Now I'm in the last year of their M.A. Human Skeletal Biology program."

"Again, that's commendable, Jayson. How did you hear about Fort Providence?"

"In '07 I volunteered for a dig at Fort Craig. You know, where the bodies of Civil War Colored troops were discovered." Jayson stood up and went to inspect the clothes rack behind a curtain. "In fact, I don't like to brag—"

"No, no, go on," Fr. Jake urged. "Brag away."

"Well, I pointed out to the site supervisor where I thought the black guys might be buried."

"And?" *Young man, I know exactly what's coming.*

"That's *exactly* where those three Colored soldiers were found." Jayson paused to let his accomplishment sink in before continuing, "Then I read about the discovery of Fort Providence in a Bureau of Reclamation newsletter. It being so new—"

"—That you decided to come and help dig out important finds," the priest finished for him.

"Yeah, kinda."

Jayson there's a school teacher here, Cynthia Plow, who's been working archaeological sites for about eight years. She was at Fort Craig the last couple of seasons, and she's the person who discovered Buffalo Soldiers' bodies here at the fort cemetery."

Jayson asked, "She's no professional 'Archie' is she?"

"Archie?"

"Archaeologist talk, Father." Jayson stroked the brim of his fedora while asking, "So. like what's her M.A. or Ph.D.? Forensic? Socio-Cultural, Linguistic?"

*Control yourself, Father, be calm.* "None of the above. K-8, Fifth Grade Elementary, but Cynthia is well informed about the methodology of digging excavations."

"Really? Bet I could teach her a thing or two the gal can't possibly know." The young man's snort bordered on smugness. He wandered toward the bedroom area and tested the bed's mattress with his hand. "This where I sleep?"

"'Fraid so, Jayson. Later today, after you get settled in, I'd like to take you to the Providencia Grocery, the closest place to buy food."

"I'm not much of a cook," he admitted with a scowl toward the small kitchen. "I just may eat out to save time, and that cabbie told me about Mamacita's place"

"Sorry, that restaurant is closed."

"Bummer. Aren't there other eateries around here?"

"I'm afraid not." Fr. Jake went into the kitchen to run a hand over the microwave oven. "I've put this appliance to many a good use."

"Yeah, right…" Jayson looked out the front window. "So where is this fort cemetery? The excavation?"

"Let's go out on the porch." Outside, the priest pointed across the street. "That's my church, San Isidro. The cemetery is at the far corner of that vacant field, to the east of where the elementary school is located…" He glanced at his watch. "It's almost eleven o'clock, so Cynthia's summer school classes end at noon. I could go there with you and introduce her."

"Father, that's okay," Jayson quickly refused. "I'd really like to go back inside and stow my gear, then hike over to look at the dig."

"Suit yourself. I'll move into the old rectory now. You can see a corner of it just to the right of the church."

"Ah…we came through a town called Belloon or Belize. Is that possible?"

"Belén, Jayson. That's the Spanish name for 'Bethlehem'."

"They have buses running there from here?"

"Not that I've noticed." Back inside the house, Fr. Jake again tried to make the young man feel welcome. "Look, Jayson, I can fix a sandwich for us at the rectory, then let's go meet Cynthia when her class lets out. She can take you over to see her dig."

"*Her* dig? Father, that's on BLM property."

"Cynthia is the only person who's worked it, but she told me that she notified the Bureau of Land Management about discovering the Buffalo Soldier bodies."

"That's why *I'm* here." Jayson edged the priest toward the front door. "Thanks for the lunch offer, but I'll just munch on a granola bar while I walk over and check out that excavation by myself."

"All right, Jayson." Fr. Jake picked an envelope off the side table where his *altarcito* to Saint Isidro had been set up before. "Here are a couple of keys to your *casita*. My cell phone number is on the envelope, if you need me to help work the propane stove—"

"That's okay, Father. I have the latest BlackBerry and an HP laptop with Windows 7 and wireless Internet. UPS is sending my other stuff."

"Then please make your rent checks out to San Isidro Parish."

"Will do." To end the conversation, Jayson put his Indiana Jones fedora back on to follow the priest out, and lock the *casita's* front door.

"Well, God Bless, Jayson and good luck."

He replied without much sincerity, "Yeah, you, too Father Jakubowski."

Before returning to the rectory and preparing his lunch, Fr. Jake decided to visit the church and offer another prayer of thanks to San Isidro for the monsoon rains.

The nave interior was cool, but humidity had brought out a lingering smell of mold that had been white-washed over on the ancient adobe walls. A *bulto* of the saint stood on a side altar with a lighted candle and wilting field flowers. The wooden statue depicted him kneeling in prayer, while a miniature angel behind a pair of oxen plowed his field. Fr. Jake knelt and recalled the legend. *The story is that Isidore, a poor Spanish farmer, had so much work to do during the planting season that he could not take time off even to attend Sunday Mass. As a reward for his pious devotion, the Lord sent an angel down to help with the plowing—* Abruptly, the priest's concentration swerved to thoughts about the schoolteacher who first befriended him on his arrival in Providencia. *Cynthia was excited about having an archaeologist working with her this summer as a kind of partner, but now that I've met Jayson Baumann, I'm quite sure he isn't going to return the honor.*

# 11 early 'fireworks'

Late in the afternoon, on July first, Armando Herrera and two of his *Hermano* friends had brought a new mattress, with not-so-new sheets and blankets, to Fr. Jake at the rectory. The three men hauled away old bedding and the pictures that Ofilia had kept or consigned to the outdoor trash pile during her *velacione* cleansing ritual.

Despite concerns about Jayson Baumann and Cynthia Plow as co-workers, and his imprudent quarrel with Don Fernando over the man's bizarre memorial to his late wife, the priest slept well enough on his first night in Fr. Mora's old bedroom. Ofilia's incensing and the pine-scented disinfectants of Carmella and Carmelita replaced most of the former unpleasant sour smells in the rectory. When the sisters had finished—and over their gentle, murmured protests—Fr. Jake insisted that they accept the thirty-five dollars he placed in an envelope for each woman. One of them—he was not sure which alliterative sister—shyly presented him with a small barrel cactus, planted in a pot.

Ofilia Herrera was less hesitant in accepting fifty-five dollars.

O

Two hours after lunchtime, on the second of July, the cobalt sky clouded over enough to obscure the sun and make it less uncomfortable to be outdoors. Fr. Jake, wearing work jeans and a white Tee, stood in his backyard contemplating the wisdom of planting a garden this late in the growing season, when he heard the familiar engine whine of Sonia Mora's Plymouth Neon. The car's tires crunched to a stop behind his Nissan on the gravel driveway. The detective had put on different pantsuit, this one a tan, 2-button flap pocket blazer that complemented her summer Baker Boy cap.

"Father Jake," she called out as she stepped from the driver's door, "I was able to get a quick court authorization to question Dulcinea Trujillo. As a female in this particular crime, and the Don's daughter, she's a person of interest. I've got her on tape."

"What about interviewing Eusebia Nevarez?"

"Unfortunately, that will have to wait. Fernando told me the nanny fell ill after lunch yesterday in Belén. When I arrived at Tru-Cor, he said she was sedated and sleeping…" Sonia glanced toward the kitchenette. "You have any coffee left?"

"I made a fresh pot at noon, Sonia, so go sit in the living room and relax."

"Thanks. I'll share what I found out with you."

As Fr. Jake filled two mugs, he asked her, "Did you question Vando Benavides and…and 'Mister Crisp' was it?"

"Yes, Mathias Crisp. I didn't do an in-depth interview with them, since Dulcinea was my primary interest. Benavides is from Providencia and the Don's oldest employee. He was hired by Isabel's father and stayed with Fernando when Isabel inherited the ranch in Nineteen ninety-six."

"Fourteen years ago," he calculated, setting down Sonia's coffee on a table next to the mohair armchair. "Careful, it's hot."

"Right, Father…" She took a cautious sip and set the mug down. "Benavides was there when Isabel was killed in that horse trailer accident."

"I recall Fernando telling us that. What about Mathias?"

"Thirty-two years old. Coloradan. Passion for horses. He got out of a bad marriage and then drifted around a bit before Don Fernando hired him. That was three years ago."

"So you have four healthy, unmarried men—"

"Pardon, Father, but we need to find the female first…a formerly pregnant woman…so we're checking area clinics. Too bad the one here in Providencia closed down in January for lack of funding. Seems it's always the needy who get screwed…" Sonia flushed at the metaphor she had blurted out. "Jeez, that was another really bad unintended pun."

"Forget it, Sonia, I know the term. You were going to play that taped interview with Dulcinea for me."

"Right. First, I did get bad news from the forensic lab about Baby Doe. The fetus was too short-term, and having been soaked in what was contaminated pond water for several hours, precluded any valid DNA testing. The lab did determine that an abortifacient was used, so it was a self-induced procedure, not a miscarriage. Mifepristone and misoprostol pills."

"Where would a person obtain such drugs?"

"Normally, from a physician. The process can be done at home, but it's usually with the supervision of a doctor. Externally, Dulcinae doesn't exhibit the post-abortion signs of pain, bleeding, and low-grade fever caused by retained residue tissue as a result of conception. I would have to establish probable cause and get another court order before a doctor could examine her."

"Let's hear what Dulcinea said in your interview."

Sonia took a cell phone-size micro cassette recorder from her briefcase and put it on the coffee table, facing the priest, then brought her coffee mug and sat next to him on the couch. After she hit the Play button, the detective's electronically distorted voice began.

"Detective Sonia Mora, Socorro County Sheriff's Department, recording Dulcinea Maria Trujillo, female, age eighteen, in the study of her father, Don Fernando de Trujillo at Rancho Truj-Cor, One Romero Loop Road, Socorro County, New Mexico. Mister Trujillo is present. Today is Friday, July second, nine-forty seven A.M., Two thousand and ten. Miss Trujillo, you consented to this interview, is that correct?"

"Yes, detective, Dulci did agree to speak with you."

Sonia clicked the Pause button to explain, "That was Don Fernando. I told him I had allowed him to be present, but not to interrupt again. Let me Fast Forward a little—"

Sonia's voice resumed, "...know any local women who appeared to be pregnant in the last three months and now do not?"

(Dulci's voice.) "How would I know of any? I never get off this property long enough to make friends with anyone."

(Fernando'voice) "Now Dulci..."

"Sir!"

"Sorry, detective."

"Miss Trujillo, please simply answer my questions 'yes' or 'no'."

"No, I don't know any girls like that."

"Were you yourself pregnant within the last four months?"

(A girl's laugh.) "Of course not. Uh...no, I wasn't. No."

"Thank you, Miss Trujillo. I'd now like to ask you some questions about your mother's death. You were five years old at the time, yet can you remember who was present at the accident besides Isabel?"

"Well…Vando was there and *nana* Eusebia. Me. That's all."

(Fernando's voice.) "Dulci, Sweetness, I was there. Don't you remember?"

"No. *Papá*, you weren't. Eusebia and you always told me you were, but I didn't believe that, even when I was small. How could I forget what I saw? You went to the barn just before the accident—"

(Fernando'voice interrupting.) "This is monstrous…. Detective, turn that damned recorder off."

After a squawking sound, the tape fell silent. Sonia reached over to click the Off button, then took a sip of her now-lukewarm coffee, but said nothing.

Fr. Jake broke the silence. "Sonia, if the girl is telling the truth, why would her father and Eusebia both insist that he was present?"

"Any ideas about that, Father?"

"None right at the moment, detective. Except I don't know whom to believe."

"It's not in the police report, either, so perhaps no one had the heart to question a five-year-old or thought it necessary. On the report, Don Fernando is listed as present at the time of the accident."

"According to his say-so, plus that of a ranch foreman and long-time family nanny."

"Right, Father Jake." Sonia replaced the recorder in her briefcase, then took off her cap and leaned back. Instead of continuing the conversation, she patted the couch's mohair cushions. "I'm surprised this old furniture looks so good. The rectory smells nice and I see those holy pictures are gone. I never did like the one of Christ, where his eyes follow you around. And I see you took off the window shades. Father Mora kept them down. It was always so damned gloomy in here."

"I'll get venetian blinds next time I'm in Belén,"

"So how was your first night here in the rectory?" she asked. "Any ghosts bother you?"

The priest laughed. "I never sleep too well the first night in a strange place, but if you mean ghosts like that La Lorona woman staring in my window, then no."

"That's good…." Sonia tipped her coffee mug to look inside.

"More?" the priest asked.

"No, thanks. Father, do I recall that on Sunday you're going to see the Civil War re-enactments of the Glorieta battle at Rancho las Golandrinas?"

"Probably not. Armando hasn't mentioned it again, and I have eight and eleven o' clock Masses."

"It's a long drive, anyhow, probably ninety miles one way. If you did go, best to stay at La Cienega overnight and come back on Monday."

"I couldn't do that." He reminded her, "I have the Adam Salazar funeral at ten o'clock that day."

"That's right. Have you seen his two friends since they were here last?"

"No. Presumably Dave and Breanna are still at the Zia Motel…" Fr. Jake stood up and listened at the front door to what sounded like gunfire outside. "What in heaven's name?"

Sonia identified the sound. "Those are firecrackers….the Fourth of July is coming up. We try to control amateur pyrotechnics, but monsoon rains were early, so, luckily, dry grasses are less apt to catch fire. There have been nasty blazes in the past that even destroyed outlying structures." The detective smoothed her slacks, then stood to put her cap on. "I should get back and write up the report of my shortened conversation with Dulcinea—"

When Fr. Jake's cell tone rang, she paused with her briefcase in hand while he answered, "San Isidro Church, Providencia. How may I help you?"

"Reverend Jacob?"

"Well, yes, close enough."

"I got your number from Armando Herrera. This is Gil Begay, you know, the Indian at Rancho Tru-Cor."

"Gilbert, of course I remember. What can I do for you?" The priest half-turned and silently mouthed "G-i-l B-e-g-a-y" for Sonia.

"Reverend, I just found out that Mrs. Nevarez…you know, Miss Dulci's nanny…that she was discovered dead in her room."

"What? Just a moment…" The priest put a hand over the speaker. "Sonia, Gilbert is telling me that Eusebia Nevarez has died."

"At the ranch? Did someone call 911? Paramedics?"

He turned back to the phone. "Gilbert, were emergency medical personnel notified or summoned?"

"I didn't see any. No sirens or anything."

"Probably not," Fr. Jake told Sonia.

"Then I should get over there. Maybe Don Fernando wouldn't object to you coming along for a blessing or whatever it is that you do to people who've died.'

"My sick call kit has anointing oil. I'll bring that and my Roman Missal."

○

The white wrought iron gate to Rancho Tru-Cor was open. Sonia parked her Neon near the driveway fountain. The basin still had not been cleaned out; the stagnant water level was low, and humid afternoon air smelled of fresh-cut grass.

Gilbert Begay answered Fr. Jake's rapping of the front door knocker and saw the priest. "Reverend, I didn't know who else to call…. Oh, hello, detective, I didn't realize you were coming too. I'm here at the house because Mister Trujillo asked me to come up and mow grass around the patio. I overheard them talking about Eusebia. See, her room faces the back—"

"Sir," Sonia requested, "please take us to the deceased woman."

"Sure, detective." Gil stepped aside to pull the door open. "Her room's at the back of the kitchen."

Eusebia's Nevarez's body, dressed in a rumpled cotton nightgown, lay on its back beside a partly thrown-off sheet. Her arms and legs had contorted as in a seizure. The woman's red, watery eyes were open in a sightless stare at the ceiling. Her grotesquely open mouth in a blotched face seemed to have uttered a final, contorted cry of anguish.

Don Fernando sat slumped in an armchair, staring at the floor. *Curandera* Queen Millie Jaramillo bent next to him with an arm around his shoulder, comforting the man. Dulcinea was not in the room.

Sonia paused at the door to ask Gilbert if he had entered the room.

"No, Ma'am," he replied. "I came inside the house to tell Mister Trujillo that I was through mowing and found him in here."

"Thank you. Please stay outside the room. Father Jake, go directly to the deceased and touch as little as possible." She turned back to Fernando and Millie. "For the moment, please remain where both of you are. Sir, can you tell me what happened?"

Don Fernando looked up at her and wiped his eyes with a handkerchief. "Eusebia… Mrs. Nevarez…felt ill when she returned from Belén yesterday. She went to bed early, and when she wasn't in the kitchen this morning, well, I just decided to let her sleep later—"

"I was the *susto*," Millie broke in to explain. "The old woman die of a fright. Maybe terrifying *sueno*, bad dream…."

"Ma'am—"

Sonia paused when Fr Jake prayed aloud as he anointed the old woman's forehead. "'…make her one with your Son in his suffering and death, that, sealed with the blood of Christ, she may come before you free from sin'."

Fernando inadvertently mumbled, "Amen."

After waiting until the priest put away his kit, Sonia asked the Don, "Sir, do you know what the deceased might have eaten yesterday that possibly could have made her ill?"

The Don looked up at the *curandera*. "Millie? You were at lunch with Eusebia."

"*Detectiva*," she said, "the old woman only eat salad, drink hot tea."

"I'm notifying the Office of the Medical Examiner in Socorro that we may have a suspicious death here—"

"Suspicious?" Fernando jumped up to protest, "That's ridiculous, detective! Why would you think such a thing?"

"Sir, Mrs. Nevarez was a material witness, who died suddenly before she could be questioned about two deaths."

"Two deaths?"

"The aborted child, sir, and that of Isabel, your late wife."

The Don's face turned a livid red. "Detective, this is an outrage! My attorney in Albuquerque will most certainly contact your superiors first thing Monday morning."

Sonia ignored an implied threat of censure that she had heard many times from other self-important detainees. "Father Jakubowski, you've finished with your blessing …your ritual…haven't you?"

"I have, detective," he said as he took off his green stole.

"Then, Mister Trujillo, I'll get crime scene tape from my C.I. kit to seal this bedroom door. No one is to enter these premises until a forensic physician from O.M.I. arrives later today."

O

Neither spoke as Sonia drove Fr. Jake back to the rectory. Both realized that besides Cervando Benavides the only other adult left who could corroborate or counter the Don's insistence that he was present at his wife's death, now was herself dead.

○

That night, Fr. Jake lay in bed thinking about the many unnerving discoveries made that day. *Sonia said that DNA testing on the fetus would not be possible. That means the paternity of Baby Doe will never be known unless his mother is found.*

*Why would Dulci insist in that interview that her father was not present at the accident, when all other indications point to the opposite? Was she a child traumatized by the horror of seeing her mother injured that horrible way and rendered unable to recall events accurately? The Don said that Eusebia hurried her away from the scene. The old woman's upset stomach is understandable at her age, yet Millie said she ate very little. Few people die of indigestion, but, hopefully, an autopsy will reveal the true cause of the nanny's death.*

*Millie didn't mention Vando. Would the ranch foreman sit and eat lunch with three women, or go to a nearby bar for a beer and burger? I'd bet on the latter. Come to think of it, could there be connection between these people? A few years ago a couple of priest friends and I went to a movie in Pontiac, John Guare's 'Six Degrees of Separation.' We spent quite a bit of time afterward discussing the implications for us, since clergymen deal with the problems of many people. A number of fellow priests spoke of chance meetings with others that altered the direction of their lives, some for the worse.*

Fr. Jake eventually fell asleep to the distant, snapping sound of firecrackers detonating in sporadic, shotgun-like bursts, and the occasional wail of descending rockets.

Toward early Saturday morning, well before the first flush of pre-dawn rendered a northeastern horizon even faintly visible, a loud sound erupted outside the rectory. It was as if an explosion had occurred that rattled his two living room window frames.

Fr. Jake abruptly awakened at the din.

An orange brightness lit up his bedroom, as a distinctive smell of gasoline and choking, greasy smoke drifted into the rectory through a partly open living room window. Barefoot, he hurried across the room to look out at his driveway: billowing orange flames and black smoke engulfed the 2005 Nissan that he had bought from Armando Herrera, five weeks before.

"My God!" he exclaimed as he went back to the bedroom for his cell phone to dial 911. "This vandalism has gone far beyond anything to do with setting off holiday fireworks!"

## 12 a 'new' old honda

As a brilliant morning sun rose over the forested heights east of the village, a stunned Fr. Jake stood alongside mechanic Armando Herrera. Both men stared, unbelieving, at the charred hulk of his automobile, now soaked in the remnants of fire suppressant foam.

"Someone," the priest finally remarked, "was very, very careless with firecrackers."

"Oh, I don't think so," Armando objected. "Your car probably was deliberately torched."

"Torched?" Fr. Jake repeated as a question and looked toward the young man with a surprised expression. "Why…why would anyone do that on purpose?"

Armando shrugged at recalling one cause of vandalism. "Sometimes kids get drunk and burn stuff just for fun."

"Fun? Setting cars on fire seems a perverted sense of Fourth of July 'fireworks' fun."

"Yeah, it isn't right, Father. Look, you got insurance?"

"I have."

"Then don't worry, I'll get you another car." Armando kicked aside a scorched aluminum wheel cover. "You musta called 911, so did the fire guys talk to you after they doused the blaze?"

"Not much. It was still dark when they rolled up their hose and mentioned that arson inspectors would come by later today."

Armando shook his head. "Those guys won't be much good at findin' out who did it. A gasoline-soaked rag, lit and shoved into the gas tank started that fire. It wouldn't leave no clues. Father, you got a weedy gravel drive here, an' all that AR-FFFP foam hosed off any footprints." He glanced back at the rectory. "Lucky you parked away from your *casa*. Father Mora's old place coulda gone up too."

"I've been leaving more room for Detective Mora's car. She comes here because we're working on the Baby Doe case."

"How's that comin' along?"

"Armando, I can't discuss it just yet."

"Yeah, I understand. That's cool.... Father, you said you wasn't havin' a five o'clock Mass today."

"Right, but we'll start again next week. Tomorrow is the Fourth of July, so I'll conduct two services at eight and eleven."

"So we won't be goin' to the Civil War re-enactments?"

"I don't see how I can, Armando."

"That's okay, the guys will doin' more at Labor Day." The mechanic extended a hand to the priest. "Father Hakub, I better be getting over to the shop, see if anyone needs an oil change. Talk to ya later."

"God bless, Armando."

"Thanks." He touched the priest's arm in sympathy. "Don't worry, Father Hakub. I'll check out gettin' a new set of wheels for you."

O

Schoolteacher Cynthia Plow rented a small mother-in law *casita* built at the back of a double-wide manufactured home about a mile south of Providencia. A retired couple who owned the property was happy to receive the extra income that a quiet young woman teacher provided each month.

That Saturday morning Cynthia—unaware of the arson at Fr. Jake's rectory, but anxious to get to her excavation site—ate a quick breakfast of yogurt, toast, jam, and tea in her pajamas. Afterward, she put on outdoor coveralls, sturdy shoes, and her boonie hat, to continue excavations at the Fort Providence military cemetery, before BLM authorities closed the site.

Outside in her Hyundai Tucson, the young woman glanced at the fuel gauge and muttered aloud, "I better get gas at Carlotta's when I stop in to buy something for lunch."

She drove north on Highway 310, then turned right at the southern loop of Calle San Isidro and past Excelencia Elementary. The amateur archaeologist's excavation site had not yet been taken over by state professionals nor closed, so she felt free to continue digging for period artifacts—or perhaps more soldiers' bodies. Up ahead, on the west side of her excavation, she noticed a tan sunshade stretched over a small plot of ground. *That must belong to the NYU anthropology major that Father Jake mentioned. Could he really be the Jayson Baumann I know?*

The thought made Cynthia uneasy as she bumped the Tucson's wheels up over the low curb and parked on grass opposite the awning. A young man with his back turned away from the street knelt on the ground, digging up turf with a trowel. She slammed the driver's side door shut and strode toward the graduate student. At the sound, Jayson turned and looked toward a young woman coming toward him. She was not smiling.

"Jayson Baumann, what the hell are you doing here?" Cynthia asked in a tone of angry disgust.

"Hey, Cyndi…" Baumann grinned and held up his trowel. "What am I doing here? Aren't you supposed to be a budding archaeologist? Can't you tell I'm excavating, Love."

"Don't call me that. Why are you over here?"

"That Polish priest told me you were digging in this area."

"Father Jakubowski. I meant, why are you here at Fort Providence?"

"I have a grant, Cyndi. Didn't Father J. tell you?"

"Yes, and after Father Jake asked if I knew you at Fort Craig, I avoided a direct answer."

Jayson wagged his trowel at her and smirked, "Why would you do that? Lie to a priest?"

"I didn't outright lie—"

"Relax, Love, I didn't let on that I knew you either. Hey, you look great now that you got rid of that mousey look." Jayson grinned and winked. "You remember that motel in Socorro…the hot time we had last year at the Fort Craig farewell party for volunteers?"

"But not 'hot' enough for you to answer any of my letters to you?"

Jayson avoided her glare and looked down to where he had cut away a layer of field grass. "Well… you know…with being a graduate assistant at NYU and all, I got pretty busy."

"I had almost started to like you, Jayson."

He glanced back up at her and grinned. "Hey, Cyndi, you're special!"

"Obviously not special enough even to get Email," she retorted, her voice cold with sarcasm. "What *are* you doing here?"

Jayson hesitated a moment, then sat back on his heels and absently chopped at the ground with his trowel. "I read about Fort Providence being found and applied for a grant to help with excavations. When I rented a place from that priest, he told me you'd discovered bodies of Union Colored troops here, like I did at Fort Craig."

"Jayson," she corrected, "you personally didn't find those Buffalo Soldiers. It was a team effort."

"Hey, wait," he protested. "I was the one told that supervisor where to dig."

"Is *that* what you tell people? So what do you expect to find here?"

Jason tossed his trowel aside, stood up, and moved closer to her. "Kind of keep this under your boonie, but during the Civil War, U.S. Cavalry units had Indian scouts working for them."

"I know all about that. They were Native-Americans."

"Yeah, that's what I just said, Cyndi. Anyway, after the war, there must have been Indians with the Colored guys stationed here, pacifying the Territories. Apaches mostly, and I figure some of them must be buried in this fort cemetery. That's what clinched my grant application."

"No doubt, with help from your alumni father knowing the right people at the university?" Cynthia reminded him. "Didn't you brag about your family being big donors to NYU?"

Jayson ignored her taunt. "Look, Cyndi, I'm not going to bother your dig. I looked it over"—he grinned at her and tipped his hat—"Hey, not bad for... for—"

"For a woman or an amateur?" she suggested at his hesitation. "Which is it Jayson, perhaps both?"

"Well, Cyndi, you really don't have an archaeology degree..." He reached out to touch her arm, but she pulled back. "Okay, look. I said I'm not going to disturb what you've done here, and anyway state authorities will take over the site. I'm surprised they haven't already done that and closed it."

"New Mexico is the land of *mañana*," she told him without smiling. "Have you forgotten that?"

Jayson shrugged and looked toward her SUV. "So where are you living, Cyndi? Maybe we could have dinner together sometime."

"I rent a small place about a mile south of here."

"And you have a car. The priest mentioned what...Belén...as a place with restaurants. If it's a late dinner we could—"

"—Stay overnight in a motel?" she satirically finished for him. "In your dreams, Jayson."

Both turned as they heard an automobile come from the direction of the highway and pull up behind Cynthia's car. Armando got out of his Chevrolet Camaro and walked toward the two.

"Hi, Cynthia," he called out. "I was goin' over to tell Father Hakub about a car he might like to buy, when I saw your car here. I came to see how you're doin'." He glanced over to acknowledge the man. "Hi."

"Armand, this...this is Jayson Baumann," she said, using a hand to hide the flush in her complexion. "He's here from New York University to excavate another part of the fort's cemetery."

"Yeah, Father Hakub told me..." He extended a hand. "Armando Herrera."

"Like Cyndi said, I'm Jayson." He nodded toward the Camaro. "Say, is that a low rider, like I hear you guys drive?"

*You guys? Does he mean every Hispanic?* Armando threw Cynthia an amused glance before replying, "Naw, it would be cut down if it was. This baby is a souped-up '87 IROC-Z that runs like three hundred an' five ponies."

"Hmmm. So," Jayson asked, "who's this 'Father Hakub' guy you're talking about?"

"Father Jake, the pastor at San Isidro," Cynthia explained. "The first part of 'Jakub-owski' shortened to a Spanish pronunciation. You're renting from him."

"Right..." Jayson looked from one to the other with a knowing leer. "So, you two are...well...you know, like, 'an item'?"

"Armand and I are *friends*," Cynthia emphasized.

"Right," the mechanic agreed. "Look, I gotta get over to the rectory. There's a '01 Honda Civic I saw advertised for sale in the *Herald*. I'll take Father Hakub to Belén so we can have a gander at it."

Unaware of the previous night's fire, Cynthia asked, "Is something wrong with his Nissan?"

"Father thinks some kids got careless with firecrackers. Fire Department says it's a total loss, but you can see that yourself. I think it was torched."

"His car was destroyed?" She looked over at Jayson. "Didn't you see or hear anything? You live in Father's old adobe across from the church."

"Musta slept through it all, Cyndi," he said with a shrug of indifference.

"Armand, why would anyone burn Father's car?"

"Well, you know, could be kids, or maybe not everybody likes the changes he's been makin' at our church."

"But to destroy his property—"

"It's okay, Cynthia," Armando reassured her, "I saw that Civic for sale in the paper this morning, so I'm takin' Father Hakub to see it."

"That's good of you. I hope it works out for Father."

"Yeah…." Armando looked toward the anthropologist and gave him a half salute. "Nice meetin' ya, Jackson."

"It's Jayson," he corrected, unsure whether or not the mechanic mocked him. After watching Armando's Camaro round the bend toward the rectory, he taunted Cynthia. "If that's your new boyfriend, did he even finish high school?"

"Jayson," she bristled at his conceit, "Armand is two things you are not. He's a top-notch car mechanic and, more important, a very nice person. Now excuse me while I get my digging tools out of the car." Cynthia walked a few steps, then turned back to him. "If you find Civil War scout remains, you'll have to notify the Native American Graves—"

"—Protection and Repatriation people," Jayson said, then sneered, "You telling me how to do my job?"

She ignored his snub and went to open the back of her Tucson and pull out her excavation tools.

A moment later, Armando Herrera pulled his Camaro into the San Isidro rectory driveway and braked behind the priest's burned-out car. Yellow tape draped the charred hulk, but no arson investigators were present to make a report.

Fr. Jake answered the knock on his door. "Armando, come in."

"Thanks, Father. Hey, I got a line on a used 2001 Honda and also brought you one of *Tia* Ofilia's smudge bundles. She thought that greasy smoke last night musta stunk up your place."

"I've had the windows open all morning."

He sniffed the air. "It does smell a lot better in here."

"That's because your aunt and her two *viejos compeñeras* did a fine job of cleaning up a real mess."

"*Bueno.* Father Hakub, you doin' anythin' really important right now?"

"Working on a Fourth of July sermon, but I could put it aside. Why do you ask?"

"It's about takin' a look at that Honda Civic for sale. You got time to drive to Belén with me?"

"Sure, Armando. Of course."

"*Bueno*. Wanna know a funny thing, Father? I called the phone number from that ad in the paper. Turned out it was Pete Gonzales sellin' the car, a guy I knew in high school."

"Really? Have you kept in touch with him?"

"Naw, Pete's a year older, but we only talked a little. He's in real estate… you know, sellin' properties. The Civic belongs to his sister, but she's out of college now and wants to sell it off."

"How much is the car?"

"He's got it listed at thirty-five hundred in the paper, but maybe I can get him down a bit, you bein' a priest and all."

"Armando, I don't expect any special clerical treatment."

"Still, I'm gonna ask Pete to let me look the car over in my shop. Can you give him a hundred dollar deposit…somethin' like that?"

"Would he take a check? The bank probably isn't open on Saturday, so I can't make a cash withdrawal."

"No, Western Savings is open until one 'o clock today, and I'm makin' a business deposit, there first. They'll even be open part of Monday, too."

"But that's the Fourth of July Holiday," Fr. Jake pointed out.

"Just the bank manager and Rod Jirón will come in. People might need extra money that day to do somethin,' or go some place. Since they closed the branch here, Mister Ramirez is pretty nice about helpin' out folks."

"Rodrigo Jirón? I remember him. A nice young man. Does he still live up at the commune at Eden West?"

"I wouldn't know."

"Okay, let me get my wallet and we'll go take a look at this Honda."

After the priest belted himself into the Camaro's passenger seat, Armando gunned the car toward SR 310, and paused at the stop sign. After he turned right he nodded his head toward a closed restaurant on the left. "Father, you hear anythin' from Detective Mora about the Feds lettin' Mamacita's open up again?"

"She hasn't mentioned it, but that would probably take a court order."

"Too bad, we need a good pace to eat here in Providencia. Me and the guys used to play guitar there on Friday nights."

"I miss the place, too," Fr. Jake admitted. "One can get fed up with frozen dinners."

Armando chuckled. "'Fed up.' That a joke, Father Hakub?"

"If so, it was unintentional, and I guess no one uses that expression these days."

The young mechanic drove on in silence before giving the priest a quick side-glance. "Pardon me for askin', Father, but you been here over a coupla months now and we don't really know a lot about you."

Fr. Jake chuckled at a long-overdue question. "Ask away, Armando."

"Okay…like…how come you came from Michigan over to here?"

"Well, I was eligible to retire last April, but wanted to keep my ministry. I told that to my Detroit archbishop but he…well…he's a bit upset with me because I have concerns about the Catholic Church, with which he doesn't agree."

"Whatcha mean, 'concerns he doesn't agree with'?"

"Armando, a bishop has to follow the church line very rigidly."

He nodded and cast the priest a knowing look. "Like you gotta agree with the boss to keep your job."

"Something like that. Actually Archbishop Sredzinski was quite fair. A priest usually is not reassigned outside his diocese, but he knew I was learning Spanish so I could communicate more easily with Mexican seasonal workers in my parish. As a favor to the prelate in Santa Fe, Archbishop Benisek, I was allowed to come here on a year's sabbatical leave."

"That means what, Father?"

"It's like a paid working vacation and…well…I'll be out of the bishop's hair for a year, or so to speak."

Armando swung the car around to pass a slow-moving tractor, then pushed his cap further back on his head. "So, Father Hakub, what are these crazy ideas you have?"

"They aren't really that crazy, Armando."

"Sorry, I didn't mean nothin' by usin' that word."

"Forget it, son. Well, for one thing, new ordinations to the priesthood are lagging far behind retirements. Fortunately, since the Vatican II reforms, we have deacons to help us. Many of them are married men, yet they can't be ordained as priests and celebrate the Eucharist. That's the central rite in Catholicism."

"But lots of non-Catholic pastors have wives. I mean, wasn't priests married at one time?"

110

"True, and that's a hot topic right now. Most people, perhaps even many priests, don't realize that in A.D 325 the Council of Nicaea discussed the issue that early. The Council voted to allow presbyters to decide if they wished to marry or not."

"So you woulda had a choice back then?"

"Yes, and priests *were* allowed to have a wife until around the eleventh century. After the seven hundreds, when abbots of celibate religious orders became popes, some began to forbid the practice."

When his driver became quiet, Fr. Jake reflected, *Like most Catholic laypersons, Armando is afraid to ask too many questions about what to believe. The ancient Hebrews had six hundred-thirteen precepts to follow. The Catholic Catechism has two thousand eight hundred and sixty five, yet priestly celibacy is not even mentioned among them.* "Armando," he pointed out, "celibacy is not a Church dogma that we are required to accept."

"It isn't?"

"No. Priestly celibacy is not a doctrine, it's considered an accepted discipline. Exceptions are now being made to ordain married non-Catholic clergymen, who wish to convert."

"Then how about maybe havin' women priests, like I hear about?"

Fr. Jake laughed at his timely question. "Please, Armando, one change at a time! Some Protestant denominations do ordain female priests. For example, the presiding bishop of the American Episcopal Church is a brilliant woman. I once heard her speak in Detroit— "

"She's a bishop?" he interrupted. "I dunno. A woman bishop…."

*Maybe a new subject, Father.* "Ah, have you met Jayson Baumann yet?"

"Yeah, I went by Cynthia's dig when comin' to see you. He's okay."

"I found him on the arrogant side, but I hope he can help Cynthia with her excavation."

Armando barely nodded agreement, then was quiet again as they passed through a flat, arid countryside laced with occasional green irrigated fields of beans and corn. Despite monsoon rains and Rio Grande *acequia* water, subsistence farming had declined; residents drove—or moved—to Belén and other locales, where work and stores were more available. "For Sale" signs dotted a number of foreclosed homes and failed roadside businesses that were tragic evidences of Wall Street banking mortgage abuses and the state of the current recession.

Clouds had built up on three horizons, heralding the promise of another monsoon rain that afternoon.

O

At Western Savings, a young teller and the manger were on duty. Armando knew both men, and Fr. Jake also had met each of them. The mechanic went to Mr. Ramirez's window to make his business deposit.

Rodrigo Jirón smiled when he recognized the priest and beckoned him over. "Father Jakubowski. Nice to see you again."

The priest grinned at him and extended a hand. "Same here, Rod."

"How can I help you?"

Fr. Jake pushed a withdrawal slip toward the teller. "I should probably take out a couple hundred for the holiday. Half of it is for a deposit on a used automobile."

"I thought you owned a car, Father."

"It was destroyed last night, Rod. I figure some kids became careless with firecrackers or rockets."

"Hmmm…" The teller seemed skeptical. "You really think so?"

"Why would anyone burn up my Nissan?"

Jirón avoided an opinion by opening his cash drawer. "How would you like the money, Father?"

"Two fifties and the balance in twenties will be fine."

While the teller processed the slip and counted the money, Fr. Jake commented, "Rod, I'm glad you're open today. I just found out that the Providencia branch had closed."

"Not enough business there," he explained. "Some other banks have offices inside a supermarket that are open until noon on Saturday. We stay here until one o'clock."

"Armando says you'll even be open on Monday."

"It's a service to our clients, Father, and frankly, I need the cash. I…I still live at the commune."

"Is Caleb Parker up there?"

"No…." Rod hesitated a moment before admitting, "We were talking about buying a house together, but I'm not sure where he's looking to do the Holy Spirit's work right now."

"How is James Parker, his father? Elder Jeremiah?"

"Still the same crusty old guy…" Jirón spread out the bills. "Okay, Father, here's your two hundred dollars."

"Thanks, Rod. God bless, and have a safe Fourth of July."

"You, too."

Two other customers came in while Fr. Jake waited for Armando to finish his transaction. As the priest slipped the bills into his wallet, he thought of what Rod had revealed about his friend. *Caleb Parker evidently hasn't yet made peace with his father. He wanted to leave the commune for work more attuned to the Holy Spirit than was recycling roadside trash. Has he found it? Rod-the-ex-Catholic is still with 'pentecostals' who have nothing to do with the United Pentecostal Church. Elder Jeremiah just took on the name for his store-front Assembly—*

Armando jarred the priest out of his thoughts. "All set Father Hakub?"

"Sure, let's go see this car."

In the parking lot, the mechanic unlocked the Camaro's passenger door. "Pete Gonzales lives on Scott Avenue, the next block over from the school. It's across Center Street, but not too far from here. Belt up, Father." Before activating the ignition, Armando turned to the priest. "We're having a *Lechóna*...a pig roast...at Ofilia's tomorrow for the Fourth. How about comin' over in the afternoon for supper?"

"Thanks, Armando, I'd like that. We Poles do the same thing, but in my part of Michigan the meal mostly was catered."

"Naw, here we build a mesquite or apple-wood fire in a pit. Buy a young *lechón*, a pig up to about a hundred pounds and.... Well, you'll see how Latinos cook it."

"Who else are you inviting?"

"Mostly *Tia* Ofilia's friends and her son's family, but probably Cynthia, and a couple guys I know who are gonna help carry the coffin at that soldier's funeral on Monday..." When Armando started the engine, glanced in the rear view mirror, and backed out of the parking space, Fr. Jake thought about his invitation to a family tradition. *Perhaps I'm beginning to belong to the community.*

○

Pedro "Pete" Gonzales was a year older than Armando and had graduated from Belén High in 2001. He lived with his wife and two small children in a three-bedroom / two-bath, single-family home on a quiet street near the city's public library.

"Hey, 'Mando *Pesado*'," Gonzales joked when he saw his former schoolmate at the door.

Mando responded in kind. "Who you callin' a pain in the neck, *Alcornoque*?"

113

"¡*Pescado!*"

Pete slapped Armando on the back. "Great you called!"

"Great you got a car to sell!" Armando laughed, then introduced the priest. "This is Father Hakub. He's at San Isidro now."

Pete—full-faced, wearing cargo shorts, and with a premature paunch bulging beneath a Plumaria-patterned Hawaiian sport shirt—extended a hand with a puzzled look. "Father, your name is 'Hakub'?"

"Father Jake, actually," he explained to the realtor. "Armando pronounces Polish-English as if it were Spanish."

Pete grinned at the clarification. "Of course, Father. And I just used up two of the five Spanish words I remember from high school on him. Sorry, but they aren't very nice ones."

"Armando told me you have an automobile to sell."

"It's there in the driveway." As they came off the porch and walked to the Honda, Pete explained, "The car belongs to my sister, but she graduated from college now and has a job in an Albuquerque law office. Consuela's making money, so she wants a newer model."

"Understandable and I need a 'new' older one."

The mechanic walked around the car to inspect it. "Mind if I look under the hood, Pete?"

"Be my guest, Mando. Go ahead and kick the tires, too. Here…start her up." He took a key off his ring and tossed it to Armando, then pulled the priest further toward the sidewalk, away from exhaust fumes. "No offense, Father," he whispered, "but he acts like he knows what he's doing."

Fr. Jake found the remark patronizing. "Armando is a fine auto repairman in Providencia. We drove here in his Camaro."

"Oh, Mando fixes cars? I lost track after we graduated. Me, I went into real estate, like my dad. He…he died a couple years ago."

"I'm sorry, Pete."

"Yeah, thanks. I took over the office and I'm doing pretty well myself." He gestured toward the house. "I bought my place on a short sale. That means at a price below the balance owned on the mortgage." The realtor grinned again as he patted the priest's arm. "Father, that's a great way to buy a house."

The priest said nothing, but realized silently, *Unless you're an owner who lost a job and were forced to sell your home on a money-losing deal.*

While Armando checked the Honda's engine, Pete told the priest a bit about his family. "Father, my wife, Amanda, and the kids…well, all of us go to Mass at Our Lady of Sorrows here in Belén. But, you know, if I have to show a client a house, I might miss going once in a while—" He paused as Armando shut off the car's engine and came toward the two men.

"She sound good, Pete," he told him, "but I'd like to check cylinder compression. Okay if Father Hakub drives the car to my shop? He can get the feel of it, too."

The realtor thought a moment before agreeing. "Sure. Fine. Hey, how about coming in for maybe a beer or some lemonade?"

"Naw," Armando refused as he handed the ignition key to the priest. "Really Pete, thanks, but Father Hakub's gotta get a Fourth of July sermon ready for tomorrow. Right, Father?"

"Yes. I…I really should get back."

"Suit your selves," Pete shrugged.

Fr. Jake thought the man seemed relieved. *What would he talk about with a mechanic he hasn't seen in nine years, or to a priest who might criticize his lapses in Mass attendance?* He took the two fifty dollar bills from his wallet. "Pete, if that's acceptable, I'd like to leave a hundred dollar deposit on the car with you."

"Sure, 'Gentleman's Agreement,' Father, no paperwork…. Hey," he abruptly recalled, "I read in the *Herald* about the excitement you guys had a couple weeks past. You know, few years ago that Tex Houston film guy came to the office and talked to my dad about buying properties in this area. Exactly what did he do?"

"Pete, I'll take very good care of your sister's car," Fr. Jake hedged, unwilling to delve into past legal or financial events with the man.

"Okay, Father." The realtor held the door open for the priest. "Stick the key in the ignition there. What were you driving?"

"A 2005 Nissan."

"My sister's Honda won't be that much different. Hope you like it."

"I'm sure I will," Fr. Jake said, "and I'll send you a check for the balance."

"*No problemo*, Father…" Pete closed the door, then looked over at Armando. "Hey, '*papanatas*'…'dimwit'," he called out. "You, Mando. Don't be such a stranger."

After a wan smile, Armando closed the door of his Camaro. "Sure, Pete. See ya around."

Fr. Jake had watched the two men and started the Honda's engine to drive back. *I think Armando is uncomfortable around his former classmate, who seems more successful, yet probably couldn't fix a flat tire if his life depended on* it. *I'll remind Armando what Christ pointed out—that a laborer is worthy of his hire, but the Lord never specifically mentioned real estate brokers.*

*Real estate....* A thought came to him as an unexpected revelation: *Could the elder Gonzales have advised Tex Houston on how to obtain land in Providencia, by using quit claim deeds? Perhaps there's something to this six stages of connection idea that I mentioned to Sonia!*

## 13 a july fourth *lechóna*

On the afternoon of the Fourth of July, as Fr. Jake walked through the San Isidro *camposanto*—a shortcut to reach the narrow gravel road leading up to Ofilia Herrera's house—a few parishioners still decorating graves in the cemetery waved to him. A family knelt around a recent burial mound and sang *Dale el Descanso, Señor,* a simple requiem hymn in Spanish he had heard in Michigan. Some *Providenceños,* who perhaps had not attended Mass that morning, bent low over their flower tributes or ducked behind tombstones. *Catholic guilt, but will they go to confession?*

Fr. Jake knew that the entry on **Sin** in the *Catechism of the Catholic Church* alphabetically listed 'Neglect of Sunday obligation" directly under "Murder" as grave sins, that is, Mortal Sins. Some priests he knew seemed to give equal importance—and eternal punishment—for committing either of the two offences. He recalled that Jayson Baumann had come to the eleven o'clock service and left early, walking out the front entrance immediately after taking communion. *He probably went to work on his excavation.*

Near the left boundary of the cemetery, two men in T-shirts and black military caps embroidered, "Gulf War Veteran," or "Home of the Brave," were so intent on digging a coffin-size hole that neither looked up at the priest. *Those must be the two young men Armando invited to dinner, still preparing Sergeant Salazar's grave.*

Attendance at both Masses had been sparse. Since it was a long holiday weekend, more families than usual had gone camping in state parks or driven to visit relatives and friends living at other locations.

When Fr. Jake crossed Calle San Isidro and started up the rutted driveway to Ofilia Herrera's house, brilliant vermillion blossoms of Indian Paintbrush

117

plants lined the edges of the gravel road. In the fields alongside, watered by the seasonal rains, the myriad of summer wildflowers that Sonia had predicted would grow now were colorful dots of purple and red sprinkled among refreshed, green field grasses and weeds. *Armando told me about Indian Paintbrush, but I should get a book on plants of the Southwest.*

Near the end of the priest's near-half-mile climb, the aroma of roast suckling pig and mesquite smoke drifted down to him. He walked a bit further on, then stopped to catch his breath where Ofilia had planted her front herb gardens. Monsoon rains had revived common medicinal or cooking herbs—*Añil de Muerto, Ponso, Cebadilla,* and oregano, sweet basil, and rosemary. Some herb plants opened delicate flowers on long stems.

Up ahead, Armando's Camaro, the Hyundai SUV owned by Cynthia, and another car had parked in front of the *curandera's* house, an adobe *casa* roofed over with sheets of rusting corrugated-steel. Draped over the railing by an American flag, her front porch overlooked Providencia and gave visitors a panoramic view of the area to the west, beyond Highway 310 and on toward the distant Rio Grande *bosque.* Fr. Jake heard voices coming from the right end of the porch and figured that was where guests at the *Lechóna* had gathered. As he walked around the side of the house, an enticing aroma of roasting pork became stronger. On Ofilia's back property, a smaller log *casita* extended into a larger herb drying shed that was sheathed in weathered, 4" x 8" plywood panels. Behind it, an ancient outdoor kiosk-sized latrine made the priest wonder if Ofilia had indoor plumbing.

Near the house, bluish smoke rose from a fire pit at one side of a flagstone patio. Armando and a somewhat older man held beer bottles as they tended the carcass of a suckling pig that was supported over the coals by two rebar rods, resting on cement blocks.

Cynthia, wearing a straw sun hat, short sleeve blouse, and stylish jeans was with another woman about her age. Both women set a picnic table with Ofilia's non-matching plates and a variety of drinking glasses. A beverage cooler was set on a bench in the shade of the house's eastern wall. A soft sound of contemporary Mexican music from a Hispanic radio station drifted from a portable radio next to the cooler.

Armando spotted the priest and called out, "Hey, Father Hakub, good you could make it! C'mon over. This here is *Tia's* son, Victor."

The auto mechanic's cousin smiled and extended a hand. "*Bienvenido,* Father. Mando speaks very highly of you."

Fr. Jake returned the man's strong grip. "A gratifying, if perhaps exaggerated, report. Victor, do you live here in Providencia?"

"No, in Socorro, Father."

Cynthia heard them, smiled as she put down a stack of plates, and hurried over to greet the priest. "Father, Jake, I'm so glad you could be here!"

He smiled back at her and nodded toward his hosts. "'*Gracias*' to Armando and his aunt Ofilia for inviting me."

"Hey, glad to have you, Father," Armando repeated. "How about a Corona?"

"Sure, why not? Thanks."

While Armando went to bring the priest his beer from the cooler, Victor used his bottle to indicate a woman at the picnic table. "Father, come meet Lena, my wife. She's over there laying out the dishes and silverware."

Lena Herrera wore a flower-print summer dress and an Albuquerque Isotopes baseball cap. She allowed the priest a shy smile from the table, then avoided conversation by scolding two children throwing a rubber ball to Ofilia's Jack Russell terrier. "Fabian… Tómas! You better not get your good clothes dirty!"

After Armando handed Fr. Jake an opened bottle, Cynthia took off her sunglasses and beckoned the priest away from the table, to one side of the house.

When they were away from the others, he asked, "You wanted to discuss something, Cynthia?"

"I…I have to be honest with you, Father. I lied when I implied that I didn't know Jayson Baumann."

"I do recall you were rather non-committal about him, but that's not a lie, or even a 'confession-able offense'."

She nodded slightly yet seemed unconvinced. "We…we were together at the Fort Craig dig last year."

"So I understood."

"At first I liked him, and then came to realize that he was only there for himself. It was a way to advance his career. There was an arrogance about him…." Cynthia's voice trailed off.

"I picked up on that trait of Jayson's."

"Right, Father. I shouldn't be critical but we…at the end of the dig there was—" Embarrassed, she glanced down and scuffed sandy ground with a sandal. "The fort's staff threw a farewell party for volunteers. There was a cash bar. I'm not proud that I—"

"Cynthia," Fr. Jake interrupted by holding up his bottle. "May I get you a Corona?"

"Okay, Father." She smiled and looked relieved at not having to explain further.

After opening the beer and handing it to her, the priest said, "There is one thing I need to ask you, Cynthia."

She stopped the bottle at her lips. "Oh? What's that, Father?"

"Do you know of any pregnant women in the area? Given the premature menstruation reported in younger girls these days, perhaps even the friend of a student at your school?"

"No I don't, Father Jake. Really...I...I'm shocked. Why would you ask me that?"

"Cynthia, at this time, I can't go into much detail about the reason."

A questioning frown creased her brow. "This has something to do with Detective Mora's investigation at Don Fernando's ranch, doesn't it?"

Rather than replying, the priest glanced toward the cooking pit. "I'd better go see how Armando and Victor are coming along with the *lechón*."

Cynthia took the hint. "And I should finish helping Lena set the table. Father, thanks for understanding."

"*No problemo.*" Fr. Jake walked to the pit and stood leeward of fragrant, yet eye-searing, wood smoke. He listened to the sound of sizzling fat on hot coals for a moment, before asking the two men, "How's the cooking coming along, gentlemen?"

Armando replied, "This isn't a big *lechón*, not even fifty pounds. *Lechón*... that's 'suckling pig' to you Father Hakub, and to maybe just a few of us eatin' today. Victor and me started the fire after Mass, around noon, so this porker should be pretty much done by now."

"That chicken wire wrapped around the carcass keeps cooked meat in place?"

Victor grinned. "Right, Father. That's exactly what it's for."

The priest gestured toward the table with his bottle. "What's served with the meat?"

"*Tia* Ofilia an' the two *viejas* that cleaned your rectory are inside makin' *calabacitas con maiz*, cornbread, probably refried pinto beans. "Well, you know," he joked, "it's pretty standard Mexican stuff. Cynthia brought guacamole and chips. Lena's special dessert is *capriotada*. That's a kind of bread pudding with brandy in it. It's *muy bueno*."

"Everything sounds *muy delicioso*."

"Yeah, Father, and we fried up some the *lechón* fat into *chicharrones*." Armando slipped on oven mitts to shift the rebars and pig carcass a little to the left, then beckoned the priest out toward the herb drying shed. "Y' know, Father," he confided, nodding back toward the house, "Ofilia is worried that the *velacione* she did in your rectory didn't take."

"You mean that it wasn't effective?"

"Yeah, she heard about your car being torched."

"And?"

"*Tia* blames Father Mora's ghost and thinks a lot worse could happen to you."

Fr. Jake reached out to hold him by an elbow. "Armando, the Church accepts that certain holy persons have experienced supernatural visions, such as…say…Don Diego in Mexico City. Back in the sixteenth century he witnessed an apparition of the Virgin Mary."

"Sure. *La Virgen de Guadalupe.*"

"Exactly. That vision is considered authentic, yet believing that the dead are able to harm a person is beyond Catholic teaching."

"*Tia* ain't…isn't…one of them, but some in *curanderismo* believe dead people can do that. Like, she thinks Millie over at the ranch has put *a mal puesto,* you know, a hex, on Don Fernando."

"That's doubtful, Armando, but the woman probably does exploit the Don's extended mourning over his wife's death. That grief *is* on the neurotic side, yet a black magic curse would be something entirely different."

He shook the dregs in his Corona bottle. "Father Hakub, I'm just tellin' ya to be careful."

*Time to change the subject.* "When are we going to eat, Armando? I'm famished."

"Pretty quick now. Soon as Fidel and Luis get up here from diggin' that grave for the sergeant's coffin, me and Victor will start slicin' up the meat. Come on over and try some *chicarrónes.* You know, pork rinds."

"Yes, my Polish mother trimmed the fat off meat and fried it as a delicacy. Look, Armando, tell your aunt that I'll be careful. And…ah…may I ask if Father Mora ever attended these family celebrations?"

"Not since a while he didn't. He wasn't too social. Like I said, Father spent a lot of time with Jesus in his private *sagrario.*"

*Just as I thought.* "Armando, I'm going to open that chapel up to the parishioners, so they can worship the Blessed Sacrament there. I'll hear confessions there, too."

"That's cool."

"Yes, and let's remember Father Mora when I bless today's food."

The mechanic grinned. "Great, Father, and the *viejas* will like that. C'mon, let's go have another beer before we chow down."

O

When the two war veterans arrived, everyone stood at the picnic tables for Fr. Jake's prayer of grace for the meal.

"Please hold hands everyone," he instructed. While the guests awkwardly complied, then instinctively bowed their heads, he grasped hands with Armando and Cynthia. "You all know that there's a Catholic prayer at mealtime. There's one in Spanish, too, but I admit that I haven't learned it yet. Since I've just met some of you here, let me make this prayer a little different. You know, as some may think, Catholicism isn't just going to Mass and Confession, and then everyone can vanish for the rest of the week, without thinking about its significance. This is a beautiful family celebration and Christ attended a similar one at Cana in Galilee. That was a wedding feast, where he performed his first miracle to help out the groom. In case you've forgotten, it had nothing to do with healing the sick or forgiving sinners. When Christ heard that the poor groom had run out of wine, he turned a hundred and twenty gallons of water into a hundred and twenty gallons of wine. That had to be one heck of a wedding reception." As the men snickered, Lena covered her mouth to conceal a giggle.

Fr. Jake continued, "The lesson was that life is to be celebrated, not just at a wedding, but that each occasion, every day, really, should be joyous." He paused to look around. "Now, I must tell you that the amount of wine was symbolic of the Hebrew prophecies proclaiming abundance in the last days. The men and ladies here who produced this *lechóna* have more than adequately followed the Lord's example." He waited for light applause to subside before concluding, "Many of you visited the graves of deceased family members before coming here, so let us also remember them and your pastor, Father Jésus Mora. May God bless him, the friends gathered here, and this food we are about to eat. *En el nombre del Padre, y del Hijo, y del Espiritu Santo, Amen.*"

After everyone crossed themselves, then sat down and helped themselves to food, in deference to a priest being present, the meal continued in a less boisterous manner. Yet everyone enjoyed this holiday break from their day-to-day routines—especially the Jack Russell terrier, who was fed constant pork scraps under the table by the two Herrera children.

When Fr. Jake finished his brandy-laced bread pudding dessert, he glanced at his watch. *A little past six o'clock.* He stood up and went to where the *curandera* sat with her nephew. "Ofilia, Armando, I can't thank you enough for a wonderful afternoon with your family and friends."

"Aw, you really gotta go, Father? Vic and me are gonna play a little guitar music."

"I should. I've not conducted a funeral here yet, and need to come up with a short eulogy for Adam Salazar tomorrow. Perhaps my breviary reading will be of help."

"Okay, Father Hakub, but remember what I warned about your car bein' torched an' all. Just be careful."

"*Si, Padre,*" Ofila added solemnly. "I come light more candle…chase off *mal puesto* for you."

"Perhaps, *Señora,*" the priest conceded to soothe the old woman, then waved to the guests. "God bless, and I thank all of you." Fr. Jake adjusted his hat down lower over his face as a shield against late afternoon sun and patted a full stomach. "Armando, if the grocery isn't closed, I'll walk off over-eating your ample meal by going down to buy milk."

"Oh, the store's open all right, Father. Hey…if you're goin' there, you mind takin' some meat to Carlotta? Poor lady had to work all day."

"Of course not. I'd be glad to."

"*Bueno…*" He turned to his aunt. "*Tia, por favor* wrap up some *lechón* for Carlotta ."

She nodded a 'Si' and reached over for the meat platter.

In a few moments, Armando handed Fr. Jake a small plastic bag with a foil packet inside. "*Hasta,* Father. And I'll check the compression on that Honda in the morning."

"*Gracias,* Armando. *Hasta luego.*"

The walk down to Calle San Isidro was easier than the climb to the Herrera house. Rather than cutting across BLM land to reach the Providencia Grocery, the priest decided to walk down the Calle and see how Jayson Baumann was coming along with his excavation.

The anthropologist's site was about fifty feet west of Cynthia's dig. Jayson sat hunched on his heels, cleaning dirt off an object with a soft brush.

Coming up behind him, Fr. Jake asked, "Have you found something?"

Startled by the voice, Jayson covered his hand, then turned. "Oh… Father Jakubowski." He wiped dirt off his knees and stood to explain, "Look,

I'm sorry I skipped out of Mass early this morning. I...I was anxious to get back to my excavation."

"*Te absolvo*," the priest replied, "yet it wasn't a sin to leave early the way you did." He motioned with the meat packet at the anthropologist's closed hand. "What were you just cleaning?"

"I...I think I'm on to something big." Jayson opened his palm to show three finely chiseled flint arrowheads. "I found these Apache points about a foot down. Beauties, aren't they? Bi-facial, flat, hexagonal cross section. Corner notched. Know what I'm talking about, Father?"

"Not really, Jayson."

"Thought so."

Taken aback by the young man's smug retort, Fr. Jake told him, "You're describing details of an arrowhead I don't know anything about."

"Yeah." Jayson ignored the priest's explanation and knelt in the dirt again. "Father, I gotta get back to digging. These are burial offerings, so there must be an Indian corpse a bit farther down."

"Well, good luck and God Bless."

"Yeah, you too."

At the Providencia Grocery and Gas, Carlotta sat behind the counter to read a Fourth of July issue of the *Valencia County Herald*. After a bell on the entrance door jingled, she turned and stood up. "Happy Fourth, Father Jake. Say, that snappy hat you bought here looks really good on you."

"Thanks, Carlotta. I'm surprised that you're open today."

"Father," she joked, "I'm sorta like a priest. Aren't clergy available 'twenty four- seven'?"

"True...true. Most of us, anyway."

"Well, at least after workin' *I* get to go home at eight o'clock." She folded the *Herald* and waved it at the canned food aisles and frozen meals in the cooler. "Whatta need?"

He handed her the plastic bag. "Just milk, but Armando gave me this pork from his *lechóna* for you."

"Oh...well, thanks. How'd that go?"

"Fine, I met his cousin's family and a couple of men who will be pallbearers at the sergeant's funeral tomorrow."

"Uh-huh." Carlotta pointed her newspaper toward the dairy section of the cooler. "Get your milk, Father, and then maybe I'll close early. Been a slow day."

After ringing up the sale, the storekeeper handed him the purchase and hesitated a moment before asking, "Anything new about what happened up at Don Fernando's ranch?"

"Nothing I can talk about."

"How about how poor Eusebia Nevarez died? Any autopsy results?"

"Not yet. It's a holiday weekend, so the medical examiner's office in Socorro is closed."

As Carlotta went to turn off the store lights at a fuse box, she called back, "Father, some folks living on Romero Loop been seeing lights in the *bosque* across from that *acequia*. They report hearing a kind of wailing and moaning, even a awful sulfur smell coming from somewhere."

"The prevailing wind *is* from the west," he said. "Are there any oil refineries over that way?"

"I dunno, but Mrs. Alvarez and her neighbor even claim to of seen a tall skinny woman, wearing a dark gown with a hood. She was checking along the *acequia*."

Fr. Jake recalled, "Sonia Mora told me the legend about a woman whose children drowned in a sluice."

"'Course, Father, that would be La Llorona. She roams around waterways, hunting for her dead kids. Some oldsters say that witch up at the Don's conjured her up."

"Ofilia mentioned the legend, yet surely, Carlotta, you don't believe that ghost story? As to Queen Millie being a witch, well—"

"Father Jake, I'm just telling you what I was told people heard and saw." Carlotta fished the front door key from her purse, and then paused to confront him at the entrance. "Wasn't there a dead baby found in the *acequia*?"

The priest's eyebrows rose. "Who told you that?"

Carlotta chuckled at his naïve question. "No offense, Father, but folks tend to clam up around priests. If you want to hear the latest gossip, come be a storekeeper."

He smiled understanding of her explanation. "Okay, I won't confirm the gossip you heard, but on second thought maybe I should stake out that sluice myself."

"Suit yourself, but don't say I didn't warn you."

"Noted." *And yours is the second warning I've gotten today.* "Well, God Bless."

O

That evening, Fr. Jake finished writing general remarks about the ultimate sacrifice that Adam Salazar, possibly a stranger, had made for community and country. The Gospel Acclamation in his breviary for July 5 brought the hope of Resurrection, an appropriate reading for a young sergeant, who gave his life in the cause of the American freedom they all had celebrated the day before: "Our Savior Jesus Christ has done away with death, and brought us life through his gospel. Alleluia.

*"Alleluia!"*

# 14 pastor haskill

Fr. Jake decided to conduct the *Misa Exequial*, a funeral Mass in Spanish for Sergeant Adam Salazar. The congregation could follow the ritual by using new July missalettes placed in the pews. Only a few *Provideñcenos* were able to attend the rites, or parishioners had not gone to the July Fourth Mass and heard about the soldier's burial. Because she taught a class, Cynthia Plow could not attend the requiem service.

Before a procession into the church and start of the funeral liturgy, several gray-haired women, dressed in black with lace *mantillas* covering their heads, prayed the rosary aloud together in their pews. Some wore jet black mourning jewelry. Several unemployed men in faded jeans and tees sat close enough to fill a rear pew. A color guard of two grizzled oldsters held American and New Mexican flags. One of the *viejos*, who wore an ill-fitting Knights of Columbus black tuxedo suit, and white-plumed chapeau, struggled to keep his American flag upright. He stood by a green banner depicting San Isidro, patron saint of the church. Long ago, parish women had embroidered the saint's image on the background cloth.

The oldster with the New Mexico state flag had put on his old olive drab Korean War 1st Marine Division uniform.

Armando had contacted four *Hermanos* as pallbearers, all veterans, who sat in the first pew. One wore a red sweatband around his dark hair. Another had on a black veteran's service cap with "Vietnam Veteran" lettered in yellow above the visor. Armando, who was not a pallbearer, sat with Fidel and Luis, the two men who had dug the grave and been at the *Lechóna*. Breanna Springer was next to them, but, oddly, David Allison, the sergeant's war buddy, was absent.

Late morning light filtering through frosted windows in the church's east wall illuminated the sergeant's coffin, which had been set atop sawhorses on the tile floor in front of the altar stairs. Undecorated, it was of finely crafted pinewood, with four oak handles attached to the sides. Armando had placed a *santero's* crucifix on a lid that was sealed shut with pegs. Allison had not brought the American flag that he said he would supply to cover the coffin.

Standing at the head of the bier, Fr. Jake sprinkled the cross with holy water while reciting, "*En la bautismo Adam, recibó el signo de la cruz....*"

The Mass continued in a Spanish that only the older parishioners could follow, and Fr. Jake's mispronunciation of unfamiliar words did not help. The day's Gospel Acclamation in English was appropriate for a funeral:

"Our Savior Jesus Christ has done away with death and brought us life through his gospel."

The Michigan priest centered his homily for a young man he did not know, on having faith. As examples, he cited Matthew's account of the woman who had long suffered a hemorrhage of blood and been cured because of her faith. The reading included the resuscitation of an official's young daughter, who was believed to have died, but whom Jesus awakened.

Afterward, Armando raised a hand. "Father Hakub, could I say somethin' about the...the deceased sergeant?"

"Of course, son, and anyone else who wishes to do so may speak on the sergeant's behalf."

Armando took a nervous breath and turned to look back at the assembled mourners. "We here didn't know Adam Salazar, not even what he looked like, but it's enough to know he volunteered to defend this country. He died doin' it and that's plenty reason for Father Hakub and us to let him get buried here in our *camposanto*. I'm proud that he'll be lying there *con mi papá y mamá...y todos los antepasados*. God bless Adam, and God bless America!"

"Thanks, Armando, that was beautiful." Fr. Jake looked around. "Does anyone else wish to say anything? Miss Springer?"

Breanna hesitated a moment, then did not stand or turn around to say, "I didn't know the sergeant as well as Davie, but if he was a pal of his, that's good enough for me."

"Thank you. Anyone else?" After a few moments of silence, the priest said, "Then let's continue with the *Liturgica Eucharista*. Please stand."

The Mass continued with the familiar actions of the Consecration, the Lord's Prayer in Spanish—which most there had memorized long ago—and the Communion Service. In a final commendation, Fr. Jake prayed that the saints and angels of God would receive the soul of Sergeant Salazar: *"Reciban su alma y preséntenla ante al Altissimo."*

As the small congregation stood for the final prayer and Amen, Armando took the cross off the coffin. The four pallbearers replaced their caps and moved from the pew to hoist the pine box on their shoulders. The men began a slow procession down the aisle, then out along the Calle San Isidro toward the cemetery. The oldsters of the flag color guard followed the coffin, while the black-clad women mourners sang verses of *Concédeles el Descanso Eterno*—"Grant Eternal Rest."

It was close to 11:00 A.M. A blazing ~~June~~ July sun, almost directly overhead, cast short, black shadows of the funeral procession onto the heated asphalt paving of the street. No breeze stirred air that smelled of hot tar, and fresh grass newly resuscitated by the monsoon rains. Fr. Jake walked with Deputy Hilario Griego at the head of the procession, a short distance after the pallbearers and coffin. Breanna and Armando were side by side behind the two men. The *viejo* in his Knights of Columbus regalia barely managed to keep his American flag upright. The other oldster in the Korean War uniform struggled to hold onto the staff of the state flag, which was looped in his belt. Following them, the small knot of gray-haired village women perspired in the June heat, yet had insisted on wearing their traditional dark funerary clothing, and taking time to honor a fallen American soldier they did not know. All sang softly in Spanish to the tune of a single middle aged violinist, *"Christo Es La Resurrección,"* a hymn of hope that they would one day be with Christ in Eternity.

Fr. Jake wiped sweat from his brow with a handkerchief, then turned to Breanna. "I didn't see David Allison at the church."

"Right," she explained, "Rev., he's all broke up about Adam. Davie's waitin' by the cemetery in our Humvee, probably wipin' off tears he don't want us to see. You know, the 'macho-guy' thing."

"I thought that he didn't know Sergeant Salazar that well."

"Aw, Davie's an old softy inside, Rev. That's part of why I love the crazy guy."

The priest smiled at the unpredictability of love. "Then, 'Amen', Breanna."

Nearing the east end of the Calle, four perspiring *Hermano* pallbearers struggled under a heavy wooden coffin that now chafed their shoulders. Looking past them, Fr. Jake was surprised to see about a dozen people up ahead, milling about in front of the cemetery gate.

"That's strange," he remarked to Deputy Griego. "Who do you suppose they are?"

Griego was equally clueless. "Father, that's maybe some of Salazar's family that heard about the funeral and are standin' over there waitin' for us."

"If so, why didn't they attend the funeral Mass? Let me go ahead and find out."

After Fr. Jake passed around the pallbearers and walked up to meet the group, several of their members raised printed signs that were too small to be read at this distance. Their chanted words also were not quite legible.

A man wearing a white summer suit, blue-and-gold tie in a "Jesus Loves You" repeat pattern, and white Stetson cowboy hat, came forward from the crowd. Sweat stains darkened the armpits of his suit, when he turned back and raised his arms in a signal that quieted the chanters. The man strode toward Fr. Jake, smiling broadly and extending a hand. He greeted the priest in an almost imperceptible drawl.

"Well, now how do, Rev'rind. We ain't here t' cause trouble, just t' do the Lord's work."

"I never expected that you would cause trouble," he responded. "Who are you and these other people?"

"I'm Pastor Hask'll...that's spelled H-a-s-k-i-l-l...of the New Zion Free Will Apostolic Assembly, in Oklahoma."

"Oklahoma?" Fr. Jake repeated. "That's another state away."

"Panhandle City, where my church is, ain't so far off, Rev'rind. Down Highway 56 to 54, then I-25 to I-40."

"I see..." *But why travel to central New Mexico?* Fr. Jake felt a mild anxiety churn his stomach. *Handsome enough man, probably around thirty-five, but looks younger. That salon tan and those sideburns make him resemble a rock star. Suit's a bit threadbare, so New Zion probably doesn't have much of a Christian radio following that donates a lot of money.* "Pastor Haskill, what exactly are you doing here? This is the funeral of an army sergeant. Did you know Adam Salazar?"

"Not directly, Rev'rind. We're just exercisin' our God-given right t' free speech."

"Actually, that's more a Constitutional right than it is Biblical. You say none of your people knew Adam Salazar?"

"Nope, but the Lord Jesus Christ tells us where we're needed."

Recalling newspaper accounts of protests at soldiers' burials, Fr. Jake felt increased concern about the group's intentions. "Pastor, tell me why you're harassing this sergeant's funeral and—"

"What the hell's goin' on here?" Armando came forward to demand. "Who are all those people?"

Fr. Jake introduced their leader, "This is Pastor Haskill from a Protestant church in Oklahoma."

"So? We're *Católica* here and plan on stayin' that way."

After Haskill abruptly turned and gave another arm signal to his followers, the lowered signs were thrust upright:

**SALIZAR BURNS IN HELL   THANK GOD FOR DEAD SARGINTS   GOD HATES USA   I.E.D. is GODS PUNISHMENT**

A child no more that six years old giggled while waving a sign that read **AMERICA IS DAMNED.** Male New Zion church members, wearing identical black Tees with "America is Doomed" stenciled in yellow on front, began their chanting again: "God…hates …homo-sexuals. God…hates… homo-sexuals. God…hates…homo-sexuals…."

The four pallbearers halted, shifted their awkward burden, and looked at each other, unsure of what to do. The Vietnam vet yelled up to the priest, "What's going on, *Padre?*"

Angry now at this desecration of the funeral, Fr. Jake confronted Haskill. "Pastor, this is outrageous! Adam Salazar gave his life so you could have the freedom to commit this…this affront to us and the military. Even if the sergeant was gay, and I don't believe you have any evidence of that, it would make no difference to the Lord."

"Really, Rev'rind?" he goaded. Haskill's youthful face took on a grimace of hate. "You ever hear of W.W.J.D.?"

"'What would Jesus do'? Pastor, he go to the sergeant's house and have dinner with him. Don't you recall Luke 7, where Jesus dined with both Pharisees and a sinful woman? Or Matthew 7, where Christ warns about not judging others?"

Haskill's tan darkened, the color intensified by his white suit and hat. "You don't try to teach me the Bible, you…you Papist lackey," he sputtered and raised a hand toward the sky. "The great Tribulation prophesied in Matthew 25:15 will smite America for its immorality and tolerance of homosexuality."

Despite a tense situation, Fr. Jake suppressed a laugh. *Papist lackey? Are Catholics still called by that obsolete term?* "Pastor," he told him as calmly as possible, "I respectfully ask that you and your congregation allow us to bury Sergeant Salazar without your...well ...your truly non-Christian and hateful interference."

As if he had not heard the priest, Haskill pulled a small New Testament from his suit coat pocket, held it up, and repeated, "The Great Tribulation prophesied in Matthew 25:15 will smite America. 'When ye therefore shall see the abomination of desolation spoken of by Prophet Daniel, standing in the holy place'—"

Fr. Jake countered, "The people who lived in London and other Russian, German, or Japanese cities that were leveled in the Second World War, have already experienced that desolation. I'm giving you a sixty-five-year-old example there, but Sergeant Salazar must have had his fill of desolation and horror by serving in Iraq."

Impatient, the *Hermanos*, shifted position again and began to mutter among themselves in Spanish, complaining about the disruption and trying to decide what to do about it.

*These are mostly Vietnam and Gulf War Vets, not prone to suffer fools like Haskill lightly.* Fr. Jake pleaded with him again. "Pastor, I ask that you and your followers return home and let us bring the sergeant to his eternal rest in peace."

Deputy Griego had heard the two clergymen arguing, and came forward to warn Haskill. "Reverend, I'm ordering ya to disperse these people or ya'll all land in jail for disorderly conduct an' trespassin' on private church property."

Haskill glared at him, but remained defiant. "Deputy, we can legally protest from a coupla hundred yards away. Besides, we obey God's law, not yours—"

The next few moments became a blur to those watching the confrontation.

Breanna Springer abruptly pulled a Glock .38 caliber revolver from her purse and pushed past Armando, Griego, and Fr. Jake. She faced Haskill to snarl, "You son of a bitch and all your fucking kind! You'll never hurt a kid again!"

At the same moment that she fired pointblank at the pastor's face, the Humvee's engine roared to life. The vehicle's heavy tires squealed as Dave Allison accelerated directly toward the four pallbearers and their coffin. The *Hermanos* saw him, dropped the pine box, and instinctively dived toward the side of the street for cover. When the edge of the wooden case hit hard asphalt paving, the sides split apart: not a dead soldier's corpse, but two 80-pound sacks of cement spilled gray limestone out onto the black asphalt.

Breanna turned her pistol and aimed toward Fr. Jake. "Rev., you're no better than any of your other child-molesting colleagues...."

A nano-second before the woman fired her second round, Griego flung his body in front of the priest: Fr. Jake was thrown back and tumbled onto the street paving, scraping skin off an elbow. The deputy's body collapsed on top of the priest, then rolled onto its back. A pool of scarlet blood seeped from the upper right front of Griego's neatly pressed, tan uniform shirt.

The stunned New Zion church members near the cemetery screamed and crouched down in terror. A few huddled behind their signs—as if the zeal of their slogans might inspire God to protect them from retaliation and physical harm.

Pastor Haskill, his face smashed and bloody, lay lifeless on the hot asphalt, perhaps having had a small foretaste of the Hell in which he so fervently believed—and undoubtedly deserved.

The aged San Isidro banner and flag carriers stood petrified, along with any women mourners and men, who had not bent down, or now lay prone on the ground to avoid becoming targets.

Armando recovered and helped the priest stand up. "Father Hakub, you okay?"

"Scraped elbow," he said, blotting blood from the wound with a finger. "I think Haskill's dead, but we need to help the deputy. Call 911."

"Shit, my cell's over at the shop.... Hey, Fidel," he yelled over to his pallbearer friend. "Go call to get a ambulance over here *pronto.*"

Both men knelt beside the fallen deputy; Armando muttered, "That bitch," as he held up Griego's head while Fr. Jake pressed his handkerchief over the chest wound to staunch the flow of blood.

Allison had screeched the Humvee to a near stop with the passenger door open. "Goddammit, get in Breanna!" he shouted at her. "This was all your idea!"

His female accomplice sprinted to the slow-moving vehicle, hopped aboard, and partly slid into the front seat. As Allison accelerated, the Humvee's sudden forward momentum slapped the heavy passenger door hard on Breanna's right leg and foot.

In passing San Isidro, Allison slowed enough to remove the pin from a fire grenade with his teeth, then flung the bomb out at the church. The grenade rolled to a stop against the adobe wall, without exploding. At the street intersection, the Survivalist camp member braked alongside Hilario Griego's patrol car long enough to lob a second grenade into the open front window. As an explosion and geyser of flame erupted from the vehicle's interior, Allison swung the Humvee to the right on Highway 310 and sped away from the burning automobile. The vehicle headed north, in the direction of Belén and Interstate 25.

## 15 late afternoon after

More abruptly than usual, Detective Sonia Mora braked her red 2005 Plymouth Neon just behind the burned-out hulk of Fr. Jake's Nissan, which still cluttered the rectory's gravel driveway. She hopped out of the car, pushed open the adobe *casa*'s front door without knocking, and stormed into the living room. Fr. Jake turned from watering the window barrel cactus that one of the *viejas* had given him at the time he paid her for cleaning the house.

"Sonia?"

"What the hell happened yesterday over here, Father Jakubowski?" she demanded, tossing her cap and briefcase on the couch. Before sitting down, she saw the oversize plastic bandage on his right elbow. "And what's wrong with your arm?"

"Nothing."

"What, 'Nothing'?"

"Okay, a little antibiotic ointment on a skinned elbow."

"Jeez, Fatherrr—"

"I'm fine, detective, so calm down. First off, how is Deputy Griego doing?"

"Stable…" Sonia leaned back, smoothed her black hair, and exhaled a breath of relief. "That .38 slug lodged in his pectoralis major, right about at the level of where *your* heart would have been, Father Jake."

"Then Hilario Griego saved my life."

"By a split second. The bullet clipped a rib, but missed puncturing Griego's right lung by a millimeter. Lucky it wasn't a .45. So, Father," she asked, half-in jest, "is there a saint for protecting your lungs?"

There was, Bernadino of Siena, but the priest ignored her sarcasm. "Sonia, in which hospital is Hilario recovering? I'd like to visit him."

"Socorro Regional. Only his wife is allowed there right now, but I'll let you know when he's taking non-family visitors." Sonia slipped a manila folder from her briefcase. "This morning, I ran a check on Breanna Springer through an Internet police records data base. You mentioned she might have had a West Virginian accent, so I started with that state. Sure enough, she came from Beckley, off US 77, which heads north and south, but pretty much from nowhere to nowhere. "Oh," she added with a straight face, "for family excitement, there *is* a coal museum in town."

"What about family?"

Sonia sifted through printed computer sheets. "Her father was a non-denominational preacher. There were multiple reports of abuse to Breanna by him, and also by a youth minister. Nothing ever was done about it. At eighteen she ran off to join the military."

"Then she *was* in the Army."

"Right, except that it didn't last long. Our gal was in basic training at Fort Bliss, where she repeatedly mouthed off to superiors, just as Billy Ray Scurry did. That got her a speedy bad conduct discharge. Breanna kicked around El Paso awhile, had run-ins with the cops in Texas and Mississippi on traffic violations, and two misdemeanors on controlled substance charges. She represented herself in court, claimed the Mary Jane was planted, which it probably was, but that defense didn't wash in Mississippi. She spent eight months in jail. Same charge in El Paso after she came back, but that one got her a suspended sentence, along with a very strong suggestion that she leave the Lone Star State of Texas and not ever return."

"That's when she hooked up with David Allison?"

"Gets a bit hazy from there on, Father, but I suspect she'd had it with being abused and harassed by religious, military, and/or civil authorities. I haven't finished checking on Allison, but there's a Patriot militia group active here near Belén. He and Springer may have gravitated from there to Scurry's Fort Liberty."

"At the 'funeral' I heard Dave Allison cuss Breanna out, then yell that the shooting was all her idea."

"Really? Sounds like she planned a revenge operation to kill Pastor... Pastor—"

"Haskill."

"Pastor *Has-kill?*" Sonia emphasized the improbable surname as a question. "That name would be funny if it weren't so tragic for him. Deputy Griego and you barely avoided being happenstance victims."

Fr. Jake murmured his grateful relief for both of them in a recollection of the morning's breviary reading, "He will shelter you with his wings. God's faithfulness is a protecting shield."

Sonia Flipped to another sheet. "We're still checking on Haskill and Allison. My guess is that Breanna Springer or, rather, she and David Allison, planned a phony funeral, notified the New Zion Free Will-something-or-other church in Oklahoma, then persuaded them to come here and demonstrate. She'll get murder and aggravated assault charges filed against her, with Allison complicit in the assault."

Fr. Jake diplomatically pointed out, "Breanna Springer hasn't been caught, and neither has David Allison."

"Well, no...." Sonia took a newspaper out of her briefcase. "I brought you the *Valencia County Herald*, which published what has been found out so far about the crime."

"I know that they tried to blow up my church, and did destroy Deputy Griego's patrol car."

"That fire grenade Allison threw at San Isidro was a dud. I suppose you'll give the saint credit for that?"

"Do you have a better explanation, detective?"

Sonia hedged, "The story's on the front page, but I haven't read all of it yet."

She let the priest scan the paper, while straightening out her file. Fr. Jake saw the lead article under a headline:

**Okla. Church Pastor Killed. Socorro Sheriff's Deputy Wounded.**

He read more of the story, then summarized, "It says that after Dave and Breanna got to Belén, they booby-trapped the Humvee. It exploded as a distraction, while they robbed Western Savings Bank and kidnapped the teller as a hostage. My God, it...it was Rodrigo Jirón! I met that young man. Rod lived at the Eden West commune."

"I know," Sonia commented, "but read on and you'll find that they had another accomplice in a waiting car. Father, when spectators ran over to watch the Humvee burn, the three made a clean getaway in the other vehicle with their hostage."

He asked, "Where would they go?"

"The big question. Allison turned right at 310, so at Belén he could pick up I-25 North or South and then Interstate 40 at the Big I."

"Big eye?"

The detective inadvertently smiled at the confusion that outsiders experienced on first hearing the term. "Father, the letter 'I' is for the intersection where north-south Interstate 25 crosses east-west Interstate 40…" Sonia glanced around the room. "Do you have a New Mexico map?"

"'Fraid not yet."

"Okay, but get one from your car insurance company or at the grocery. Just a minute—" Sonia went outside to her Plymouth and took a road map from the glove compartment, then came back and spread it on the coffee table. "Okay, here"—she pointed to Highway 310 at Providencia—"The perps could get on I-25 at Belén and drive south to Socorro…T or C… Las Cruces, and on to the Republic of Mexico. That's roughly a hundred-eighty miles that have several Border Patrol checkpoints." She moved her finger up on the map. "I-25 north goes through Albuquerque, Santa Fe, Las Vegas, Raton, and then you're in Colorado. An alternate route is to take I-40 through Tijeras Canyon to SR North 14, then on to Santa Fe, Española, and Taos, with a possible detour…well…here…" Sonia pointed to Highway 285 with a clear-lacquered nail. "This route leads straight on to Alamosa in Colorado. Or…*shit!* This was so well planned that anywhere in between could be a temporary hideout. We don't even know the make or model of the vehicle an accomplice is driving."

"The state police would have to stop every car that has four passengers."

"Four?" Sonia frowned her disbelief. "Don't be naïve, Father. They might drop off the accomplice, kill Jirón, dump his body, and put on disguises. Like maybe a Kirtland AFB Airman and his new bride heading for a Colorado mountain honeymoon. Cops respect military guys, or don't you watch CSI?"

The priest returned her mischievous question with his own quip, "Not since I've watched you at work, detective."

"Okay, Father. I had the Belén P.D. check out the Zia Motel. That room the couple rented was clean."

"Why," Fr. Jake asked, "would Breanna, a West Virginian, contact the pastor of a church in Panhandle City, Oklahoma, just to disrupt a funeral? Haskill wasn't her father."

"No, but perhaps it was Oklahoma's proximity to our state?"

The priest scanned the map, which included a three-county section of northwestern Oklahoma. "Panhandle City is way up here, detective. Surely there are...or were...other soldier's funerals in the eastern part of New Mexico that those New Zion church members could picket more easily." He ran a finger along a line of larger towns in the state that were roughly parallel with Haskill's hometown. "For example, "Clayton ...Springer... Raton, even Taos." Fr. Jake looked up to quiz Sonia. "Detective, there's a town named Springer in this state?"

"Yes and it's central to the ones you mentioned."

"What a morbid coincidence with Breanna *that* name would have been. So, detective, where do *you* think they went?""

Sonia impatiently tapped a pen against her folder at his implied criticism of progress in apprehending the fugitives. "Father, we've got an APB, All Points Bulletin, out..." She glanced toward the kitchenette. "You have any coffee left?"

"Made a fresh pot at noon. Sonia, just relax on that couch." As Fr. Jake went to fill her mug, he called back, "You weren't able to question Vando Benavides about the horse accident, were you?"

"No, just about Baby Doe."

"Let me get something to show you with your coffee."

"Is it fattening?"

He chuckled with Sonia at a mock concern that masked their feeling of helplessness about the mock-funeral tragedy. "I don't think you need to worry about that, detective."

As Sonia folded up the map, she commented, "Father Jake, I'm a woman. We worry about stuff like that."

The priest returned to the living room, put two coffee mugs on the low table in front of the couch, then stood to pull his Daily Roman Missal from under an arm. "I've mentioned that I read this breviary each morning and sometimes try to figure out if a Biblical passage might predict what's in store for me that day."

"And...?" Sonia asked, then gently blew on her coffee.

"Today's reading has Hosea criticizing the Samaritans as apostate Hebrews rebelling against God's plan for Israel. Verse 8: 7 reads, 'When they sow the wind, they shall reap the whirlwind'."

"Hosea? Samaria? Father, could you explain? I'm not biblically following you."

"Then let me backtrack to the beginning. The prophet Hosea is difficult if you take the Bible literally and aren't familiar with the ancient writer's symbolic imagery."

"Go on."

"Ready for this?" At Sonia's slight nod of assent, he continued, "The Lord orders Hosea to marry a harlot and have children by her. Their names are symbolic and refer to the northern kingdom of Israel, which had turned to idolatry and offended God. Hosea abandons his wife, but then is commanded to take her back, just as God will forgive Israel. In Chapter Eight, Hosea takes on Samaria, which was in the northern kingdom of Israel and had a separate sanctuary where their people worshipped God."

"How did that happen?"

"The Samaritans had rebelled against the anointed Davidic dynasty with its temple at Jerusalem, and set up their own sanctuary."

"Like this Pastor Haskill's Protestant 'Assembly of Whatever' may want to replace the Catholic Church?"

"They could hardly do that, detective," he said, then chided her. "That's not very ecumenical of you."

"Okay, what about this whirlwind? We call small ones 'dust devils' out here."

Fr. Jake settled in an armchair across from Sonia. "Inadvertently, Pastor Haskill and his misguided followers may well have reaped what they sowed."

"Meaning?"

"What happened yesterday was so fast it could have taken place inside a whirlwind…" The priest reached over and took a sip of his coffee before asking, "Sonia, have you heard of an idea called, 'Six degrees of separation'?"

"Sort of," she replied defensively, "but do enlighten me further, *Padre*."

"I used to speculate about the premise with Al Franzek, a good friend in my Michigan parish. It basically postulates that everyone is about six steps away from any other person on Earth. If you investigate 'a friend of a friend,' say, you might connect any two people in six steps or less, and so on. In 1990, John Guare wrote a play about the concept that I saw performed at my college."

Sonia clutched her mug with both hands and sat upright. "Father, I think I see where you're taking this. If Pastor Haskill could be the youth minister who molested Breanna, and she tracked him down to Oklahoma—"

"—And," Fr. Jake continued, "to help carry out her revenge, she encountered Dave Allison, Billy Ray Scurry, then Jirón, a bank employee who could supply escape funds. Griego, number five, had interacted with Scurry, but accidentally got in the way."

"And you, Father Jake, might be number six. As a clergyman, you were one of the woman's targets."

He nodded remembrance. "Breanna said so herself before firing at me."

After a period of silent thought, Sonia put down her mug. "Father, I wonder if we could apply that six degrees of connection idea to the Baby Doe and horse trailer accident cases."

"You mean to help identify possible suspects?"

"And/or victims."

"Right, Sonia. Let's see..." Fr. Jake counted on his fingers, "There's Don Fernando, Isabel, the deceased nanny, Eusebia...little Dulcinea. That's four persons, so who's left, Cervando Benavides or any of the other ranch workers?"

Sonia added softly, "Or, Father Jakubowski, perhaps you as number six? You're now involved in both cases, directly or indirectly. Someone destroyed your car, and it wasn't by accident."

"Armando thinks it probably was kids having perverted fun."

"I doubt that. Locals would know your Nissan was a priest's car and leave it alone."

"Then who? In so short a time, have I made *that* many enemies?"

"Don Fernando for one," the detective said. "You've criticized his wife's shrine, so a person like him, who usually gets his own way, can be vindictive. You heard him threaten to go to my superiors over what I said about his wife's accident."

"I can't imagine the Don going to that length. Besides, he'd contact the archbishop, not torch my car."

"Father, Millie Jaramillo sees you as a threat to her *curandera* treatments for Dulci."

"Millie? The woman would trip over those long skirts trying to set fire to my car," he quipped.

Sonia put on her cap and stood to leave. "Make a joke of it Father Jakubowski, but as a law officer, I'm advising you not to be a fool. Isn't there something about that in the Bible?"

"There is, Sonia, and I'm sorry for being flippant. I promise to take care."

"Okay, Father, I'll be in touch."

After the detective left, a chastened Fr. Jake took the coffee mugs back to the kitchen muttering, "I do believe there's something in Proverbs about 'Fools die for want of sense'."

# 16 eusebia's fatal salad

Now that Fr. Jake pretty much had settled into his rectory, he decided to celebrate a morning Eucharistic Service for himself. He called it a "Kitchen Mass" that would be in addition to the daily readings from his breviary. The priest set up his portable Mass kit on the kitchen table to begin. At the communal prayers after the gospel, he added a petition for the safety of Rod Jirón. Nothing had been heard about the young bank teller who had been taken hostage during the bold robbery at Western Savings by David Allison, Breanna Springer, and their unknown accomplice driver.

This morning Fr. Jake recalled that the day's gospel reading in which Matthew listed the names of Christ's twelve apostles had prompted a favorite sermon in his Lake Sirius, Michigan, parish. He had begun his homily by reminding a congregation of residents and summer vacationers that, of course, there was symbolism in the choice of a dozen persons, and that Holy Scripture could be interpreted on several levels. Jesus chose twelve followers —the number of the Tribes of Israel. Modernizing the gospel account, and drawing chuckles from his congregation, he pointed out that Christ had not sat behind a CEO's desk, read the apostles' résumés, interviewed them about any previous experiences that might be useful to his mission, fielded questions about salary or benefits, and afterward politely hedged, "Thanks, I'll let you know." No, he had encountered the men and merely said, "Follow me."

Six were lake fishermen, perhaps two sets of brothers, among them Simon Peter and Andrew; James and John. The other two were Bartholomew and Thomas. These men probably were neither very poor nor illiterate. Five may have lived in Bethsaida, at the northern shore of the Sea of Galilee, where excavations uncovered fine stone houses, gold jewelry, and amphorae of imported wines. As it was in Michigan, he added that lake fishing was a good business in ancient Judea! Although Aramaic was the area's common language, all Jewish males could read and understand enough Hebrew to pass their coming-of-age Bar Mitzvah rituals. Most who attended synagogues were familiar enough with Mosaic Law and the Prophets to reject Jesus' early claim to have been their fulfillment, and even to throw him out of Nazareth as a man possessed, a lunatic.

Incredibly, Jesus chose Matthew to be a companion. Based in Capernaum, the man was a hated tax collector for both the Roman occupiers and Herod, their client king. "Caesar" estimated what amount the tax would be, and collectors could retain anything above that sum, which they could extort from disgruntled citizens.

Judas, Simon the Cananean, and Phillip may have been Zealots, a subversive political group dedicated to ending Roman rule by violence. Not a few Hebrews were willing to die by the sword to overthrow Roman rule.

The work done by James, son of Alphaeus, is unknown, but he may have been the first bishop of Jerusalem and at odds with St. Paul over the direction the Way should take in admitting gentiles. Thaddeus interrupted Jesus at the Last Supper to needle him about the nature of divine predestination, a query that went unanswered.

Fr. Jake had ended his Michigan homily by pointing out that the men Jesus chose as disciples ran the gamut of human experience—hard work and faith, yet also doubt, greed, denial, betrayal, and cowardice—and, all but one, ultimate martyrdom for their beliefs. Biblical scholars considered these traits as proofs of the authenticity of the Gospel accounts about Christ. Unlike those mythical consorts of pagan gods, the twelve followers of the Messiah were men in a human condition, and the Son of God had willingly taken that same physical burden—

A persistent knocking on his front door interrupted the priest's morning reverie. He opened the portal and saw Sonia Mora impatiently pacing the small porch.

"Come in, come in, detective." He stepped aside and suppressed asking if she wanted coffee. *I've been teased about that.* "Has there been progress about Eusebia's case?"

"Yes, yet there's always a lot more crime on holidays….drunken brawls, shootings, car accidents. I was assigned other cases, so I'm kinda beat." Sonia was in uniform: black slacks and shoes, short sleeve shirt. She put down a briefcase, took off her Baker Boy cap, and settled back on the couch. After noticing the candles, chalice, paten, and missal on the kitchen table, she asked, "What's all that church stuff, Father Jake?"

He explained, "I started saying a Mass here in the rectory today, yet it's about time that I began a daily eight o'clock service in the church."

"I see." Sonia glanced around at the priest's residence as she smoothed a hand over the couch's mohair upholstery. "This place looks and smells quite livable now that my uncle's messy housekeeping was tidied up. What was your Michigan rectory like?"

"My rectory?" *Sonia seems in no hurry to tell me why she came today. She does look very tired.* He sat in an armchair opposite the detective and began his answer with a question, "How old is this adobe?"

"Oh, I'd say it's been around seventy-five to a hundred years."

"That ancient? My rectory was a lake cottage about an hour north of Detroit, and probably built by an autoworker in the nineteen-thirties for a weekend and summer get-away." He commented on her timing. "Sonia, just before you came, I was thinking of my parish and about a sermon I used to give."

"Do you miss Michigan?"

"'The Great Lake State'? I do like the lakes, even though I'm not much for swimming or fishing. Probably a good thing, because after cottages are opened up in summer and vacationers start to arrive, I don't have much time for either activity."

"You must visit sick people in hospitals. The Socorro P.D. has a chaplain we also use for those occasions."

"Yes, and I do Oakland County-Southfield Detention Facility counseling. I try to meet with the inmates once a week, about how not ever to be behind bars again."

"Is that why you priests don't marry? Way too busy to have a wife around?"

Fr. Jake laughed. "I tried to explain that to Armando. Priests could and did marry for over a thousand years of Christianity. It was a cultural thing back then."

"Ministers still do, and"—Sonia glanced down to self-consciously trace the crease in her slacks—"pardon me for saying, Father, but you really care about people. I think you'd make a good husband for someone."

"Thanks, but it would be a hard life for both of us. I've known wives who divorced Protestant clergy-husbands for that very reason." *Sonia surely didn't come just to talk about priestly celibacy.* "Detective, what sort of news do you have to share?"

She tried to hide a blush by smoothing her hair. "Sorry, I got off the subject. Father, I went over to interview the Torrez couple, see if they knew anything about Baby Doe."

"Victoria and Juan, Don Fernando's Mexican workers."

"Right, except that since then Lorenzo Lujan told me that the couple never showed up last Saturday for a ride back to the ranch from Belén. He thinks that Baby Doe is Victoria's aborted child, and they both were frightened by my investigation."

"And skipped down to Mexico on a bus?"

"That's what he told me. Valencia County deputies reported a lot of southbound holiday traffic."

"What do *you* think?" Fr. Jake asked.

"They're both legally documented migrant workers, so no problem with them traveling back and forth, yet they might not be sure about how American justice works. At this point, I'm not going to speculate about the couple."

"Wise. Oh…" The priest recalled his conversation with Carlotta. "I…I hesitate to tell you this. Sonia, but Carlotta at the grocery told me that some residents living in proximity to the *acequia*, the sluice, reported wailing and seeing strange lights in the *bosque*." The priest grinned at the thought. "No doubt it was La Llorona haunting the woods."

Sonia did not join in his mirth. "You seem skeptical, Father, yet don't you have similar legends in Poland?"

"Well, yes, there was *Rusalka*, a kind of female, lake-dwelling demon. One version is that she's the ghost of a young woman murdered by a lover, thus her soul haunts the water until the death is avenged. Of course, I'm also skeptical of that folk tale."

"So to what reason do you attribute these unusual sightings that people report?"

"A prank, of course. As a detective, isn't that what you would think?"

"Right away I would wonder who would benefit from what you call 'a prank." Sonia wagged a playful finger at him. "Any ideas on *that* thought, Father Jakubowski?"

*She's serious.* "I suppose a prankster could be having, well, perverted fun, on hearing about the fetus."

"Halloween isn't until another four months, and that sounds like a lot of work just to make a joke. Also we've kept Baby Doe's discovery low key, so not a lot of people outside of the Don's ranch know about what Benavides discovered." Sonia reached down to open her briefcase and pull out a file folder. "I have Eusebia's autopsy results here."

"I was about to ask. What do they reveal?"

"A toxicity report found oleandrin, that is, 'cardiac glycoside,' in the old woman's system."

He spread his hands in a helpless gesture. "English, please."

"Nerium Oleander."

"But that's a flower, isn't it?"

"Actually, Father Jake, it's a flowering shrub in the dogbane family and toxic in all its parts. I'd bet there's a few of those deadly bushes planted on the Don's property."

"But how would Eusebia ingest it?"

"Leaves mixed in a salad, I'm thinking."

"But enough to kill her?" he doubted. "Detective, that's hard to believe."

"You're correct, Father..." Sonia held up the file. "There's a report in here by the Toxic Exposure Surveillance System...TESS for short. Despite oleander's poisonous reputation, there are very few instances of human deaths. However, Eusebia was found to be severely diabetic."

"Those nasty skin blotches made me suspect that. I'd visited parishioners in the hospital with that disease and terrible skin condition."

"Yes, and one of the two thousand-nine deaths reported in *Forensic Science International* was of a diabetic gentleman with a high blood level of cardiac glycerides. In other words, oleandrin poisoning."

"Still—"

"Father, I was skeptical, too," she quietly admitted. "Yet the autopsy also indicated that the old woman was suffocated, just to make sure she was truly dead. We'll undoubtedly find dried spittle stains on a pillow in her room. Oh," Sonia added, "and TESS reports that a proper concentration of Nerium extract is safely used in parenteral and topical applications."

"Parenteral?"

"Medical term for a substance taken into the body other than through the digestive tract. I'm betting that any competent *curandera* would know that."

The priest thought a moment before suggesting, "Such as Millie Jaramillo?"

Sonia nodded her head. "Such as Queen Millie Jaramillo, Father Jake. And she mentioned that the vic ate a salad during lunch in Belén."

# 17 millie vs. fernandi

In a furious mood, Lareina "Queen Millie" Jaramillo clutched a fringed Mexican shawl tightly around her shoulders and paced the ranch's kitchen floor.

Don Fernando and Dulcinea had not joined her for breakfast. With Eusebia Nevarez dead, no one had cooked her favorite dish, a New Mexican omelet of mushrooms, green chile, ham, and Monterey Jack cheese. The *curandera* had finished dry toast with marmalade, and now glanced at the kitchen clock. *¿Qué hora es? Diez y media.* "Perhaps Fernandi go riding," she told the timepiece, "but he should be return by now."

Millie left her dish and knife on the table, along with the jam, then went to listen at the closed door of the Don's study. A rustling sound and voices inside indicated that someone was in the room. She twisted the doorknob and found the portal locked.

"Fernandi?" she called, rapping on the door with a graceful hand. "Fernandi, Millie *es aquí*. What you are doing, *amante?*" After she did not hear a reply, the woman snarled, "Answer, Fernandi, or I get with *mucho enoho*. A great anger."

"Dulci and I are busy," came a muffled, terse response by Don Fernando.

"*Mierda*," she muttered under her breath, then appealed to his daughter, "Dulcinea? Dulci, *mi niña*. Por favor, *abierto la porta por* Millie."

After a brief, muted discussion inside the room, the girl slowly opened the door. Millie frowned in surprised disbelief as she looked past her: Fernando had almost cleared the side table of his wife's photographs and mementos. Most of them lay packed in closed boxes; only one carton still was open.

"*Dios*, what you doing?" Millie demanded, brushing Dulci aside to enter and look around. "Fernandi, *su deshacerse del memoria de su esposa.* Millie yanked a photo of Isabel out of the open box and set it on the table again.

"No!" The Don snatched the picture back and replaced it with the others.

Millie placed her hands on both hips in defiance. An angry scowl creased her forehead as she whipped a braid of dark hair over her shoulder. "Why you do this, Fernandi?"

He closed the box's cover and held his hands over it. "I finally realized that the priest at San Isidro was correct when he said that my continual grief over Isabel's death is unhealthy. I also dreamed that my wife forgave me—"

"Dream? Me, *I* will tell you what dream means," Millie insisted. She stepped toward him, her right hand clenched against her chest.

Fernando ignored her response. "Dulci also thinks we should put the shrine away. You've been here over four years, treating her, and she's no better than when you came." Don Fernando turned his daughter. "Dulci, I'll have a couple of ranch hands, maybe Matt and Lorenzo, clean out that fountain and make it beautiful again." He drew his daughter close and slid an arm around her shoulder. "Then you and I will go to Belén and buy a half dozen koi fish. We can put screening up around the rim to keep away the snakes."

"I'd like that *Papá*—"

"Dulcinea, ¡no!" Millie screamed. "Fernandi, the girl has *susto, desasombro.* Fright sickness that I must still treat to make her well again."

"Millie, you've 'treated' my daughter long enough," he objected without looking at his Mexican mistress. "I now realize that both of us have been hampering…yes, *hampering*…not helping, Dulci. Now get out and let us finish packing these things."

"Fernandi, you be sorry you throw Millie away." she threatened, her brown and blue eye ablaze with angry reproach.

"I'm not throwing you out," Fernando countered in his defense. "With Eusebia dead, perhaps you can take over the job of housekeeper for us."

"¿Casera?" she scoffed. "Me, housekeeper, Fernandi?" she repeated, then flung another threat at him, "You think Queen Millie, *curandera*, who study in *Mejico* with the great El Perito at shrine of El Niño Fidencio, will clean house now? ¡*Jamás!* That will be never!"

"Then I'm sorry, Miss Jaramillo—"

"Ha! Fernandi, I am now to you 'Miss Jaramillo' and not *querida* Millie *mi amante?*" The woman's body shook with rage as she spat out, "*¡Metete un pelo en el culo!*"

At the vulgarity, the Don flushed to a mahogany hue and grasped his daughter's hand. "Come, Dulci. Let's go see about cleaning out that pond. And I think spending a few days or more at our summer cabin near Jemez Springs would be restful."

"Oh, yes, *Papá!* We haven't been there in so long."

"Then, Dulci, let's plan on going!" Fernando's face brightened in an enthusiastic smile as he kissed his daughter's hand. "Vando could bring Chorro, and Bombóna for you, in the horse trailer. We could explore mountain pathways and get away from this ranch for awhile."

"*Que bueno, Papá*. That would be such fun."

"Then let's go tell the men to get ready."

As the two pushed past Millie to go out the door, she turned to hurl a final insult at the Don. "*¡Cabrón! ¡Trasto antiquo!*"

Fernando ignored the woman's rant, and silently guided his daughter into the hallway and toward the fountain pond in front.

Livid with anger at her lover's scorn, Millie dumped the boxes of the dead Isabel's memorabilia on the floor, furiously kicked them around with one dainty foot, then the other, and stomped out through the back patio toward Cervando Benavides's room in the bunkhouse.

When Millie entered the frame building, she saw the TV-recreation room cluttered with Styrofoam coffee cups and empty beer or soft drink cans. Flies circled around bits of pizza and french fries on paper plates—leftovers from the three ranch hands' Fourth of July holiday meals. "That *Mejicana* woman is told to clean here," she muttered to herself, "but *nada*. No do good job. I tell Cervando get rid of her."

She tried the doorknob on the foreman's room, the first one to right, and found it locked. On the chance that the *jefe* was inside, she called at the door. "Vandi, *Abierto la porta*. Open. Millie want to come in."

In moments, the lock clicked. The bleary-eyed, unshaven foreman opened the door and peered at her with eyebrows arched in surprise. "What brings ya here now, Millie? Somethin' wrong?"

"*Si...*" The woman pushed past him and paced the room with her arms crossed, clutching her waist. "Where is the *Mejica?*" she demanded.

"Vickie? On Saturday Lorenzo drove her and her husband to shop in Belén—"

"TV room is like *cochino*, pig house."

"Yeah, Vicki's usually pretty good at cleanin' it, but she ain't here. They was supposed to meet Lorenzo for a ride back to the ranch, but never showed up." Vando chuckled at his theory. "Stupid jerks prob'ly skipped back to Mexico because that was her dead kid I found in the *acequia*." Vando wavered as he peered at the *curandera* with bloodshot eyes. "Millie, did ya come here to ask about them?"

"¡No!" She stamped her foot in frustrated anger. "Fernandi throw me away like old serape. Queen Millie no stand for that. Queen Millie no be throw out!"

Puzzled, half drunk, the ranch boss brushed his moustache with a hand. "Whatta ya mean the Don threw you out? What happened he should do that?"

"That new *padre* at San Isidro, *Jakob*-somebody, he tell Fernandi my treatment of Dulci not good. Shrine to Isabel no good for both..." Millie grasped his beefy arm and began to sob. "He want me...now be...*casera*. Only housemaid!"

Vando patted her hand. "Now simmer down, Millie.... Here"—He reached over to push aside a *Playboy* magazine on the unmade bed—"Sit... sit here an' tell me about why he's doin' that to ya."

She half-smiled at him and settled down, smoothing the pleats in her broomstick skirt. After the *curandera* sniffled again, Vando pulled a soiled blue kerchief from a jeans pocket and handed it to her. Millie dabbed at her nose, but kept his handkerchief in one hand and gazed at the floor. "Vandi," she asked coyly, "what happen when Isabel die?"

"What happened?" He flopped down next to the woman and the mattress edge sagged. "Well, that accident was a long time ago, Millie. You heard the story before."

She reached over and placed a hand lightly on his knee. "Vandi, again tell what happen," she coaxed in a seductive voice. "Tell to Millie."

"Well...like...like I said, we was loadin' a stallion into the trailer when it bolted an'...an' kicked Isabel in the head. It was a accident."

"*Detectiva* say doctor find round hole...injure...in neck of horse." The *curandera* looked directly into Vando's red-rimmed eyes and moved her hand up toward his crotch. "Vandi, you there. Who hurt that *caballo*?" Despite an open window, the foreman perspired in the breezeless July heat of the fetid room. Stinking of sweat, and breathing more rapidly, he placed his rough hand over hers. Millie toyed with his stubby fingers, while moving both his hand and hers higher up on his thigh. "Vandi, what happen?" she insisted again, her whispered voice velvet smooth, enticing. "*Amante*, tell Millie," she coaxed, leaning over to brush his lips with her tongue.

"Isabel...Isabel, she sick," he said, his voice hoarse. "Don Fernando told me she wasn't goin' to live very long."

"What sickness, Vandi?" she murmured, stroking higher inside his thigh.

He squirmed at her arousing touch. "I...I don't know. "It had a funny name. Wait...I kept somethin' about it that the Don threw away in the barn trash."

When Cervando half-stood to walk to a bedside table, Millie noticed the unmistakable bulge in the front of his jeans and pulled him back. "Not now, *amante*. Stay sit down, show me later." She pushed him back on the bed and lifted her voluminous skirt to straddle his legs. "You not tell anyone anything what I ask, Vandi, and Millie promise make you happy."

"I...I won't tell."

Realizing the extent of the man's arousal, she added a coquettish suggestion, "Vandi, I not like that *norteño* priest."

"*¿Padre Jakub?*" Cervando breathed in shallow gasps now, his massive hands groping beneath her skirt. "Wha...whatta ya want me...to do about it?"

"Maybe after now Millie make you happy, you think of something," she whispered, and bent down to unzip his fly. "Vandi, after you happy, then you do something to *norteño padre* that make Millie happy. *¿Si, amante?*"

"*Si*," he mumbled thickly. "Make...make me happy."

## 18 socorro regional hospital

Detective Sonia Mora called Fr. Jake on the evening of July 8 to tell him that Deputy Griego was allowed to have two visitors, other than his wife, at the same time. She said she would come over at nine o'clock in the morning and drive to Socorro Regional Hospital with the priest.

O

When Sonia arrived a half hour early, Fr. Jake was reading the day's entry in his breviary. He heard the crunch of tires on his driveway gravel, put the book aside, and went out to meet the detective. Her red Plymouth had been cleansed of its usual coat of dirt and mud spatters.

"Sonia! You had your car washed!" Fr. Jake exclaimed, hands raised up in wonder.

She grinned at his sham surprise. "Yeah, Father, even I occasionally get tired of all the grime."

"Come in and have—"

"—No coffee, thanks." She had anticipated his presumed offer. "I stopped for some on the way."

"Fine."

"I will come inside though." Sonia slipped her briefcase off the passenger seat and got out of the car. Inside the rectory living room, she spotted Fr. Jake's open breviary on a table next to his armchair.

"Father, were you reading your prayer book?" she asked, while putting down the briefcase and taking off her cap. "Hope I didn't disturb."

"No, no. I had just about finished."

"Still trying to find out what might happen on the day you read the entry?"

"Detective, it's *not* a horoscope," he pointed out. "The Bible pretty much covers all of human experience, thus there might be a coincidence and I—"

"How's that going?" she broke in, reluctant to face a possible lecture.

"Probably about fifty-fifty accurate."

"Those are pretty good odds, Father, so what's in store for today?"

"The reading is from Matthew's gospel, about how the Apostles were sent out like sheep among wolves. To survive, they had to be cunning as serpents, but gentle as doves."

"So, as a priest does that snake part actually apply to you?"

He went along with her ribbing. "Occasionally, so watch out!" Fr. Jake picked up the breviary to read the end of the passage. "Sonia, the next part is meant to be prophetic. 'Brother will betray brother to death, and the father his child; children will rise against their parents and have them put to death'." Christ goes on to say, "'If they persecute you in one town, take refuge in the next. And if they persecute you in that, take refuge in another—"

"Sounds like Allison and Springer trying to elude capture."

"Right, detective. You know, Scripture can be applied to anything going on today. Look at what's happening with rival tribes in Africa."

Sonia expanded the reports of unrest, "And those Iraqi Sunni and Shiite clans."

"Yes, even Christians keeping guard over the holy places in Israel too often quarrel over ridiculous questions of jurisdiction, such as who cleans what and when."

"Then maybe that is an appropriate reading, Father. Look, I...I didn't want to upset you, but there's bad news about Mister Jirón, that teller at Western Savings."

"Rod? What happened?"

"A Santa Fe sheriff's deputy noticed a lot of ravens gathered in a field off Highway North 14, between Golden and Madrid."

"Sonia, I don't know the area you're talking about."

"It's northeast of Albuquerque. Here, I brought you a map." Sonia slipped the chart from her briefcase and unfolded it on the coffee table—"We know Allison was headed toward Belén and I-25, but not which way he would turn when he got there. Now we realize it was north on the freeway, and then east along I-40. They got off at Exit 175 and drove north." Sonia pointed to a red X she had drawn on the map. "The deputy discovered the victim's body right about here."

"That's terrible! Th…the poor young man."

"Tragic, Father, and I realize you knew him," She said. "Look, knowing there would be an APB out, Allison probably kept to the speed limit, and the limit is seventy-five MPH, except through Albuquerque, where it's ten miles slower…" Sonia flipped open her note pad and read off calculations. "I figured two hours max with the bank robbery and the…and Jirón's murder."

Still shaken by her report, Fr. Jake asked, "How was Rod killed?"

"Execution style, Father. Look, let's not dwell on that, but try to figure where the fugitives went next."

*I'll dwell on it long enough to say a prayer for his soul.* The priest ran an index finger up along the highway. "'Madrid' is the next town? The Spanish who first settled there must have thought big."

"It's a family name and became a nineteenth century coal mining town that lasted into the 1950s. Today it's an art lover's destination. Incidentally, the name is pronounced 'Mad-rid.' Since turquoise was discovered a few miles further on, the tourist guys in Santa Fe thought that naming this highway 'The Turquoise Trail' sounded cool."

"I see that the road ends in Santa Fe at Interstate 25. To the right, the freeway continues north into Colorado."

"Yes, the border is about three to three-and-a-half hours further on." Sonia pointed to a smaller road leading northwest. "However, they also could have driven through Santa Fe and taken Highway 84/285 to Colorado. It's a bit shorter, but probably might take as long."

Fr. Jake wondered, "Wouldn't a New Mexico license plate stand out in Colorado?"

"We don't know what plate was on the getaway vehicle, but the answer is 'not necessarily,' since a lot of our tourists go up there to cool off."

"But wouldn't driving through a city like Santa Fe run the risk of being stopped by the police?"

"Yes, that could happen."

The priest leaned forward to examine the X. "Sonia, your map shows a gravel road near the murder site. It leads back across to I-25."

"That's an unimproved road that goes to Santo Domingo pueblo, Father. 'Tewa,' as it's now called. But why," Sonia questioned, "would they waste time heading northwest on a secondary road, Father?"

He sat back again. "Detective, you think priests spend all their time lounging in a rectory and thinking about what to say in next Sunday's sermon?"

"Go on...."

"I was sixteen when I got caught up in the nineteen-fifty-six *Poznań* riots. It wasn't a political demonstration. Polish workers basically wanted better factory conditions and a decent pay that would adequately feed their families."

"And?"

"And, detective, the workers quickly learned how to fool the UB secret police who came after them. While they seemed headed for Mickiewicz Square to protest, some doubled back and stormed a prison to free a few of their leaders."

"So you're suggesting the fugitives might have taken that road back to I-25 as a diversion?"

"Perhaps, and, look, at Bernalillo, this Highway 280 heads north, toward Colorado."

"Let me see..." Sonia picked up the map. "Near Cuba they could go up to Chama on 112, or across the Navajo Reservation on 550, then on to the border..." She shook her head. "Naw. Not much traffic that way, so they'd be sure to be spotted by the Rez cops."

"What about Highway 4?"

"That road is quite mountainous and goes on to Los Alamos, then back to Highway 84/285."

"What's at Jemez Springs?"

"Vacation homes, mostly," she told him

"With this recession, quite a few cottages might be unoccupied."

"Right, Father, and I suppose you're thinking comfortable hideaways." Sonia put down the map as she recalled a previous event. "Come to think, last year a serial killer used one of the empty cabins up there as a hideout. A sheriff's deputy was murdered trying to arrest him...." She checked her watch. "Speaking of deputies, Father, it's time we left to see Griego. Fold up and stash your map and we'll be on our way."

○

Sonia took a short route over the Rio Grande River to Socorro, a journey all too familiar for the petite detective since the murder of her priest-uncle in May. She drove the few miles to Highway 60 in silence, then turned her

Plymouth to the right, toward the river and the access ramp to Interstate 25 South.

When the car rolled over the river's bridge, Sonia gestured to the priest's right. "Father, there's the muddy Rio Grande."

"And my first real look at the water." Below the span, ochre mud flats lined the river banks. Several bare sandy islands broke the surface of shallow July water. Stalks of red salt cedar grew among the lush vegetation of the neighboring *bosque*. "Sorry," he commented, "but it's certain to be a disappointment for people who know the Spanish name means 'Big River."

"Oh," she protested, "but it is *grande* down Texas way, closer to the Gulf. Father, you should read 'Great River,' Paul Horgan's history of the southwest. The book is several years old, but comprehensive, and he writes kind of poetic-like."

"Cynthia Plow lent me a couple of volumes about the Civil War's Glorieta action."

"She'd have Horgan's book." Sonia drove silently again until they reached the Bernardo exit to I-25. Highway signage indicated that Socorro was twenty-five miles to the south. "Father, you haven't been to Socorro yet?"

"No, but the Spanish word means to aid or help, correct? We have the English derivative, 'succor'."

"Right, and if I remember Horgan correctly, the original seventeenth century mission was named 'Our Lady of Aid," or something similar. The church today dates from around 1815. It's named after Saint Michael. Mom...mom used to attend services there."

"Sonia, you've confided in me about both of your parents' deaths."

She acknowledged the fact with a slight nod and changed the subject. "Father, you keep talking about that Polish riot you witnessed. In fact, you mentioned it at the rectory. Well, guess what? In Sixteen-eighty, the Indians kicked the Spanish out of New Mexico, clean back down to El Paso. It's called the Pueblo Revolt, which lasted twelve years before the Spaniards returned for good. Well, anyway until the Mexican War."

"Sonia, I'll be sure to read Horgan's book, but let's get back to the present. You told me that you work out of Socorro."

"The Socorro County Sheriff's Office on Market Street."

After leaving the freeway's merge lane, Sonia gunned her Plymouth to the 75 MPH speed limit. Low, sand-colored mesas on the right hosted scrub vegetation. On the river side, a wide belt of green trees and cultivated fields followed the fertile bed of the Rio Grande. Nearing San Acacia, cottonwood trees in full leaf marked a settlement that surely had a water source. A herd of fenced-in longhorn steers grazed just beyond the roadway. Five miles from Socorro, a small New Mexico State Police station simmered in the growing heat. Fr. Jake asked about a sign that flashed by too quickly to be read; it had pictured a black bat with wings spread out.

"BATmobile, Father," Sonia explained. "That would be capital B-A-T, 'Breath Alcohol Testing' vehicle. Those are DWI sobriety checkpoints that help identify drunk drivers. That's a big statewide problem."

"So I've discovered in my short time here. Both Armando's parents and Don Fernando's in-laws where killed in drunk driver accidents."

"I know." At Exit 150, Sonia swung the car to the right and slowed down while approaching California Street/Highway 60. Beyond a "Welcome to Socorro" sign, the city's main thoroughfare was a colorful mosaic of filling stations, fast food restaurants, small businesses, and motel signage. She braked behind traffic stopped at a College Avenue red light signal. "The college designation refers to New Mexico Tech. You probably noticed that big white 'M' on the mountain to your right."

"Yes, I wondered about the significance of that."

"Every spring Tech students race each other to climb up and put new paint on it."

"A 'write of spring' so to speak."

"'Write'?" She caught his pun and smiled. "You could say so. After the light changes, look to your right again. Four blocks from here, you'll catch a glimpse of the old San Miguel mission church. Here we go...." As Sonia slowly accelerated, she decided, "Think I'll hang a right at the street to the old plaza. All these original Spanish settlements have grassy parks, where guys and gals could strut their stuff and show off on Sundays." She turned right and crawled the car around three sides of a tree-lined square. A bandstand stood in the center.

"Nice," Fr. Jake remarked. "We also have these public squares in the Midwest."

"All American, huh, Father?" she wisecracked, then maneuvered onto a street to her right. "We'll take a short cut past the Municipal Court."

The parking lot of the plain adobe-styled court building was half-filled with Socorro County Police or Sheriff cruisers. After Sonia honked her horn at an officer standing next to one, he looked over and waved back. "Cops can't miss my red car, can they?"

He laughed. "No way, detective."

At Highway 60 Sonia turned the Plymouth and crossed BN & SF tracks, which began to parallel the highway. Neither mentioned a recent incident at the Burlington Northern and Santa Fe tracks, south of Providencia: drugs were being smuggled from Chihuahua, Mexico, to New Mexico inside a counterfeit railroad service truck.

O

Despite being located across the railroad tracks from a dusty and noisy industrial zone, the 36-bed Socorro Regional Hospital made a valiant effort at being an oasis of greenery and calm amid daily traffic of exhaust-emitting commercial trucks and noisy freight trains. The front of the building faced barren rock outcroppings; beyond them, to the west, a cluster of industrial buildings blocked a view of the mountainous landscape. Patients' rooms were located at the rear of the hospital, where windows gave a peaceful view of a distant, bluish mountain chain.

Sonia pulled into a parking lot that served several medical buildings, including a mental health facility. A tree-shaded garden of sculptural work, in the diversified style of civic "1% for the Arts" projects, spread out near the main entrance walkway. On the opposite side, a patio that had been walled high enough to block out the industrial view offered five tables for staff use.

As the two walked to the door of the one story, pueblo-style building, Sonia remarked, "Father Jake, I'd say Griego was pretty lucky to be havin' visitors just five days after he was shot."

"I agree, Sonia. I'm anxious to see the deputy and personally thank him for saving my life."

"Same here, Father, and I'm hopin' he's had a little time to think about where our perps might have headed."

*Sonia is in macho mode to see Griego,* the priest realized as the automatic entrance doors swung inward.

The modest waiting room provided a prominent gift shop directly ahead. Corridors on either side led to patients' hospital unit rooms. An arrow pointing toward the reception desk graced a wall sign reading, "Visitors Sign In."

At the desk, Sonia greeted a dark-haired, olive-skinned woman of about forty, whom she knew from previous visits. "*Buenas Dias*, Dolores. How ya doin'?"

"*Bueno*, doing good, detective," she replied, eyeing her priest companion's Roman collar. "You both here to see Deputy Griego?"

"Yes. This is Father Jakubowksi."

"Father—"

He smiled at the receptionist. "Father Jake' will do, Dolores."

"Pleased," she responded. "You a police chaplain, Father?"

"Not really, but I know Deputy Griego and am very grateful to him."

The receptionist looked back at Sonia. "Deputy's in 105, to the left. Miranda's with him."

"*Gracias*, Dolores."

"Oh…" She pushed a visitor's ledger toward the priest. "Father, would you please sign in?"

"Of course."

Although venetian blinds in Room 105 were drawn to dim the room, morning light filtered into the room. Deputy Sheriff Hilario Griego, wearing a light-blue hospital gown—to which he had pinned his sheriff's badge— lay propped up by pillows to reread the June 6 issue of the *Valencia County Herald*. An attractive dark-haired woman, in early middle age, wearing a white blouse, slacks and sandals, sat in a chair next to him. Miranda Griego worked on finishing a floral design printed on embroidery hoop fabric.

Fr. Jake nodded to her as he entered the room, then grinned as he went to gently squeeze the hand on the wounded officer's uninjured side. "Deputy, it's so good to see you sitting up."

Griego put his newspaper aside. "Aw, thanks, for comin' Father. You shouldn't a taken the trouble."

"Nonsense, it's highly probable that I owe my life to you."

The deputy waved at Sonia, then shook his head while recollecting, "Y' know, Father Jake, everything happened so fast…" He gestured toward the seated woman. "Oh, this is *mi esposa*."

The priest extended a hand. "My pleasure, Mrs. Griego."

The deputy said, "Jus' call her Miranda, Father."

His wife flushed, then held her embroidery hoop in one hand and half-stood to return the priest's handshake. "Father, thank you for coming to see Hilario."

"Miranda, I recall that your husband mentioned you when he questioned me about Father's Mora's death."

"Yeah, Miranda," the deputy said, his voice a bit sheepish. "I guess I told Father you're always buggin' me about goin' back to church with you."

"Hilario...show some respect to Father," she warned, shaking the hoop at him as she sat back down.

Griego turned back to the priest. "I see you got a bandage on your elbow there. That from the shooting, Father?"

"Just scraped it a bit when I fell." He pulled a clear envelope from his shirt pocket. "Deputy, I brought you a medal with Saint Michael. It's quite large and shaped a bit like a police badge. He's patron saint of law enforcement and the military."

"I know..." Griego took the medal and held it to his chest. "Thanks, but I'd have to be hit smack in the middle of this for it to be of much help—"

"Hilario!" Miranda glared at her husband. "Hilario, I'm not telling you again to respect Father!"

"Hey, deputy, how ya doin'?" Sonia intervened, mimicking her macho-detective talk. "Y' know, ya gave everybody a real scare. That slug came a millimeter or two from puttin' ya inside a body bag."

"Aw, I'm okay, detective," he shrugged. "I was jus' readin' again about what happened at that fake funeral."

"It ain't all in there," Sonia told him. "The perps made a clean getaway."

"Oh?" Griego's eyebrows rose as he leaned to lay the medal on his side table. "You still ain't found 'em?"

Sonia reverted to normal speech. "Not yet, deputy. Father Jake and I were speculating at his rectory about where they might go. Griego, from what you've read, do you have any ideas about that?"

"Me...if it was me robbed that bank in Belén, I'd high-tail it to someplace where I could get lost quick. Like straight to Colorado on I-25. Or maybe take I-40 right into Texas."

Sonia was quietly somber. "Griego, that teller's body was just found on North 14, not far from Madrid."

"Sonuvabitch! Then they gotta be headed for Colorado."

"Father Jake thinks that's exactly what the perps want us to believe, Griego, but maybe not right away."

He looked toward the priest. "Whattaya mean, Father?"

"Deputy, the murder of Pastor Haskill was well-planned, and the 'perps', as you call them, those responsible, are clever. Law enforcement authorities have no idea of what kind of car they have nor of a state license plate. It could be Alaska, for all we know, and I'd bet all the car paperwork is in perfect order."

The deputy glanced back at Sonia. "Detective, that don't leave us much to go on."

"Exactly, Griego. Father Jake speculates that they might hide out in New Mexico until the heat's off. You really think they might have high-tailed it up to Colorado?"

"Wouldn't you, detective?"

"I suppose," Sonia half-heartedly agreed.

Griego changed the subject. "What about that Baby Doe case?"

"Latest is that Eusebia Nevarez, Don Fernando's old nanny to his daughter, was poisoned."

"Dead? Poisoned by who?"

"We don't know, but Millie Jaramillo is a person of interest. I need to question her next."

The deputy recalled, "Didn't you pin the old lady as a prime suspect in the accident that killed the Don's wife?"

"Eusebia was a witness, not a suspect, and the last one other than five-year-old Dulcinea."

The deputy whistled at the thought. "So whatever's goin' on, the daughter better be kept alive!"

"You're absolutely correct on that one, deputy." Sonia reached for his good hand. "Uh, look Griego, I wanted to see how you're doing, fill you in. Now hurry up and get back on duty!"

"Hey, detective, this place is pretty boring. Am I right, Miranda?"

"Me, I kind of like the peace and quiet at home," she joked, yet reached over to hold her husband's arm. "Father, can you please say a prayer so Hilario'll get better fast?"

"Of course…" The priest bent to place both hands on the deputy's head, and then closed his eyes to recite, "All powerful and living God, hear us as we ask your loving help for Hilario Griego. Restore him to health so that he and his wife may again offer joyful thanks in your church. Grant this through our Lord Jesus Christ, your Son, who lives and reigns with you and the Holy Spirit"—Miranda joined in for the ending—"one God, forever and ever. Amen." Fr. Jake straightened up and replaced his hat. "God, bless, Deputy… Miranda."

Sonia added, "So long, Griego. Take care now."

"You, too, detective, an' Father, don't take any wooden *centavos*!"

"I'll try not to."

On the way back to the car, Fr. Jake remarked, "The deputy seems to be coming along quite well."

"And you made his wife feel better."

"All three of us were quite fortunate in that incident."

Seeing the deputy had eased some of the fears that the shooting had spawned. Both were silent until they were near the Highway 60 exit. Just before the off ramp, a green highway sign marked distances to Albuquerque, Bernalillo, and Santa Fe.

Sonia pointed to it and told the priest, "Bernalillo is the turnoff that goes toward the Jemez Mountains."

"It would be less than an hour away," Fr. Jake calculated, "and that's where I thought the fugitives might head."

Sonia deftly swung her Plymouth onto the Highway 60 exit lane. "Nice thought Father, but I'm with Griego on this one. Ain't gonna happen. Definitely ain't gonna happen."

# 19 jemez springs

Driving north on Interstate 25, from Albuquerque toward Colorado, the Jemez Mountains appear as a low, craggy, bluish range, some fifty miles distant as a raven might fly. Yet the most impressive view of these mountains, which actually are the rim surrounding a nineteen-mile-wide caldera of an extinct volcano, was taken in June 1991, from the space shuttle *Columbia*. The spacecraft flew directly over what now is the Valles Caldera National Preserve, where the pyroclastic flows that resulted from two massive eruptions, 1.6 and 1.2 million years ago, are dramatically revealed. Today, the "Super Volcano" is a government experiment in public land management: the lush area's expansive mountain meadows host hiking trails, photographic adventure trips, camping, fishing, and seasonal elk and turkey hunts.

Natural hot springs abound in the vicinity. Inside the village of Jemez Springs, and to its north, public or private mineral springs and spas attract many visitors. The village itself mostly hosts a public bathhouse, art galleries, a few restaurants, and a feed store. Nearby stand the ruins of Jemez Mission, a 16th century Franciscan church built to serve the Pueblo of Jemez—now called Walatowa in the native Towa language. Further on, the Soda Dam, a natural limestone cavern spouting a waterfall, is surrounded by hot springs that leach out from the slippery ground at the site and along a stretch on a shoulder of the highway

O

Don Fernando shifted a small suitcase to his left hand and knocked on his daughter's bedroom door. "Dulcinea, it's your father."

"*Si, papá.*" In a moment the girl opened the door. After she kissed her father's cheek, Dulci pointed to summer clothes spread out on her bead. "I'm picking out what I want to take to our cottage."

"Good girl. I brought your hard case to carry everything in."

Dulci seemed eager about her forthcoming trip. "I'm excited that we're going. When will we leave, *papá?*"

"I hope by ten in the morning. Vando will drive the F-150 to pull the small horse trailer, but I want Gilbert to go along, too."

"He's sweet."

"I'm telling him about our going to the Jemez next." With a final glance around the room, Don Fernando told his daughter to ask for anything she needed, then closed the door behind himself.

Neither had mentioned Millie Jaramillo.

Gilbert Begay waited in the family room of the main house, work cap in hand, when his employer beckoned to him from the hallway.

"Gilbert, can you spare a minute in my study now?"

"Sure thing, Mister Trujillo."

In the room, Fernando took a seat behind his desk and toyed with a ball point pen a moment before looking up. "Gilbert, there are a couple of delicate things I'd like to discuss with you."

"Yes, sir."

"I...I believe that Cervando's drinking is getting out of hand. Victoria has brought me vodka bottles from your TV room trash that I'm sure are his. Would you agree?"

The Navajo twisted his Purina Mills cap and glanced down. "Mister Trujillo, I don't believe that's for me to say."

"I understand. Guess you ranch hands stick together. Well, no matter, I know what's happening with him." The Don gestured toward the room's interior. "You've been in my study before, haven't you, Gilbert?"

"Yes, sir, I have."

"Then you can see that I've taken down that...that...well, the shrine I had built up to my late wife." He reached over to turn a framed photo toward the Navajo ranch hand. "I'm just keeping my favorite picture of us together here on my desk."

"Ah...a ...she was a beautiful woman, sir."

"Indeed." Fernando caressed the photograph with the back of his hand a moment before continuing, "Gilbert, without going into details about it,

I've decided not to let Miss Jaramillo treat my daughter's illness any longer. She can stay on as housekeeper if she wishes. Probably won't, but—" He stood up and took his Stetson off the back of a chair. "The reason I called you here is because my daughter and I are going to spend some time at our summer cottage near Jemez Springs. I don't recall. Have you been up there?"

"No, sir, not to your place I haven't, but I've been to the Springs."

"Good. We'll bring Chorro and Dulci's mare, Bombóna. Cervando will drive the 150 pickup to pull the horse trailer, and I'd like you to ride along with him."

Gil objected in a pained voice, "Mister Trujillo, there's lots of ranch work to do right here."

"Lorenzo and Matt can handle that for and day or two." The Don's voice became more forceful. "Look, I need you to keep an eye on Cervando's drinking. Both of you stay at the cottage overnight and drive the pickup back the next afternoon. Do you have a cell phone?"

"No sir, I don't."

"I'll lend you one so I can call when we're ready to return here. A week… maybe two, I should think."

"Understood, sir." Gil adjusted his cap back on. "Anything else?"

"Just that my Dulci wants Father Jake to come along for a day or two. He's willing and can ride with us in the BMW up to Bernalillo. Now, we should leave in the morning by ten o'clock. I'm anxious to get to know my little girl… that is…my daughter again. Would you tell Cervando to ready the Featherlite 2-Horse trailer by then?"

"Of course, Mister Trujillo."

"Ah… don't let Dulci see the horses being led aboard the trailer. You see, there was an accident involving her mother."

"Sir, I've heard about that. I'm sorry."

"Yes…. Well, I'll tell Cervando to rendezvous with us around eleven-thirty for lunch at the Open Range Café in Bernalillo. Father Jake then can continue on with you, since Dulci and I will drive to Los Alamos for some shopping." Don Fernando put on his hat and reached over and shake his employee's hand. "Thanks, Gilbert."

"No problem, Mister Trujillo."

○

After Gilbert Begay did most of the work of coaxing the two horses aboard the trailer, Cervando Benavides slid behind the driver's seat of the

Ford F-150 pickup. It was a little past ten o'clock. Fernando, his daughter, and Fr. Jake waited in the Don's white 2008 BMW for the truck and trailer to begin moving, then drove off ahead of the two men. They would meet them at Bernalillo's Open Range Café, an hour or so away.

Vando was silent while driving with Gilbert the distance from Providencia to Belén: he brooded over what Millie Jaramillo had said to him two nights before about "making her happy by taking care of the *norteño padre* at San Isidro." She had made him happy, yet just what did she expect him to do?

Once the truck had passed through Belén traffic and exited onto northbound I-25, the ranch boss abruptly elbowed his companion. "Gil whatta think of that new priest at the church?"

"Father Jake?" He shrugged his opinion, "I don't go there, but I guess he just does what priests do."

"Yeah, but why is he snoopin' around here with that woman detective?"

"Think it might be because she asked him to? You did find a human fetus in the *acequia* didn't you, Vando?"

Instead of replying, the foreman accelerated into the center lane to pass a Walmart truck exiting on the right to Los Lunas. "Millie don't like him," he muttered.

"Queen Millie probably sees him as a threat to her voodoo 'cures'," Gil replied. "Not that a lot she does with herbs isn't legit. Our *Diné* people are also pretty savvy about using plant remedies."

"They been talkin' again about what happened to Don Fernando's wife."

"Vando, that was long before I came here, but weren't you there at the accident?

"Yeah, I was."

"So what did happen?"

"Simple. Stallion bolted, kicked Isabel-Maria in the head, an' she died."

"End of story, then…. Hey!" Gil abruptly braced himself against the dashboard. "Watch your driving! You're tailgating that motor home up ahead way too closely."

"Aw, screw 'im…" Vando slowed down a bit to regain the right lane, then nudged Gil again. "Guy, reach back and pop me a Bud from the cooler."

"No way, man! We haven't even reached Albuquerque. Mister Trujillo said we'll stop for lunch in Bernalillo, and I wouldn't touch any booze there either, if I were you."

"You *ain't* me," the foreman bristled, "an' don't forget it." He muttered a cliché about "dumb Indians" under his breath, clicked the radio on to a

Mexican music station, and hunched down over the steering wheel. Gil settled back on the seat to pull his Purina Mills cap over his eyes and nap.

O

The Open Range Café' in Bernalillo was crowded with office workers from City Hall. When Gil came in with Vando, he spotted Don Fernando, Dulci, and Fr. Jake seated in a corner booth, finishing glasses of ice tea.

"Sorry if we're a little late, sir," he apologized.

"That's fine, Gilbert," Fernando told him. "We've finished eating, so Dulci and I will head for Los Alamos. You'll take Father Jake on to our cottage with you."

"Where I'll straighten out the place," the priest said. "After not being used for awhile, the cottage definitely will need to be swept out."

"Thanks, Father," the Don said. "Gil and Vando can settle Chorro and Bombóna in the corral, then, if you really want to help out, you could tidy up."

"I like to be useful."

Gil said, "Mister Trujillo, I'll have to buy fly spray for the horses and also a few bales of hay."

"Charge anything you need to my account at Ponderosa Feed in Jemez Springs." The Don stood up and took out his wallet from a leather suit coat pocket. "Ready Dulci?"

"Yes, *papá*. Could…could I say hello to Bombóna outside?"

"Of course, darling." Fernando handed Gil a twenty-dollar bill. "You and Vando have lunch, and we'll see you at the *caseta* late this afternoon."

"Thanks, Mister Trujillo."

Don Fernando had made sure he did not leave enough money even for one beer. While the two men gulped down Rangeburger Specials and drank iced tea, Father Jake looked through a rack of flyers near the entrance. Most advertised New Mexico tourist attractions, including the Jemez Mountains and Jemez Springs. *It seems to be a beautiful recreational area, with a river, hiking trails, even this Fenton Lake for camping.*

Vando grumbled about the tip that Gil left the waitress, which had used up the twenty dollars. Gilbert also made sure that the foreman did not sneak a beer from the truck's cooler. In a foul mood, Vando swung the truck and trailer onto Highway 550 and headed north toward San Ysidro village and the turn off to Highway 4.

Fr. Jake was given the passenger window side, with Gil sitting in the center. The landscape flattened out with the outline of the Jemez Range gradually looming larger on a distant horizon. Vando remained in sulking mood. Gilbert sat up straight and pushed his cap back. After the truck passed the Santa Ana and Zia reservations, without either man commenting, the priest finally held up a twenty-page summer guide to northern New Mexico he had found in the rack.

"We're heading into mountainous scenery that we don't have in Michigan."

"It's nice," Gil agreed. "Father, I noticed that bandage still on your elbow. What happened?"

"There was trouble at that supposed funeral at San Isidro on July fifth."

"Yeah, I read about that. How's the deputy doing?"

"Recovering well. I saw him a couple days ago at Socorro Regional."

"They ever catch those responsible?"

"Not yet, Gil."

Vando broke in, "It ain't so peaceful as it looks up there in the Jemez. They got a guy breakin' into empty cabins, stealin' TVs an' stuff, then sellin' it off."

"That's true," Gil confirmed. "He also eats whatever he can find, mostly stale breakfast food, so the newspapers call him the 'Cereal Bandit'." He chuckled at the name. "That's a take on 'Serial Killer—"

"I get it, Gil," Fr. Jake said, "and it's nothing for anyone to joke about."

"Right," he conceded, "but he's probably more of a nuisance than really dangerous."

Vando disagreed. "That could change if deputies corner the guy like a rat."

Fr. Jake surmised that the odds were against anything dangerous happening, but kept silent about mentioning it.

Shortly after turning onto Highway 4, they passed older homesteads with abandoned cars in most yards, directions to a nearby winery, and the San Ysidro Catholic Church. Presently, a roadside sign welcomed travelers to The Pueblo of Jemez, where recent housing gradually gave way to the more rustic homes in the older pueblo. Eroded cliffs on either side were brilliant red ochre. When a large building, the Pueblo of Jemez Walatowa Vistor Center, appeared on the left, Gil said they would gas up there on their return. Father Jake could then go in and look over authentic Native

American jewelry, pottery and rugs, but joked that "some cheaper tourist items were labeled 'Made in India'."

As the highway approached the village of Jemez Springs, enormous cliffs of red limestone dotted with piñon and juniper trees bordered the road. Several day-camping sites that lined the babbling Jemez River, gave way to older homesteads set amid the more recent houses of retirees.

At Jemez Springs, the road curved past a church roofed in corrugated steel, two art galleries, and the Cowpoke Bar. Vacant booths of a weekend art fair dotted the town square. Beyond another bar, a small, adobe-style building housed Ponderosa Feed & Tack. A wooden porch, centered on the entrance, ran almost the length of the store. A shed to the left held stacked bales of hay. Vando pulled the white pickup with a Rancho Tru-Cor logo on the doors into the front parking lot and stopped parallel with the highway to accommodate the trailer.

Gil turned to the priest. "Reverend, we have to check on the horses and I need to discuss something with Vando." He pointed to the tack store, "You mind waiting in the shade over there under that porch? Can you read a book or something on the bench?"

"I have my breviary. Let me get it out of my carry-on."

"Good. I won't be a minute."

Fr. Jake sat on the metal bench, noting that Gil argued with Vando before they got out of the truck's cab. The two men walked on opposite sides of the trailer to open the twin back doors, then entered to look in on the horses. When both men came out, they went to a bar next door, rather than in the feed store. The priest read aloud a sign that faced the street above the entrance, "'Bonnie's Blue Belle Bar & Bar-BQ * Pkg'. An interesting, if awkward, alliterative name." He glanced down at his watch. "Almost One-thirty. Well, 'Reverend,' you intended to question the Psalm for today, July Twelve, so..." Fr. Jake opened his missal to a white ribbon that marked the page and re-read, "'Happy are those who suffer persecution for justice's sake'." He looked up at surrounding mountains flanked the highway, dark green with ponderosa pines. "I doubt the verse will apply here in this beautiful landscape."

Gilbert Begay came out of the bar first. Vando, holding a brown paper bag, loped after him, went straight to the F-150, and slumped inside.

"Reverend, sorry that I kept you waiting," the Navajo apologized.

"No problem, Gil, but isn't our driver coming in the feed store with us?"

"No. Despite my warning, he'll guzzle a *cerveza* from the cooler, stash that vodka he bought somewhere in the cottage, then head right back to this bar next door."

"'Bonnie gave her establishment an unusual name."

"She's Scotch and the food's not bad. That's good because there aren't that many eateries in the Springs."

"You've been in the Jemez before?"

"I once spent time here doing forestry work, like clearing away brush to help control forest fires." Gil swept a hand at the wooded mountains. "Hard to beat the scenery and it's cooler in summer than the Rio Grande Valley."

"That must have been a back-breaking forestry job."

"Yeah, but mostly I missed being around horses."

"Gil, what are you purchasing in this feed store?"

"I noticed we were low on fly spray for the horses and there'll be more flying bugs and mosquitoes up here. Ready to go in, Reverend?"

The priest closed his missal and stood up. "Let's go."

A young Native American man from Jemez Pueblo stood behind a cash register set on a display case. He wore a black short-sleeved T-shirt, similar dark-color cowboy Stetson, and faded jeans belted with a turquoise-studded silver buckle that matched his watch band. Gil nodded to him and looked for the fly spray in a room that smelled of fresh hay and disinfectant.

Fr. Jake walked around metal shelves of various colors and sizes that lined the walls to display red and blue plastic buckets and an assortment of livestock items. Aside from the fly spray Gil mentioned, bottles and jars identified equine hoof thrush and white line remedies, turpentine medications, Horse Calm to soothe equine anxiety, and Rain Trot Treatment—all products that catered to horse owners.

An alcove held several saddles on stands. Horse tack supplies hung from pegs. A back wall displayed the long yellow rain slickers that were ubiquitous in Cowboy Hall of Fame oil paintings of stoic cowhands huddled next to horses in gray, vertical rainstorms.

After the ranch hand made his purchase, Fr. Jake called him over to a center aisle display. "Gil, what are these? They look like old fashioned ice picks bent at right angles, but have a flattened end."

Gil grinned and took one off the display. "That's right, Reverend, you're from the city. This is a hoof pick. Some of them come with a small brush attached to the handle."

"I thought a pick would be more pointed."

"This type is flattened so you can use cotton to swab medicine into, like a horse with thrush. That's a smelly hoof infection."

Fr. Jake noted, "But the blade could be ground down to a sharper point."

"Sure. In fact, Vando has one like that in the big horse trailer at the ranch."

"I see." He replaced the tool. "Its purpose is quite clear now that you've told me."

"Let's get to the cottage," Gil said. "I brought along a new hunting bow I'd like to try out in the woods around there."

"Fine, and I'll dust whatever needs to be dusted at the place."

When Vando saw the two men returning, he shoved his empty beer can under the front seat. No one spoke as he made a U-turn back onto the highway and headed north. The pickup passed the modern Motherhouse Church serving a convent of cloistered nuns. To the right, ruins of the ancient San José mission were now a New Mexico State Monument. The Soda Dam, a sizeable limestone formation, spouted a waterfall from inside a dark cave. The smoothly sculpted mound was a natural formation, yet its effect suspiciously resembled a cement Disneyland attraction. Fr. Jake respected the strained silence between the two men without interfering, yet vowed to return and explore these multi-attractions.

Just before a green and white highway sign identified Battleship Rock, Vando slowed down the truck. Without activating a left turn signal, he abruptly swung onto a forest road, then shifted into a groaning 2$^{nd}$ gear as the road climbed steadily upward for about a mile. At a wooden post with three red reflectors at the top, he bounced the truck and horse trailer to the right, onto a rutted driveway marked by a deteriorating sign that needed repainting.

Tru-Cor Lane
PRIVATE!

Gil commented, "Reverend, I guess this is the place. Hope it's not too messed up. No one's been in there for quite awhile."

"With you and Vando away, I'll have the whole cottage to myself!" the priest jested.

Gil laughed. "Yep, and it'll be quiet enough for you to sneak in a nap."

## 20 *caseta* tru-cor

Gilbert mouthed a few less-than-complimentary remarks in Navajo, but held back from actively criticizing Vando as the moody foreman over-maneuvered his truck toward a one-story wooden building that was visible beyond a stand of tall ponderosa pines.

Built in 1991 and raised two-and-a-half feet off ground level, Don Fernando's three-bedroom, two-bath *caseta* had a screened-in covered porch built across the front. An open deck ran along the left entrance door side. Five acres of forested land surrounded the cottage, with a small horse corral, equipment shed, and carport/storage structure in the back.

Since his wife's tragic death, thirteen years earlier, the Don rarely had visited the property. Stark signs of neglect were evident in the peeling paint, torn screens and dirty windows. Mud Wasps buzzed around a clay nest tucked beneath side eaves. Hailstones and winter snows had damaged the roofing, causing melt water to stain the wood-paneled wall of an interior family room.

Vando braked hard enough near the corral to send his beer can rolling forward from under the seat. Still scowling, he flung himself out of the truck's cab and headed toward the trailer's back doors. "Let's get these *caballos* out an' in the corral quick-like," he ordered, "then unhitch the damn trailer."

Gil noted a depleted water trough inside the enclosure's fencing. "The horses will need to drink."

"Fernando had a guy turn on the well pump," Vando snarled, "so you fill the tank, Mister Navajo Man. Me, I'm heading for Bonnie's and it ain't to guzzle water."

"Just watch your drinking," Gil warned, "and bring back the load of hay I paid for at the feed store."

The ranch boss glared at him. "Don't need you tellin' me what to do."

"Just do it, Vando. And I *am* telling you that Mister Trujillo should get here by maybe five o'clock. Right now, it's already past two, so you better be back by then."

"Aw, screw you...."

"Gil," Fr. Jake asked to interrupt the argument, "do you have a key to the cottage?"

"Right here...." He searched a key ring attached to his belt and picked one off. "It has a 'C' for cottage written on a piece of adhesive tape. Reverend, I'll get my stuff and your suitcase out of the back."

"Thanks." Chorro was being led into the corral, when the priest walked onto the side deck, tried the door, and found it unlocked. "Gil," he called back, "this door wasn't locked."

"Probably that water pump guy. He knew we were coming."

"Okay..." Fr. Jake picked up his suitcase, stepped inside and set it down on the floor of a pine-paneled family room. He glanced around at the rustic interior, then went to inspect the rest of the cottage. The kitchen was opposite the room, on one side of a counter. A hallway led to a master bedroom / bath area on one side. Two smaller bedrooms opposite shared a bathroom built adjacent to them. A bed in one of the rooms was unmade, as if slept in.

When Fr. Jake came back to the family room, he noted that its furniture was protected with bed sheets, except for half of a Santa Fe-style couch that faced an uncovered TV screen. *Someone's definitely been in the cottage, and Gil thinks it might have been the water pump man. The place smells less musty than it should, but that could be because New Mexico air is drier than in Michigan, even here in the mountains.* Yet the priest felt a persistent sense of uneasiness as he looked in a pantry alcove and found cleaning supplies, a broom, and dustpan. A box of crackers alongside a few cans of food stood on nearly bare shelves. *Don Fernando said he'd be shopping in Los Alamos, so he'll probably bring more food. I'll take the covers off the furniture, do some sweeping.*

After Fr. Jake heard the Ford pickup's V-8 engine start up, he glanced out the open door. Chorro and Bombóna guzzled swirling water from the corral's trough, which was being filled by a green hose. The horse trailer stood nearby. Vando, in the driver's seat of the truck, released the brake and gunned the Ford bouncing down the driveway. *He certainly didn't lose any time in heading for Bonnie's!*

Gilbert shut off the water, then came inside with a quiver of steel-tipped arrows strapped to his back. He grinned and held up a new Take Down Bow. "Saved up and made this baby from a kit," he boasted. "Standard model, but that's all I could afford. Still, Bubinga handle, Black Locust limbs under clear glass.... Heck, Reverend, that's all technical stuff. I need to go out and do some actual shooting."

"Gil," the priest alerted him, "one bed looks slept in and the kitchen table was used lately. Cracker crumbs and ants. Do you suppose the Cereal Bandit was here? Perhaps he's still around?"

Gil suggested a more plausible reason. "Reverend, it's likely that the water pump man has a girlfriend. We know he had a key to the place, so when Mister Trujillo told him to open up, he just came a in few days early—"

"I get it... '*Cherchez la femme*'!" Fr. Jake's laugh was uncertain. "Gil, you're probably right, so go try out your bow. I'll fold up these sheets on the furniture, start cleaning up, and maybe consider that nap you mentioned."

"You sound a little worried, Reverend. Are you sure I can leave you alone here?"

"I'm sure. Go! Go! Vamoose, Gilbert!"

O

Fr. Jake's unease had been tempered by the time he finished putting the inside of the cottage in order. He had just sat down on the couch with a tumbler of water, when he heard the sound of an automobile whining up the gravel road to the cottage. He put down the glass and stood up to check his watch. "Three-forty-three. Seems like the Don and his daughter are returning early." He glanced around the family room, straightened a chair cushion, then muttered, "Looks pretty decent now," and went to open the front door.

A surprised Breanna Springer stared at the priest a moment, then recovered quickly enough to bring around a Colt M1911 .45 caliber pistol that she held behind her back. The woman leveled the gun at Fr. Jake's head, while she smirked a sarcastic greeting. "Hi Rev. Ya just gotta believe it's a small world, don'tcha?"

# 21 death in the jemez

Breanna grinned as she waved her automatic pistol in the priest's face. In a frigid tone that reflected the ice-blue of her eyes, the West Virginian ordered, "Rev., place your hands on your head like you see in the movies, and step outside this door."

He complied and walked out onto the deck. At the top of the stairs, Breanna looked around the priest to yell down to her companion. "Hey, Davie! Guess who I found in our cottage!"

David Allison walked around a corner of the house and stopped in surprise. "Well, I'll be damned, Brea! It can't be Reverend what's-his- name."

She laughed at his reaction. "You bet it is, sugah!"

Fr. Jake glanced back over his shoulder. "How…how did you find us, Breanna?"

The woman's immediate reply was to prod the priest's back with the Colt. "Walk down them stairs, Rev., and then near to that yonder tree line up ahead."

Fighting back a rising panic, Fr. Jake stumbled as he stepped off the bottom stair of the porch. Breanna laughed at his awkwardness, then limped down after him to answer his question. "How did we find you, Rev.? Lady Luck, I reckon. Davie and I were having a beer at Bonnie's, in the Springs, when this Hispanic guy name of Van-something starts bragging about how he's opening a cabin for his boss up the highway. I started sweet-talking the jerk and figured he might be referring to the place where we been hiding low until this Haskill thing blows over. Coming here and seeing that horse trailer was a give-away. We were gonna take our stuff out, but, Rev., I sure never expected to find you here." Breanna jabbed his back again with the gun barrel. "Now get movin' and keep your hands up there."

*How can I stall her?* Clasping his head with both hands, Fr. Jake glanced back. "Breanna, I notice that you're limping. How did you injure yourself?"

"When Davie accelerated away, that open door on the fucking Humvee closed back into my leg and foot."

Allison, walking behind, heard and taunted the priest. "You rebuild your burned church yet, Reverend? Man, I wish I'd seen that place go up."

"Son," Fr. Jake replied, "your grenade was a dud. San Isidro protected his own."

Breanna again sharply jabbed the priest in his back with the Colt's barrel. "Don't give us that religious shit! That fucker, Haskill, said his screwin' me was the will of the Almighty."

Fr. Jake objected, "The pastor was tragically wrong and not typical of—"

"Shut up, dammit!" Breanna screamed, with another vicious jab of the pistol.

*What else can I say to stall…perhaps change her mind?* Fr. Jake recalled the reason the woman came to New Mexico. "Breanna, we now know that Pastor Haskill was the youth minister who sexually abused you back then in that West Virginia church."

"So? I just said that."

"What you did in killing him was terribly wrong, but Deputy Griego is recovering from your bullet wound. Considering the circumstances, a court might treat you with lenience over Haskill's death."

Breanna cackled a dry laugh and turned to Allison, behind her. "Hey, sugah, hear that? The stupid Rev. here wants me to turn myself in."

David Allison seemed to have second thoughts about killing the priest. "He…he might be right, Brea, and I…I told you not to shoot that bank teller."

"Yeah, well, Davie, he was a witness and could of fingered us. Besides, if and when they find a corpse, a bunch of coyoties will of got to it. The cops won't know who it was."

Fr. Jake sounded more nervous than he intended when he told her, "Breanna, the police have found and identified Rod Jirón's body."

"Really? Well then, you, Rev., are another witness that definitely has got to go."

"Brea, don't…" Allison's protested was weak. "Let's just get the hell out of here and head north."

"Shut up, dammit, and don't be dumb," she snarled at him. "The Rev. probably saw our Colorado license plate, so every cop between here and the Canadian border would be out looking for us."

The three had reached a grassy clearing about twenty-five feet from dense underbrush that grew at the edge of the Ponderosa forest, when the woman told Fr. Jake to stop.

"Kneel down, Rev.," Breanna ordered without emotion in her command. "Ain't you church types supposed to be good at that?"

"Brea," Allison pleaded again. "Let's just tie up the Reverend and leave. That Hispanic guy might come back any minute with the cabin's owner."

The woman ignored him and pushed down on the priest's right shoulder with her gun. "Rev., I said kneel down, and keep your fucking hands on top of your head."

Trembling from genuine fright as he sank to his knees, the priest absurdly worried about soiling his trousers. *I could try to stall Breanna some more, but David is right. Vando, or even the Don and his daughter might return. She would murder them all without blinking an eye.* Through his fear, he thought of the early Christian victims of persecution and how stoically most had faced their martyrdoms. In his own dangerous experience in Poland, during the Poznañ uprising, he had read underground newspaper reports about summary executions by the communist *UB Urząd Bezpieczeñstwa* secret police. *I wondered then how their victims faced imminent deaths? Now my time has come to find out.*

"Young woman…let…let's get it over with," Fr. Jake stammered.

"Now you're talkin', Rev…" She grinned and called back to Allison. "Davie, get that shovel out that we saw in the shed."

Although his body shook uncontrollably, Fr. Jake managed to ask, "You… you'll have me dig my own grave?"

Breanna affected a comic West Virginia stage drawl. "Naw, we'll jus' drag ya over yonder and cover y' up with forest moss and leaves, all nice and cozy-like. When a coupla .45 slugs come out through your face, Rev., ain't nobody gonna even recognize who ya are. We'll muss up the house an' the cops will figure some homeless weirdo killed ya, then robbed the place, like's happened up here before."

Numb thoughts continued to flood the priest's mind. *So that's it? Then that makes today's Psalm almost reassuring in a final way: "Happy are they who suffer persecution for justice's sake. The kingdom of heaven is theirs." Whenever I prayed with people who breathed their last in accidents or hospital sick rooms, I always wondered how they felt about dying. Now I pretty much know.* Overcome with a panic he had only felt during the Polish riots, Fr. Jake instinctively recited the ending of the second most familiar Catholic prayer. "…Holy Mary, Mother of God, pray for us sinners now and at the hour of our death—"

"Godammit, hurry up, David!" Breanna yelled to him. "My gun hand's getting awful tired."

Fr. Jake felt the cold muzzle of the pistol slide down to his middle cervical vertebra, and heard Allison's distant reply.

"*Shit,* Brea, I'm looking for it!" After a pause, he called back, "Here, I found the bugger."

"Okay, good. Now trot it the hell over to me." When her accomplice walked up holding the shovel, she ordered, "Throw it down. You're gonna have to help me drag the Rev.'s body over yonder."

"Breanna," he urged again. "Maybe we—"

"I told ya to shut up, Davie! Shit…" She poked her military pistol hard against Fr. Jake's neck. "Reverend, you just turn your head toward me *real slow* and then I'll—"

Breanna Springer never completely voiced her final order to the kneeling priest: if the woman heard the deadly swish of an arrow, she would not live long enough to tell anyone how it sounded. As a steel-pointed, feathered shaft sliced through her neck, dark blood from both severed carotid arteries spurted onto Fr. Jake. Eyes wide in shock, her mouth coughing blood, Breanna's body swayed a moment, then, pulled down by the weight of her military pistol, she slumped down alongside her intended victim. Far from her home state, bent on revenge, Breanna Springer lay on the ground, legs twitching, as if attempting to escape eternity in her final death spasms.

David Allison barely had time to cast a panicked look from her fallen body toward the forest's edge, before a second arrow lodged in his right shoulder joint. He bellowed in pain as he clutched at the quivering shaft. Struggling to pull it out, Allison dropped to a kneeling position that mimicked the priest's.

Stunned, Fr. Jake, rose on one trembling knee and turned toward his fatally wounded would-be assassin. With a priest's instinct, he extended a shaking hand in a sign of the cross over the dying woman's head and stammered a prayer for her immortal soul. "Lord of forgiveness…and … and mercy, may our sister, Breanna, enter…the kingdom in peace and… and light, where…where your saints live in glory. We…ask this through our Lord Jesus Christ…your Son, who lives and reigns with you…and… the Holy Spirit, one God, for ever and ever."

"Reverend, save your breath, about saving her here or in the Hereafter," Gilbert Begay counseled, as walked from the tree line, holding his hunting bow. With a glance at the woman's now-still body, he ordered, "Don't touch her gun, Reverend, but go clean yourself up while I bandage the guy's shoulder and call to turn him and the woman's body over to the Jemez Springs police."

Breathing in short hyper-ventilated gasps at his narrow escape from being killed in the last few minutes, Fr. Jake slowly stood and looked toward another New Mexican who had saved his life. "Gil…thanks, but I…I need to call Detective Mora and …and tell her about…what happened."

"Reverend, where's your cell phone?"

"In…in my suitcase."

"Okay, but you calm down first," Gil said. "What you need is an hour in my sweat lodge, but right now just strip off your shirt and wash up in the horse trough. Then shower inside and only afterward call your detective. The Jemez police should be here by then, and she may want to talk with an officer on the phone."

Still numb from shock, the priest hesitated. "Gilbert…Gil…how did you return? I mean…just in time? You're Native American, so was there some instinct, some…well… supernatural tip-off that I was in danger?"

"Oh, yeah, Reverend, there sure was. In the forest there, Coyote sent me a vision of you in big trouble."

"Truly, Gilbert?"

"Naw, I'm kidding. My bow has a thirty-pound pull so, after two hours, my arm just got tired. As to my coming here when I did, you probably were praying to be saved, or maybe just plain luck was involved." Gil patted the priest's back. "Now go get cleaned up, Reverend Jake, while I deal with the guy's shoulder and cover the dead woman's body with one of those sheets inside."

O

When a somewhat calmer Fr. Jake rang up Sonia Mora, Gilbert Begay had placed one of the bed sheets that covered cottage furniture over Breanna Springer's body. Dave Allison rubbed his head with a left hand as he sat at the kitchen table and moaned at the pain in his bandaged shoulder.

After three rings, Sonia answered, "Sheriff Detective Mora speaking."

"Sonia, it…it's Father Jakubowski."

"'Jakubowski'? How formal, *Padre*. You having a good time in the Jemez?"

"Sonia...Breanna Springer and David Allison were hiding out in Don Fernando's summer cottage."

"What? Say that again."

"Yes. It...it's true. Breanna and Dave are up here."

"Then, Father, you were correct about where they might go, or at least that it wouldn't be directly to Colorado. But what's the connection with Don Fern—?"

"Detective Mora," he interrupted, his voice impatient, "I called to tell you that Breanna Springer is dead. David Allison is wounded."

Sonia paused a moment, as if opening her notebook and locating a pen. "How did that happen?"

"I...I'm still shaking. She had a .45 caliber pistol and was about to.... Well, it would have been execution style."

"You, Father Jake?"

"Yes, but by the grace of God, Gilbert Begay came back from practicing with his hunting bow, and...and...." The priest's voice choked up at the recollection. "Sorry—"

"Okay, Father, just take it easy," Sonia advised. "I'll get details later, but did someone call the Jemez police?"

"Gil did. Gilbert Begay called. They...they aren't here yet."

"Have them contact me, since there's an APB out on the couple. Are Don Fernando and Dulcinea safe?"

"He and his daughter haven't returned from shopping in Los Alamos. Now I don't suppose they'll want to stay on here."

"Didn't Cervando Benavides go with you?"

"Yes, he drove us, but at the moment he's drinking in a Jemez Springs bar."

"Sonia reminded him, "Mister Benavides is a person of interest in the horse trailer incident that killed the Don's wife."

Fr. Jake updated her. "Detective, perhaps he's more than that now."

After a pause she urged, "Go on, Father Jake. What do you mean?"

"Sonia, do you know what a horse hoof pick is?"

"Actually, despite being a 'city girl,' I do. Why do you ask?"

"I saw one in a Jemez Springs tack supply store. You recall that veterinarian's necropsy report on the stallion that killed Isabel Trujillo?"

"*Vencedor?*"

"Yes, that's it. I'd forgotten the animal's name."

"Father, what about the report?"

"The vet had found a small, unexplained puncture on the right side of the animal's neck."

"Yes, I know, but it couldn't be caused by a hoof pick because the blade is flat, not pointed."

"I thought of that and asked, Gil. He told me that Vando had ground at least one pick to a sharp point, and it's still in the trailer where *Vencedor* was being loaded. Doesn't that upgrade him to 'suspect'?"

"Padre, yer catchin' on fast," she mimicked, then added. "Seriously, Father, I...I'm so relieved that you're all right. You and I will talk later about exactly what happened, but right now have a lieutenant, or the police captain at Jemez Springs, contact me about Springer's death."

"Gil killed her with a hunting arrow and wounded Allison. Will he be arrested?"

Sonia avoided a direct answer. "Father, have the police call me after they've taken statements from you and everyone else involved in what happened."

"All right...Sonia."

For once Fr. Jake ended his call without repeating, "God Bless."

## 22 'harden not your hearts'

While statements were taken from Gilbert Begay and Fr. Jakubowski, Cervando Benavides was brought from Bonnie Belle's Bar—amazingly sober—and confirmed the story about a man and woman, total strangers. He admitted that he had told them about the location of *Caseta Tru-Cor*.

Don Fernando and Dulcinea returned from Los Alamos just as a Paramedic Fire and Rescue ambulance took Breanna Springer's body, and a handcuffed David Allison, to a clinic in Jemez Springs. The Don ordered his daughter to stay in the BMW, while he went to find out why an emergency vehicle and the Jemez Police were at his cottage.

"What happened?" he demanded of a policeman standing at the bottom stair that led up to the entrance deck. "Why are representatives of the law here?"

"Sir, are you Don Fernando?" the officer asked.

"Yes, this is my cottage. I asked why law enforcement was here?"

"Sir, one of your ranch hands killed a...well...an intruder, and probably saved the life of a priest. He was presumably your guest."

"Father Jake?"

"A Father Jakubowski, I believe." The officer moved away. "Sir, go inside. Captain Flynn is questioning the men involved."

"Mike Flynn is here? I know the captain." Seated at the kitchen table, Flynn, Fr. Jake, Gilbert, and Cervando glanced up as the Don entered. "Mike," he demanded, "what the hell went on here?"

"Oh, 'afternoon, Fernando…" Captain Michael Flynn stood to extend a hand and express regret. "Sorry that we have to meet under these circumstances."

"What circumstances? Mike, why is my ranch hand, Gilbert, in handcuffs?"

The Captain gestured toward Fr. Jake with his pen. "Don, I'll let this priest tell you about that."

Fernando faced him. "Father, what's this that the officer outside said about someone saving your life?"

In explaining, Fr. Jake's voice still quavered. "Evidently, Dave Allison and…and Breanna Springer were…were staying in your cottage—"

"And who are they?"

"The two individuals involved in the July fifth shooting of that Oklahoma minister during a supposed funeral at San Isidro. They also robbed Western Savings in Belén."

"Impossible!" Fernando challenged the priest's report. "You say they were living here, and yet I don't even know either one."

"It's true," Captain Flynn attested. "According to Father and Mister Begay, the woman he killed was about to execute the priest when he…" Flynn paused to exhale a breath of admiration. "Hey, Don. Your Indian ranch hand is pretty damn good with a bow!"

Fernando looked toward him. "Gilbert, what is he talking about?"

"Sir," he said quietly without looking up from his hands, in handcuffs and folded on the table. "I guess it's that I happened back from target shooting just in time."

"Amen!" Fr. Jake added loudly. "Gil absolutely saved my life."

Fernando glanced back at the captain. "So, Mike, why is Gilbert in handcuffs?"

"Don, Mister Begay admits to killing the woman."

"From what I just heard, he saved Father Jake's life," he objected. "Gilbert should get…get a commendation."

Flynn chose his response carefully. "I realize we're friends, Don, but the law's the law. I can't hold Mister Benavides, but I have to arrest your ranch hand."

The Don told him, "So be it, Captain, but I know your Judge Gallegos well enough for him to stay at my cottage whenever we hunt elk in the Valles Caldera. I'll get him to authorize a cognizance release." Fernando glanced at his watch. "It's late Monday afternoon, but if he's not in court, I'll go to his home. Gilbert will be my responsibility after that."

Captain Flynn was firm. "Do what you must, Don. If Gallegos okays a recognizance release, please pick up Mister Begay at the jail."

"Vando will damn well have to do that, because I plan on staying here with my daughter." Fernando turned back to Fr. Jake. "Gilbert would be in house arrest, so would you go back with them to Providencia and keep an eye on him for me?"

"Of course. He seems a fine man."

Don Fernando agreed. "I trust the Navajo completely, or I wouldn't do him this favor."

Captain Flynn pushed their statements back toward the priest and two ranch hands. "Reverend…sirs…sign these, then, Mister Begay, we'll head back to the village."

"Captain…" Fr. Jake handed him Sonia Mora's card. "The Socorro detective investigating the two fugitives would like you to call her."

Flynn tucked the card into a shirt pocket without reading it. "Sure, Father, soon's I have time."

○

Despite the seriousness of the charge, Judge Zachary Gallegos, a long time friend and hunting companion of Don Fernando, considered his personal ties with the ranch owner and his willingness to vouch for his employee, and quickly authorized the cognizance release. Gilbert Begay was to remain at Rancho Tru-Cor until his eventual arraignment in a Sandoval County Courtroom.

○

Dark monsoon clouds gathered later in the afternoon, obscuring the upper third of the surrounding Jemez slopes and promising moisture that would do much to help control fires plaguing the state's forests. Heavy rain began falling when Vando and Fr. Jake picked up Gilbert at the Jemez Police station. Don Fernando went out to shake his hand and wave the three men off, then joined his daughter in the BMW and returned to their cottage. As a precaution, Captain Flynn assigned a police car to stand guard in the *caseta*'s driveway during the night.

O

The three men were silent on their return to Providencia, each reliving in their own way the afternoon's fateful events: Gilbert, grateful that he had saved the priest's life yet, ironically, facing a possible murder charge and prison sentence; Fr. Jake, reliving in his mind the image of Breanna Springer holding her pistol to his head, then the woman's legs twitching as if to outrun death, even as her pierced, bloody throat gurgled her last breaths. Vando, hunched over the truck's steering wheel, clenched his teeth and drove the speed limit on the rain-slick highway—fortunately in light traffic.

The ranch boss did not stop for gas at the Jemez Pueblo Walatowa Center. In his twisted memory, he alone was responsible for the capture of the fugitives, yet had not received proper credit. That "honor" had gone to his Indian ranch hand.

When Vando dropped Fr. Jake off at his rectory, a crimson sun had set shortly after 8:00 P.M. Bright summer twilight would last at least an hour. The priest lugged his carry-on inside, then walked across to the church building. The afternoon rain and its attending clouds were gone, revealing a red "sailor's delight" sunset. Cooler air carried the overwhelming fragrance of juniper and sage, a scent that was reminiscent of a macho aftershave lotion.

At the church's entrance, Fr. Jake rubbed a scorched wooden door panel that he left as it looked after an arsonist's recent attempt to torch the building. The vandalism was unsuccessful, thus the charred door stayed as a reminder that San Isidro had protected his namesake church. Faithful parishioners believed this was so.

The interior nave was cool. Since the *norteño* priest's somewhat abrupt arrival in mid-April, parishioners had cleaned the old church as best they could. The reclusive pastor he was sent to help had been murdered; given the priest shortage in the Archdiocese of Santa Fe, Fr. Jake now was pastor *pro tem* at San Isidro.

In the three months since he arrived, the Michigan priest tried to make his Masses more in line with the reforms of Vatican II, and "user friendly." Up-to-date missalettes and a rack of religious pamphlets were placed in the vestibule. He scheduled a Saturday five o'clock Vigil Mass. Armando Herrera and his musician friends helped parishioners sing hymns in both English and Spanish. Cynthia Plow was organizing after-school Faith Formation classes for the fall. He had not yet installed a more private Confessional area for the Sacrament of Reconciliation: at present, pews had been removed and the space curtained off with Zapotec blankets. A priest faced away from the penitent. Yet he hesitated to disturb the villagers' over-crowded array of saints' statues set on a *banco* along one wall—Fr. Jake felt it important that traditions of the largely Hispanic congregation be honored and preserved.

Warm light filtered in from west-facing windows as the priest knelt in front of a *santo* placed at a side altar of the sacristy. The carved wooden image represented San Isidro, a 17th century Spanish farmer-saint who was the church's patron. "Isidore," he murmured, "I again may owe you my thanks. Gilbert Begay, who has not much use for our religion, and possibly even priests, quite miraculously saved my life today. I ask that you help me be a good shepherd to your flock, while I finish my assignment at your church. Help me bring them to a greater understanding of what it means to truly love the God they worship, and to love and forgive their neighbors as they would themselves." He repeated aloud the next day's Gospel psalm. "'If today you hear his voice, harden not your hearts.' Amen."

Fr. Jake crossed himself, then stood and lighted a votive candle for the soul of Breanna Springer. Exhausted by the day's events, he returned to his rectory, took a sleep-aid pill, and hoped for a restful night's sleep.

## 23 cervando' s revelation

On Tuesday, July 13, at precisely 9:00 A.M., Detective Sonia Mora pulled her Plymouth Neon up into the rectory driveway and got out of the car.

Fr. Jake opened the door, but before he could speak, she said, "Sure, I'll have coffee."

"You knew I would ask that question?"

"Does the earth go around the sun?"

The priest chuckled at what others had noted about his habit of offering the beverage to everyone who visited. "I guess answers to both questions are pretty predictable."

"'No comment,' Father."

Sonia wore a woman's four button, flap pocket, military-style tunic and slacks, in a light olive shade that complemented her complexion. She took off a matching Baker Boy cap, smoothed her glossy black hair, and sat on the couch with her briefcase at one side.

"How is Deputy Griego?" Fr. Jake called from his coffee maker.

"Went home yesterday, and he'll be off maybe another three weeks. The real question is, 'How are you today, Father'?"

"I'm good….took a sleep aid…slept pretty well." The priest came in to place steaming coffee cups on the low table in front of the couch and sat in his armchair opposite.

Sonia noticed his breviary on the lamp table next to the chair. "So what's your prayer book say is in store for you today?"

"Well, in Matthew's gospel, Jesus reproached several ungrateful towns where he had worked miracles, because they refused to repent."

"Ungrateful? Father, your 'miracle' happened yesterday."

"And I am grateful, Amen. But the point of that story was that forgiveness is always available, if you're not too bull-headed to ask."

"Even for Breanna Springer?"

"Sonia, remember what Mahatma Gandhi warned? 'An eye for an eye and a tooth for a tooth, and soon the whole world will be blind and toothless.' So, yes detective, 'even for Breanna Springer'."

Sonia took a sip of coffee. After she had talked with the priest about the events in the Jemez cottage, the detective still found it difficult to lose her professional skepticism. "Father Jake, speaking of Springer and Allison, it's almost beyond belief that you would have run into the two fugitives at Jemez Springs."

"Breanna Springer was a troubled person who eventually survived by charming and conning people," he pointed out. "Consider how she convinced me to conduct a funeral for a non-existent Gulf War soldier, and that was just to take revenge on an abusive minister."

"Yes, but their happening to be in Jemez Springs?"

"I agree that she and David went to that locale might seem unusual, yet remember when we looked at your map? It's a round-about way to reach Colorado, yet they could have picked up Highway 550 from the Jemez area. It runs straight to Durango."

"You did point out that possibility," Sonia admitted, "and the police report stated their getaway vehicle had Colorado plates."

The priest continued his speculation. "I'm sure the couple went to local realtors. Breanna no doubt sweet-talked them about wanting to rent a small place for a honeymoon, family reunion, or some such event. Lay low for awhile in an empty cabin. They would have gotten a list of available places and stumbled on Caseta Tru-Cor, while looking at some of them. At Bonnie's Bar, Breanna found out in less than an hour that Cervando Benavides was talking about Don Fernando's cottage, and she realized they would have to leave."

"You're right again, Father, and maybe an example of 'six degrees of separation' jelling together?"

"You mean Pastor Haskill...Breanna and David....Deputy Griego, Cervando, plus myself?" Fr. Jake's expression over his coffee cup was skeptical. "Detective, I might not go quite *that* far."

"Okay, *Padre*, and speaking of Mister Benavides, I obtained a warrant yesterday to search that horse trailer. If the hoof pick is still inside, I'll impound it as evidence and question him." Sonia finished most of her coffee, put on her cap and stood up. "Let's drive over to Rancho Tru-Cor and find out about the pick."

He reminded her, "Fernando and Dulci are still up at their Jemez cottage."

"Fine. As I said, I have a warrant to search that trailer."

O

No work yet had been done to clean out the fountain koi pond, and the main ranch house was deserted. The priest and detective walked in a wide circle around the stables and barn at the rear, then over to the barracks-like building where the ranch hands lived. With a description and license number of the trailer from the accident report, they found the horse transport parked behind the bunkhouse—a place where Dulcinea could not see it and be reminded of the vehicle in which her mother was killed.

Bits of dry hay lay on the floor of the aluminum interior, but otherwise the trailer looked unused. A double saddle rack was at the far end, where a black compartmented bag hung on the wall between them.

"I'd never been in one of these horse trailers," Sonia acknowledged, "but I looked them up on the Internet. Some have inside dressing and tack rooms. Ah…what I hoped to find probably is on that back wall." She walked ahead of the priest up to a canvas storage container. "This is called a brush bag, but the pockets could hold other tools."

Fr. Jake noticed thin strands near one side and held her back by an arm. "First let me use my knife blade to clean away that spider web."

"Thanks, Father. It could be a Brown Recluse."

After searching the bag's top compartments and finding two equine combs and brushes, Sonia reached in a bottom pocket and pulled out a six-inch, red-handled hoof pick. "Presto! Here's a hoof pick."

"But with a regular flat tip," the priest noted. "That pick has not been altered."

"Right. Perhaps in this last pocket? Hey! What have we here?" Sonia held up a rusted steel pick with a worn blue handle. "This tip *has* been ground to a sharp point."

"And looks like it hasn't been used in maybe thirteen years?"

"Father, we may just have our murder weapon. I'll slip this in my briefcase, then let's find Mister Benavides."

Inside the nearby barn, Mathias Crisp and Lorenzo Lujan sat on square bales of hay, listening to Vando as he sucked on a stem of alfalfa and bragged about his part in helping capture Breanna Springer and David Allison.

"I was the one let them two *alcornoques* know where the *caseta* was. They went right to where I told 'em."

Zo asked, "And you said the cops was waitin'?"

"Well, sorta. They came around later an'—"

"Excuse me, Mister Benavides," Sonia interrupted him. "May we go to your room, where I could ask you a few questions?"

"*Si, detectiva.*" Vando beamed at the invitation and muttered to the two ranch hands, "Told ya I was a important witness." He stood and turned back to Sonia. "You wanna talk about what happened at the *caseta* up north, right?"

"No, sir, not exactly. Captain Flynn faxed me his report about that incident in the Jemez. This is about a different matter."

"Differ'nt?" The *jefe's* grin faded. "I dunno. My place is kinda messy."

"Sir," Sonia insisted, "may we go there to talk?"

Annoyed at the intrusion, Vando brushed a hand over his moustache and led the way to the bunkhouse in silence. The TV room was cluttered with beer cans and food scraps on used paper plates; Victoria and Juan Torrez had not been seen for over a week. He unlocked his door and made a quick swipe at pulling a blanket over his unmade bed.

"*Detectiva*, I…I been kinda busy…"

"Sir, I'm not here to criticize your housekeeping." Sonia indicated a chair. "May I sit there?"

"*Bueno.*" The foreman snatched a magazine off the seat, then sat on the side of his bed and nervously fingered the rosary around his neck.

"I'll take that other chair," Fr. Jake said.

Sonia opened her briefcase and pulled out a manila file folder. "Sir, we're probably going to re-open the case about Isabel Trujillo's death."

"*¿Por que?* Why? It was a accident. Cops said so."

"You and the girl…Dulcinea…are the only two witnesses to the incident left alive."

"Eusebia took Dulci inside right away," he protested. "She didn't see nothin'."

"Sir, the five-year-old witnessed enough to have caused a traumatic arrest in her pubertal development."

"Arrest? What, you gonna arrest Dulci?" Vando glanced toward the priest.

Fr. Jake explained to him, "The detective thinks you know more than you've told the police."

"I told 'em it was a accident."

"Mister Benavides, were you were standing at the head of the stallion?" Sonia asked.

"Yeah, so?"

"And Isabel Trujillo was on the right rear side of the horse?"

"I told the cops that a million times. Why you askin' me again?"

Sonia moved her chair closer to the ranch foreman and leaned forward. "I'm asking because, as Father Jake said, I don't think you told the police a complete story." She reached in her case and took out the rusty hoof pick. "Sir, do you recognize this grooming tool?"

Vando's normally ruddy complexion blanched. He squirmed on the bed and stammered, "Wh…where d' you get that?"

"You could answer that question yourself." Sonia laid the blue-handled pick on the bed beside him, and then flipped to a page on her report. "The veterinarian who did the necropsy on *Vencedor* discovered a circular puncture on the…the brachiocephalicus muscle of the stallion's neck. I believe that sharpened hoof pick caused the injury and that you likely were responsible."

"*¡Dios no, detectiva!* W…why would I even do that?"

"To make the horse rear up at the shock and lash out with its hind legs…" Sonia held the veterinarian's report up close to his face. "Mister Benavides, tell me why you caused that puncture wound."

Vando slumped forward with his coarse hands resting on both knees of his jeans. He stared at the floorboards, his usual husky voice almost inaudible. "Don Fernando, he told me Isabela was sick. Said she wouldn't live much longer."

Sonia leaned back and glanced toward Fr. Jake. "Sir, what kind of sickness did Don Fernando tell you about?"

"I don't know, *detectiva*. It…it had a funny name I never heard before."

"You don't recall what that was?"

Vando glanced up at her and shook his head. "Isabel looked like she hurt all the time. Wasn't happy no more…. Always tired because she had trouble sleepin'." The ranch foreman's eyebrows rose as he remembered. "Wait, I kept somethin' about it the Don threw in the barn trash bin."

He slid over on the mattress to a bedside table and rummaged through the contents of a cluttered drawer. After pulling a glossy brochure from the bottom and shaking off tobacco shreds, he handed it to Sonia. "Here, *detectiva*. Here it is."

She read the title, then held it up for the priest to see. "Father, Isabel Marie Trujillo suffered from chronic fibromyalgia."

"Fibromyalgia?" Fr. Jake reached for the brochure. "My God, there's no cure for that condition. I've seen its debilitating effects on patients in Michigan hospitals. Some treatments may reduce the symptoms, but the effects on a body are multiple and horrendous. Even a kind of 'brain fog' can occur that hampers mental acuity. I mean, that major depression Vando described in Isabel is common in almost all the cases."

Sonia remarked, "Don Fernando could afford the best medical care available for Isabel's condition."

"Except that its causes are controversial at best," Fr. Jake cited. "Some physicians don't consider fibromyalgia a disease, yet the symptoms won't improve over time, so the quality of an individual's life may become, well, zero. I'd hate to read statistics on the number of suicides related to the condition."

"Or mercy killings, Father?" Sonia turned back to Cervando. "Mister Benavides, it's perhaps understandable that you wanted to put your employer's wife out of her miserable existence. Isabel was a beautiful woman. You were infatuated with her, so you took a chance that the horse's kick would kill her, and it did so. Yet, murder is unlawful no matter what the rationale or excuse is for the act—"

"¡*Dios no!*" Vando sprang up from the bed so abruptly that Sonia pulled back her chair and held the file up as a flimsy shield. "No!" he shouted again, clutching his rosary beads. "*Maria Purisima*, I swear it weren't like that! Don Fernando, he...he was the one said he would fire me if I didn't do it!"

## 24 jason's dig

"Vando, that …that's impossible!" Fr. Jake blurted. "Don Fernando was…is…still deeply in love with his wife! He never would have—"

"Fatherrr…." Sonia gently warned against his interference. She closed the veterinarian's report, put away the pick, and stood up. "Thank you, Mister Benavides, we'll talk about this again. Gilbert Begay's room is three doors down from yours, is it not?"

"Yeah, he's the last one. Gil's in there now."

"Thank, you. That's all for the present."

Vando stood up, his shoulders drooping. "Th…then I gotta get back t' work."

In the hallway, Sonia watched the man shuffle away, then turned to the priest. "Father, I'd like to talk with Gilbert about what happened to you in the Jemez."

He was confused at Sonia's apparent indifference to what they both heard. "Aren't you going to call Vando on his lie?"

"He did admit to killing Isabel, didn't he?"

"And you heard him."

"I heard what he said."

"You don't believe the man?"

Sonia avoided an opinion. "Father, let's go talk to Mister Begay."

When Gil opened his door in response to a knock, Sonia asked, "Sir, what happened near Jemez Springs isn't my case, but may I ask you a few questions? Father Jakubowski is with me."

Gil pulled the door open. "Detective, no lawyer told me not to say anything to anyone. Come on in."

Soft Native American flute music and a pleasant scent from a smoldering sage bundle filled the small room. Gilbert apologized for wearing only a bathrobe. "Sorry, detective, I spent time in my *táchééh*, my sweat lodge and just came out"

"Yes, I remember seeing it when I first spoke with you."

Fr. Jake remarked, "Gil, I hope it helped you relax. Everything will turn out fine."

"Yeah, sure, Reverend. Amen." Begay took an open can off his bedside table, shook the contents, and held it out. "Have some pistachio brittle candy made right here in the Land of Enchantment. You want to sit down, detective? Here, I'll move these magazines off that chair for you."

"That's fine, sir," Sonia told him.

Gil pointed with the can. "Reverend, sorry, but you'll have to sit on the bed with me."

"I'm good with that." *Gil sounds understandably nervous at being questioned.* Fr. Jake scooped up a handful of brittle and settled on the bed. "I like that flute music."

"Paul Horn and Carlos Nakai exploring Canyon de Chelly." Gilbert sat on the bed a short distance apart from the priest. "Now, what does both the law and the church want to talk about? The facts are plain that I killed a woman and I've admitted I did. Two witnesses will confirm that, right, Reverend? You're one of them."

"Gil, you saved my life. Of course I'll testify on your behalf."

"Mister Begay…" Sonia took out her spiral notebook and a pen from the briefcase. "I presume the car with the Colorado plates was the one that an accomplice used after the bank robbery to get away from Belén. The Jemez police will check the VIN number and probably find it was stolen, but the driver is still on the loose. He…or she…may have left the area, or might have been away somewhere else when the incident happened."

"Sonia," Fr. Jake recalled, "I only saw one unmade bed in the cottage."

"And you don't think Breanna went in for a threesome?" She caught herself and flushed. "Oh, sorry, Father…."

He laughed again at a layperson's general reaction to mentioning illicit gender encounters. "That's right, priests aren't supposed to know anything about s-e-x."

"Guess I forgot about you hearing confessions."

"Sadly, fewer and fewer of them," Fr. Jake said.

Sonia turned back to Gilbert. "Sir, you didn't notice anything, either in the feed store or at the *caseta* that might suggest a third person. Someone who might be that driver?"

Gil swallowed a mouthful of chewed pistachio brittle. "Sorry, detective."

"Thank you." Sonia closed her notebook. "At the time you're arraigned, Father Jakubowski will be a witness, also David Allison. He may cop a plea with the D.A. or not be offered one, because that bank teller hostage was executed. I'll be asked to testify about the murder of Pastor Haskill and wounding of Deputy Griego, which happened in my county. Perhaps even about that bank robbery as part of the phony funeral caper, although Belén is in Valencia County."

Fr. Jake tried to reassure the Navajo ranch hand. "Gil, there's no way this possibly will go to trial. You'll be exonerated of any crime."

"Yeah, Reverend, thanks," he replied with little conviction.

"Look, Gil..." The priest reached over to touch his arm. "How about coming to my place for lunch? Would that be all right, Sonia?"

"Under the supervision of a man of the cloth? Why not?" she agreed. "Just bring Mister Begay back before curfew."

"Fine. And, Gil, I won't talk 'religion.' It's that your pantry is probably bare. Lunch won't be fancy, and I'll fix something simple, maybe *quesadillas*. How about it?"

Gilbert shrugged his neutral acceptance. "I guess so."

Sonia slipped the notebook back in her briefcase and stood up. "I do have to drive Father back to his rectory."

"Then let me get some duds on and I'll meet you outside."

While they waited for him, Fr. Jake mentioned to Sonia, "You were very sympathetic toward Gilbert."

"I wouldn't want to be in his shoes, Father, yet frankly, isn't a case like this always...or at least, hopefully...about justice rather than punishment?"

"It's supposed to be, but you read about miscarriages of justice every week."

Sonia was hopeful. "With luck, one less in that particular week of his arraignment, and yet there's still major prejudice against Indians. Native Americans."

"But the area where he...where the killing took place, is named after an ancient Navajo tribe."

"Gilbert isn't Towa...a Jemez native, Father."

The two glanced around at the stable and barn area of Don Fernando's ranch. Overhead, Cumulus 'fair weather' clouds already began to merge into massive, cauliflower-shaped groupings that brought afternoon monsoon rains. Although barely mid-morning, the fields had heated enough to give off a grassy, sweet aroma. Yellow cowpen daisies now carpeted large parts of the alfalfa pasture. The distant irrigation sluice, swollen by upstream rains, gurgled loudly in its various channels. Vando, Zo, and Matt were nowhere in sight.

Gilbert came down the bunkhouse steps wearing clean jeans, a cotton shirt under his denim jacket, a tan cowboy hat, and polished boots.

Fr. Jake chided him in jest, "Gil, you didn't have to dress up for me."

"Had to put on something, Reverend," he said with a slight smile.

The three bypassed the stabling area in walking toward Sonia's Plymouth. After driving down the ranch's drive and turning left on Romero Loop, she paused at the intersection with Highway 310, to let a generic gasoline tanker pull into the grocery store's pump island. In the front seat, Fr. Jake looked for traffic to his right, toward Excelensia Elementary School. A Socorro Sheriff's black and white SUV blocked access to the next street over, where a line of trucks and cars had parked. Emergency lights flashed on a fire department truck. At the head of the line, a KOB-TV4 television news truck had its mobile Camcorder pointed downward, toward whatever was happening in the adjacent field.

He nudged Sonia. "Something's going on in the area of the Civil War cemetery. I hope Cynthia and Jayson are all right."

"Hmm. Let's check that out." Sonia swung the car around, then turned left toward the blocked street entrance. She slowed enough to hold out her sheriff's department identification for a bored deputy at the entrance. He recognized her.

"Hey, detective 'Sunny.' Yer lookin' pretty cute today," the deputy quipped, his grin just short of a leer.

"That's good," she retorted, "'cause I sure feel pretty and cute. So do I get to see what's going on up there?"

"Be my guest..." The deputy mock-bowed and made a sweeping hand gesture for her car to pass.

Fr. Jake wondered, "Sonia, do you get dissed much like that?"

"Just from a patronizing A-hole or two, Father, but that's okay. I'll just wait until they need a great big legal favor from me."

The detective eased her car along the outside of the parked vehicles until she was abreast of the KOB-TV4 truck, and then braked to a stop. "Ma'am," she called out to a tall, blonde-haired female reporter writing in a notepad. "Ma'am, I'm a Socorro County detective. What's happening here?"

The woman held up her pad. "Some college guy found arrowheads and an Indian skeleton buried in an old Civil War fort's graveyard."

Fr. Jake asked, "Jayson Baumann?"

"Yes, that's his name, but he won't let us see the actual remains. It'll be on the Channel Four ten o'clock news."

Gilbert leaned forward from the back seat. "Detective, I'd like to see those arrowheads."

"So would I." Sonia turned off her car's engine. "Let's go take a look."

She opened the driver's side door and stepped out. Fr. Jake and Gil walked around the Plymouth to an area marked off by blue excavation tape. The entrance flap was closed on a tent Jayson had built over his dig. The anthropologist himself stood nearby with a KOB television cinematographer, where a shoulder Camcorder focused on a cardboard box holding five flint arrowheads.

Cynthia Plow, watching nearby, saw the priest, and called out to him, "Father Jake, over here!"

"Sonia, you know Cynthia," he reminded her. "She's the teacher who discovered those bodies of Buffalo Soldiers stationed at Fort Providence."

"Yes, I remember."

"Isn't this exciting?" Cynthia enthused. "Jayson says he probably discovered the body of a Native American Apache, who served as a Civil War Army scout."

Gil asked her, "Have you seen the remains?"

"No…"

Fr. Jake introduced him. "Cynthia, this is Gilbert Begay. He works at Don Fernando's ranch."

"Hello…" She shook his hand. "No, I haven't even seen Jayson's excavation. He put up that tent a few days ago to keep monsoon rains from flooding his dig."

The cameraman stopped filming and stepped away. Jayson looked up and noticed the priest. "Hey, Father J.," he called out and walked over with his box. "I hit pay dirt. Discovered some artifacts and one, maybe more, bodies of Civil War Indian scouts."

The priest introduced his companions. "Jayson, this is Detective Mora and Gilbert Begay."

"Hi." He tipped the box of arrowheads toward them and grinned. "Aren't these beauties?"

"Gilbert is Navajo," Fr. Jake told him. "May he take a closer look?"

Jayson hesitated a moment before agreeing. "Sure, I guess. Pick one up if you want."

While Gil examined a slender arrowhead, he remarked, "I heard you say you'd struck 'pay dirt.' Do you expect to sell these, Mister Baumann?"

"Well," he hedged, "you know, it…it's just a figure of speech."

"But you are familiar with the Native American Graves Protection and Repatriation Act?"

"Yeah, sure I know all about it. I'm a graduate assistant in my last year of the human skeletal biology M.A. program at NYU. That's New York University to you."

"NYU Graduate Assistant in Forensic Anthropology!" Gil whistled appreciation. "Impressive." He handed back the delicate pointed flint and looked up at Jayson for the first time. He was not smiling when he said, "Mister Baumann, you should recognize these as Woodland Indian Lowe Points. Narrow flaking and shoulders, flared stem. Hexagonal cross section. This one probably is Iroquois, and unlikely to be found in a late nineteenth century Southwestern grave site."

"Hey, man!" Jayson fumed as he snatched back the arrowhead. "You calling me a cheat? A…a liar?"

"No, sir, I'm not," Gil answered pleasantly. "I'm just implying that you're honestly mistaken. And as far as the Repatriation Act goes, this is BLM land, so you can't remove anything you find here without permission from—"

"You think I don't know that?" Jayson broke in, his face crimson under a suntan. "Listen, who-ever-you-are. I have an NYU and BLM permit, so you just go F-yourself."

Fr. Jake held up a hand to intervene. "Jayson, that's enough! Gilbert is only concerned about the possible desecration of an Indian burial site."

"That's correct. Mister Baumann, how long have you been excavating here?"

"He came on July first," Cynthia replied. "Isn't that right, Jayson?"

"Something like that," he muttered.

"Today is July thirteenth," Gilbert pointed out. "That was a mighty quick arrowhead find, and you're concealing a skeleton you say you found."

"I don't want it contaminated. What are you…" Jayson clenched his jaw and right fist, then took a step toward Gilbert. Fr. Jake stepped between the two again and whispered through his teeth, "Gentleman, that TV-4 cameraman is catching all this. You'll be lucky not to be on the evening news. Now shake hands, both of you, until there's been more time to work everything out."

"Sure…" Gilbert extended a hand, but Jason turned away with his box of flint points and ducked down to go inside the tent.

Cynthia remarked, "Jayson goes off track quite easily."

"Another fouled-up Indian-White Man treaty," Gil quipped.

Fr. Jake turned to Sonia. "Detective, you can go back to Socorro from here. I need to buy a couple of lunch items, so Gil will walk to the grocery with me, then over to my rectory. I'll drive him back to the ranch after we've eaten."

"As you wish, Father. I have to contact Don Fernando now and have him come down to Socorro for questioning on Monday. Sorry that everyone's Jemez vacation is being cut short."

"Yet this might clear up the circumstances of Isabel's death."

"Might, Father. I'll be in touch." Sonia turned to walk back to the Plymouth. "Nice seeing you, again, Cynthia."

The teacher raised her hand to wave goodbye. "Same here, detective."

Fr. Jake asked Gil, "Is that okay? I mean the walking part to the grocery? I didn't really ask you."

"Sure, Reverend. Let's go."

## 25 tracking la llorona

When the two men entered the grocery, Carlotta Ulibarri sat behind her counter on a high stool, reading the *Valencia County Herald.* "Hey"—She put the paper down and stood up—"I though you both went to the Jemez for some time out."

"We did," Fr. Jake told her, "but unfortunately had to return early."

"Guess that's none of my business. What can I do for you?"

"Thanks, Carlotta, I can find everything I need. I have cheese, so… tortillas, chips, salsa. Gil, lemonade is in the fridge. That okay?"

"Fine with me, Reverend."

After Carlotta rang up and bagged the priest's purchases, she recalled, "Father, remember I told you about folks reported seeing La Llorona at the *acequia?*"

"I do, yes. Why do you ask?"

"Well, she's still there, looking for her drowned kids, moaning and groaning and all. Comes from the north along the far side of the *acequia.*"

"I also remember that you told me not to meddle in what I didn't understand, and that these same folks reported that Millie Jaramillo is a witch."

"Maybe, but did you ever stake out the ditch like you said you might do?"

"I…I ever got around to it," the priest admitted. "No."

"Then, Father, maybe you oughta find out what's going on?"

He picked up his plastic bag. "Carlotta, does Llorona appear at any particular time?"

She rubbed her chin, thinking about his question. "Wait a minute, come to think…. I believe most ladies said it was on Sunday nights."

Fr. Jake promised, "I'll keep that in mind, Carlotta. God Bless."

"Bye," she said, and went back to reading her newspaper.

As the two men walked to the rectory, Gilbert asked, "Reverend, what's all that Llorona business about?"

"You know about the fetus that Vando discovered in the ranch's section of the irrigation sluice. Detective Mora questioned you about it."

"Right."

"Well, there's a Hispanic legend about a Weeping Woman who haunts sluices in search of her drowned children. Carlotta says that resident near the *acequia* have spotted moving lights, a hooded figure dressed in black, strange moaning noises, a sulfur smell and so on, but that's probably all nonsense."

"Interesting, though."

"Other cultures have such a myth," Fr. Jake said. "We Slavs have Rusalka, a kind of ghostly female spirit of a young girl, who was drowned in a lake by her lover and haunts it to seek revenge."

Gil recalled, "I've read that Aztecs had a legend about a weeping woman searching for her family. We Navajos have myths about mountain spirits, but I can't think of a similar drowning story."

At the rectory, Fr. Jake made *quesadillas* of cheddar cheese and *salsa* spread on a tortilla, then micro-waved them until the cheese melted. He served the food with corn chips and lemonade.

Before eating, Fr. Jake crossed himself, and bowed his head to softly recite, "Bless us, Lord, and these your gifts…."

"…Which we are about to receive from thy bounty," Gil continued.

Both men ended the prayer in unison. "Through Christ, Our Lord. Amen."

Fr. Jake picked up his fork. "So, Gil, you know the Catholic blessing for meals?"

"Yeah, I was baptized at Our Lady of Mercy in Chinle. In fact, the Franciscans usually gave us their own baptismal names."

"The priest was a Father Gilbert?"

Gil added to the probability, "With a German-sounding last name I forget."

"I don't know much about you. If it's not prying?"

"Reverend, you want to get to know your flock. Is that it?"

The priest shook his head as he laughed. "Relax, I'm not trying to re-convert you. What it is, Gil, is that everyone has a story."

"Okay." Gil leaned back, swallowed, and wiped his mouth with a napkin. "Mine began in Chinle, Arizona, thirty-eight years ago."

"Tell me about Chinle."

"It's on the Navajo Rez, just over the New Mexico line. The original word is Navajo and they told us in school it means something like 'Place where clean water comes out.' That probably refers to Canyon de Chelly. The town is on the canyon's western rim, just off Highway 191."

Fr. Jake leaned over to pour him more lemonade. "Go on, Gil."

"Sure I'm not boring you...Father.?"

'Not at all." *First time he hasn't called me 'Reverend'.*

"Funny thing," Gil continued, "is that Chinle is in Apache County, and our immediate Navajo ancestors were Apaches. At some point they split off from the others and called themselves *Diné*—'The People'.'"

"What about your own family?"

"My daddy died pretty young of tuberculosis. To help my mother and two smaller sisters, I dropped out of Chinle High School at seventeen and worked for our local burger joint. But I always liked horses and hung around stables whenever I could, even helped out at a vet's clinic."

"Gil, dropping out of school must have been a hard decision for all of you."

"Yeah. After about ten years, I gave mother most of the money I'd saved and headed for that forestry job in the Jemez. When that didn't work out, I tried my luck in Albuquerque. The State Fairgrounds had a racetrack and horses, but turned out that I didn't like the big city. Five years ago, I met Mister Trujillo at the track and he hired me to work here." Gil finished his lemonade held up the empty glass. "Pretty much 'End of story'."

"Thanks, Gil, but let's say 'End of story' for now. You're still a young man and know a great deal on the subject of Native Americans."

"Which makes me wonder about Jayson Baumann's finds." Gil put down the glass and pushed aside his plate. "Father, back to what Carlotta said about those reported nighttime sightings at Mister Trullijo's irrigation ditch."

"All right. What about them?"

"Those folks must have seen something."

"Gil, why would someone impersonate Llorona, a weeping lady out looking for her drowned children?"

"Guess you'd best ask them." He paused a moment before venturing, "Did you really tell Carlotta you'd stake out the *acequia?*"

"I guess so, but I was just talking big."

"Father, why don't we do that? She said the figure shows up mostly on Sundays and goes north to south. I'd wait some place down past Romero Loop, in case she showed up."

"Come to think of it, there's a *morada*, an unoccupied chapel, in the woods that's south of the Loop's first turn north."

"Good place to hide a costume and scurry back home?"

"Hey..." Fr. Jake reached over to shake Gil's hand. "You may be on to something. Since you'll be here, let's take a chance on Sunday night. That's July eighteenth and the *morada* is close enough so that you can walk back to the bunkhouse."

"Meet you at the Romero Loop turn around nine," he agreed. "It should still be light enough to find that chapel." Gil stood up to leave and tugged on his cowboy hat. "Thanks for lunch, Father."

"My pleasure, Gilbert. I'll call Sunday afternoon to remind you. Now let me drive you back to your 'house arrest'."

# 26 jayson's folly

Cynthia Plow's six-week summer school classes would end on Friday, July 16th. As she predicted to Fr. Jake, the New Mexico Office of Archaeological Studies had closed her excavation site until professionals in the field could continue attempting to locate any remains of Civil War-era Buffalo Soldiers that yet might be uncovered.

After class on Thursday, the elementary school teacher sighed as she slowly drove her Hyundai Tucson past her excavation trenches—now protected from rainy weather and the public by a tent with "No Trespassing" signs planted outside. Further on, Cynthia pulled her SUV over the curb and onto weedy grass just beyond Jayson Baumann's dig. The NYU grad assistant had built a smaller tent over his own recent excavation. "He's not outside," she mouthed to herself, "but I'd like to talk more with Jayson about those discoveries that he called a press conference to publicize."

Cynthia slid off the car seat and walked back to an area marked off with the blue excavation tape he had "borrowed" from her. "Jayson," she called out, "are you inside the tent?"

"Just a minute," came a gruff response. In a few moments he came out— unshaven, wearing dirt-stained jeans, an NYU T-shirt, and a now-battered Indiana Jones fedora. "Whataya want, Cyndi?"

"Nice, friendly question, Jayson," she chided. "You look perfectly awful!"

"I'm sleeping in the tent to guard the dig." He looked back toward the excavation, then back at her. "Cyndi, look, I'm really busy."

"Did you find any new artifacts?"

"As a matter of fact, I did. That Apache Indian scout was buried with objects he valued, like those arrowheads  I found them by brushing dirt away from the skeleton."

"May I see?"

Jason hesitated, then gave her a half-nod. "Not the remains, but wait here a minute." He went back through the tent flap and returned this time holding a wooden box. "I found these around the body." As he slid off the cover, he warned, "Don't touch."

"I know better, Jayson." Cynthia pointed at mud-crusted artifacts. "Are those eagle feathers? That's a brass Seventh Cavalry forage cap insignia. More scraps of blue uniform…a calico shirt." Her eyes narrowed in suspicion as she looked up at him. "Jayson, did you keep some of the Buffalo Soldier items we found last year at Fort Craig?"

"What the hell are you implying?" His question bore menace in its tone.

"Gilbert Begay said the arrowheads you claim to have found here were Woodland points."

"The guy's Navajo, so what would he know about Apache arrows? Most of the Army scouts were from that tribe." Jayson slid the top back to close the box. "Okay, Cyndi, you had your look, and I told you I was busy."

Unwilling to pursue her speculation at this time, she said,. "Okay, I'll leave you to it."

Jayson softened his tone, "How about that dinner in Belén I promised you?"

"You didn't promise me anything, Jayson, and I certainly didn't agree to anything."

"Girl, you might wish you had," he smirked, then turned away to stoop down and push aside his tent flap,

Suspicious and upset, Cynthia decided to talk to Fr. Jake. She found the priest in his church, arranging cowpen daisy blossoms around the San Isidro *bulto*.

"Cynthia…. Nice surprise!" he exclaimed, after he saw her enter. "So you're through with summer school?"

"Not until tomorrow. Father,I think Jayson Baumann is faking his discovery of those remains of what he claims is an Apache Army scout."

The priest reacted with skepticism. "Surely, Cynthia, he's not that stupid."

"I worked my site for months before finding anything," she contended. "He comes here and discovers artifacts and he says a skeleton in...well... in literally several days."

"Have you seen anything besides those arrowheads he showed us?"

"I just came from there. What he had in a box could have been stolen at Fort Craig...or...if those *are* Lowe points, from a New York University collection. As a grad assistant, he certainly had access to whatever they have stored in boxes that are cataloged, shelved, and rarely opened."

Fr. Jake still hoped to give the young man the benefit of a doubt. "What would be his purpose? I mean, it would be a serious set back to his career if he's discovered to have 'salted' an excavation. Isn't that a term used for planting false artifacts in a dig?"

"Correct, Father, but you know better than anyone that hubris can cause people to do strange things."

"I suppose that authenticating a find does take a lot of time."

"It does, Father, and meanwhile Jayson would be acclaimed for his discoveries."

"Risky business."

"True, but he might chance it. Oh, on another subject, Father, yesterday was Bastille Day. You know, the French Revolution and all."

"Yes."

"It's the last day of summer school, so when classes start again in August, I'm having the children bring in a food from around the world. Well, not every country. A boy and girl team will pick names out of a bowl, but could you come then and bring something Polish?"

"Ah...like *pierogi?*"

"Sure, and talk to the class a bit about what it was like for you in Poland."

Fr. Jake felt pleased at her interest. "I'd be happy to do that, Cynthia."

"I'll remind you at the Sunday Mass before school opens."

"It sounds like a fun learning project."

O

On Friday, Fr. Jake's phone rang. It was Gil saying that a friend of his who was with an Indian Graves Repatriation bureau was in town. Could they come over Saturday and visit Jayson Baumann's excavation with him present? The priest agreed on 10 o'clock in the morning.

O

A few minutes before ten on Saturday, a black, four-door 2010 Ford Focus pulled up in Fr. Jake's driveway. When he answered knocks on the door, Gil stood outside with a tall Native American companion, who carried a briefcase. The ranch hand was in his work jeans, but the man wore a tan summer suit. His white shirt displayed a modest silver and turquoise bolo at the throat. Similar Native American jewelry decorated his wristwatch strap. It was somewhat unusual that he wore his black hair neatly braided to fall on each side of his head.

Gil introduced him, "Father Jake, this is Jim Eagle Feather. He's with the Indian Graves Repatriation Bureau in Santa Fe."

"*Hootah niyá...*" Eagle Feather smiled as he tipped a doeskin-color cowboy hat. "Pleased, Reverend."

The priest reciprocated his smile. "My pleasure. Come in, come in."

After the men stepped in to his living room, he indicated the couch. "Gentlemen, may I get you coffee?"

"We're good," they refused, pretty much in unison, as if forewarned, then laughed along with Fr. Jake.

"Yes, I've been told that I am little pushy about that. Now, does one or both of you need my help with something?"

"Sort of, "Gil replied. "Jim wants to talk with Jayson Baumann about his discovery in that excavation, and since you're his landlord—"

"The parish is, actually."

"Okay. Jim, why don't you explain your visit?"

"Gladly..." Eagle Feather took off his sunglasses and hat, then smoothed his braids with a hand. "Reverend, as a field agent of the Bureau, it's my job to investigate any claims about finding alleged Native American grave sites. Since Baumann is Catholic, Gil here thought having his pastor with him at an interview might relax the young man."

Fr. Jake felt mild surprise. "You're interviewing Jayson? Will that be in Santa Fe?"

"Reverend, perhaps I misspoke. I'd just like to go over to Mister Baumann's excavation and have an IGRB procedural talk with the man."

"IGRB?" the priest asked.

"Sorry for the professional lingo. 'Indian Graves Registration Bureau'."

"Sure, if it would help, I'd be happy to accompany you. In fact, I'd like to know more about Jayson's find myself. Cynthia Plow told me he's sleeping at the site."

"Commendable, and probably to prevent looting." Eagle Feather stood up and replaced his hat. "Reverend, is this a convenient time?"

"Good as any, if y'all don't want cawffee," Fr. Jake drawled.

The men chuckled again. "Let's drive over," the agent said.

At the excavation site, Jayson was squatted a short distance from his dig, reading assembly directions for erecting a wigwam from a mail order kit. He had put up a tripod of three poles; six others and the structure's cone-shaped canvas cover lay on the ground next to him. The grad student scrambled up, feeling apprehensive at noticing a car pull up at the curb and seeing three men get out. He was relieved to recognize Fr. Jake and Gil. "Father, what's going on?" he asked the priest.

"Jayson, you've met Gilbert Begay. This is Mister Eagle Feather from a bureau of graves repatriation."

Gil ignored Jayson, but Eagle Feather stepped forward to briefly flash an ID wallet with an attached gold badge, and extend a hand. "Mister Baumann."

"Sorry, my hand's dirty. Wh…what's this all about?"

"Sir," Eagle Feather explained, "I'm excited that you've uncovered the possible grave of one of our Apache Army scouts."

Suspicious now, Jayson turned defensive. "Yeah, and what about it? How did you even find out?"

Gil reminded him, "You called a press conference that was shown on our local television news. Remember, you said you found Apache points—"

Eagle Feather intervened. "Sir, could we talk about your excavation?"

Jayson glanced around. "I…I don't have anything for us to sit on."

"The curb over here will do nicely," the agent suggested. Fr. Jake wondered why he hadn't chosen his car seats, but gamely joined the three men on the uncomfortable cement street border. "Mister Baumann," Eagle Feather began, "I'm particularly interested in your discovery because I'm Jicarilla Apache. Many warriors of the *Tinneh*…'My people', if you'll indulge me…enlisted or were hired by the Department of the Army as scouts. The Army Reorganization Act of 1866 authorized President Johnson to employ a force of Indians in the Territories. In fact, when I leave here, I'm going on to Fort Wingate, outside of Gallup, to research who might have been assigned right here at Fort Providence." He clicked open his briefcase and held up an envelope to show Jayson. "You must be familiar with Photo Number 87797 of the U. S. National Archives?"

"N…no."

"I see…" Eagle Feather eased a glossy 11 x 14 print from the folder and handed it to him. "The photo shows twelve Apache Scouts at Fort Wingate. It's in black and white, but notice the dark jackets on nine of the men. Presumably, blue Union Army issue, combined with white trousers and knee-length boots. Regulation uniforms, yet their head coverings are different. Some men wear more or less regulation Army hats, but others sport the headbands peculiar to our males at that time." After a pause to let Jayson study the picture, the agent asked, "Sir, have you found remnants of any of this clothing?"

"I…I have some…some blue cloth," Jayson stuttered, "and a Seventh Cavalry insignia. Actually, I…I'm still uncovering what's around the skeleton."

"Excellent! I ask because it's generally unknown to the public that names exist of Indian Scout enlistments. These are in records of the Adjutant General's Office. Entry 93 of an Index to Enlistment Papers, Indian Scouts, 1866-1914."

Gil added, "And, Jim, you're hopeful that Jayson's find might be identified."

"Precisely." He took back the picture, replaced in its folder, then handed it to Jayson. "If you wish, Mister Baumann, you may keep the photograph."

"Thanks, Mister…Mister Eagle Feather."

The agent smiled acknowledgement as he took out a three-ring binder. "Jayson. May I call you Jayson?"

"Sure."

"Jayson, there is another formality. As an NYU Anthropology grad assistant, you're certainly familiar with NAGPRA, Public Law 101-601, 16 November 1990. That would be the Native American Graves Protection and Repatriation Act."

"Sure, I know about it." Jayson's tone again bordered on suspicious belligerence.

"Sir, I'm required by law to read some of the pertinent statutes…." Eagle Feather grinned innocently at the grad student. "You know, kind of like the Miranda Law, although you certainly aren't being charged with anything." Jayson shifted position; sitting had become painful on his coccyx, and he did not respond. The agent continued, "Since you're familiar with the law I'll just skim the highlights. Let's, see…. Ah…. 'Ownership'." He read, "'Intentional Excavation and Removal of Native American Human Remains and Objects. Under paragraph (d). Notify in Writing the Secretary of the Department…having primary management authority." He looked back at Jayson. "That would be the Bureau of Land Management. Sir, have you notified BLM as instructed?"

"N…not yet."

"I see. Hmmm… 'Illegal Trafficking in Native American Human Remains and Cultural Items'—"

Jayson interrupted, "Mister Eagle Feather, can I show you what artifacts I have found? So far, mostly arrowheads, blue wool cloth, scraps of a shirt, and maybe a cloth headband."

"Clothing?" The agent pulled away from him, glanced around, and affected a low voice. "Jayson, do you know how the victim died? Are there any visible bullet wounds in the head, torso, et cetera?"

"No. I…I haven't excavated very far down."

"Sir, many soldiers of that era succumbed to various diseases, smallpox being the primary killer and possibly present in your finds. I'll have to contact the bureau's forensic anthropologist to come out in a few days and test your site. Meanwhile"—He slipped an orange sign from the briefcase and handed it to Jayson—"Meanwhile, I must quarantine your excavation and strongly advise you not to continue."

Eagle Feather returned his NAGPRA notebook to the briefcase and stood. Gil extended a hand to help Fr. Jake up. Stunned, Jayson remained seated, staring at the quarantine sign.

"Well, I'd best be on the road. *Nahodootiil*, Jayson," Eagle Feather said, then looked toward the field where parts of the wigwam lay. "Hey, just ask Gilbert here, if you need help with putting up that *tipi*."

After the three men were in the car, Gil shoved Eagle Feather's shoulder. "Jim, for 'good bye' you said in Navajo, 'It looks like it's going to rain'." You don't know Apache do you?"

"Whattya mean?" Jim demanded, feigning indignation. *Dal'é…nakki… tai'… díí'… Áąshdlai*. I could probably count up to ten if I wanted." He glanced at his watch, started the engine, and eased the Ford slowly toward San Isidro. "I'll drive Father Jake to the church, but I've got to get back to the studio in Santa Fe."

"Okay, Jim, thanks," Gil said. "I'll walk back to the ranch, or Father Jake can drive me."

Puzzled, the priest asked, "Gil, I'll gladly take you back to your place, but Jim, didn't you say you were going on to Fort Wingate?"

Both men shared a quiet laugh before Gil admitted, "Father, James Joseph Eagle Feather is an actor in a film being shot in Santa Fe. Again, Jim, who is it you're playing?"

Eagle Feather affected a serious pose. "I'm a savvy 'Redskin' lawyer fighting an oil company trying to scam mineral rights on pueblo land."

Gil said, "I'm pretty sure that now Jayson Baumann will pack up his bones and leave."

"He claims to have a skeleton," Fr. Jake told him. "Where would he have gotten that?"

Jim replied, "Our prop department can order a bag of plastic human bones in the Internet for a few dollars, but you can buy the real thing on the Asian black market."

"Jayson wanted immediate publicity, maybe to impress his father or professors," Gil speculated. "The media wouldn't recognize a Lowe point from a grouting trowel."

"Gilbert, the arrowheads were a dead giveaway to you," Jim said.

"Probably bought in a New York pawnshop."

The New Mexican actor stopped his car in front of San Isidro church and let the two men out. As they stood watching him pull away, James Joseph Eagle Feather winked and raised one hand in a solemn mock-Tonto salute. *'Tay'ee kimo sabe'.*"

# 27 la llorona lujan

On Sunday afternoon, July 19, Fr. Jake called to remind Gilbert Begay of their plan to confront the Weeping Woman at nine o'clock that evening, if she should appear along the *bosque*. The Navajo ranch hand had not forgotten.

O

That night a pale quarter moon rose shortly before midnight. After using a flashlight to help tramp their way through entangling *bosque* underbrush to the *penitente* chapel, the two men had waited patiently outside the *morada*, annoyed and harassed by flying moths, their ears deadened to the unending chirps of night insects. Their eventual reward was to hear a wailing noise in the distance, the sound that Carlotta had said neighbors described. Now, stiff from sitting on stumps since 9:30, when darkness set in, they stood up and noticed a light bobbing toward them among the Cottonwood and Mexican Elder trees.

Barely containing his excitement, Fr. Jake whispered, "Someone's coming, Gil. Let's hurry inside."

"That's a bright L.E.D. pocket flashlight," he mouthed back.

The inside of the small room retained a lingering smell of sulfur. Gil shined his light on a sandstone altar at the far end of the chapel.

Fr. Jake whispered, "We could hide behind that."

Gil murmured a reply, "There *was* someone impersonating Llorona, after all."

"Carlotta said a lot of residents think it's Millie Jaramillo out frightening people."

"Wouldn't be surprised, but why?"

"Shhhh."

A figure paused in the doorway—a dark silhouette hardly revealed by the faint moonlight behind. Dressed in a black gown and dark hooded cloak that covered the head and face, a human form shined a bright, wide-ranging light around the interior, as if searching for intruders. Satisfied after a moment that nothing had been disturbed, the shrouded figure entered the sacred chapel. The near-apparition placed the flashlight it carried on the rough wood of a full-sized Good Friday cross, laid across two saw horses, shook out of the costume it wore, then hopped up far enough to sit at the lower end of the cross.

Wearing only long-johns, Lorenzo Lujan wiped white makeup off his face with a sleeve, then pulled a hand-rolled cigarette from his underwear's breast pocket. After striking a kitchen match on the cross to light the paper end, he blew bluish smoke that swirled in the flashlight's white beam.

"What the?" Gilbert stormed from behind the altar to demand of his ranch companion, "Zo, you *idiota*, what in hell do you think you're doing?"

"*Mierda…*" Startled, Lorenzo dropped the cigarette, grabbed his flashlight like a pistol, and pointed it toward the voice. After he recognized the face of his fellow worker, he exclaimed, "*Cabrón*, what the fuck *you* doin' here?"

Fr. Jake came up to the men. "Lorenzo, are you the one who's been imitating La Lorona all this time?"

He slid off the cross. "Aw, shit, you here, too, *Padre?*"

"Why have you been frightening some of the local residents?" the priest asked him.

Lorenzo bent down to retrieve his cigarette. "Millie Jaramillo pays me. Today, she told me to make sure I do it like right now. Late tonight."

"Tonight?" Gil repeated. "Did she tell you why you should do it tonight?"

"*No, baboso*, I don't know why tonight. I jus' do it for the *dinero*, the cash."

"So," Fr. Jake asked, "Millie is back at the ranch?"

"*Si, Padre*, didn't you know?" The ranch hand re-lit his cigarette before continuing. "The Don, he came from Jemez on Friday. He went to Socorro yesterday 'cause that *detectiva* wants to talk with him on Monday."

"Did Dulci go to Socorro with him?"

"No, he told Millie she should take care of her while he's gone."

Fr. Jake felt his stomach protest an unhealthy arrangement. "Don Fernando's daughter was left alone with Millie?"

"Ain't no one else here, *Padre*."

"That could be a problem because of the quarrel Millie had with Fernando. Gil, we better get back to the house. Lorenzo, you bring that flashlight and walk ahead of us."

"Yeah, I been doin' this a lot, an' made a path outa here."

After he stamped the cigarette butt with a boot heel, Gil and Fr. Jake followed him outside. Guided by Lorenzo's wavering light beam, the men stumbled through thick *bosque* vegetation until they reached Romero Loop. Nearby, the *Acequia Madre*'s loud gurgle was unmistakable: now augmented by monsoon rains further north, the swift waterway overflowed its banks in places as it raced southward toward the Rio Grande. To avoid tramping diagonally across dew-wet fields and soaking his boots, Lorenzo followed the stream's edge, toward the gravel walkway that led up to Rancho Tru-Cor's main house. Just before the turnoff, he stopped and motioned back with one hand, a signal for his two companions to listen.

A woman's sobs sounded from the direction of the sluice, louder than the current's flow.

Lorenzo turned his flashlight toward the outline of a kneeling figure, faintly visible in the moonlight. "¡*Madre de Dios!*" he gasped, when the beam illuminated the frail body of Dulcinea Trujillo, who knelt on the ground a few feet away. "¡*Esta la hija de Don Fernando!*"

Sobbing, wearing only a soaked nightdress, the starveling girl looked toward the voice, then slumped forward onto the dew-drenched grass.

## 28 dulci' s story

Fr. Jake ran forward to ease the girl's head and shoulders upright. "Dulci, why are you outside in a night dress? What…what happened here?"

Shivering, the girl looked up at him, and pointed toward the *acequia*. "Millie. Millie Jaramillo."

"Millie?" Puzzled, the priest motioned to Lorenzo. "Check the sluice. Try to see what Dulci is talking about."

At the waterway's edge, Lorenzo searched the swollen shoreline with his flashlight, turned the beam on the opposite bank, and finally ran the light along the middle of the fast-moving current that streamed past. A short way down, he illuminated the red iron sluice gate. "Somethin' ain't right…" he mumbled and walked to the wheel mechanism that controlled the water flow. *Dios*!" he exclaimed, making an instinctive sign of the cross and pointing at the water. "*Esta la cuerpa de la bruja!*"

The unmistakable back side of Millie Jaramillo's long colorful skirt undulated with the sluice's muddy current. The head and upper body were underwater, but long strands of black hair waved atop the stream.

"Millie drowned? That's what Dulci tried to tell us," Fr. Jake said.

Gilbert Begay saw the figure, eased himself down the muddy bank, and waded waist-high into the sluice's current. He ducked under and held his breath while reaching around to feel an area where the woman's head and shoulders should be. After tugging at the body a moment, he stood upright, coughing water. Gil looked back at the two men. "Jesus Christ! Millie's head is caught tight in the round opening of the sluice gate! Sh…she did drown."

As Dulci lay supported by Fr. Jake, severe convulsions that shook her body alarmed him. "We've got to get this girl to the house and call 911. Can you walk there, Dulcinea?"

She nodded feebly. "I...think...so."

Gil struggled out of the *acequia* with his clothes and boots soaked, wringing water from his hair He gasped as he shook his head. "Nothing we can do for the *curandera* woman now except find out how this happened." He came over to the priest. "Here, Father, I'll get Miss Dulci up and we'll both help her get to the ranch house."

At the end of the entrance hall, lights were turned on in the kitchen. "Let's take the girl in there," Gil said. "There's a phone at the far end. Zo, you call 911."

"Dulci," Fr. Jake asked the shivering girl, "where is your bedroom?"

"It's past my father's study, but...but I'd like to sit here at the table." She shuddered again and clasped her upper body with crossed arms. "Maybe bring me a blanket. I'm so ...so cold."

"I'll get one," the priest said.

Zo completed his phone call and came back. "It's late Sunday night, so I hada leave a message. Them paramedic guys may hafta come all the way from Belén."

Gil said, "If they didn't contact the sheriff's office, they can tell us about getting them here."

Fr. Jake brought back a blanket from Dulci's bedroom and wrapped it around the girl's shoulders. She refused anything hot to drink, yet, now inside her house, swathed in the warm covering, Dulci gradually stopped shivering and became calmer. The priest sat across from her at the table to gently ask, "Can you tell us what went on down there?"

Dulci sniffled and reached for a paper napkin to wipe her nose. "My... my father told me he had to go to Socorro on business tomorrow and that Mille would stay with me overnight. I knew they had a fight, so I thought that was weird, but he said he didn't want me left here alone." She looked over at Gilbert. "You were here when they fought."

"True, Miss Dulci, but I didn't hear much of what it was about."

"Despite that," Fr. Jake continued, "how did Miss Jaramillo treat you?"

"She was nice, made rice and beans for supper. I was nervous because my father was away, and didn't eat a lot. Millie noticed and made an herb tea of some kind for me. Then she brought a piece of paper and said she had *curandera* magic, so that I wouldn't be so upset."

"Magic?" Fr. Jake glanced over at Gilbert. "What did she do?"

"Millie told me to fight the *mal ojo* by writing on the paper about how I loved my father and missed him, and that I hoped he would come home safely on Tuesday. Then she put the rolled-up paper in a jelly jar, mumbled something in Mexican over it, and said we'd go down to throw it in the *acequia*. It would float to the Rio Grande and past Socorro, where he was staying. She said her magic words would keep him safe, but we had to do this after dark, just when the moon appeared in the sky."

Gil scoffed, "Miss, that's all just nonsense."

"I thought so too, but didn't want to make her mad. Oh, and Millie kept having me drink more of that tea…" Dulci pointed to the sink board. "Look, there's my cup."

Fr. Jake got up and brought a gilt china tea cup over to the table. About a quarter inch of amber-colored liquid, flecked with dark leaf specks, remained at the bottom. "Gil, find some plastic wrap to put over this and we'll show the police."

Dulci volunteered, "It's in that drawer below the blender."

The priest sat to continue his questioning. "So you and Millie went outside just after the moon appeared?"

"Yes, but…but…I remember that I felt sleepy and kind of dizzy. My mind was spinning— I…I don't want to talk about the rest."

"Dulci," Fr. Jake gently insisted, "it's best if you remember now. The police may ask you the same questions."

"All right…I guess." The bulimic girl looked down and traced a geometric pattern on her blanket with a finger. "When…when we got to the *acequia*, Millie wasn't friendly any more. She grabbed my arm and said my father made her pregnant. He ordered her to abort the baby with medicines and throw it in the water. Millie did that like a ritual, but realized it was an evil thing, and said now she was going to get even with my father by drowning me, just like her *niño* died. She said Llorona was watching and I…did hear her wailing across the water." Dulci reached for the priest's hand. "I really did, Father Jake."

He squeezed her hand to reassure the girl. "Dulcinea, that was Lorenzo you heard on the other side of the sluice. What happened next?"

"I…I remember I felt sick. Millie pulled me toward the water and I tried to fight her off. We fought on wet grass. It was slippery and…and she tripped on her long skirt and fell backward into the water. I fell, too, but she was in front of me."

Gil noted, "That dress Millie wore and her jewelry were heavy."

"That would have dragged her down," Fr. Jake realized. "Then what, Dulci?"

"Millie started to drift down toward the sluice gate and...and sink. I managed to crawl back up the bank where...I...I guess I fainted. When you found me, I had just come to and thought about what happened—" The girl began to weep as an emotional recollection convulsed her body.

Fr. Jake released her hand. "Dulci, that's enough for tonight. Get into bed until the emergency crew arrives. They'll take you to a hospital for tests to make sure you're all right."

"Father," she pleaded, while standing up, "will you wait until they get here?"

"Of course, Dulci. And I'll call your father at Detective Mora's in the morning."

"Thank you. It's so late now and he'd be worried."

The priest pushed his chair back and stood. "I'll tell your father that, on his way back from Socorro, he should stop at the hospital and bring you here. We're just glad you're safe."

The girl managed a wan smile. "Thank you both."

"Try to sleep, Miss Dulci," Gil said. "The paramedics won't get here for awhile." After she left the room, he checked the cupboard shelves for a can of coffee. "I'd like to brew some java that will keep us awake until the emergency crew is here."

"That's good," Fr. Jake joined in. "I don't think I could sleep, thinking of that poor woman trapped underwater."

Lorenzo yawned. "I'm beat an' ain't waitin' for coffee. Goin' to the bunkhouse."

Gil warned him, "*Atún*, you better have your story straight about Llorona when the cops question you."

"*Anda a bañarte.* "Take a hike, Navajo guy," he joked in the amiable way the two men teased each other.

"Thinking back on what Dulci told us," Fr. Jake said, "it seems that Millie drugged the girl to make her go down to the sluice with her. That's odd, yet it had to be something like that."

"Millie was a *curandera*, so she would know how." Gil picked the tea cup off the table. "Lucky we have a sample of what Dulci drank, and there's a strainer by the sink with leaves inside the mesh." He lifted the plastic film covering the cup and sniffed the liquid. "Chamonile or passionflower, definitely mixed with valerian root. Peppermint to make it drinkable." He tipped the cup toward the priest. "Smell, Father."

"Peppermint all right, and something not as nice."

"That's the valerian. Could be as much as fifteen hundred milligrams of that, which would make a highly potent sedative."

"And the girl did claim to have passed out." Fr. Jake thought a moment before speculating, "Gil, what you said makes me think Dulcinea's explanation was a little too pat, a bit contrived."

"What?" Surprised, he looked up at the priest, "Why would you think that?"

"I hear confessions."

"And?"

"You'd be astonished at how many 'The-devil-made-me-do-it' rationalizations I hear, some even for what aren't actual sins. That was quite a story our Dulci told us."

Gil thought about what the priest suggested. "I guess the girl wouldn't *have* to have drunk that tea."

"No, she could have poured it down the sink when Millie wasn't looking and left that sample for anyone to find."

"Another funny thing," Gil remembered. "I've always heard Dulci call Mister Trujillo '*Papá*'. Tonight she always said, 'my father'." Gilbert Begay's hand trembled slightly as put the tea cup down. "Father Jake, I…I find it hard to accept what all that could mean."

"That Miss Dulci might not have told us the whole truth?"

"Right, but…but what would make her do that?"

"Or *who*, Gil?" the priest wondered aloud. "Also, why she…or they… would concoct such a tale, and that's to say nothing of wanting Millie dead."

## 29 the corpse in the sluice

As Fr. Jake had promised Dulcinea, he waited for the emergency personnel to arrive and take her to Belén's Presbyterian Hospital for observation. He had not seen the girl again before she was driven off in a Fire & Rescue ambulance. Gilbert Begay had brewed the coffee, then returned to his room in the bunkhouse shortly after.

It was near three-thirty in the morning, when the priest went to retrieve his parked Honda Civic from Romero Loop. The high desert night air felt chilly. Overhead, a vast expanse of July stars shimmered as distant mini-jewels of varying size and brilliance. The Milky Way's broad, luminescent sweep was pierced by the occasional brief slash of a plunging meteorite. In Michigan, the priest had always regretted not taking a course in astronomy at the nearby Cranbrook Natural Science Museum, which was not far from his Lake Sirius parish. *In Michigan at this time of year nights are much warmer and more humid than here. Even constellations there don't seem as bright. In many ways, New Mexico does have a kind of unique enchantment, although I haven't yet had much chance to see and enjoy it.*

Once Fr. Jake returned to the rectory, sleep would not come. Lying awake, his mind over-stimulated by the horrific events of that night, and still mentally living his narrow escape from death in the Jemez, less than a week earlier, he finally glanced over to see his bedside digital clock blink 4: 53. *No point lying here like a store dummy.*

He swung out of bed, put a sweater over his shoulders, brewed coffee, then sat in his pajamas for an early look at the day's reading in his breviary. Although the Farmer's Almanac listed sunrise on July 19 at precisely

6:00 A.M., a pale, yellow-rose flush of pre-dawn already silhouetted the mountainous eastern horizon outside his kitchen window.

"The First Reading is from the prophecy of Micah," he murmured aloud. Hearing his voice… any voice…was a simple way to counter the loneliness inherent in a celibate priesthood. "Micah," he repeated after a sip of coffee. "Not my favorite Old Testament guy…fiery, reproachful, vindictive. In the prophet's thinking, honey isn't better than vinegar for catching flies or followers. His passage shows the Lord as plaintiff against an uncaring Israel. Micah asks what offerings it would take to make the people acceptable in God's sight—even the sacrifice of a child?"

The verse made him recall Dulci's story of how her father had ordered Millie to abort their unborn child, who was a direct result of fornication. Uneasy and chilled, he re-read Micah in a whisper. "'Must I give my first-born for what I have done wrong, the fruit of my body for sin?' Millie's vicious revenge on Fernando for spurning her was to drown Dulcinea, his first-born daughter. *The verse is for today, and we've had the accidental death of Millie, while she attempted to drown Dulci. Can that be more than a prophetic coincidence?*

Stunned at the parallel circumstances of the reading, Fr. Jake closed his breviary without continuing on to the gospel. He glanced at his watch. *Almost six o'clock.* He laid the missal aside and went to his *altarcito*, the flower-decorated "little altar" that *curandera* Ofilia Herrera had shown him how to build for his cottonwood San Isidro statue. The priest struck a match and lighted a candle at the saint's feet. "Isidore, I see that your field daisies are a bit withered, so I'll pick fresh ones later this morning. You… you were a big help to me awhile ago. Can I count on you again to clarify what Dulcinea Trujillo told us about the…the body in the sluice? Indicate in your own way whether it was true or not?"

In considering the attention that Catholics gave to statues, Fr. Jake always remembered that too many outsiders believed that the faithful prayed to the images. They did not, and if skeptics looked up "Saints" in the *Catechism of the Catholic Church*, they would find them explained under "Holiness," subcategory, "—Activity in the Church." The saints' stated purpose was to help the faithful know the Holy Spirit: "In the witness of saints through whom he manifests his holiness and continues the work of salvation." Admittedly, that concept was a bit abstract for distraught petitioners, who felt that saints should better spend their time helping find lost articles or curing sickness, and even assist in finding a job. Ironically, many of these same skeptics never left a home in the morning without reading their horoscopes in the newspaper, or pocketing whatever objects they considered to be their good luck charm.

As the priest went back in the kitchen for his second mug of coffee, a brilliant sun broke the horizon and suffused a pinkish glow into the room. Colored dots of light danced around the walls, reflected from the faceted crystal prism that Cynthia had given him to hang in his window. The bright diversion and hot coffee made him feel a little less uneasy on that early Monday morning.

O

Shortly after nine o'clock, Fr. Jake rang up Sonia Mora on her cell phone.

"Detective Mora, Socorro Sheriff Department."

"Sonia it's Father Jake."

"Good, I was about to call. The hospital notified me about what happened last night. Are...are *you* all right?"

"I'm fine. It's Dulcinea Trujillo I'm concerned about."

"She's had a physical exam and toxicology screening tests taken. Nothing too serious, beyond some dehydration and, of course, considerable mental trauma. The nurse gave her a mild sleep aid."

"Does Dulci's father know about what happened?"

"Yes, and I've finished interviewing him. Don Fernando is here right now being processed to go home. He said he'll stop by Belén Presbyterian to pick up his daughter. The hospital will give him that toxicology screening to bring to me when I get to the ranch."

"Did the Don admit to what Vando told us?"

"Can't tell you over the phone, Father, but what he did say will blow your mind! The medical examiner will still be at the drowning site and I'd like to talk with him. And, oh, I'm bringing Deputy Griego along. He still has a couple weeks medical leave, but the guy's 'chompin' at the bit,' as they say."

"It will be good to see him, Sonia."

"Be there around ten thirty," she estimated.

"God Bless."

O

The detective and deputy arrived at the rectory close to the time that Sonia had planned. She wore the olive, military-style pants suit she had on a previous visit. Hilario Griego, who looked thinner, had not put on his deputy's uniform, but wore chino slacks and a bright Ginger Blossom-design Hawaiian shirt. His right arm was sheathed in a blue canvas sling. Fr. Jake asked him about it.

Griego explained, "Docs, they don't want me movin' this arm too much."

"Understandable. Coffee, both of you? Fresh pot?"

"Thanks, Father, but we're good," Sonia refused, but smiled at his predicable offer.

"I need to stand after last night," he said, "but you sit on the couch. Sonia, I'm anxious to hear what Fernando said that would blow my mental state. Hope that's only a figure of speech…. No, I shouldn't jest, my mind is discombobulated enough as it is, just thinking of all that's happened lately."

The deputy interjected, "Speakin' of that, Father Jake, I heard you had a close shave in the Jemez."

Sonia frowned as she sat down. "Griego, I don't think Father wants to be reminded of that so soon."

"No, it's all right, detective," the priest said. "Yes, Hilario, with that gun at my neck, I recall praying, but Gilbert Begay showed up just in the nick of time."

Griego laughed at a possible joke. "Close shave…nick. That's real good, Father."

Sonia sighed and rolled her eyes. "Deputy, can we get back to why we came here?"

"Uh…sure, detective." He looked away and pretended to adjust his arm sling.

"Father, as I told Griego on the way over, it was a short interview. Fernando admitted that he knew his wife suffered from fibromyalgia. He said she had studied all about the condition and became terribly depressed. Her physical health rapidly deteriorated."

"All the symptoms of the condition. Go on."

"Well…then Fernando took a letter out of his briefcase and pushed it toward me."

"Maybe," Griego warned, "y' should sit down for this, Father."

"It's that 'mind-blowing'? All right."

After the priest settled in his armchair, Sonia continued, "Fernando told me Isabel wrote this letter to him, saying that she did not want become an invalid or live as a burden to him and their daughter. If it was God's will, she wished to die in a manner stated in the letter."

"Sonia, you don't mean being kicked to death by her favorite stallion?"

"Crazy, Father, totally far out, but exactly what she wrote. Fernando said he tried to talk her out of doing such a thing, but she was adamant."

"That's quite unbelievable, yet if true, it had to involve Cervando Benavides, just as we thought." At Sonia's nod of assent, the priest continued, "Then the foreman was being truthful when he told us about the hoof pick."

"If so, Father, that's where it gets legally sticky. Isabel wrote a kind of suicide note. Correction, an 'assisted suicide,' which is a Fourth Degree Felony in this state."

"Wouldn't the Don have an obligation to void her request and not be part of it?"

"Father, I can't vouch for his mental or emotional state at the time. Dulci did say that just before the accident her father left the trailer and went into the barn."

"Sonia, it's understandable that he didn't want to witness his wife's horrible death. Yet, he could have sent Eusebia and the child away."

"As distraught as he must have been, would he think clearly? A psychiatric exam at the time might have been helpful, but would be meaningless now."

Fr. Jake finished the last of his cold coffee, then put the mug down on the end table. "Sonia, do you believe the letter is genuine?"

"That, Father, is the sixty-four thousand dollar question."

"Yes, and we both heard Cervando confess complicity. What's the punishment for a Fourth Degree Felony?"

"After a judge sifts through all the evidence during a trial, it's really up to him or her. Sentences generally are between six and eighteen months in prison."

Griego asked, "This is a second vic found in the *acequia*, in what, about three weeks? Right?"

Sonia confirmed his question. "Baby Doe and now Millie Jaramillo."

Fr. Jake wondered, "Have you heard whether or not Fernando returned to Rancho Tru-Cor this morning?"

"I haven't, Father. Let's go find out, and besides I'm anxious to talk with the Medical Examiner at the scene."

When the three reached the ranch in Sonia's car, Don Fernando's white BMW was not in his driveway. She doubled back and parked nearer to the *acequia.* A white crime scene van was next to the medical examiner's car and a sheriff's department paramedic ambulance.

On seeing the van, Sonia whistled astonishment. "That's a Socorro Police mobile walk-in CSI lab. The Don must have considerable influence in the department."

"Detective, you saw how he was able to get Gil released in a few hours."

"True, Father, so why am I surprised?"

Yellow crime scene tape extended fifty feet on either side of a privacy screen set up around the body. Gilbert Begay and Lorenzo Lujan stood together, well away from where the dead woman had been retrieved. Fr. Jake signaled toward them with a hand wave. Gil nodded back. Lorenzo, his back turned, threw pebbles into the sluice.

As Sonia and Fr. Jake stepped behind the screen, a portly, white-haired man she didn't recognize looked up from a report book. "Hey, little lady," he warned, "you can't come in here. This is a crime scene, and Father, you're too late to help our vic."

"Detective Mora, Socorro Sheriff's Department," she told him. "I'm investigating the 'vic'. Are you a new M.E.?"

"Mora? Right, and I speak some Mexican, *Detectiva Mora.*"

"*Bueno* for you, *médico,*" she deadpanned.

The doctor's jowly face had bushy eyebrows, eyeglasses, and a grayish moustache that followed the droop of his mouth. He pushed back a well-worn brown fedora and closed his book. "I'm newly retired from the Chicago P.D. and now living in San Acacia with the missus. That's a place south of Socorro."

"I know where it is."

"'Course you do." The doctor stood up, but did not extend a hand. "McMurtry. The regular M.E. doc is on vacation, so I'm filling in part time."

Sonia said, "This is Father Jakubowski."

"Jacku-baw-ski," he mispronounced. "We had lots of Po-locks in Chicago."

Fr. Jake went along with a comment he often heard. "I know that it's a hotbed of us there. What a shame."

McMurtry grinned. "Aw, *Padre,* I'm just pulling your leg."

"Doctor McMurtry," Sonia asked in her professional tone, "what have you discovered?"

"Well *detectiva*, divers pulled the female vic's body out of the water a little over an hour ago, then left her to me. Crime lab guys back there are processing any evidence found on or around the scene." He glanced back at the priest. "Lucky it's too late for you, *Padre*. She isn't looking pretty at all."

"Doctor," Sonia continued, "Father Jakubowski was here last night with those two other witnesses standing over there."

"That so, *Padre?*"

"Yes, I arrived with Gilbert and Lorenzo a little after midnight. The victim… Millie Jaramillo…was in the water. Gil tried to pull her out, but gave up after a few tries."

McMurtry smoothed a hand over his mustache. "That's 'cause the vic's head was jammed in the sluice gate opening and the current kept her bobbing up and down. As you can imagine, slamming a face against steel don't do a complexion much good. In fact, those two ranch guys had trouble ID-ing the vic. They said those were sure enough Jaramillo's clothes and black hair, but her features were too battered to be positive."

"Understandable," Sonia added, "since the victim also was in the water about nine hours."

McMurtry looked surprised. "Who told you *that* C.& B. story, *detectiva?* It was more like a twenty, twenty-one hour soak."

"Are you sure? Father Jake said that Dulcinea Trujillo told him the victim accidentally fell into the *acequia* around midnight. That would make it no more than…than maybe ten hours max."

McMurtry's reply was belligerent at being contradicted. "That 'accidentally' part might be right, detective, but you doubting my word about the time of death?"

"Of course not…doctor."

"If so"—McMurtry smirked and reached over to lift the sheet away from the dead woman's head—"Wanna see the vic's face?"

Sonia called his bluff, "Sure, I'll take a look. Your job's almost done and mine is just beginning."

Taken aback by her unexpected response, McMurtry pulled aside the upper part of the sheet. A woman's battered, swollen face and bruised shoulders confirmed the M.E.'s appraisal. "'Course an autopsy will confirm if she was dead or alive when immersed. In Chicago, I covered lots of drownings that happened in Lake Mich. Pathological changes are tricky in such deaths, so we look for lake water and debris in the lungs—"

"Thank you, Doctor McMurtry," Sonia interrupted to end the session.

"You're welcome." He had started to tug the sheet back in place, when Fr. Jake stopped him. "Doctor, I'd like to say a short prayer over the deceased."

"Be my guest." McMurtry shrugged disinterest and stripped off his latex gloves to close his medical case. Fr. Jake bowed his head a moment, silently recited a prayer, crossed himself, and then got up. The M.E. pulled the sheet back down and stood. "Okay, I'm releasing the vic's body for autopsy." He smoothed his moustache again with a hand and touched his fedora's brim. "Guys, have a nice day."

After McMurtry was outside the screen, Sonia expressed her opinion—before Fr. Jake could ask. "Patronizing Son of a B."

"*Detectiva*, as a 'Po-lock' I've experienced that, too, yet in his long career perhaps the good doctor suffers from having seen one routine corpse too many?"

"Always lookin' on the bright side, eh, Father Jake? No, it's a generational thing. People around your age…" Sonia caught herself. "Sorry, I once said you were different. Let's go talk with Gilbert and Lorenzo, then wait for Fernando to come back with his daughter."

The two ranch hands stood motionless as Sonia and the priest approached.

"Gentlemen," she asked, "did the M.E. question you?"

Gil replied, "Mostly about identifying Millie."

"That was Millie's clothes, all right," Lorenzo confirmed. "But, Jeez, her face was all…." He held his stomach as his face scrunched up. "Eeeeew."

"Gilbert?"

"Detective, Zo saw Millie more than I did. I couldn't recognize her, although I did think she was a bigger woman."

"Detective Mora and I just had a short look at the features," Fr. Jake said. "Terribly swollen and battered."

Sonia summarized the time frame. "According to Dulci's story, the victim would have been in the water about nine hours. Yet Doctor McMurtry determined that possible submersion could be over twenty hours."

Gil calculated, "Detective, that's long enough for Mister Trujillo to kill Millie and still get to your interview in Socorro on time. Remember they had a fight."

"If…he…drove from the Jemez earlier than necessary. Interesting…." Sonia dismissed the two men, "All right, you're both free to go, but CSI will question you further."

"That poor woman," Fr. Jake sympathized as he walked with Sonia back to her car. "No matter what you thought of Millie's treatments for Dulci—"

Sonia mused about what she had heard, "Gilbert brought up a salient point, so I'll definitely quiz Fernando about the time of his return to the ranch."

"Evidently, as Gil said, the two of them did fight tooth and nail."

"Right, Father, but isn't it strange that Queen Millie could barely be identified? Well, as the doc said, an autopsy will determine who the vic is and what happened to her." Sonia looked back toward her car. "Okay, Father, let's drive up to the house and wait for the Don."

Shortly after Sonia parked her Plymouth along the driveway, Don Fernando pulled his BMW up behind her. He stormed out of the vehicle and went around to open the car door on his daughter's side.

When Sonia got out to meet him, he shouted, "What is it now, detective? You most certainly aren't going to question Dulci!"

"No, sir. Father Jake and I just wanted to see how she's doing after last night."

"Doing?" Fernando grabbed a manila envelope off the back seat. "Here's the damned toxicology report you wanted about how Dulci is doing. Right now, detective, she's going inside to rest. Then, in a day or two, we're going back to the Jemez and continue our vacation."

Sonia took the envelope. "Sir, aren't you going to ask about Millie Jaramillo?"

"Why should I? That *gorrón* of a *bruja* died after drugging and attempting to murder my daughter. She can go to straight to hell!" He noticed the priest sitting on the Neon's passenger side and went around to speak with him more calmly. "Father Jake, my daughter is safe, so perhaps there is a God after all. We'll talk." He returned to his car and pulled the girl toward the house. "Come on Dulci, let's go inside."

Sonia walked back to sit in the driver's seat of her Plymouth. "*Enojado que una gallina mojada,*" she muttered.

Fr. Jake looked her way. "Detective, I caught 'wet' and 'hen'."

"Then you can guess the 'madder than' part. I'll definitely have more questions for him when Fernando returns from his Jemez off time." She held up the envelope. "I asked for a toxicology screening of only blood and urine, not a complete post mortem, or even stomach contents. Those take a lot longer. Father, if you have that Swiss pocket knife with you, will you slit the top of this envelope for me?"

"Sure."

Sonia slipped the form out of the envelope and studied it a moment. "Good, it's by Liz Long. She always writes clarifying notes to me. Let's see…. 'Subject underweight for her age…CBC blood count shows definite indication of bulimia. Possible hypothyroidism, which could account for the subject's delayed menstruation….' What's this?" Sonia's voice rose in disbelief as she slowly read the next entry, "'Acute dehydration, which made passing urine difficult. The small sample obtained contained no traces of the valerian-based sedative reported to have been ingested by the subject'."

"But," Fr. Jake objected, "Dulci told me that Millie forced her to drink a lot of herbal tea."

"Let me check her CBC again…" Sonia studied the rest of the report, then looked over at him, her eyebrows raised. "Father, neither did Dulcinea Trujillo's blood sample have any trace whatsoever of that sedative. The girl simply was lying to you."

"Then, if she might not be Millie, who was the woman who drowned in the sluice?"

"Hopefully, autopsy results will help provide that answer, Father Jake, but they won't be available as quickly as this toxicology screening."

# 30 don fernando' s conversion

On Thursday, July 22, Fr. Jake finished his usual bran and banana breakfast, washed down, of course, with coffee, then settled in his armchair with the breviary to read the entries he would use in celebrating what he had come to call his morning "Kitchen Mass."

The First Reading was from Jeremiah. The prophet wrote of the Lord telling him of his affection for Israel, of leading the people to a fertile country, which the Lord complains that they immediately defiled. This debasing primarily was spiritual: the priests who administer the Law ignore the God of Israel to prophesy in the name of Baal and useless idols. In compelling desert symbolism, the Lord accuses Israelites of abandoning him, the "fountain of living water," to build for themselves leaking cisterns that hold no water.

*If I were preparing a sermon on Jeremiah, I would parallel that Seventh Century B.C. text with today's misuse of the land, destruction of forests, waste of natural resources, an over-emphasis on today's material idols, and a generally declining church membership—*

The ring of his cell tone intruded on the priest's thoughts.

"San Isidro Rectory, Father Ja—"

"This is Don Fernando," the caller broke in. "Hope I'm not disturbing you, Father. Have you finished breakfast?"

"Yes, I'm fine. How can I—"

"Father Jake, I've been thinking. I suppose that Detective Mora told you about that suicide message of my wife? The note Isabel wrote?"

"She did. I'm sorry she came to that and—"

"No, no. Listen to me. I've done nothing but blame God all these years, perhaps not only for her death, but also by asking why she had to contract the disease in the first place. Isabel was a good woman. Why would she have to suffer from fibromyalgia?"

"Don, these difficult questions always arise at such tragic times."

"I suppose that's true, yet now that I understand more about the disease, I realize it can be a physical...even a genetic problem."

"Disease entered the world—"

"Right. Father, Dulci and I are back at our cottage in the Jemez and, frankly, having the time of our lives. Riding our horses, talking late into the night. Dulci had her nineteenth birthday this week, so we had a quiet celebration. We'll stay here about another week, but when we do return, may I make an appointment to talk with you about... well...about coming back to San Isidro?"

"Delighted, Don, and no appointment needed. If my car's in the driveway, just show up at the rectory door."

"Father Jake, thanks so much. Well, *Buenas dias* for now."

"*Buenas dias*. God Bless."

As the priest pressed the off button on his cell phone, he thought aloud, "Hmm, sounds like Fernando is returning to the fountain of living water. It's a bit strange that he didn't have Dulci say something to me, but she may be worn out from finally having the time of her life.

"Yet, in the light of what she told Gil and me, the girl's toxicology screening results are puzzling. Even if an autopsy of the victim will take time, as Sonia suggested, we may know more about what happened that night after the Mobile Crime Lab report about the crime scene is ready."

O

After celebrating his Kitchen Mass, Fr. Jake walked over to the church. Cynthia was in the vestibule, opening up a box of August seasonal liturgy missalettes that had arrived.

"Good morning, Father," she said. "I found these by the church door, where UPS must have left them."

"Thanks, Cynthia. I don't think I've seen you since last Thursday."

"After my classes ended, I drove to Albuquerque for a few days, to visit my parents."

"Are they well?"

"Fairly well. Mom just turned sixty-two and I guess that's kind of a milestone in applying for Social Security and all."

He laughed his understanding. "I remember it well."

"Father, I've been reading my Faith Formation textbook, so I'll be starting lesson plans for that class I'll be teaching in September."

"Wonderful! I'll make a formal announcement on Sunday about parents registering their children."

"Thanks, Father." Cynthia turned to stack the Mass booklets on the table.

*I might as well mention the many changes attempting to take place in the Church by progressive Catholic groups. I think she'll be receptive.* "Cynthia, I'm afraid that textbook you have may be obsolete by the time those children are in college."

She looked back at him in surprise. "What do you mean, Father?"

"I tried to explain some of this to Armando, while we were on our way to Belén to buy my Honda. Cynthia, I'm sure you've welcomed many reforms of the Vatican II Council, which met from Nineteen sixty-two to Nineteen sixty-five."

"I was born about twenty years later, Father, so I don't remember the pre-council church, but my parents liked the new direction. My dad was career Air Force, so we moved around a lot, but on one Base chapel I served as an altar girl."

"Exactly. Not every priest agrees on having female servers, but many parishes do allow them. Also, in having women participate in the Washing of the Feet ritual on Holy Thursday. That would be only proper because lay women today are very active in running parishes. Some groups advocate allowing women in the Diaconate and, in fact, there's no church law prohibiting that from happening. When the children you're teaching grow up, there well may be a married priesthood."

Cynthia put the books down and leaned against the table to face him. "Doesn't the Episcopal church have woman deacons and priests?"

"Yes and deaconesses are mentioned in the letters of Paul. Despite his mistaken reputation of not liking the female sex, the greetings that begin the apostle's letters, include influential women converts. And he tells his Corinthians that the gifts of the Spirit—meaning wisdom, healing, prophecy, and such—all are distributed individually to men *and* women as the Holy Spirit wishes. Not just to males, as church authorities would have you believe."

Cynthia recalled, "Father Mora would say a quick mass, then go into his *segrario*. I admit that it wasn't very satisfying for me."

"A Eucharist should be reverent, of course, yet also the joyous inward and outward communal experience that Jesus proclaimed. Sadly, I've seen Vatican reforms steadily eroded by members of a conservative Curia in Rome."

Cynthia suggested, "Maybe you should organize an evening class about that and the Council reforms."

"Well, such classes were held in the early years of the council," he said. "Detroit happened to have an archbishop who supported the reforms one hundred percent."

"Not so much here?"

"I imagine the changes have taken solid hold at many New Mexican parishes. This is a conservative one, so right after I arrived in April, well, you remember, the deacon told me they didn't want anything changed in the way they did things."

Cynthia insisted, "You've made changes for the better, Father."

"Hopefully, but regarding the Episcopal Church you mentioned, one of their vicars, whom I knew in Michigan, a learned theologian, told me…in a comradely way, of course…that his church had implemented all of the reforms of Vatican II."

"You hear the term 'Cafeteria Catholic'."

"That's become a media buzz term. An informed conscience is the determining factor in making spiritual decisions, always has been since the time of Aquinas. But then, Jayson Baumann went to an exclusive Catholic school, yet he's quite rigid and not very favorable toward our Vatican II changes."

Cynthia thought about what Fr. Jake had told her. "Speaking of Jayson. I didn't stop by his dig before coming here. I wonder how he's doing?"

"I haven't seen the young man since Jim Eagle Feather spoke to him last Saturday."

"Eagle Feather? Who is he? I left for Albuquerque on Friday right after school."

"Then you missed a lot of action around here that weekend. Mister Eagle Feather said he worked for an Indian Graves Repatriation Bureau. He quarantined Jayson's dig after inspecting it, but also, an actual tragedy is that Millie Jaramillo may have accidentally drowned in the sluice at Don Fernando's ranch."

"What? Th…that's terrible, Father! How did her drowning happen?"

"Cynthia, it's an ongoing investigation. I can't say too much because it might not be accurate, but we could go see Jayson. Knowing him, despite the ban, he'll still be working his site."

"Sure, I can come back here later and finish up."

As they walked across a field that led from the church toward the excavation site, Cynthia asked, "What was the reason for Jayson being shut down?"

"It seems that a lot of soldiers died of smallpox back at that time, so Mister Eagle Feather thinks some of the material Jayson claims to have found might be contaminated by smallpox virus."

"The graves inspector said that?"

"Word for word, Cynthia."

"Strange…. BLM authorities saw what I was doing and that was never a problem with my excavation. I'm digging not very far from Jayson."

"There's a bit more to the story, but let's walk over and see if our grad student is there."

James Eagle Feather's orange quarantine sign was pinned to a door flap of the tent protecting the grave site. A short distance away, a *tipi* that the archaeology grad assistant had been constructing still lay unfinished.

'Jayson," Cynthia called as she squatted at the tent's entrance. "Jayson… you in there?" She looked back up at the priest and shook her head. "No answer, Father."

"Let me untie the flap…." Fr. Jake knelt and crept inside the entrance after Cynthia. Jayson's digging trowel and an excavation brush lay on a mound of dirt, but a rectangular, three-foot-deep grave site was empty.

Cynthia leaned over to run a hand inside the pit. "There's no skeleton down here, yet even Jayson wouldn't have lied about finding one. He'd be exposed too easily."

"Eagle Feather said human remains such as bones can be bought on the Asian black market."

"So Jayson might have gotten a skeleton and brought it to be buried here?"

"Possibly. Cynthia, let's check the house. I'm betting that he's gone back to New York and I didn't even hear him leave."

As Fr. Jake predicted, no one answered his knock on the door, and the *casita* was vacant. "Our grad assistant must have called a cab driver and told him to come pick him up in the middle of the night."

Cynthia recalled, "I accused him of stealing a Seventh Cavalry button and pieces of blue wool cloth from the Fort Craig excavations. Now I'm positive his dig was a set-up."

Fr. Jake was not as sure. "I wonder if Jayson thought he'd get away with showing professionals what Gilbert Begay said were Woodland points?"

Cynthia said, "The arrowheads wouldn't be conclusive evidence, since it couldn't be proved that his Apache scout hadn't traded for them. That would take time, yet under the Repatriation Act, the skeleton and any artifacts quickly would be returned, probably to the Jicarilla Apache Reservation up at Dulce. They would perform their own re-burial ceremonies."

"And, meanwhile, our grad stud would reap all the glory of discovering a site."

Cynthia laughed at the priest's apt description, "Exactly, yet it seems that Jayson opted out a third of the way through his grant and decided to go back and tell people that he didn't find anything."

"Or, per the quarantine, so he wouldn't contract smallpox," Fr. Jake added.

"The state forensic archaeologists will determine that. Hey, wait..." A sudden thought came to the elementary schoolteacher. "Now, I don't believe he even *had* a grant, and that his father paid for his trip out here."

"I'm sure that you're correct, Cynthia."

"Meanwhile, I have nothing to do at my dig."

Fr. Jake asked, "With, what, a month before school starts again? Cynthia, let's just leave it at that and go finish up at the church. This morning, part of my reading from Jeremiah was the Lord saying something like, 'No sooner had you entered my land than you defiled it and made my heritage detestable'."

Cynthia said, "That certainly describes Jayson's work with the Buffalo Soldiers at Fort Craig, and now here with a non-existent Apache scout."

As Fr. Jake walked across the street with Cynthia to the church, he recalled, "In today's gospel, Jesus fears that the people look without seeing and listen without hearing or understanding."

"Our Jayson again!"

"Okay, Cynthia, enough gossiping. I've got to get a sermon ready for the five-o'clock Saturday Mass. Oh, but I did get an encouraging phone call from Don Fernando this morning."

"About what, Father?"

"He and his daughter are still vacationing in the Jemez, but when he comes back he'd like to talk to me about joining San Isidro again."

"Wonderful! And he'd bring his daughter back in with him."

'Amen!" As the priest checked to be sure that his altar missal was marked at the proper readings, his mind also was on what he had kept from telling the schoolteacher about Jayson abandoning his dig. *Eventually, I'll let Cynthia know that Jim Eagle Feather was an actor and that Jayson deservedly was prevented from his carrying out his deceit. What's of greater importance is the possible murder of Millie Jaramillo.*

## 31 the barbed wire fence

On Saturday morning, Fr. Jake skipped his Kitchen Mass because he would celebrate a full Eucharist for the congregation at five o'clock that afternoon.

Shortly after moving into the rectory, the priest began to throw pieces of wheat bread outside his kitchen door, for birds to snatch up. These morsels were from an inexpensive wheat sandwich loaf that he bought from Carlotta and dubbed, "Bird Bread." Soon, a variety of jays and finches—even a family of raucous crows—appeared each morning for a handout. He thought he had interpreted the ebony birds' cries: a first crow to arrive would sound three caws at three to five second intervals. These seemed to alert his mates that food was available, or if the priest was late, a signal for the tall, two-legged creature in the doorway to throw out food. Four to five frantic caws warned of danger, as when feral cats occasionally slinked onto the sandy ground to eat the bread—or stealthily crouch nearby as potential hunters.

After a second cup of coffee, which Fr. Jake finished as he read his Daily Missal, he closed the breviary. While cutting two slices of bread into small cubes for his birds, the priest realized he had not seen Gilbert Begay for a week. *After I toss these out, I'll walk over to the ranch and see how he's doing. He may act nonchalant, yet surely the man's concerned about when he'll receive notice of a forthcoming court arraignment.*

The priest threw the bread pieces into the yard and watched from the doorway as birds fluttered down from nearby piñon trees: jays were the quickest to snatch up the bread; crows the most wary; small finches seemed perpetually nervous as they pecked at crumbs.

"I wonder how our friend Gil is doing?" the priest asked several jays, experts at stealing food from under the beak of any crow strutting on the ground. "And do you suppose the Don is back, and yet hasn't called me about returning to church? It's time I went and found answers to both questions."

Fr. Jake drove his Honda past the Providencia grocery, planning to stop for food on his return from Rancho Tru-Cor. He was half way up the ranch's driveway when he saw that Fernando's BMW was not parked in the circular drive in front of the house. "Then he and Dulci aren't back from the Jemez," he thought aloud, "but that looks like a couple of ranch hands working across the pasture and along the sluice. Gil is probably one of them."

The priest left his car parked in the drive, took out a small package to give Gilbert, and walked down to meet the two men across an alfalfa field that was yellow with cowpen daisy blossoms. Two Arabian horses, Diablo and Velocita, grazed on fresh grass at the pasture's far end. Delicate horsetail clouds laced a cerulean-blue sky, a backdrop for the myriad green hues in the Rio Grande *bosque*. Insects hopped away from the swish of his shoes, and a sweet scent of sun-heated field grasses filled an early air whose coolness would dissipate into high July afternoon temperatures. As he had at one point in the spring, the priest paused to admire his surroundings. The green trees and vegetation could reflect a similar scene on a hot July day in rural Michigan, yet without the Lake State's suffocating humidity.

At the north end of the sluice, he could see the two workers erecting a barbed wire fence along the near bank. One man was Gil; he didn't recognize the other, but it was not Lorenzo, a smaller man with hair distinctively braided at the back of his head. After the two ranch hands noticed the priest walking their way, both paused to mop sweat from their faces with bandanas and wait for him.

When he came closer, Fr. Jake called out, "Gil, how are you? I thought you might be lonely for company, and I brought you a package of Carlotta's special roast piñon coffee."

"Thanks, Father…" He took off a heavy leather glove and extended a hand to shake the priest's, and take the coffee. "I been keeping busy. Mister Trujillo called from Jemez Springs and asked me to put up a barbed wire fence along his length of the ditch."

"So the Don and his daughter haven't returned yet?"

"Not that I've seen." Gil indicated his companion. "Matt here is helping me with the fence."

In contrast to his clean-shaven companion, Mathias Crisp grew a moustache and goatee to ornament his face. He put down his posthole digger and pulled off a glove. "Pleased, Father."

"Same here, Matt. I believe that now I've met all you ranch hands." Fr. Jake eyed the steel posts, tools, and coils of fencing wire lying on the ground. "That looks like difficult work you're doing."

"Putting up barbed wire fencing is hard enough," Gil agreed. "Even with the right tools, like that posthole digger, a tamping bar, and post pounders, it's not an easy job. Mister Trujillo just doesn't want any more accidents happening down here at the *acequia*."

"I can understand that."

"Yeah," Gil remembered, "right after I started working here…Miss Dulci, I think she was twelve and taking care of a foal. One night it somehow got out of a pen, fell in the water, and drowned. She found it in the morning. Poor girl stayed shook up about the animal's death for a long time."

"Dulci was already depressed," Fr. Jake remarked. "That's when the fence should have been put up."

"That's what I thought." Gil lay down the coffee package on a denim jacket he had taken off, then pointed at the south end of the waterway. "We're going clear down to Romero Loop, past where the woman's body was found." He looked back at the priest. "So, Father, anything new on the Jaramillo drowning case?"

"Not that Detective Mora has told me about. She's waiting for autopsy results on the …the 'vic'…as that medical examiner called her."

Matt said, "Gil told me about that night, but I can't figure out how he and Zo couldn't tell it wasn't Millie."

"There were only the woman's clothes to go by," Fr. Jake explained. "The face was mutilated beyond recognition. I saw her—"

Abruptly, the distant engine of an approaching aircraft sounded in the air. All three shaded their eyes to watch a black speck in the bright sky to the south become large enough to be recognized as a helicopter flying their way. The rotorcraft approached in a straight line, yet, instead of passing over the men, the pilot began a descent that circled the ranch house. Frightened by an unaccustomed loud noise, the two Arabians galloped to the pasture's most distant fence and nervously paced back and forth along its length.

"Looks like that pilot's checking out a landing place," Gil said, the loud chatter of rotor blades almost drowning out his words.

Fr. Jake raised his voice to shout, "I wonder if Don Fernando hired a helicopter to fly him and Dulci back here to the ranch? Let's hope there's no medical emergency involving his daughter."

Gil shaded his eyes again. "I can't make out any passengers in the cabin."

On its third pass over the pasture, a sleek EC 120 Eurocopter briefly hovered above a level area in the field east of the men, then descended to land a scant fifty feet from the main ranch house. The priest and two workers turned away from flying ground debris of dirt and sticks kicked their way by the main rotor's downwash.

"What the…?" Just as Fr. Jake ducked to avoid being struck by a small branch, he read the name **Helitransporte Méxicanos / Esperanzo** painted on the red, white and green side of the rotorcraft's fuselage. "That helicopter came here from Mexico!"

Now farther away from direct rotor wash by the idling craft, the men straightened up and turned in time to see Don Fernando come out of the ranch house entrance; he carried a heavy suitcase and pulled Dulci by the other hand. Both of them, with Millie Jaramillo behind, dashed down the porch stairs and sprinted toward the helicopter. The Mexican pilot scrambled from his cockpit seat to hold the right side cabin door open for his three passengers.

When Fernando noticed the priest and his two ranch hands, still running, he let go of his daughter's hand to pull a pistol from his leather jacket's pocket and fired shots at each one. None hit the men.

Stunned, Fr. Jake could only stare at what was happening. *Don Fernando and his daughter are supposed to be vacationing in the Jemez, and Millie Jaramillo is thought to be dead. They're still persons of interest in possible murders, and it looks like they're heading for Mexico. That helicopter has to be kept from leaving the ground….* "Gil!" he shouted, as he looked around. "How can we stop that thing from taking off?"

Afterward, the priest would not recall how he thought of the coils of barbed fencing wire he had seen lying on the ground, or that he noticed a spinning rotor chambered in the Eurocopter's tail boom, or even that he yelled, "Gil…Matt! Throw that smallest coil of wire into the rear…into that…that back propeller!"

The two ranch hands heard him and swiftly reacted: using both gloved hands, they picked up a loose quarter-coil of barbed wire and ran to heave it into the rotor, then drop to the ground face-down, with hands clasped over their heads.

An unearthly screech sounded as fencing wire twisted itself around the spinning rotor blades. Lethal sections of barbed steel spikes shredded the aluminum tail boom and flew forward to penetrate the craft's thin walls. Don Fernando had tossed his suitcase into the cabin and was helping Millie climb into the craft, when several barbed missiles struck him in the head and neck. He fell forward, his torso halfway into the cabin. Injured by the lethal strands, the *curandera* toppled backward off the entrance step and onto the grass next to the skids. As the pilot held open the door, bits of barbed metal penetrated the left arm of his leather jacket. His scream of pain went unheard in the screeching din.

Dulcinea Trujillo, standing farther off, slowly backed away from a deadly perimeter that was fanned by the overhead rotor, then abruptly turned and ran toward Fr. Jake. He held onto the trembling girl, who tightly clutched him as she numbly repeated, "I didn't want to leave. I didn't want to leave."

In moments the damaged tail rotor jammed, stopped its spinning, and forced an engine stall. As the whining rotor overhead slowly ceased turning, the unearthly noise abated into a deadly silence.

In shock at what happened, Fr. Jake gently pried Dulci's hands away from his arm and called out, "Matt, take...take the girl around to the back of the house, away from this. I...I'll call Detective Mora on my cell."

Gilbert Begay sprinted to the helicopter and gave the pilot his bandana. The Mexican stripped off his flight jacket and wrapped the cloth around bloody wounds soaking his arm. At the copter's open door, Gil's glance at Fernando's bloody head injuries was enough for him to determine that the man probably was dead. Barely breathing, Millie Jaramillo lay unconscious on the ground. He helped the pilot down from the doorway and sat with him on grass a short distance away.

"*¿Habla inglese?*" Gil asked the Mexican.

"*Si*, I know Ingleesh."

"Then, what happened? Why are you here?"

"*Señor* Trujillo, he call me, come take heem and *Señora* Jaramillo to Méjico."

"Where in Mexico?"

"Esperanzo. Place where *La Curandera* leeve."

"So he was trying to escape New Mexico with her and Dulci—"

Fr. Jake, more composed now that he had phoned for help, came over to the two men. "Gil, Sonia will alert the sheriff's substation at Bernardo, then get here herself as soon as possible. Deputies and a Paramedic unit should be here in about ten minutes.

"Good. Millie looks badly injured, and I'm pretty sure Mister Trujillo was killed. But…him using that gun on us—" Gil's voice trailed off in disbelief.

"What a terrible tragedy." Fr. Jake noticed the bloody bandana on the pilot's arm. "Is he badly injured?"

"No, but medics will have to dig out some barbed wire. He says he was hired to bring Mister Trujillo and Millie to her town in Mexico. Pilot, what's that name again?"

"Esperanzo, *señor*."

"Right. Millie Jaramillo came from there."

"Then she wasn't drowned and Fernando planned all along an escape to Mexico with her. By doing that, he could avoid further questions about his wife's death."

"It looks that way, Father."

"Even his call to me about coming back to San Isidro was a lie."

"The saint probably won't like that," Gil remarked without betraying a smile.

"No…" Fr. Jake looked to the north of the main house, where the ranch workers' bunkhouse was located. "Where's Vando?"

Gil shrugged ignorance of his boss's whereabouts. "Haven't seen him all morning, but it's still early. He might be sleeping off a vodka binge."

Fr. Jake realized the man was the last adult witness to Isabel's accident. "Quick, let's check his room."

The bunkhouse recreation room had been straightened up, which still puzzled Gil. "Vando wouldn't clean this place, Father, and it's been like this for over a week. I haven't seen Victoria or Estaban Torrez, but maybe they came back on their own?"

"I suppose that's possible." Fr. Jake motioned toward Vando's room, "Try his door."

The portal was locked. Gil pounded his fist on the wood and called out his foreman's name, without receiving a response. He looked back at the priest. "No answer, Father."

"Gil, he may know what's going on with Fernando and Millie. If he's in his room, it's important that we talk to him."

"Okay. Stay here while I give the stables a quick check. If Vando isn't there, I'll bring a two by four and batter down his door."

254

Gil returned with a heavy wooden framing stud. "He wasn't around, Father, so stand back." After the Navajo's blows splintered wood around the door knob, air reeking of stale cigarette smoke and alcohol fumes filtered into the hallway. After Gil loosed a final, battering smash, the lock shattered and the door slammed inward.

On his rumpled bed, the rigid body of Cervando Benavides lay on its back, his arms and legs contorted into unnatural, almost swastika-like positions. Under his thick mustache, a sickly grin twisted the man's mouth and revealed uneven teeth. A half-full vodka bottle stood on his bedside table, with a drinking tumbler of thick Mexican glass lying unbroken on the rug next to the bed.

"'Strychnine Grin'," Gil said, brushing flies away from Vando's mask-like face. "Someone poisoned him, so, Father, I guess that rosary he wears didn't help much."

"It's an important sacramental, Gil, not a good luck charm you put on as decoration."

"Okay...sorry."

Fr. Jake studied the ghastly tableau a moment. "I was correct about someone wanting to eliminate the last witnesses who were involved in his wife's accident."

"Eusebia and now Vando...."

"Right, Gil, and after what we've just seen and heard, I'd wager that the 'someone' was Millie Jaramillo."

"Then that wasn't her who drowned in the *acequia*. And the Mexican pilot told me what was going on out there with Mister Trujillo renting the helicopter. Father, do you think Ofilia may have a point in thinking Millie hexed Don Fernando?"

"Any 'charms' undoubtedly were sexual, and not black magic." Fr. Jake made a sign of the cross and murmured a brief prayer over Vando's body, then turned away. "Gil, let's go back and see if the police and paramedics have arrived."

Curious spectators, who had heard the helicopter approach and saw it descend—a distinct novelty in Providencia—stood gawking at the edge of the pasture. Fr. Jake noticed Cynthia Plow standing next to her SUV, parked on the road. He hurried over to her.

"Cynthia, I'll explain later, but Dulcinea Trujillo was involved in this accident. She's around the back of the house with Matt, one of the ranch hands, but she needs a woman with her at this tragic time. Could you go help?"

"Sure, Father."

In the wail of a siren and flashing red and blue lights, a patrol car from the Socorro Sheriff's Bernardo substation bounced across the uneven field toward the downed helicopter and braked near the wreckage. A Paramedic Fire & Rescue truck followed close behind.

Two sheriff's deputies stepped out of the car and came toward the priest.

"I'm Father Jake," he said to the first officer, a sergeant whose name badge read Montoya.

"Yeah, *Padre*," he replied. "Detective Mora told us you'd be here. The department's heard all about you."

"What the hell…heck…went on here?" the other deputy asked.

"The owner of the ranch…Fernando Trujillo, along with his daughter and…and mistress, planned to get to Mexico on that helicopter. You can question their pilot for the whole story, but medical personnel need to check all of them. The daughter survived, but her father, and possibly Miss Jaramillo, are…or will be…dead."

Montoya nodded. "All right, thanks, *Padre*."

The sergeant and his deputy went to examine the wreckage of the disabled rotorcraft. While paramedics treated the pilot's arm and attempted to revive a still-unconscious Millie Jaramillo, the undulating wail of a siren and a flashing red Mini Light Bar on the roof of Sonia's Plymouth Neon, announced the woman detective's screeching arrival in the driveway of Rancho Tru-Cor.

## 32 aftermath Mass

Sonia left her driver's side door open and sprinted across the field to the accident site. Concerned about the priest's unnerving call, she saw him standing alone, staring at the helicopter's wreckage.

When she reached him, the detective asked, "You okay, Father Jake?"

Still unnerved by the tragedy, he stammered, "I...I'm all right. It's the others—"

"Just a moment..." Sonia noticed the two sheriff's officers and yelled to the one she recognized. "Sergeant Montoya! Put 'Do Not Cross' police line tape up around that copter."

"Heard you, detective," he shouted back. "We were just going to do that."

"Good, and keep those gawkers away. I don't want souvenirs taken that'll wind up on E-bay." She turned back to the priest. "Not a formal statement, Father, but take a few deep breaths, then, in a nutshell, tell me what happened."

"Sonia, there's more than the helicopter crash. After preventing take-off and accounting for the passengers, Gil and I went to the bunkhouse and found Cervando Benavides dead in his room."

"What!?"

"Detective, he...he was poisoned."

"A whole new ball game then," Sonia clichéd. "Father, let me go tell Montoya to secure the ranch bunkhouse with crime scene tape and get a couple more deputies out here. Also he should notify an M.E."

Fr. Jake took the interval to walk around, taking deep breaths to relive stress, and doing an exercise by waving his arms. *relieve*

Sonia returned, grim-faced, sighed in exasperation, and took out her notebook and pen. "Father, I need those deep breaths I saw you taking. Okay, the accident first. How did you even happen to be here?"

"I came over to see how Gil was doing and brought him piñon coffee. He and Matt were putting a fence up along the sluice. We were talking when that helicopter came from the south, circled the ranch house a few times, and then landed. I thought some emergency involving Dulci might have prompted Don Fernando to return here with his daughter."

"But that wasn't the case."

"Definitely not!" Fr. Jake emphasized. "As soon as the helicopter landed, Fernando ran out of the house with his daughter and Millie Jaramillo. They were going to board..." He paused to catch his breath. "Actually, Dulci saw us and started backing away. Her father threw a suitcase into the cabin and then tried to help Millie climb in."

"Go on."

"I...I knew we had to prevent that pilot from...from escaping to Mexico with them."

Sonia indicated the wreckage with her pen. "He's the man over there with Gilbert?"

"Yes."

"I'll question him at headquarters. Okay, Father Jake, I know this is upsetting, but take it slow."

"Sonia, everything happed so quickly. After Fernando took shots at us and missed, all I could—"

"Hold it there, Jakubowski!" Sonia grasped the priest's arm. "You men were shot at?"

"Yes. All I could think of was to yell for Gil and Matt to throw a coil of fence wire into that rotor at the helicopter's tail."

She looked toward the Eurocopter's destroyed tail rotor. "Knocking out that rotor was *your* idea?"

His nod of remembrance was painful. "After they threw the barbed wire, all Armageddon broke out. Dulci ran toward me to get away—"

"Okay, Father, I can guess the rest. You say there's a suitcase inside the cabin?"

"Fernando carried it in one hand and pulled Dulci toward the copter with the other. Millie was running behind them."

"Let's go take a look." Sonia tried to avoid blood that stained the Eurocopter's open door and trampled grass underneath the cabin. She climbed onto a skid strut and pulled the case toward her. "I'll have Montoya tag this and put it the Don's study for now."

Fr. Jake noticed Cynthia and Matt bringing Dulci back. "Sonia, here's Fernando's daughter..." Father Jake went to meet the three and walk with them back to the detective. The bulimic girl looked pale, yet seemed calm now. "Dulcinea," he gently told her, "I'm sorry, but your father is dead. Millie Jaramillo is seriously injured and may not survive."

"My father's dead?" the girl repeated in a numb voice.

"I'm afraid so, Dulci."

"My sympathy," Sonia offered. "I'll get a hospital report on Miss Jaramillo, but, Dulcinea, while I'm here, may I ask you about what happened?"

Still dazed, the girl answered as if not hearing the question. "My father... he was trying to get to Mexico with Millie. I didn't want to go. I...I told Father Jake—"

"That's true," the priest confirmed, "but if you're too upset to talk now, Detective Mora probably can wait."

"No, I'm all right." She looked back at Sonia. "What do you want to know?"

"Dulci, let's go back to my car to talk."

Cynthia said, "I'll return to school now, Father Jake. When we heard the helicopter, I was getting my room ready for classes, when school opens next month."

He thanked her. "You helped a lot, Cynthia."

"Okay, Father." Before leaving she turned back to the girl. "Dulci, you can stay with me tonight if you want."

"No, I think I'd like to be here at the ranch."

"Okay, but let's get together soon. I'll call you tomorrow for sure."

Sonia went over to give Fernando's suitcase to Montoya. "Sergeant, tag this and put it in the victim's study. End of the first hallway and to your left."

He grinned. "You got it, Detective Mora."

As the three walked across the field toward Sonia's Plymouth, Dulci asked the detective, "Could we sit on the edge of the fountain for your questions?"

"Of course. We can talk there just as well."

The fountain's stagnant water gave off a noxious odor of algae and decaying leaves. After Dulci swatted mosquitoes away, she picked up a small tree branch to stir green scum floating on the surface a moment, then threw in the stick and turned to lean against the rim. "Funny, my father and I were going to fix this up, put fish in the pool, and now he's dead."

"Again, I'm sorry," Sonia sympathized. "Please tell me what was happening with that Mexican helicopter."

Dulci sniffled. "I didn't find out we were leaving this morning, until we got back from the Jemez last night and he parked the car inside the garage. *Papá*...my father...told me we were going to live at Millie's village in Mexico."

"Then Miss Jaramillo wasn't dead? She didn't drown in the *acequia*."

"No."

Fr. Jake asked her, "But, Dulci, what's that story you told Gil and me about what happened at the sluice?"

"My father rehearsed me to say those things to make everyone think Millie *was* dead. When I refused to do it, that made him very angry. Like the sweet little five-year-old girl he thought me to be, I always did whatever he wanted. I...I guess that I still needed to please him, so I did tell you that story."

Sonia summed up the girl's statement, "As part of your father's scheme to escape to Mexico, he wanted everyone to believe that Miss Jaramillo was no longer alive?"

"Yes, because he planned for us to live there with her."

"Yet she fought with your father," Fr. Jake contended. "Don Fernando threatened to throw Millie out, or she could choose to stay on at the ranch as housekeeper."

"I heard them," Dulci said, "but I'm not sure that fight was for real."

Sonia asked, "So who is the dead woman in Miss Jaramillo's clothes?"

"Probably Vickie Torrez."

The detective reached out a hand to her. "Thanks, Dulcinea. I'm sure you're upset and exhausted, so we'll wait to talk again later on."

The girl went back to stand at the edge of the driveway and look around, then turned back to Sonia. "My father's dead, so do I own the ranch now?"

She had not expected the question. "Dulcinea, it's too soon to see what kind of will Don Fernando left, but in all probability you do."

"I see. Detective, I...I'm going inside to lie down now."

"Are you sure you're all right?" Fr. Jake asked her. "Perhaps you shouldn't be left alone."

"The ranch hands are here, so I'll be okay." Dulci half-smiled at him. "After all, I *am* nineteen years old now."

"That's right, and your father told me you had a birthday at the Jemez cottage. Well, as you wish, Dulci, and God Bless."

She murmured thanks and turned to go into the house.

Sonia said, "Come on Father Jake, I see your car is parked over there."

As he walked back to his Honda with her, the priest commented, "I'm afraid Dulcinea Trujillo doesn't sound that broken up about her father's death."

"Could be shock, denial, or perhaps she's even relieved, in a way."

"Relieved, Sonia?"

"I'm pretty sure Dulcinea didn't want to trade New Mexico for life in Old Mexico."

"That's probably true, yet so much is unanswered. This *must* have something to do with Isabel Trujillo's death. Don't forget that Vando undoubtedly was murdered by Millie to silence him."

"Good sleuthin' Father," Sonia panned. "'Course it does. All the adult witnesses are dead, and we're left with three conflicting accounts of Isabel's death."

Fr. Jake held up an index finger. "Such as, One, a mercy killing by Cervando Benavides."

"Number Two,' Sonia counted. "Assisted suicide, per a real or forged note by the deceased."

"Murdered on orders to Vando by his *patrón*, Don Fernando. That's number three."

The detective added, "And don't forget five-year-old Dulci insisting that her father wasn't present at the actual accident scene. I'd say that covers numbers two and three."

"Detective, your own sleuthing for the facts is cut out for you," Fr. Jake said. "My five o'clock Mass today won't be a memorial service, but we'll say extra prayers for the victims and survivors, Dulci in particular. Care to attend?"

Sonia pulled her cap further down to shade her eyes and looked away. "I'd like to, Father, but must finish securing the two sites and talking with that pilot. I jotted down what Dulcinea told me, but I also need to get statements from Gil and Matt."

"Just thought I'd ask. Detective, what comes after that? The investigation?"

"Because this involves the crash of a Rotorcraft, the NTSB...National Transportation Safety Board...will send investigators, a 'Go Team'. And since this affair might hide suspected criminal activity, the FBI may get involved. The Safety Board itself has no power to arrest perpetrators."

"Strange thing," Fr. Jake remarked. "Fernando evidently forgot, or didn't know, that the fence was being erected at the same time that his means of escape would arrive. Otherwise, no one would have seen him leave."

Sonia quipped, "You giving credit to San Isidro for that, Father?"

"Not just yet," Fr. Jake retorted amiably and opened his car door. "I'll be in touch later. God Bless."

O

The priest's afternoon Mass was crowded. Others than *Providenceños* had heard about the helicopter crash, so a number of people who were not parishioners came in the hope that they would learn more about what happened at the wealthy, reclusive Don Fernando's ranch.

Fr. Jake only told the congregation that details of the helicopter crash would be available in due time and kept his homily short. The gospel for that Saturday's Vigil Mass was Luke's account of when the disciples asked Jesus how to pray. His answer was the familiar "Our Father," a prayer totally memorized by both English and Spanish speakers in the church. The gospel included Christ's exhortation to be persistent in praying: "For the one who knocks will always have the door opened to him."

Just before the Elevation of the bread and wine, Fr. Jake noticed two distinguished-looking men quietly enter the church and sit in a back pew. Both wore white summer suits and shoes. One had on a tie made of gold silk; the other man's neckwear was silver. The priest's first thought was that they might be Mormon missionaries, yet at the Consecration both had knelt with heads bowed. When both men took Communion, he deduced they were Catholic.

After Mass, the two strangers waited in the vestibule for the priest. Both had identical light-tan skin tones and smooth, wrinkle-free complexions that made judging their ages difficult. The shortest man's flowing blond hair resembled that of an angel in a Renaissance Botticelli painting. The taller of the two parted his white hair in the middle—a somewhat obsolete style.

He stepped forward and extended a hand to the priest. "A pleasure to meet you, Father Jakubowski."

*His hand has the feel of…of warm velvet, and he knows my name.* Fr. Jake returned the greeting, "Welcome to San Isidro, gentlemen."

"Thank you." The white-haired speaker turned to introduce his companion, "My associate, Gabríel."

*Spanish pronunciation, accent on the second vowel.*

The angel-haired man shifted a briefcase he carried to his left hand. "Pleased, Father."

"Likewise. Is…is there some way I can help you?"

"There is, indeed, Father." The white-haired man with the golden tie paused to glance around. "Nice little church you have here. May we sit in the nave while we talk?"

"Of course. A few hours ago, there was a helicopter accident nearby and I—"

"We know."

"You know? Then has this something to do with insurance? Are you with a company?"

"In a way, I imagine." He glanced half-amused at Gabríel, then took his business card from a leather case. "We're with EQUUS, Equine Unified Sanctuaries. Our organization's purpose is to salvage and shelter abused, aged, or discarded horses."

"I see." Fr. Jake read his name. "And you are 'Miguel 'Izzy' Martín'?"

"Yes, and you correctly pronounced my surname, Father, so you're coming along quite well in learning Spanish. Now…may we sit toward the center of the church, perhaps opposite that colorful Confessional that's draped with Zapotec blankets?"

"That's temporary, Mister…or *Señor*…Martín. I'll set up a space for the Sacrament of Reconciliation in the *Segrario* built by my predecessor."

"Father, formalities have a proper place, but just calling me 'Martín' will be fine."

"Very well, Martín" *He knew my name, that I study Spanish, and about the accident. Both men have saints' names and rehabilitate abandoned or otherwise abused horses. What can they possibly want from me?*

After the priest was maneuvered into sitting between the two men, an incense-like fragrance was apparent on their bodies. Gabríel opened his briefcase and handed a manila folder to his companion. Martín toyed with the papers inside a moment before saying, "Father, you're not aware that Don Fernando de Trujillo has sold his ranch."

*His question sounded like a statement.* "No. I...I'm stunned to hear that. Hadn't the slightest clue."

"The Don listed his property without a realtor and under a box number in the Arabian Horse Association newsletter. Gabriél, if you will, please...."

"EQUUS," he explained, "is expanding nationwide, so when we received a description and photographs of Rancho Tru-Cor property, its water rights, existing ranch home, equine facilities, and so forth, we made the Don an offer of one million dollars."

"A million? I...I haven't any idea of property values outside of my previous parish in Michigan."

"It *was* a fair sum," Martín emphasized. "Don Fernando accepted, yet on rather odd terms. He insisted on a cash down payment of two-hundred fifty thousand, but paid in thousand-dollar bills. The balance was to be deposited in a Mexican bank account. Gabriél express-mailed him closing papers to sign, along with the money in a sealed suitcase. We never actually met the Don, nor have we seen his ranch."

"Fernando was killed in the accident." Fr. Jake recalled the chaotic scene. "It was horrific...Fernando and his...well...his mistress, tried to board the helicopter. The... Wait, gentlemen, he had a suitcase with him! Detective Mora ordered it taken to his office. If that held the money, we should get over there as quickly as possible!"

Outside the church, Gabriél opened the door of a white 2010 Ford Mustang with the EQUUS logo on the side—the mythical horse Pegasus, flying skyward over two green hearts. *Appropriate vehicle name.* Fr. Jake ducked into the back seat of the two-door automobile.

After Martín buckled himself in the passenger seat, Gabriél started the Mustang's engine. When Fr. Jake leaned forward to tell him directions to Rancho Tru-Cor, the driver said he already knew the way—despite Martín having told the priest that they had not visited the property.

At the ranch, Gabriél parked the Mustang in the driveway. The men got out of the car in silence and walked to the crash scene. The yellow police line tape Sonia had called for surrounded the downed helicopter, but no deputies were present as guards.

The three had a only a few moments to look at the wreckage, before the sound of a tractor engine came from the direction of the *acequia* They turned to see a Bobcat Mini Loader jolting up the field toward the house. Lorenzo Lujan drove the tractor, with Dulcinea Trujillo sitting next to him. The front bucket was empty.

As the machine neared, Fr. Jake gave the ranch hand a signal to kill the engine. After it sputtered into silence, he walked over to the riders. "Dulcinea, what's going on?"

"I'm getting rid of stuff in my father's study that I don't want to keep," she told him in a defiant voice,

"Young lady," he warned, "this is a crime scene. You shouldn't be doing that."

"Why not?" she demanded, with a new tone of authority. "I'm the owner of the ranch now, aren't I?"

"Not exactly, Dulcinea, and these gentlemen are here to explain about that. What were you and Lorenzo doing at the sluice?"

"Throwing in the old junk my father had in his study. All those pictures from that shrine I had to pretend really was my mom. I hated it."

Fr. Jake felt alarmed now. "Did you find a suitcase?"

"Oh, sure, full of more pictures, I guessed. It was the last thing we dumped in the water."

"Yeah," Lorenzo chimed in, grinning. "And everything is gonna float down the Rio Grande and end up in the Gulf."

"Dulcinea, shall we go inside?" Fr. Jake asked, as evenly as he could. "These gentlemen have something to tell you."

Martín beckoned to Lorenzo. "Zo, why don't you also come in?"

The ranch hand nervously fiddled with his hair braid in back before agreeing, "Sure…I guess."

Inside the house, Martín led the way through the entry hall and straight to the family entertainment area. Father Jake recalled the large room where he and Sonia first had questioned the Don about Baby Doe. He silently noted, *Those two mounted onyx heads with the staring glass eyes are gone. Probably the first things Dulci threw out.*

"Please, all of you sit down," the white-haired man said in a kindly voice. "My dear Dulcinea, we have business to discuss with you."

"Me? I don't even know who you are." She glanced at Lorenzo. Despite having been called by his nickname, his eyes and shrug indicated ignorance of the two men's identities.

Martín explained, "This has to do with your father and the ranch, Dulcinea, yet I'll start by talking about your mother."

Dulci looked surprised. "You…you knew my mom?"

"Isabel Trujillo," he continued, "suffered a debilitating disease, yet in the thirteen years since she died the medical profession has made good progress in treating her ailment. Had she chosen to live—"

"My mother was sick?" Dulci broke in to ask. "My father never ever stopped talking about her. 'Mom this, mom that.' I think *he* was sick, too."

"He was," Martín affirmed gently, "but your father's illness was pathological."

"Patho....? What does that mean?"

"Dulcinea, grief normally accompanies the loss of a loved one, yet Don Fernando's years-long dysfunction is named Prolonged Grief Disorder. However caused, he was traumatized by the death of his wife and tried to deny its reality by maintaining a shrine to her. Your father treated you and Isabel as if she were alive, even by having you say good morning at the shrine each day."

"I...said I hated doing that."

"Dulci," Fr. Jake further explained, "Mister Martín is saying that in an attempt to freeze time your father continued to treat you as a five-year-old."

"Exactly, Father." Martín turned back to the girl. "Mrs. Nevarez tried her best to nullify the physical effects of his misplaced sense of love for you. However, late puberty, your bulimic tendencies, isolation from peer groups, all these were debilitating results."

Tears had moistened Dulci's eyes at the mention of Eusebia Nevarez. "After what happened, I was scared of horses."

"Understandable," Fr. Jake remarked. "You were a small child."

The girl wiped an eye with her hand. "Nanny told me not to be afraid, and that *Vencedor* didn't mean to hurt mom. It was an accident that happens to horse owners. So...so I learned to ride and groom Bombóna. My father did encourage that."

Martín remarked, "The one thing Don Fernando did correctly."

"Nanny Eusebia gave me books on self-esteem. I read them and slowly realized what *papá*—" She stopped and put a hand to her mouth.

"It's all right, Dulci," Fr. Jake told her. "Fernando insisted that you always call him by the name you used as a child."

"Yes, and he also thought Millie could cure me."

Martín continued, "Subconsciously, your father wanted to help you, yet didn't know how. When Miss Jaramillo came along and convinced him that she could cure you, he fell under her spell, although that's really the wrong term. A magical 'hex' was not involved, and *Curanderismo* has many valid healing techniques."

Fr. Jake mused, *Yet there undoubtedly was a sexual side to the arrangement.*

Martín nodded toward him, "Correct, Father. Dulcinea, it's time for the truth now. Miss Jaramillo became Don Fernando's mistress."

"I know," she admitted. "Millie's bedroom was next to mine. He...he wouldn't...do it...in his and my mother's old room, but I heard them. I...I almost felt happy for my father."

"Dulci," Fr. Jake said, "Don Fernando called me from the Jemez cottage. He said he wanted to come back to church, to San Isidro, and that you were having the time of your life."

"Not true!" she contradicted him. "He called so you wouldn't suspect anything. We fought most of the time there and had arguments about going with Millie to live in Mexico. I...rode Bomboná when I could, to get away. At night, after he thought I was asleep, he made a lot of phone calls."

"Those were to me," Martín affirmed. "We were closing the ranch deal."

"Lorenzo," Fr. Jake asked, 'did you know any of this about your *patrón* going to Mexico?"

"*Maria Purissima, no!* Millie jus' paid me to be Llorona."

Fr. Jake, skeptical of a girl who had lied before about being drugged, asked, "But, Dulci, what about that story you told Gilbert and me about Millie fighting with you, falling in the sluice, then you finding her drowned?"

"Millie told me to put on a night dress and sit by the ditch to watch for the person pretending to be Llorona. She said she wanted to catch them. That dead woman wearing her clothes was already in the water."

"Then Millie was still in the ranch house, while we were there with you?"

Dulci nodded. "My father came the next day, then we all drove back to Jemez Springs that night."

"And he arranged the sale and method of getting to Mexico from there."

Martín and Gabriél stood up. "Father Jakubowski, it's time for us to leave."

"Of course, and I should go, too. Dulci, please don't throw anything else out."

"I won't," she promised.

After Gabriél went outside to bring their automobile around, Martín pulled an envelope from his suit pocket and handed it to the girl. "Dulcinea Trujillo, you're nineteen years old now."

"How did you know?"

Without answering, he continued, "We'll need a manager here at our equine sanctuary. Since you're familiar both with horses and this ranch property, I hope you'll agree to take the job."

Dulci glanced at Fr. Jake and fully smiled for the first time, yet was suspicious. "But, Mister Martin, I don't know anything about running a place like that."

"The main thing, Dulcinea, is that you love horses. That envelope tells about our organization, and I'll send someone from EQUUS to train you in our methods. Also, a woman nutritionist will work with you on improving your eating habits. I'm sure Gilbert and Mathias will stay on." Martín looked sternly toward Lorenzo. "I'll have a talk with you, sir, about impersonating that weeping woman."

"But I—" For once Lorenzo "Zo" Lujan had nothing insulting or even clever to say.

Martín closed his briefcase. "Dulcinea Trujillo, what's your answer?"

"I...well...sure. I'd love to stay here, if you think I can do the work."

"I'm confident you can..." Martin looked at the priest. "Am I right, Father Jakubowski?"

He smiled at the girl. "Dulcinea, you'll make a splendid manager, and Cynthia will be a helpful friend."

"I hope so, Father...Father Jake."

"Then, God Bless."

Back at the rectory, Gabriél pulled the Mustang up behind Fr. Jake's Honda. Martín got out of the front seat to let the priest leave the back on the passenger side, then extended his hand. "Father Jakubowski, I'll be sure to let Archbishop Sredzinski know that you're a fine priest."

"Thanks." *He knows the archbishop of Detroit and every detail about the ranch and the people working on it. Even my thought about the Don being intimate with Millie.* "Martín, if I may ask, how did you learn so much about me and Rancho Tru-Cor and, well, just about everything concerning the people here?"

The man laughed. "Father, our Sanctuary office staff has an excellent vetting process. What they can discover about a person or place is...is... well, for me, it's quite miraculous."

*Miraculous?* Fr. Jake bent down to ask Gabriél, "How did you know the way to the ranch without ever having visited the place?"

The driver grinned and pointed to the car's instrument panel. "Father, haven't you ever heard of G.P.S.? Global Positioning."

"Oh…sure…of course." *Those answers will have to suffice for now.* The priest took out the EQUUS business card that had been given him. "Gabriél, Miguel, and Martín are names of saints, yet, Martín you never explained the origin of 'Izzy'."

"Izzy?" The man chuckled at a question he heard many times. "Since I used to be teased about my real name, I kept a nickname the kids gave me at school."

Fr. Jake felt his question still unanswered. "Mind telling me that real name?"

Martín settled into the Mustang's front seat, closed the door, and looked up at the priest. "Father, you of all people should know that it would be 'Isidro'."

As Gabriél backed the car down the driveway to the street, Miguel Isidro Martín looked out his side window, waved, and called out, "God Bless, Father Jake!"

## 33 august 1 / san isidro ?

When Sonia Mora pulled her Plymouth Neon into the driveway of the San Isidro rectory, the pert woman detective wore the work clothes she had put on to clean out her uncle's rooms in June—plaid summer shirt, belt-less denims, leather sandals, and a signature Baker Boy cap of tan twill cotton.

As the first sprinkles heralding an afternoon monsoon shower darkened the drive's pebbles, she got out of the car, shielded a manila folder against her shirt front, and made a dash for the front door.

Fr. Jake noticed her arrival and held the screen open. "Come in, come in, detective, you'll get all wet. Doesn't anyone out here own an umbrella?"

"Maybe for the sun, Father…" She took off her cap and shook out glossy black hair, while apologizing, "Hope I'm not disturbing your Sunday."

"When you called, Sonia, I said you wouldn't. I haven't seen you in… what…a week?"

"Just about."

The rectory smelled pleasantly of lingering scented smoke from a sage bundle that tempered a reek of mold in the long-neglected adobe whenever wet weather came. A stronger strumming noise on the metal roof promised an increasingly full, if short, rainfall.

Sonia glanced up. "That won't last."

The priest agreed with her assessment. "Even I've figured that out by now. These 'monsoon' rains don't stay as long as storms do in Michigan."

"Fast learner of New Mexican weather…" Sonia slumped down on the couch, exhaled in fatigue, and laid the folder next to her cap.

Still standing, Fr. Jake asked, "Ah, Sonia, I know how you feel about my coffee, so I opened a bottle of Australian Chardonnay I bought in Belén. Care to share?"

"Love a glass, Father, I'm bushed. This was my day off and I not-so-smartly spent it cleaning my apartment."

When the priest returned with the wine, he apologized, "Served in resale shop glasses that don't match, I'm afraid."

"Long as they don't leak…" Sonia held up the wine he handed her. "*Salud*, Father."

"*Salud…Naszdrowie*," he toasted in Spanish and Polish, sampled in unison with her, then sat back in his armchair. "So, Detective, what's the latest? You know, I've hardly slept, remembering…feeling guilty, really… about the two deaths I caused at the helicopter. I… I've prayed, certainly—"

"Father Jake, we'll hash that out a bit later." Sonia put her glass on the coffee table and held up the folder. "I have a final autopsy report on Baby Doe's parentage. More than more than likely, the mother *was* Millie Jaramillo."

"How do they know? I thought DNA couldn't be determined with that early a fetus."

"True, yet pathologists did identify traces of a natural plant abortifacient in the tissues."

"A plant that a *curandera* like Millie would know about."

"Exactly, Father. To protect confidentiality the plant's name is blackened out on the report they gave me, but there are several known species used in self-induced miscarriages or abortions."

"So that part of what Dulci told to Gil and me that evening was true, and Don Fernando is the father." At her slight nod, Fr. Jake continued with a question he had long thought about. "Detective, could Baby Doe be released to me? I'd like to hold a funeral mass and burial in the San Isidro cemetery."

"That probably can be arranged, Father."

"Then, that leaves only your investigation into Isabel Trujillo's death."

"Father, in reopening the case," she explained, "I did find out that Isabel's parents had left the ranch solely to her. She hadn't yet made a will that included the Don, but since her death was deemed an accident, no further investigation was made about his possible involvement. On her death, Don Ferdinand Trujillo de Sevilla inherited Rancho Tru-Cor."

"And all witnesses to her 'accidental' demise are now themselves deceased." Father Jake sipped from his wine glass before asking, "Sonia, what were you going to tell me about my involvement in the helicopter deaths?"

"Father, it's true that what you and those ranch workers did to keep that copter from taking off resulted in the deaths of two individuals."

"Or homicides? Detective, I…I said that I take full responsibility for that and I've agonized over it—"

"Father, let me finish. Had the two victims lived, they would have been charged with the murders of Eusebia Nevarez, Victoria Torrez, and Cervando Benavides. Since Dulcinea would probably testify that she strongly resisted going to Mexico, and was no longer a minor, a kidnapping charge would be added. All that aside, the fact that Don Fernando fired gunshots that could have killed you, Gilbert Begay, and/or Mathias Crisp, would make a self-defense plea viable."

"Legal jabberwocky!" the priest scoffed. "The plain fact is, Sonia, that because of me, two people are dead."

She retorted, "Father Jakubowski, would justice have been served had they escaped? There's no statute of limitations on murder, and Don Fernando was correct in assuming that a new investigation into his wife's death would take place. The D.A. was preparing to empanel a grand jury. He'd argue that to avoid prosecution the Don and his mistress came up with an elaborate, pre-mediated scheme to flee the country."

"Well, when you put it that way—"

"Father, you're not drinking enough of your Chardonnay."

"All right." The priest took another sip, then sat back in silence to think about what the detective had implied.

Sonia cocked an ear toward the ceiling. "Rain stopped. These minimal showers aren't unusual…" She put her glass down and paused to listen at another sound outside. "I hear a car pulling up behind mine. Are you expecting anyone else?"

"No…" Fr. Jake stood and walked to the window. "It's Armando and his aunt."

When he opened the screen door, the young mechanic seemed embarrassed. "Hope we ain't…aren't disturbin' you, Father Hakub. *Tia* Olfila wanted me to bring her over to see you." Armando looked past the priest. "Oh, hi, Detective Mora."

"Hello." Sonia stood and gestured to them. "Come in. I was just getting ready to leave."

Fr. Jake said, "Armando, I've been meaning to tell you that I sent a check to Pete Gonzales for the Honda."

"He didn't tell me."

"I suspected not…" The priest turned to smile and clasp the aunt's hands. "Ofila, your nephew said you wanted to talk to me?"

"*Si, Padre.* I come see how my *velacione* work for you. You need new one?"

Fr. Jake encompassed the rectory space with a hand. "No, I think everything is fine."

The old *curandera* flashed him her most innocent smile. "New *velacione* only twenty-five dollar."

"You and your two friends did very well, Ofilia. I've not seen a ghost of Father Mora yet."

"How about spottin' La Llorona?" Armando asked the priest, half in jest.

He recalled what had happened. "Well, Armando, at least Gil and I caught Lorenzo Lujan wearing her dress and smoking her cigarettes."

"Father Hakub, I coulda told you that. Zo was over at the shop braggin' about how Queen Millie paid him to be her. I think she had some kind of hex on him. Y' know, Millie didn't like you, and Zo was the one torched your Nissan for her."

"What? And you didn't tell me?"

The mechanic flushed and looked down at the rug. "You…you didn't ask me."

"Fine, Armando." *Guess I need to understand there are areas an outsider can't penetrate when they haven't been born in the right place. I can live with it…Armando's a good man.*

Ofilia walked over to Fr. Jake's *altarcito* to check the freshness of a vase of cow pen daisies that decorated the wooden saint's shrine. "San Isidro still here, *Padre.* You take good care of the *santo*?"

"*Si*…yes. He…the saint….has even helped me a lot lately."

"*Bueno*…" Ofilia turned to quiz Sonia. "You, *detectiva.* You have *altarcito* in your room?"

"No…not yet," she admitted; the old woman's questions could be blunt, even intimidating.

This time Ofilia's smile was guileless. "Fifty dollar, *detectiva*, I come to Socorro. Make nice shrine for you—"

A similar sound of tires crunching gravel in the driveway spared Sonia from committing to a home altar. Fr. Jake checked the window again and saw a man getting out of a white Ford Mustang. The car was like the one in which Gabriél had driven Izzy Martín to Providencia. He went over to meet the new arrival at the door.

"Father Jakubowski?" a dark-haired man of about thirty asked.

"Yes. You are…?"

"Here, Father…" He handed the priest an EQUUS business card. "I'm Rafael Smith-Garcia. Mister Martín told you that someone would come to help Miss Trujillo with details about managing one of our sanctuaries. That would be me, and I'll stay at least a month."

'Welcome, then." The priest stepped aside. "Please come in, Mister Garcia."

"Father, just 'Rafael' will be okay."

*Rayfee-el. Not the Spanish pronunciation.* "Fine then, Rafael, and I'm Father Jake. There just happens to be some people here you should meet. This is Detective Mora, who investigated the recent helicopter tragedy."

Sonia reached for his anticipated handshake. "Pleased, detective. I've heard about that unfortunate accident at the ranch."

"Sir, it's an ongoing investigation."

Fr. Jake introduced the others. "Armando Herrera is a fine auto mechanic, and his aunt Ofilia is a practicing *curandera*. If you ever feel ill at the ranch—"

Ofilia promptly cajoled the newcomer. "*Señor* Rafaél Garcia, maybe you hurt some place now? *Mi sobrino*, Armando, have *medicamentos* in car outside."

Rafael smiled at the old woman's brazen salesmanship. "Thank you, Ofilia. I'll be sure to keep that in mind while I'm here."

Sonia leaned down to pick up her cap off the couch. "Father Jake, I should be going. McMurtry did finish his report on Cervando Benavides. I'll share it with you later, but Gil was correct in attributing strychnine as the cause of death."

Armando said, "Yeah, I heard about that from Zo. Weird…" He looked over at the priest. "Father Hukub, you sure got yourself in the middle of somethin' since you came here. We never had nothin' bad goin' on like this before."

Sonia corrected him, "Armando, maybe you just never heard about the other crimes? Don't blame Father Jake."

"I'm not blamin'—"

"Good night, Sonia...." The priest stepped over to open the door for her and end the discussion. "Safe trip home. God Bless."

"Thanks, Father. I'll be in touch."

After the detective left, Ofilia squinted at Rafael and resumed her questions. "*Señor*, why you here?"

"*Tia*..."Armando scolded. "That's not polite to ask."

"It's all right..." Father Jake answered for the visitor. "Mister Garcia represents a company that just bought the Tru-Cor ranch."

"*Rancho* sold?" Ofilia's mouth worked her gums a moment. "He buy *Isabela*, too?"

"Isabela?" Confused, Fr. Jake looked toward her nephew.

"Father Hakub, don't you remember? Vando told you they give names to *acequias*? 'La Chica,' 'Tres Caballos'...kinda like that. Don Fernando, he named his for Isabel, his dead wife."

"I do recall that now."

"Yeah, I always thought that was on the weird side."

Ofilia grasped Rafael by the sleeve. "*Señor* Garcia, now you need *velacione* for *Acequia del Muerte*. She looked over at Fr. Jake. "*Que no, Padre?*"

"The 'Sluice of Death'?" At the ominous-sounding translation, an uneasy feeling shivered through the priest's body.

Rafael asked him, "Father Jake, what is this *velacione* that Ofilia mentioned a couple of times now?"

"It's a *curanderismo* cleansing ceremony for a dwelling and evidently even for irrigation channels like a sluice. Ofilia 'purified' this rectory after the priest living here was murdered."

"Father Hakub," Armando said, "Vando showed us that unborn *niño* he found in the ditch, and I heard about a woman just bein' drowned down there. Lotta animals like a *javelina* or *coyote* been found floatin' in that *acequia*."

The priest recalled another incident. "Gil told me about a colt of Dulci's that once drowned there."

"*Si*," Ofilia complained. "Long time *Padre* Mora he no bless *acequia* no more." The old woman glared at Fr. Jake. "You, *Padre* Hakub, are *norteño* priest. In Mitchigen you no bless *un salto en la primavera?*"

Armando explained, "*Tia* means, in Michigan don't you bless water in springs, like we do here every June?"

"On October fourth I...I do bless animals for the feast of St. Francis."

"We do that too, but water's a lot more important in New Mexico."

The priest was skeptical. "You're telling me that putting Isabel Trujillo's name on the sluice was some kind of curse?"

"I'm only sayin' that Carlotta's warned you not to fool around with what you don't understand."

"Right." Fr. Jake raised his eyebrows as a question and looked toward Rafael.

"Ah...Father...EQUUS respects whatever customs local residents have in places where our sanctuaries are located." He turned to Ofilia. "*Señora*, I'll be here for a month, so we'll schedule a *velacione*, for the waterway first thing."

"*Bueno...*" Ofilia's smile widened. "You got good name, Rafaél. You just no say it right."

Armando coughed to suppress a smile. "*Tia*, it's time to go. I'll talk with Father Hakub about that *velacione* and *acequia* blessin'." He opened the screen door for his aunt. "Come on, *Tia*," he urged. "Good luck, Mister Garcia. Hope we'll see a lot of each other. 'Bye, Father Hakub."

He waved a hand. "Thanks Armando, Ofilia. God Bless."

After the two left, Father Jake invited Rafael to sit on the couch. "Can I get you wine or coffee? I tried Carlotta's piñon roast and bought a pound. Quite good."

"Sure, coffee, why not?" Rafael settled down on one side of the couch, where he could look into the kitchenette. While the priest prepared the beverage, his visitor commented, "That was quite an introduction I had to local customs, Father Jake."

"I'm still learning about them myself," he called back.

Rafael glanced around the modest room, until the priest came in and set two steaming cups on his coffee table. 'It's very hot, Rafael. You might want to wait a minute."

"Thanks. Father, I just understood a little about what was said just now. Was that irrigation ditch named after a deceased woman?"

"Yes. Thirteen years go, Isabel, the ranch owner's wife, died in a terrible horse trailer accident."

"And people believe her 'ghost' is still haunting the ranch?"

"Rafael, I'll introduce you to Carlotta at the grocery, so you can talk to her about the paranormal. Ofilia's ritual and my blessing the sluice won't hurt a thing..." He tipped his head toward the man's cup. "Try your coffee now."

Rafael took a cautious sip. "Very good. Pinion you say?"

"'Pin-yon.'"

The man had another taste and put his cup down. "The professional woman, whom Izzy told you would work with Miss Trujillo, will arrive tomorrow."

"Good. Dulcinea needs all the help she can get, physically and psychologically."

"Father, EQUUS deals with maimed animals, yet we also hire maimed humans to work with them. If chosen well, it can be a symbiotic relationship beneficial to both."

"I found Mister Martín...Izzy...to be a most sympathetic person."

"Izzy? Yes, he's the founder of EQUUS and totally devoted to the rescue of abused equines." Rafael paused as if considering his next words. "Father Jake, if I may say so, Izzy does have one...well...peculiarity. He has us take a saint's name as a kind of security ID password. For example, my father is Hispanic and my given name really is Rudolfo."

"I see. Well, that explains the name of his associate, Gabriél."

Rafael seemed puzzled. "Sorry, Father. Who?"

"Gabriél. The man who came with Miguel Martín. With Isidro."

"What was his surname?"

"Come to think, he didn't mention one. Gabriél drove a white company Mustang like yours."

"Sorry, doesn't register, and yet I thought I knew everyone working for us." Rafael continued where he left off, "I was talking about Izzy. I mean the man gives one hundred and ten percent of himself, twenty-four / seven. A lot of us even consider him a saint."

"A saint?" Fr. Jake looked toward the *bulto* of San Isidro, standing on his *altarcito*. In dim afternoon light, the wooden statue almost seemed to be smiling. "Rafaél, I just might be able to understand the incredible significance and implication of that designation."

## 34 the equus 'milagra'

A little over two weeks later, Detective Mora pulled her once-again-muddy Plymouth Neon into the driveway of San Isidro rectory. She brought final reports on the Baby Doe and Isabel Trujillo cases to share with the priest—and also a personal development on which she wanted his opinion.

Fr. Jake had spent much of the interval since the first of August on renovating Fr. Mora's old *segrario* into a quiet space where parishioners could visit the Blessed Sacrament, as they did in many Mexican churches. In their spare time, Armando Herrera and his *Hermano* friends contributed materials and worked on the chapel, which included a separated area for the Sacrament of Reconciliation.

After Sonia came inside the rectory and settled on the couch, she pulled an envelope from her folder and held it up. "Father Jake, I...I finally received a letter from Juan Herrera."

"Good, from that handsome F.B.I. agent, who was transferred to Washington D.C."

"Actually, Juan's D.E.A. Drug Enforcement Agency."

"Right. How is he? Weren't you hoping to hear from Juan back in June?"

"Juan explained his lack of correspondence, but I won't go into that. Father Jake, he...he wants me to visit him in D.C. over the Labor Day weekend."

"Splendid! Can you get away? Is there any free time coming to you?"

Sonia was offset by the priest's unexpected enthusiasm. "Probably, since I haven't taken real vacation time in over a year."

"Any 'official business' you could conduct while you were in Washington?"

"Fatherrr," she chided amiably. "I don't operate that way."

"You liked Juan, didn't you?"

"We did hit it off on that Survivalist drug bust, but I'm not sure if I want to get too involved with a law enforcement guy."

"I know, Sonia, you told me about your father's suicide. He had retired from police work, yet, since crime was still rampant, you said he didn't think that he had done much good during his career."

"Guess I'm not talking entirely about crime here."

"About going to visit Juan, then? Sonia, the church has poked into Catholic bedrooms far too long. I mean, read the statistics. Ninety eight percent of Catholics—"

"Father, pardon for interrupting, but I know the statistics."

"So what are you asking me?"

"I'm not really sure."

"You're a good person, Sonia…" The priest thought a moment before saying, "You know, synagogue authorities criticized Christ for hobnobbing with the 'IRS' agents of his time, or with people who forgot to wash their hands before eating. Both actions were against Jewish Law. Also, being the same room with, as we might say today, 'Ladies of shady character' drew criticism."

Already restive, Sonia shifted position on the couch. "Father Jakubowski, you usually have a point to make."

"I'm coming to that. By the time they all ate dessert together, every one of those 'sinners' felt vindicated by Christ's overwhelming forgiveness and love. Don't you feel that way?"

"I don't know…."

"Okay." *Different subject.* "How about a piñon coffee, Sonia? It's almost fresh brewed." At her willing nod, Fr. Jake stood up to fetch the beverage. "So did you bring me anything more of interest in that folder?"

"The M.E. is ready to release Don Fernando's body. Dulcinea Trujillo will be notified by mail, but I wondered if you wanted to tell her first and talk about a funeral."

"Thanks, I will. How about Baby Doe?"

"That's in the paperwork, too."

"Then, I think a joint service, father and son, would be appropriate."

When Fr. Jake came back with two mugs of coffee, Sonia told him, "As you suggested, I went to look for Isabel Trujillo's grave in the Socorro cemetery."

"What did you find?"

"She's buried in a plot next to her parents. Except for routine maintenance by the cemetery staff, both graves seemed abandoned. The Don evidently never visited the wife he claims to have adored."

"The reason could either be guilt or denial as an abnormal effect of his Prolonged Grief Disorder."

"Right, Father. That will remain part of the mystery." Sonia tasted her coffee. "Good. Oh, by the way, Queen Millie's body was cremated and her ashes 'extradited' back to that Mexican village."

"May the *curandera* rest in peace."

"No Hell? No Purgatory?"

"Judge not—"

"—or you'll be judged," Sonia finished. "I know."

"It's an overused cliché, yet many people create their own 'hell' here on earth."

She sipped her coffee and thought of a current example. "Jayson Baumann seemed to be one of them. Selfishness and greed motivated him to falsify a burial site. Have you heard from the guy again?'"

"No, and I won't, but I can pray that God gives him the grace to change attitudes. Cynthia Plow might have helped him do so, yet he spurned her help."

"Oh, speaking of Millie …" Sonia reached into her briefcase and brought out a paperback book. "I've been reading up on *curanderismo*, since that's been involved in what's happened over here in Providencia. I want you to read this, especially about *mal puesto*."

He looked at what was written on the volume's back cover. "Didn't Dulci mention that condition as related to one of Millie's treatments?"

"Exactly, Father, yet it seems that a person can either be helped or harmed through that particular folk cure invocation."

"You mean Millie could keep the girl in her present child-like state?"

"Possibly. A legit *curanderismo* treatment for *mal puesto* normally is helpful, but Millie used it as a means of control over both Dulci and her father."

Fr. Jake whistled amazement. "Yet it seems that the girl struggled to escape that control. She definitely did not want to go with them to Mexico."

"For sure." Sonia finished her coffee and put the mug down. "I'd like to go see how the girl is doing now that the she's getting professional guidance."

"I was thinking of that, too. Soon as you're done with business, we'll go over to the ranch."

"Father, "Sonia asked, "weren't you interested in that idea of six degrees of separation to find a criminal? How did that work out?"

"In connecting persons to find the killer? Sonia, you were pretty much with me all the way. We connected Dave Allison and Breanna Springer to Haskill because she tracked him down. Tragically, Deputy Griego and Rod Jirón became involved."

"And you, Father Jake, were number six at that Jemez cottage."

"I was lucky there was a number seven. Gilbert Begay."

"I'd say, *very* lucky." Sonia continued, "The investigation into Isabel Trujillo's death was more complicated."

"There was Isabel, Don Fernando, Eusebia, Cervando Benavides… That's only four," the priest counted. "Is Dulci too young to be included?"

"Not entirely, but no thanks to her father's obsession, the poor girl suffered the most long-lasting effects."

"Millie Jaramillo came along later," Fr. Jake said. "Finding Baby Doe began the investigation and Millie turned out to be the unborn child's mother. Had she not believed as a *curandera* that the fetus ritually would be washed into the Rio Grande, Baby Doe would never have been found. Or if you, detective, hadn't thought of re-reading that necropsy report on *Vencedor*."

She shared credit, "It was you, Father Jake, who made the connection with that sharpened hoof pick."

"In truth, Sonia, I suppose anyone would have six friends or acquaintances they could connect, and yet can you branch a concept like that out into a wider world?"

"Father," Sonia quipped, "that's what Facebook friends are all about."

"So I've heard." He laughed and looked at her cup. "More coffee?"

"No, I'm good."

"Then let's go over and see how our Dulcinea is doing."

"Fine…" Sonia replaced the folder and letter in her briefcase. "Father, have you heard more from that representative of the horse sanctuary who came over the afternoon I was at the rectory? Rafael, was it?"

"Rafael Smith-Garcia. He's over there now, but I haven't met the EQUUS woman employee who is helping Dulci. While I rinse out these cups, Sonia, why don't you move your car? I can drive for a change."

"Father Jakubowski," she reminded him in a feigned reproach, "I'm a cop and never go anywhere without my Plymouth. As a TV commercial warns, 'Don't leave home without it'."

"Of course, the car has your police radio, siren, flashing red roof light, et cetera. I should have remembered. I'll drive my Honda to the ranch and you won't have to come back here."

"That'll work."

"By the way, I've finished making Father Mora's old *segrario* into a place where all parishioners may venerate the Blessed Sacrament. I'll hear confessions there, too. Care to see it first?" When Sonia hesitated, Fr. Jake realized his blunder. "Of course, that's where your uncle's body was found."

"No, it's not that," she said. "I was thinking that my uncle forgot why he became priest and could have made those change years ago for his parishioners."

"Sonia, even one of the Pope's titles is 'Servant of the servants of God'."

"Father Jake, I'd like to see what you did."

The small room attached to the side of the church smelled of fresh paint. Chairs and kneelers faced an altar with Fr. Mora's monstrance set on top. Worshippers could spend time with the Sacred Host, or just recite a rosary and meditate. To the right, a wooden partition had a screened window that separated penitents going to confession from the priest who sat behind it.

Fr. Jake explained, "Even with that 'barrier,' many parishioners go to a different church to confess."

"The local priest would identify their voices?"

"There's truth in that I suppose, but confession is not a game of 'Who's who?' We just listen to sins, and 'sins,' then give out penances." He opened the *sagrario* door." Shall we leave for the ranch?"

"All right." Sonia glanced around a final time. "I…I like what you've done to my uncle's old hideaway."

"Father Mora did the best he could."

"You can't always use that excuse, *Padre*. Let's go."

At the ranch's entrance gate, the Tru-Cor name had been replaced by that of the equine rescue company.

**E Q U U S**

**Equine Unified Sanctuaries**

The priest and detective parked their cars near the fountain. A babble of water sparkling in the sun indicated that the pond mechanism had been repaired and the basin cleaned. In the clear water, speckled orange-and-white Koi fish slithered among lily pads and nosed up for food. Mosquitoes no longer arose to harass visitors.

Fr. Jake met Sonia at her Plymouth and pointed toward the *acequia*. "I see that Gil and Matt have finished fencing off the sluice. Detective, six months ago I might have joked, 'That'll keep the ghosts out'."

"Now you're not so sure about a hex or phantom woman snooping around?"

"Are you?"

"As I said, Father, I'm a cop. I normally don't deal with the paranormal."

The priest pushed his gambler hat a bit lower against the sun and pointed toward the north pasture. "That looks like Dulci over there working a horse with Rafael. And that must be the girl's woman tutor with them."

They walked closer to watch the team, until the woman noticed them and broke away from the training session. Dark-hair cut short, with an olive skin, she wore jeans and a denim jacket that had the Pegasus EQUUS logo sewn on one pocket. Fr. Jake thought she resembled a Vatican II-era nun who now ministered outside a convent.

"Welcome, Father Jake and Detective Mora. I'm Miriam," she told them and then laughed. "Don't be surprised that I guessed who you were. Rafael told me you'd be coming to visit."

"Of course. A pleasure, Miriam." Fr. Jake exchanged handshakes, as did Sonia, then asked, "How is Dulci coming along?"

"Quite well, Father. Her appetite is better, so she's gained some weight. She no longer bites her nails down to the quick. Our afternoon talks…we don't call them therapy sessions…our conversations center on gaining self-confidence. Dulci's work with abused equines is designed to reinforce that."

Sonia approved, "I'm sure that gives her a sense of being useful."

"Correct, detective, by helping a sensitive animal she loves and that reciprocates in its way." Miriam pointed to the sanctuary's logo on her jacket. "Two green hearts for trainer and animal, yet, like Pegaus a free-spirited mythical horse, that's a goal not always realistic or achieved. Dulci's own recovery won't happen overnight, but she's a courageous individual who is willing to try."

"I plan to hold a funeral Mass for her father and…and Baby Doe. Would she be ready for that?"

Miriam looked toward the girl. "Here, let me call Dulci over. You can ask her yourself."

Dulcinea Trujillo wiped perspiration from her face with a bandana as she walked toward the priest and detective. She smiled and greeted them cordially. "Hello, Father, Detective Mora. It's nice to see you both."

Fr. Jake complimented the girl. "You look content, Dulci, so you must like it here."

"Very much. Our own Arabians were always well-kept, so I never realized how badly some other horses might be abused."

"This is a sanctuary," Miriam explained. "The most horribly mistreated equines are brought here and will remain for the rest of their lives. Our horses are never given back to previous owners, nor, for that matter, sold to anyone."

Half-seriously, Fr. Jake thought of a parallel. "*La vida llena*…'A full lifestyle', as assisted living facilities like to advertise, but here it's for horses."

"Father, isn't that great!" Dulci exclaimed, then told him, "Cynthia called and invited me to come to your five 'o clock Mass with her next Saturday."

"Dulci, I'm pleased that you'll get to know her. And I…I'd like to discuss planning a funeral soon for your father."

"Sure, we can do that. Gil said he'd like to go to your Mass, and maybe we can drag that goofy Lorenzo along. About Matt…well…I don't know."

"I'd be delighted to have *all* of you there!"

"Okay, see you then, Father. I've got to go finish working with *Milagra*. Rafael said I could give the mare that name. It's a Spanish feminine for 'Miracle'."

"I know, Dulci, and all considered, *Milagra* is a very appropriate name."

"I should get back now."

Fr. Jake shook the girl's hand. "I'll visit you again. God bless…."

"Thanks. Bye, detective."

"Take care, Dulci."

Miriam watched her run back to the mare, then turned back to her visitors. "Dulcinea has quite a bit of money coming from the balance of what EQUUS paid for this ranch. We've put it in a trust fund, so she'll only receive a salary here, until she's twenty-one."

"It sounds like you've thought of everything," Fr. Jake said.

"Thank 'Izzy' for that," Miriam replied. "He's up on every detail. We'll soon be running ads to hire team leaders for training positions here."

"That should help the local economy," Sonia predicted. "Even cut back on theft crimes."

"Hopefully…" Fr. Jake extended a hand. "Thank you, Miriam. While I'm still here at San Isidro, I'll check on Dulci's progress."

Miriam shook his hand. "Thanks, and you might say a prayer to the saint for her. Actually, for all of us."

"Will do," the priest promised. "God bless, now, Miriam."

"Goodbye, Father…Detective."

Walking back to their cars, Fr. Jake felt pleased with what he had seen. "Dulci seems well on the way to 'rehabilitation,' Sonia, if I dare call it that."

"Right, Father, I agree. And the girl will have to decide what to with that seven hundred and fifty thousand dollars that she'll inherit in two years."

"Could have been an additional two hundred-fifty thousand," he recalled. "I guess we'll never know what happened to the money that Lorenzo dumped into the river." At her Plymouth, Fr. Jake grasped Sonia's hand. "Say hello to Juan Herrera for me, detective, and stay in touch."

"As sure as death, taxes, and crime exist, Father Jake, I will be in touch." Damp-eyed, Sonia gave the priest an impulsive hug and light kiss on the cheek. "See ya around, *Padre*…."

The Michigan priest tipped his gambler sunhat to her. "See ya around, *Detectiva*."

# Epilogue

On Tuesday, October 12, the following article appeared in the Brownsville Gazette:

### Thousand Dollar Bills Wash Ashore Near Brazos Island

*The Associated Press*

BROWNSVILLE, TX — After a shrimp fisherman reported finding several thousand dollar bills floating in the waters off Brazos Island, a crowd quickly gathered on the beach. A number of lucky searchers waded back out of the surf clutching additional amounts of currency. Police cordoned off the area and summoned FBI, DEA and Treasury officials to the site. On condition of anonymity, a DEA official declared the money to be part of a failed Mexican drug cartel operation. An FBI spokesman said the bills were counterfeit, possibly of South or Central American origin. Treasury agents are tracing the serial numbers. None of these efforts deterred the public, as boats equipped with lanterns appeared offshore during the night. Other citizens swept onto the beach with flashlights, under the pretext of digging for clams. Law enforcement officials urged finders to bring any recovered currency to Hidalgo County police or sheriff's stations. No reward for doing so has yet been announced.

Local residents saw the bonanza as celestial insurance against future hurricane damage and lighted votive candles in their homes. An elderly gentleman reported his find to be a miracle performed by a favorite saint, whom he refused to identify. A besotted resident argued that the money found on Columbus Day was "The cache from a sunken Spanish treasure galleon, brought to light on the explorer's birthday."

# Discussion Guide

The questions below provide fodder for discussion of this novel for better undersanding of the plot and historical setting.

1. The novel has a map of the immediate area surrounding fictional Providencia. By having a New Mexico map or road atlas you can follow the story locations.

   - Highway 304, running between Belèn and La Joya, was renumbered to fictional Highway 310. Providencia is about halfway between. What might the actual village be named?

   - You can follow Interstate 25 from Belèn to Bernalillo, then on to Jemez Springs. But Allison and Springer take I-40, detour to Highway 14, then, south of Madrid , they cut back to I-25.

     –What makes Fr. Jake think the fugitives may have taken such a roundabout way to Colorado ?

     – How many New Mexican or visitor readers explored the Jemez area and Los Alamos ?

   The Valles Caldera National Preserve is an experiment in public land management, well worth a visit.

2. Chapter 1: When Fr. Jake and Detective Sonia Mora clean out the Fr. Mora's rectory, what more do we learn about him?

3. Chapter 2: Detective Mora and Fr. Jake are faced with 3-month-old fetus that was aborted or miscarried, then discarded in a sluice—a moral and criminal offense. Mora quotes the Statute to Don Fernando: "Human fetal remains shall be disposed by incineration or interment," yet he is more interested in talking about the effect his wife's death had on his faith. Is this a common reaction?

4. Chapter 4: Millie Jaramillo is a Mexican-trained curandera, one of the folk healers widely used by poor residents of the Southwest. People coming from Mexican or European healing or superstitious traditions may continue them here. Do you recall any of these in your family?

5. Chapters 6/32: Dulcinea Trujillo is a victim of her father's Prolonged Grief Disorder. Have you known anyone who exhibited symptoms of this pathological condition? What happened to them?

6. Chapter 14: The funerals of soldiers and others have been picketed by some church groups as doing "God's work." How do you feel about that? What alternatives could Breanna Springer have employed in confronting Pastor Haskill?

7. Chapters 22/29: Some non-Catholics believe that statues of saints are idols to which Catholics pray, rather than to God. Fr. Jake's particular saint is San Isidro and the priest ponders the Church tradition of invoking the aid of a saint, versus the horoscopes and good luck charms in which many people have faith. San Isidro 's "help" has never been supernatural. How did you feel about what Fr. Jake believes may be the saint's intervention and how it came about?

8. Chapter 24: New Mexico has 19 Native America pueblos. Is it typical of a young tribal member like Gilbert Begay to leave the Rez and strike out on his own? How could Reservations be made more self-sufficient by employing tribal members in an industry?

9. Chapter 26: Recent excavations in New Mexico uncovered the remains of "Buffalo Soldiers" — African-Americans who served in the Civil War, and afterward in the western Territories. Native-Americans were employed as scouts. In 1990, such excavated remains were protected by extensive Congressional repatriation legislation. Where might Jayson Baumann obtain illegal artifacts?

10. Chapter 32: Do you agree with Detective Mora's reasoning in trying to ease Fr. Jake's agonizing over having caused two deaths?

11. Chapter 32/34: EQUUS is a horse sanctuary ranch, where abused equines are sheltered for the balance of their lives. There also are horse rescue ranches, where mistreated or unwanted animals are restored to heath, then found new owners. New Mexico has nine State-sanctioned facilities, all in need of volunteer helpers. Would that interest you?

# About the Author

An artist and writer, Albert Noyer was born in Switzerland but raised in Detroit, Michigan. He pursued an interest in art at the Detroit's Wayne State University. After working as a commercial artist, he taught art in the Detroit Public Schools high school technical/vocational program, plus taught art history part-time at a Catholic college. Noyer retired to New Mexico with his wife Jennifer, where he began writing and exhibiting his watercolor paintings and woodcut prints in regional exhibitions. His artwork has been featured in the *New Mexico Magazine* and in the *Mature Life in New Mexico* supplement of the *Sunday Journal*. He is a member of SouthWest Writers, Sisters in Crime, Croak & Dagger, the New Mexico Watercolor Society and New Mexico Veteran's Art.

Noyer first published an A.D. fifth century historical mystery series, the Getorius and Arcadia Mysteries. Yet-unpublished is a retelling of Julius Caesar's conquest of Gaul, from the viewpoint of a Celtic youth caught up in the Romanization of the country. He set these novels in the fifth century, an era that is now seen as critical in creating religious and political institutions that survived into modern times. *The Ghosts of Glorieta,* published by Plain View Press in 2011, was his initial contemporary mystery novel and the first novel in the *Fr. Jake Mystery* series.

CPSIA information can be obtained at www.ICGtesting.com
Printed in the USA
LVOW11s1920090913

351653LV00004B/109/P